To Mary

NO TUMBLED HOUSE
Part I. The Young

Cover design = BAD editing

Reg P. Topsho

NO TUMBLED HOUSE

Part I. The Young

PATRIC TEMPLE

"Keep the young generations in hail,
And bequeath them no tumbled house."

from 'The Empty Purse'
by George Meredith (1828–1909)

Although this novel is set in an historical context, the characters are entirely fictitious and any likeness in name or personality, to persons alive or deceased, is co-incidental.

NO TUMBLED HOUSE
Part I

Copyright © Patric Temple

First published in Great Britain 1993 by
Lionel Cox, Mersea Island, Essex.

Typeset in 10/11pt Baskerville

ISBN 0 9520878 0 4

Made and printed in Great Britain by
The Guernsey Press Co. Ltd., Guernsey, Channel Islands.

Dedicated to the memory of
MARGARET CUMMING INCE

Part I. The Young

Chapter One

The low granite farmhouse was awake. A lamp moved slowly across each of the five upper windows, disappeared momentarily before lighting in turn the four lower windows and finally emerged at the back of the building where it remained static, suspended from a nail outside a stable and illuminating the interior through the open top half of the door.

Swallows nesting in the eaves of the stable flitted hysterically from the nest to their usual vantage point on a washing line that straddled the yard and from where their shrieked admonitions to their unfledged young disturbed the entire bird population of the area. A thrush perched on his song post at the top of a gale-smitten ash informed the world that the humans had decreed a pre-dawn dawn, while a shiny cock blackbird lazily searched the earth at the edge of the gravel yard for early rising worms.

Crabs, disturbed by the vibrations created by the human world and their domestic animals, emerged from their subterranean sleeping places, alert, but curious, their stalked eyes aware of every movement and their soft, shell-protected bodies absorbing each tremor that rippled from the farmhouse to the sea. Ancient ancestors of the vigilant crabs had lived beneath the foundations of the old farmhouse thousands of years before man had invented time. Too advanced and too highly evolved to require words or language, they transmitted to each succeeding generation the history of this farm, farmhouse, beach and sea that they owned. They knew, intimately, each of the water channels that men called ley lines, carrying mountain-fresh water, alive with minerals, to meet in a pond beside the mound on which the farmhouse stood. They had seen the first upright two-legged mammals erect a great stone monument in the centre of the pond and witnessed the delight of these new creations at each full moon when the huge monolith cast its shadow across the almost still water. They knew about the great stone shrine with its pile of bones that lay beneath the mound and they had observed the erection of the mound and the excavation of the ditch that carried sea water away from the sacred relics — when the sea had first encroached on the verdant plain below. They had viewed the building of wooden huts and their disintegration, and they had been spectators at the construction of the immense granite wall with its impressive, tapered archway. Generations of crabs had lived and died before the existing house had been built, and that pre-dated any history of the area. Generations of crabs had followed the annual arrival of eels to feed and mate in the pond before making their perilous journey to the distant sea to drop their eggs in special, foreign, deep water, and they could not fail to be aware of the vast colonies of dragonflies and damsel-flies that controlled most of the pond life — and gave their name to the farm, and to the owners.

Unaware of the myriad of eyes watching from the beach, the cows made their way up from the low pastures towards the gate nearest to the yard, knowing they would be relieved of the burdensome filled udders earlier than usual; hens and ducks sleepily roused themselves; pigs stirred hopefully, but with the infinite patience of their breed, re-settled in their dwelling until such time as they would be freed and able to scavenge the meadows.

While the tide slid slowly down the sand behind them, the crabs felt the first tremors of movement towards the beach; the gentle tap, tap of two human feet accompanied by the heavy clop, clop, clop, clop of a horse's hooves followed by the rhythmical rolling of a two-wheeled object. Through the archway the crabs saw the earth-disturbers appear from the shadows, skirt the front of the building, and, by the light of a lantern, follow the pathway towards the arch. The crabs were no longer interested; no danger would result from this particular pre-dawn sortie; this was no fishing expedition intent on interfering with the sand-dwellers; this was the mate of the human they had seen drown while trying to rescue one of his species from a furiously angry sea; this was a harmless object with only one real flaw — a habit of collecting small like samples, some of which were crab-collectors and others crab-molesters.

The thrush informed the world that the first streaks of dawn had arrived over the horizon while the blackbirds competed for vocal supremacy. The swallows, comforted by the departure of the interlopers, busied themselves preening before commencing the battle for food against the fly-catchers and the regiments of insect-eating dragonflies, which they relished, but rarely caught.

The cause of the morning's disturbance led the horse and buggy through the archway where the lantern light flickering on the undressed stone produced a sparkling starlight effect, enhanced by the graceful dragonfly sculptured from a huge block of pink granite forming the centre of the symmetrically curved roof, twinkling with embedded fragments of star-shaped quartz. The woman stopped at the tapered entrance to place a small sprig of gorse in a honey-pot that stood in a curved recess, a benitier, whispering while she did so, "For la Bellule," before passing beneath the head of the dragonfly, la bellule. She did not know whether the offering was intended for the farm, the farmhouse, the family or the artifact above; all her life she had made her offerings with no thought of their pagan origin. Her sharp, grey eyes had noticed a collection of 'offerings' left by the children she was about to meet after an absence of more than three months. Before climbing lightly into the buggy she allowed her gaze to wander over the sparse common land, the beach, the gently ebbing tide and across the tranquil water to the slither of light — to the mating of sea and sky.

A quick glance backwards assured Aurora O'Donaty that light already illuminated the arched entrance to her home. She raised one arm and waved at the house on the mound, knowing that her daughter would be watching the bouncing lantern, then flicked the reins on the back of the old bay mare, and the buggy creaked and trundled along the rough track that curved close to the perimeter of the formidable wall that enclosed their home.

Roxana's eyes followed the dancing speck of light. She knew her mother would stop and extinguish it when the path left the wall. She appreciated, without understanding, her mother's need for the solitude of the lonely track across the common and around the edge of that wild coast before dawn. For Roxana, serenity and fulfilment were achieved by service, and she busied herself removing the warming bricks from each of the six freshly made beds, preparing breakfast and laying the huge oval table in readiness for the six young travellers her mother would be meeting, and welcoming back to their home.

Aurora breathed in the tang of the sea, watched the changing patterns of the lightening sky, wrapped her shabby ulster closer about her legs and felt excitement and tension sliding from her mind, her stomach and her slightly chilled legs. The calm, smooth air belied any possibility of an impending storm, as did the tranquil sky, but waves of excitement slid slowly through her body, like the wavelets creeping up the beach below, and out of sight. She knew that this meeting of the children would be different. An era was coming to a close. Her son and her nephew had completed their schooldays. All night they had been aboard the boat she was on her way to meet, not as child passengers, but as men travellers; no longer wearing school uniform, but probably uncomfortably squeezed into the 'mufti' they had taken back after Easter. Soon all the children would be grown up, perhaps they would all have left their home, even left the island altogether. "Then 'La Bellule' will indeed be a tumbled house," she whispered to herself.

Gamma, the mare, hearing the whisper and perfectly aware of their precise position, stopped. They had reached the rocky promontory where they always stopped. Aurora shook herself, physically and mentally, and thought, "The house has been since the beginning of Time, and will outlast Time," knowing that 'House' and 'Family' were synonymous to her. She sat, hunched over her knees and recalled how 'La Bellule', house and family, had almost tumbled, but, by some miracle it seemed, revived and become revitalised, and all through the great sculptured insignia that decorated the archway to the walled farmhouse, and was also their family insignia; that great sparkling dragonfly, product of unknown

4

and unrecorded hands at a time when magic walked with nature when man ate to live and killed only to survive, and believed in omens whilst understanding the universe in which he lived. "Understanding?" queried Aurora, "Or respecting?" The promontory pointed like an arrow at the thin slither of light on the horizon, and a velvet silence draped the world in which she sat re-savouring the day 'La Bellule' was saved from dissolution.

It had been her father's birthday and she and her younger sister, Tera, had been busy all day preparing a feast worthy of the man who had been left with two tiny girls to bring up alone, who had farmed his land, increased his livestock, educated his two daughters and somehow continued his profession as a writer — for twenty years. Aurora knew that her sister intended cajoling their father into allowing her to find a job away from the desolation and isolation of the old farm, preferably in England, or some other place distant from the island; Tera longed for 'life', for rewarding admiration of her undoubted beauty and talents, and for some hope of marriage. Perhaps because of her conscience, or perhaps as a part of the cajoling, Tera had elected to do all the final preparations for the feast by herself, so Aurora had gladly escaped from the kitchen into the sea-fresh air, intending to refresh her body and soul by wandering along the beach, invitingly spacious and wide due to an exceptionally low spring tide. Bare-headed, untidy and wearing her apron, she had been discomforted to the point of idiocy on finding two extremely elegant young men standing inside the archway, gazing upwards at 'La Bellule'. In turn they questioned her about the sculpture, and when she made no reply repeated their queries in French, evidently taking her for a local girl, a servant of the household.

Aurora, brought up on mythology, had to restrain herself from thinking that these were messengers sent by Poseidon, or perhaps Vikings returning from Valhalla to conquer the islands their gods had failed to subdue. She had never seen such tall, blond men, such deep blue eyes, nor such golden-bronze skin.

"I'll take you to father!" she at last gasped, before leading them along the gravel drive, around the corner of the house to the barns and stables where her father's voice could be heard imploring some recalcitrant cow to do something. After calling "Tera" through the open back door, she fled to the safety of the beach.

On her return Aurora had found the two strangers in their shirtsleeves, dishevelled and sharing a bottle of wine with her sister and her father, all four laughing together and evidently enjoying an exchange of anecdotes. It transpired that the two strangers, so inhospitably abandoned outside the barns, had been able to assist, expertly, the difficult birth of a large bull calf. During the birthday feast to which they had been invited, they described their home — a farm in far away Tasmania which they had both left in the very capable hands of a brother, five sisters and their mother, while they had followed in the wake of another brother and joined the army. Having completed their training in England they awaited their posting to regiments and decided to visit the islands during their leave, since so many Tasmanians had their roots in these offshore islands. "We have lodgings in Town," said Rex, the younger of the two, "and our landlord noticed our rings, and told us about the dragonfly in the archway to this farm, so we came to see it for ourselves." The two young men then held out their right hands and showed their host and the two girls the dragonfly engraved in the heavy gold signet ring each wore.

"It's the odonata, the family of dragonflies from which we get our name, except that it has, through the years, become O'Donaty — our name, I mean, and I'm Rex, the youngest and least of the tribe," boomed the owner of that name.

"Strange," said the girls' father, "because our name is La Bellule, French for dragonfly."

Aurora smiled to herself, not quite ready to move from the wild spot she both loved and hated. A lasting friendship, a romance and a knitting together of the two families had been forged that day; forged between two families a world apart and through the pagan insignia to which they all made their offerings without a thought of meaning or reason. She had often wondered if the house itself somehow controlled their fates; gave then extracted payment, then gave again. Certainly Tera had her wish — to leave the boredom of the farm. A marriage was arranged between her and Rex

O'Donaty, but before it could take place he had been posted to a regiment and Tera sailed alone with her dreams, her hopes, her trousseau and her father's blessing to India. Rex never arrived. His regiment had been diverted to the Sudan to perish with Gordon at Khartoum. Tera had not returned home, but worked as a governess to various families, was courted by most of the many eligible bachelors and admired by all until she eventually agreed to marry the most persistent of her followers, Augustus O'Donaty, the eldest of the brothers, the most ambitious and the most successful of the brothers, and now the father of an apparently inexhaustible supply of progeny — for Aurora to bring up and five of whom, she was about to meet from the daylight mailboat.

Leo, the other gallant who had helped at the birth of the bull calf, had eventually resigned his commission, married Aurora, settled on the farm and worked it, giving her father time to indulge in his writing to the end of his stoical life.

Aurora shivered again, flicked the reins and set the mare plodding once more along the rough track towards the less pleasant bumpy cobbles that formed most of the coast road. The mare also had her memories. She knew that at three seasons of the year she always made this pre-dawn journey from which she would return with one other passenger; some sat quietly like the mistress; others bumped and bounced and jangled the buggy behind her; she felt too old for the elastic livestock nowadays. She had another memory when her cargo was too still. The night of the Great Shipwreck when the sky was rent with lightning, thundering drums and painful cannonades of wetness and she was young and inexperienced, but she had dragged that wet still human burden from the arrow-point of the promontory to the yard between her own welcome stable and the open kitchen door.

Gamma pricked up her ears, hearing the soft, as yet, braying of the many tethered donkeys, then closed her nostrils on catching a whiff of the rummaging goats. Soon they reached the ancient ruins of a castle, planted at a time when sea split the land in two at this point and a small fishing village had grown beneath the remnants of the castle walls. The air became heavy with powerful, competing

7

odours of vraic and tar opposing manure and garbage, and throughout and over all the unique smell of fresh caught fish.

"How strange," thought Aurora, still pursuing her backward look at her life, "How strange and how unpredictable are our lives. There's Augustus risking his life every other day, surviving, rewarded with medals and honours, already an elderly man, but active as ever, breeding his children only to part with them for most of their childhood. And there was Leo, set on a life of tranquillity on the isolated farm, dying young in the sea below our home." The buggy was close enough to the sea wall for Aurora to make out the dim shapes of the boats and the nets draped over them already washed and drying after a night's work. "We each have what we wanted, perhaps," she continued ruminating. "La Bullule Odonata has been truly good to us. Tera has the gaiety, the social life and doubtless the admiration she so craved; Augustus has his career; I have the large family I wanted instead of the two only; and Leo? Has he not the peace he so craved? How fortunate we are."

The sky was lightening rapidly with long thin pink and yellow streaks, lighting up all the other islands to the east and marbling the canopy above. A quick scan behind her assured Aurora that no smoke had yet shown on the horizon. She had no wish to hurry, but she had to park early on the quay and ensure a place for Old Pierre who would be leaving the farm shortly with the big cart horse and the trailer to carry five of the children and all the luggage.

Fishermen called out greetings to La Bellule in patois, French or in English as she rattled through the village. They knew where she was going and why; they knew all about the family's struggle for survival in the past; they watched the children growing up and many had even watched La Bellule grow up, and been on the beach the night of that fatal storm; they had not been able to launch their boats in the swell, none of them could swim, so they had to witness, helplessly, while the big, blond foreigner swam to his grave. Their sharp eyes noticed the shabby buggy; the even shabbier driver, and the well-groomed mare; when fishing off Bellule Bay they saw the crumbling paintwork of the house on the mound; these were all things they could understand. They understood perfectly why one sister should care for the offspring of another, unfortunate enough to be married to a man in some distant, alien land, but they could NOT understand why the children should be sent away, across the sea, a wild and treacherous sea, three times a year, to attend school. There were plenty of schools on the island. To the fishermen, mostly of Gallic extraction, it was a terrible waste of good money, but worse, far worse in their eyes, it was cruel to inflict such misery on fairly innocent youngsters. They did NOT know that La Bellule thought as they thought; they did NOT know that she reached the depths of the most profound misery herself when the children sailed away or that her return to the farm was almost unwilling, knowing that the house would feel dead. Her daughter Roxana felt the same, but she would busy herself clearing their rooms and beds, making piles of mending, bundles of washing and once those tasks were performed she would be knitting and sewing for their return. Aurora just wrote letters to the children and to their parents and awaited the arrival of the letter each would be forced to write every Sunday.

The fishermen knew all that. There was little they did not know about La Bellule, farm, family and animals. Old Pierre fished with them and Very Old Pierre had fished with some of them; they smoked their crooked wooden, or straight clay pipes together and they and their ancestors had done so since the families existed; they had all crammed into Old Pierre's cottage on the farm the night a son and heir was born to La Bellule; none of them had fished during the subsequent terrible nights and days while Aurora fought death; they had each given their blessing to the infant when Old Pierre's wife carried him to the cottage to hand over to another fisherman's wife while she took to her bed and her son, Pierre was born; both boys received the same blessing, half Christian, half pagan; both boys went on their first fishing expedition together; both boys were taught sea-lore, celtic lore and a deep respect for nature, the elements and humanity. The fishermen's daughters had played with Roxana and now their grandchildren were being taught by her. Soon, the old men knew, they would be watching the tentative courting — and they would watch their

9

granddaughters; they foretold remarkable futures for each of the children. What neither Aurora nor the fishermen knew was that their world was about to be changed, and life would never again be quite the same. Roxana busily stirring porage in the huge double saucepan knew, and was quietly preparing for it, but hoped her mother would be able to enjoy this last summer holiday with the children.

Re-living the past had not dulled Aurora's alertness to her surroundings. She noticed that the tide was still ebbing. The mail boat would be carefully sliding through the Heads a few minutes after the tide turned, unless it was obliged to wait in the deep water beyond the harbour wall because there was too little water. She studied the beach far beneath, the small puddles left by the receding water, the light leaping from stone to stone moving with the rivulets. Gulls screamed and performed aerobatics, glided to land, fought and squabbled and made their ungainly way from titbit to titbit. There was no need to hurry although she could see the steamer's smoke clearly above the horizon. It was a very low tide; exceptionally low for July. Or was it? Had she made a mistake in her calculations? Aurora felt panic. Perhaps she hadn't allowed enough time. She set Gamma into a steady trot and pulled out the great silver hunter she always wore around her neck. It had been Leo's, and before Leo had it, it had been his father's. She flicked open the cover; the hands pointed to twenty minutes to six. There was plenty of time, but she kept Gamma trotting until they reached the outskirts of Town.

The wheels of the buggy rolled noiselessly along the tarmac road and soon after passing the derelict old chateau, houses, two storeyed high, replaced the low cottages, indicating the precincts of the town. After swinging gracefully around a wide curve Aurora was able to see the full splendour of the town that had literally grown up around a port, a natural haven, rising tier upon tier in erratic angles and heights, overhung with flowering shrubs, vines and trees. "Just like the Hanging Gardens of Babylon," thought Aurora, "except they had been designed by one master mind and Town was a flowering of the individualism of those who had built it. The church clock was visible and Gamma halted, as always, to drink at the great granite trough and splash some water across her face, sensing the heat that would be almost uncomfortable before she passed this way on the return journey. Aurora climbed stiffly down from the buggy and led the mare the rest of the way, turning to her left along the quay until she found the ideal spot to park. After turning horse and buggy she sat on the sea wall and watched the mailboat, visible beneath its umbrella of smoke. While she watched, her mind went back six years when she had sat in the same spot with Gamma and the buggy beside her, for, as she liked to recall, the most momentous arrival she had ever witnessed.

On that day six years before, she had been as excited as she was this day. Her sister and the unknown brother-in-law were arriving, complete with what seemed like a retinue of gradated young. She had not seen Tera for twenty years — longer than they had lived together before her sister had sailed for India. It was the year the all India Moslem League had been founded, she recalled; Augustus had talked constantly and disparagingly about it, she remembered. When the steamer had finally docked and the gangplank rolled to the quayside, she had become aware of bystanders gasping. Across the gangplank swept the most elegant, and most beautiful woman imaginable, followed by a short, stocky, but equally imposing man in full military regalia. To Aurora's confusion, they walked straight towards her — in all her inelegant shabbiness — and she found herself face to face with her own sister. Behind them had stalked a bustling nanny holding the hand of a tiny replica of Tera; a fairy-like child with golden curls, and Tera's two year old daughter, Anna, behind them had followed the tall, slender Lex, sparkling with excitement and flashing observant eyes holding the hand of rosy-cheeked five year old Rolf. After an interval Frank had appeared, just ten years old and manfully struggling with his mother's hat boxes. While they collected in a shy bunch around this new aunt, all of them kept glancing amusedly back at the boat where the bystanders were being treated to a solemn pantomime as the six year old twins walked from each crew member to the next, shaking hands, finally repeating the performance on the bridge where the Captain was seen to bend and kiss Una. The crowd loved it. Augustus and the two older boys showed

11

disgust, the nanny mentioned indiscipline under her breath, and Tera turned to her sister with her unquenched charm and said, "You see, they really do NEED to go to boarding school." Aurora had not been at all sure, herself, but she knew they had bewitched her.

A year later Aurora had watched her sister depart from the same quay, with Anna, the nanny and a new baby, Marc. Augustus had preceded her to India by a few weeks. The children had all been left at school in England, and her own son, Rex, with them. She was to be in loco parentis, care for them during the school holidays — and a generous allowance paid into her bank each month by way of compensation. A new and absorbing, oh and so rewarding, a life had then begun for herself and Roxana. Throughout each interminably long term they planned for the next holiday. The old farmhouse seemed to smile beneath the noise, the damage to its structure, the sadnesses that only children feel, the laughter, the fighting, the hating and the love. For Tera's children this was home; this was security; here was understanding; here was, perhaps, a maternal love they had never known. For their aunt, here was fulfilment in the large family she had needed.

While she was dreaming, a heterogeneous cluster of people had been collecting between Aurora and the quay where the mailboat would berth. A few motor vehicles noisily barked into position, jostling with horses and carriages, carts and buggies. Pierre arrived and slowly backed the cart and horse in line with the buggy, then filled the twisted pipe he held in his teeth, and with one match, lit it. "They've had a good trip," he remarked between drags.

The ship slid past the harbour wall, startled the livestock for miles as it hooted its intention to enter the Heads, slowly squeezed through a gap that seemed too narrow for it and to the accompaniment of shouted commands glided to its appointed berth, welcomed by shrieks and salutations from the quay. A creaking and groaning indicated the unwillingness of the gangplank to give up the ship's liberty by attaching it to shore, then, and quite suddenly, the first passengers were walking across it, to be embraced by those awaiting their arrival. Aurora had seen the dim outline of the six children earlier, but they would have luggage to collect. She and Pierre waited, eyes glued to the two gangplanks. Suddenly Rex was beside her, a quick hug, and all that did not need to be said in the two pairs of eyes; the old grey eyes and the young dark hazel eyes.

"Is it all right, mother, if Una goes back in the buggy with you? She has something to tell you," asked Rex, as he stepped up to greet Old Pierre.

Aurora thought about these arrangements as the children's 'pecking order!' They arranged amongst themselves that Rex should have a few moments alone with his mother; he was always first ashore while Lex organised the baggage and the other children; Rex was always last to go on board at the end of each holiday; the others came ashore in their 'arranged' order; turns were strictly taken as to who went home in the buggy, and it was, by rights, Rex's turn. Aurora had a gift denied most mothers; she very seldom questioned the children; she trusted their decisions over all small matters and many important matters; she encouraged them to discuss, even argue over important issues. She was filled with the sense that this arrival would be as memorable as that other one, six years before. Certainly this sleek haired, moustached figure was a surprise. With that thought Aurora received another in the person of her nephew Lex, towering over her, lifting her off her feet, swinging her round and planting an exuberant kiss on each cheek before returning her to the security of the cobbled quayside. She looked up at another moustache, another carefully flattened head of hair and into a pair of eyes as blue as those of the two vikings she had encountered in the archway in front of the old farmhouse, a lifetime before. Before she had time to absorb the impression she found Frank and Rolf were at her side, both so undemanding and so quiet they could easily become overlooked. The younger boy was already as tall as this older brother who, like Rex, would never grow to any great height, but was perhaps the most reliable member of the tribe. Aurora knew that Frank would bide his time and later, long after they all arrived home, she would find him by her side, greeting her in his own withdrawn fashion, whereas Rolf would remain close to her until pushed aside by the extravagant bouncing of the twins dislodged him. The twins were always last off the boat, already quarrelling before they

13

reached their aunt and usually attracting amused attention. Another surprise was in store for Aurora. She did not recognise Ivan until he spoke; he was as tall as Lex and his voice had already deepened; his vivacity had, however remained unchecked, as indeed had his loquacity. He towered over Una who looked pale, smaller than ever beside this beanpole of a twin and strangely shrivelled. One thing had not changed, though. Ivan was impeccably neat with every button done up, his hair darkly smooth, his tie carefully tied and hanging straight down, tucked inside his navy raincoat. Una had every button undone, her hair half in and half out of its plaits, her hat hanging behind her turned in collar by the elastic that appeared to be twisted around her school tie. Where Ivan had clearly outgrown all his clothes, Una seemed to have shrunk inside hers, and after greeting her aunt and Old Pierre she rubbed her cheek and hair against Gamma's mane, holding a dilapidated gladstone bag in her hand while her brothers handled cases, tin trunks and cricket bags into the cart before piling on themselves.

Rex sauntered across the quay having checked that each piece of luggage had been brought ashore. "All right for us to leave, Mother?" he asked, helping her into the buggy, then turning to his cousin he said, "Come on, Una, in you get. Everything'll be all right. Oh yes, and having MY place in the buggy does NOT mean you can have the yellow egg!" After which he leapt up beside Old Pierre and the two horses moved slowly along the quay towards the town which blazed with the sunlight winking from the myriad of windows.

"It was MY turn to sit by Old Pierre," said Una, shivering while she hunched herself forward trying to cover her wrinkled black-stockinged legs with the battered leather bag. Aunt and niece silently watched the bumping heads perched on the luggage ahead until they turned into the coast road and had to allow a motor car to pass. Neither spoke. They trundled along the quiet road, for most of the boat traffic had long since dispersed.

Gamma's hooves beat out a steady rhythm while the gulls screamed their morning concert to the world. The sun was above the horizon and the day cloudless, but the child beside Aurora sat twisting and untwisting a knotted and none too clean large handkerchief, while the normally restless feet and chattering tongue were still and silent.

"I'm going to be sick!" gasped Una. She had left the buggy before the wheels stopped rolling, sped across the road and hung over the sea wall, making a generous offering to the scavengers wheeling above.

"We'll take the coast road and let the others arrive first," Aurora decided, slowing the pace, to Gamma's surprise and disgust.

Aurora said nothing as offerings were made five more times. When they reached the promontory she stopped the buggy and they sat side by side, seeing the sunlight sparkling on a granite wall surrounding the farm. It was to the woman's credit that she still made no comment when Una announced, "It's all right now. I'm only sick six times."

"Oh," said the aunt, as casually as she could contrive, "You're used to it are you?" Her mind was trying to search out all the ailments that this might foretell.

"Only at school," came the reply. "It's just part of school."

"I see!" But she did not see, so picked up the reins to drive on to that welcoming house, high on its mound, but before she had signalled Gamma to proceed, a thin, urgent voice stilled her movement.

"Aunt Rora? Aunt Aurora, I've been expelled!"

Una watched her aunt's face, waiting for the shock, disappointment, disgust, or even anger to change that calm demeanour.

"Never mind darling, you're HOME now," was all she said as horse and buggy sped for home.

Silent tears streaked the thin pale face, and while the boys poured into the yard, perturbed by the delayed arrival, Una stood beside Gamma, wiping her face surreptitiously on the beloved mare's sleek mane. Once they were occupied with stabling the horses and clustering around their aunt, Una slipped through the kitchen and up the stairs, where, having divested herself of most of her clothes she lay on her bed, held her aching head together and finally slept, but the boys' voices in the yard below rang in her ears with their reassurance.

"You do understand, Aunt Rora?" asked Lex. "She didn't DO ANYTHING, really."

"It was OUR fault," cut in Frank.

"And we just had six of the best," added Rex.

"Ivan had them, actually," the accurate Frank adjusted.

"Yes, WE had the reprimand, all of us," said Lex.

"Oh indeed, don't forget the reprimand," Ivan's voice boomed and squeaked.

"She's been sick. I can smell it. I'll have her egg."

Rolf asked, "Why? She's only sick at school. Not at home."

"Breakfast!" called Roxana from the kitchen door.

Chapter Two

The boys trooped into the kitchen, rinsed their hands in the sink and sat in their accustomed seats, circling the table each side of Aurora. "What's wrong with Una?" asked Roxana, giving a final stir to the porage.

"She was sick all the way home," her mother explained. "She's gone up to her bed to sleep it off." Roxana made no further comment, but walked round the table ladling porage from a glittering copper pan into each willow-patterned bowl. A large basin of rich brown sugar passed from hand to hand followed by a jug of the yellow cream provided by their own cows.

After the silence of voracious appetites being appeased, Rex beamed at his mother, his sister and then from face to face around him, and voiced the general and unanimous opinion. "Ah! It's good to be home," then, as an afterthought, "And it's ME for the yellowest yolk!"

One by one as the picture appeared on the bottom of each porage bowl the owner carried it to the sink and served himself from the top of the great black range. Ivan elected to serve his cousin and his aunt, creating mirth and relaxation with his exaggerated mimicry of a waiter he had seen some eight years before in a Bombay hotel.

Aurora sat, overwhelmed with happiness behind the massive brown teapot dispensing the refreshing liquid, watching her beloved family, and feeling utterly at peace with the world. She knew they would all remain for as long as two hours over this first meal of the holiday, talking, laughing, filling in the gaps left by their Sunday letters. She had never been to any sort of school herself and this extraordinary life these young people led once they left the sanctuary of the island seemed to her like a mixture of Jane

17

Eyre's Lowood, Oliver Twist's orphan home and a battle ground or barracks. Headmasters and Headmistresses were evil dictators, all except sport, art and music teachers were tyrants, as indeed were prefects, yet two prefects sat before her and they seemed to her to be unusually gentle and benign. School Chapel was, it seemed, not the place of holiness and righteousness, but the place where evil deeds were planned. During seven years she had become almost immune to the tales of misdeeds and misunderstandings, but suddenly she had been faced with the fact that her niece had been constantly sick and nobody had told her; the child, though very small, always appeared to be exceptionally healthy. In addition, Roxana was a teacher and had none of the luridly described evil tendencies attributed to those who taught these pupils.

The plates on the table thinned, and the pile in the sink grew, but bread and honey was still being passed from plate to plate. Cups were being filled and refilled.

"I've taken the day off, mother," announced Roxana.

Knives rested on plates; bread remained in mid air between plate and mouth and six pairs of eyes stared in disbelief at the speaker.

"Roxana!" ejaculated her mother. "You NEVER take a day off, not even when you are poorly. Why?"

"It isn't every day my brother leaves school; it isn't every day my cousin leaves school; and . . . and it's St. Swithun's Day . . ." she finished lamely.

Aurora distinctly saw Rex wink at his sister, watched in turn, each of the faces surrounding her trying to affect surprise. "A conspiracy is it?" she asked. "Well, let us hope that the saint won't let you all down and permit rain to fall." The crockery groaned in the sink and the hungry young continued attacking bread, honey and home produced butter with gusto, while Aurora replenished the teapot, thinking, "They have surprises for me have they? I have one for them, as well."

Her daughter read her thoughts and asked in an undertone, "When do we tell them?"

"Not yet. Wait for Una and Pierre," she whispered back while the boys were deep in talk about the merits of differing aeroplanes.

Eating had at last ceased. Cups were passed from hand to hand for refilling, and even Aurora's steady hand and placid exterior were shaken when she heard Rex ask, "Is it all right if we smoke, mother?"

All eyes focussed on her face; she heard Roxana's surprised intake of breath, and she wished Leo were by her side.

"Of course you may," she heard herself say.

Three pipes were pulled from the depths of three pockets, a tobacco pouch passed from Rex to Lex to Frank, and after much pushing down in the bowls of the pipes, much flickering of matches and sucking sounds, smoke filled the kitchen, and she asked, "How long have you been smoking, then?"

"About seven years," answered Rex nonchalantly.

"Ever since we went away to school, actually," added Lex.

"Survival," explained, or did not explain, the laconic Frank.

The smell of pipe tobacco was one of the many things Aurora had missed since Leo died; she noticed the experienced handling of the three very different pipes, and she realized with overwhelming sadness, that she really did not know these young people who were her very reason for being.

Una walked into the kitchen, her eyes like slits, but her walk more jaunty than it had been. While accepting a cup from her aunt she said, "Oh, there's a terribly strange smell upstairs," to the world in general.

"I expect it's your sick," suggested her unfeeling twin.

"No it's not," she retorted, "I threw my dress and coat out of the window."

"I take it you are back to normal; your customary argumentative self?" asked Frank.

Roxana, who adored her little cousin asked, "You don't do things like that at school, do you?"

Before Una was obliged to reply Old Pierre walked into the kitchen followed by a dark, handsome young man in a fisherman's Guernsey and blue cotton trousers.

"It's Pierre. It's Young Pierre," they almost shouted, leaving unfinished cups of tea scattered across the table as they pumped the young man's hand up and down, thumped

19

him on the back, and generally showed him how welcome he was — and their personal regard for him.

Old Pierre watched with pride. Rex and Pierre studied each other, mutual appraisal on their faces. "Moustache eh?" said the visitor. He winked, adding, "and legal smoking eh? Pipe now is it? Try one of your old friends," with which he handed him a battered packet of French cigarettes, which, after Rex had taken one, he proceeded to pass around the other youngsters. Ivan, seeing his aunt was in conversation with Old Pierre, took one, lit it and strolled across to the barn. His nonchalance was shortlived. He was stopped in his tracks by the unusually peremptory command from his aunt. "No, Ivan! Absolutely no, no, no! No smoking in the barns or near the barns — EVER." She returned to her conversation and the others exchanged slightly mystified looks. Their aunt had NOT forbidden him to smoke — and he was not thirteen!

Their aunt's voice obtruded on their amused silent interchanges. "Come on now, all of you. It's MY turn to shock and surprise you. Follow me."

They followed her through the kitchen door into a stone paved entrance hall, guarded on the sea side of the house by a massive door that would no longer open, past the piled up luggage and under the tourelle — the spiral staircase that faced the useless door. Underneath it was a newly painted door; a door where only a wall used to exist. Aurora threw open the door and stood back to watch the effect on her family. A small window faced the door and sunlight sparkled and danced from brass taps, pristine white walls and all the necessities of a well-equipped bathroom.

"A proper bathroom. Inside," breathed Una.

"No more boiling water in the copper. No more bathing outside in a force ten gale."

"Privacy." Frank, after making that comment, asked, "How?"

"The ship came HOME," explained their aunt. "The ship, Old Pierre's imagination and Young Pierre's skill, and here it IS. A REAL bathroom, not a corner of the wash-house."

"But, Aunt Rora," Lex asked, "What about your bedroom? It must've shrunk somewhat!"

"It's quite large enough for one, thank you, Lex. Come and see."

They all inspected the shrunken bedroom, then Roxana's next to it, and then Young Pierre said, "And NOW, Mother's expecting you at the cottage — all of us — to show you what the ship brought US."

In silence they trooped through the house, followed the gravel path through a gate in the wall that surrounded the kitchen garden, along the hedgerows to the line of cottages at the far end of the property.

Marie Roche was standing in the porch of her cottage, the open door showing the cheery living room within. After welcoming each in turn she lead them proudly through the adjoining kitchen, threw open a door and disclosed an identical bathroom to the one they had all been admiring at the farmhouse. A brown flowerpot stood on the low windowsill, and the room was sweet with the smell of thyme growing in it.

"You see," she said, once they had all viewed and offered their congratulations and aired their delight, "Thanks to Monsieur Leo, La Bellule and young Pierre."

"And Old Pierre," added her husband. "Don't forget Old Pierre."

Laughing, they returned to the living room where Marie served them with red wine and fruit cake. When Una declined anything, she looked hard at the slitted eyes, asking, "Not well, ma pauvre?"

"I've been sick," explained the child.

"Not YOU, Una" asked Young Pierre in disbelief. "You're NEVER seasick; not you, nor Ivan. Never."

"Just school-sick," said her twin, helpfully.

Marie studied the eyes again. "A headache, eh? It's the migraine. I know it. Blind, then sick and then headache . . . eh?"

Una nodded, ashamed at her infirmity being publicised.

"I have the cure," she heard the kind voice continue. "A tissane. One minute all of you while I make a tissane. Come." Una followed her into the kitchen, returning a few minutes later with a steaming cup of liquid in her hand, a smile on her face and without the fear that had been her

21

constant companion for years. She was not going to go blind; she was NOT slowly becoming blind; she had a little, a very little, health problem, just like Ivan, her twin, had a problem with his attacks of asthma. It was nothing. Marie had a cure, and anyway, she never had any little problems at home, and school had dispensed with her. Her eyes began to open and her skin stopped shivering if anyone touched her. It was a wonderful, sunshiny day. She looked around her and asked, "Where's Thor?" She had just realized that the old sheepdog had not greeted her.

The silence and the covert looks passing from eye to eye, answered her ill-timed question.

"I see," she said. "He's dead!"

She thought, "they're all waiting for me to scream, shout at them, throw a tantrum, as they call it. Well, I can't. I couldn't even cry. I've got a huge ice peardrop inside me." She wiped the stickiness of the tissane that had spilled over her hands, all the way down her faded kilt and studied the pattern of wrinkles made by her black stockings on her legs and heard her aunt say, "We waited for you to come home Una; we thought you could choose another dog."

Una did not answer. She thought, "Another dog! ME choose another dog? I don't want ANOTHER dog. I want Thor."

"I think we'd better arrange the holiday chores," suggested Aurora, then you can all change into more comfortable clothes." Removing stiff collars, ties and jackets while they walked, the boys followed the Roches and their aunt round the perimeter of the meadows. Either Pierre or Aurora pointed out broken fences, clogged ditches and uprooted trees. By the time they reached the yard outside the kitchen there seemed to be a formidable amount of work to be done. "And just one other thing," Aurora added, "I thought you boys might make a partition in your room as a little room for Una . . . and a door, of course." Her sharp eyes did not miss the well-concealed, but evident relief on the faces of the two younger boys.

"What a good idea," said Rex.

"There you are, Una," agreed Lex; "no need in the future to climb trees, scramble over rocks or hide in the cromlech for a 'thinking place'; you'll have your own. What's more, when I'm rich I'll buy a generator and put electric light in this house, then you'll have your own light . . . eh?"

Ivan interrupted with, "Better than those candles you tried to . . ." He saw the withering looks being showered on him by his brothers and cousin and stopped short before finishing tamely, "you THOUGHT of making."

"Let's shift the trunks up to our rooms," enjoined the ever-resourceful Rex.

Una showed her gratitude by tackling the washing up, unbidden, while Roxana, stirred a large cauldron of stew, before remarking to her cousin that they would have to eat bread and cheese for lunch as the stew could not cook in time. She then asked, casually, "You'd like to have your own little room wouldn't you?"

The exuberant answer was all the instigator could have hoped. "And, I'll TRY to be tidy. I'll TRY to be helpful. I'll just go and rinse out my cloak and dress. Perhaps I could just drop them in the trough — there isn't MUCH sick on them . . ." Roxana knew that Una would not change overnight — if ever.

"Hang them on the line to dry, then we can scrub them with vinegar, before you go back to school."

"I'm not going back. Ever. Really and truly, Roxana. They've written to Aunt Aurora, and to mother and father. They don't want ME back, this time. It isn't just me not wanting to go back to THEM."

"You haven't been EXPELLED, have you?"

"Yes! And I've told Aunt Rora."

Shouts from up the stair took them both into the hall below, in time to hear Ivan's angry voice demanding, "Come on, Lex, let me have ONE of your shirts. I can't get into any of mine."

They looked up the stairs to see Ivan, like a scarecrow, arms extending from a shirt several sizes too small, legs protruding beneath trousers that ended at his calves.

By the time they reached the top of the spiral Rex was saying, "It seems I shall soon be LAST to wear the clothes you wreck. Justice does NOT exist."

Aurora, arms laden with roses, joined Roxana in the hall as Una sped up and around and around the narrow stairway;

and Aurora heard the irregularly pitched voice of Ivan shouting, "Come ON, Lex, just ONE of your cricket shirts, you won't want them anymore when you're flying."

Rex's deep voice could be heard below, saying, "Shut UP, Ivan."

Rolf appeared at the top of the tourelle, while from the room on the other side were sounds of scuffling, deep breathing and, intermittently, "Keep out of this, Una; you'll get hurt! Scram." A heavy bump followed and, simultaneously, the girl was propelled across the landing and collided with her younger brother.

Aurora dropped the roses, lifted the brass gong that hung inside the front door and rang it vigorously, before lifting her voice into the heights above and calling, "Lunch is ready. NOW."

Upstairs there was complete silence. Slow footsteps could be heard descending the stairs, while Roxana and her mother moved on swift feet, placing food, plates and knives on the bare kitchen table. The boys had, from their earliest days, been taught that to arrive later than five minutes after the call to the table constituted grave discourtesy to the ladies. Following the three elder boys was Ivan, wearing a pyjama top and football shorts and at the fifty-eighth second of the fourth minute Rolf and Una appeared, Rolf holding a blood-stained handkerchief to his nose.

Aurora looked at the innocent victim and asked, playing for time, "Who did it?"

"Me," said Una with alacrity and some pride.

"Me," said Ivan, without pride.

"Me," said Frank, adding after a suitable pause, "It was my impetus, Ivan's propulsion and Una's interference."

"History in miniature," added Rex.

"Precisely!" Lex threw in. "A pacifist politician starts a war, the military hierarchy produce the weapons, issue orders through the ranks, and the innocent, non-combatant suffers."

Silence and stillness accompanied by stares at the speaker followed the speech.

"Say all that again, Lex," said his aunt.

Lex repeated, with a few additions, his previous statements.

Roxana's usually imperturbable face wore an expression of some distress, and she looked from face to face around the table, from the inscrutability of Frank's to the alertness of Rex's, the mobility of Lex's to the blandness of Rolf's, from the agitation of Una's to the excitement of her twin's, resting, finally, on the hurt bewilderment on her mother's wrinkled little face.

At last Aurora spoke. 'I think there is a lot of explanation needed . . . NOW. Eat, then TALK; all of you."

The inevitable large cups of tea circled the table, bread was cut in thick chunks, butter, cheese and any other desired spread was collected from the larder, and they ate, hungry again after the not inconsiderable distance they had walked, backwards and forwards, crossing and criss-crossing the land as well as the inspection of the perimeter wall and fences. Aurora had completed her meal long before the rest of the family so she decided to talk first.

"Yes," she began, "The ship that came home. It was more a mine than a ship. A mine somewhere in Australia. An opal mine in South Australia. Your grandfather died there, his goldmine having failed, but the mine was never sold, and he had bought, or given, shares for each member of his family when he expected to make his fortune. I think the husband of one of your aunts out there took over the mine and found opals. Black opals. Anyway, there it is; there is the mine and it is making money and we get dividends from our share. Thus we now have a bathroom. The Pierres have a bathroom. Roxana is going to have a bicycle, and I think we could do with a couple for the farm. We have a new fishing boat and I think, I just think, mind you, we might buy one of these motor vehicles — for the farm. Gamma and Alph are growing too old for much more heavy dragging. I think you three elder boys and Young Pierre should look into that. Oh yes, and Ivan IS to have some suitable shirts and trousers — holiday wear."

Aurora could not have confused her family more if she had set out to do just that. They sat and gaped. They saw the familiar old-fashioned and adored head of the household, always predictable and thoroughly conservative, now providing the household with bathroom, indoors and fully plumbed and before they had absorbed that innovation they

25

find she has also provided the same luxury for her cottagers and, even more revolutionary, she was proposing adding one of the hated motor cars to the farm's already non-existent machinery. The bombshells they were about to explode would seem almost trivial behind this.

"This is the machine age, mother," her son gently teased. "One day ALL farmers will have vehicles instead of horses; everyone will have electric light supplied by a central generator; aeroplanes will carry the mail to the islands and everything will move at twice the speed, no three times the speed it does to-day."

"Well, I don't think I want an aeroplane in the top meadow."

Frank had been busily polishing his glasses, indicating a big decision was slowly revolving in his mind. He replaced them on his face, brushed the thick wavy hair from his forehead, stiffened in his seat and, in his quiet voice said, "Aunt Aurora, I'm not going to military college. I'm not going in the army." Having made his speech, so carefully rehearsed, he again removed the spectacles and thus was unable to see expressions of faces around him. He rubbed and polished and shone, his head bent and his expression shielded. "I'm a pacifist, " he said.

Roxana broke the silence. "Frank," she said, "how can YOU be a pacifist? You walk round the farm with a shotgun and shoot anything that moves. You're going to join Rex at the military college next year. Uncle Augustus has assured you of a commission in his regiment, and you read every book written about India and the army there. You must be an authority on military campaigns the world over. That isn't pacifism, is it?"

Frank replaced the spectacles he had been methodically polishing, adjusted them with care and replied, his voice slow, each word considered. "I've changed. I see the futility of war. I've decided to be a doctor. I would rather prevent pain and mend people, than destroy them . . ."

"But why?" queried Aurora. "Why this sudden change, Frank? Of course I AGREE wholeheartedly with you . . . but your father? What is he going to say?"

Rex interpolated, "They've ALL written to Uncle Augustus and Aunt Tera. You should hear from them any day now, I should think."

"No," disagreed Frank. "We wrote three weeks ago. We won't have a reply before the middle of August — even the end."

"Well, Frank, explain, if you can," his aunt urged.

Frank pulled at his pipe, phrasing and re-phrasing the words in his head, watching the tenseness of the other young people. At last he said, "We met this chap, this old man; he'd been all over the world in the army. A VERY old man. He fought in the Crimean War, saw the Charge of the Light Brigade. He was even with the army sent to relieve Gordon at Khartoum. He told us what it was like to be an ORDINARY soldier. He told us what it was like to be a prisoner, and he told us what he THOUGHT it must be like to be a free man one minute and then have your country and your farm taken over by foreigners with firearms." Frank stopped. He had never made such a long speech in his life.

In the silence that followed Frank felt the congratulation of his fellow-conspirators flowing towards him.

"I can't see anything wrong with those sentiments, Frank," his aunt encouraged, "but, of course, your father has ambitions for you . . . rather different from your sentiments, hasn't he?"

Lex encouraged his brother to complete his confession. "Go ON, Frank, old man. You may as well tell Aunt Aurora EVERYTHING. We agreed on that."

Unwillingly and even more hesitantly Frank, feeling as if he exposed his soul, burst out. "I want to be a missionary, Aunt Aurora. A medical missionary. Like that chap Schweitzer, you know. In India. I didn't tell father that bit, but we did agree, all six of us, that we must tell YOU."

"It's all Una's fault," said her twin. "She found the hermit . . ."

"Ivan!" There was no mistaking the command in Rex's voice. He faced his mother and pleaded, "We'll explain Una's part in all this later. It IS long and complicated."

Ivan, quickly roused to anger, and with normal thirteen year old aggressiveness, added to his earlier gaucheness by saying, "And what'll be the use of missionaries when the war comes. You know what The Beak said at the leaving service. 'And now boys, war may be merely days away.'"

"Could you find some food, Roxana," asked Rex, "like toffee, to stuff the mouth of this young oaf?" He then joined in the laughter that followed Ivan's clever impersonation of their Headmaster. Mollified by the applause, Ivan tackled the tray of hard, sticky toffee that Roxana produced from the larder.

Aurora took a deep, deep breath before asking, "Now, am I to understand that each of you has some sort of confession to make? Some alteration in your future careers? Rex?"

The answer came back as soon as the question was asked, "Not me, mother! I'm not filled with imagination. I'm a simple straightforward sort of chap. Like Rolf. I go to military college in September. I'm more phlegmatic than these others. I expect I'll end up a General when I'm eighty. You don't have to worry about ME. I'll just help keep the peace in the greatest empire the world has ever known — and leave the Franks of this world free to 'convert' the natives and, hopefully cure diseases like leprosy, malaria, cholera and the rest. Frank can bring me quinine from time to time."

"Not worry!" thought Aurora, "not worry, when MY son, of all the young around MY table, has decided to join the most scattered army in the world. And you, Rolf?" she asked.

"Oh me, Aunt Rora, me? I'm not ambitious either. Not me. I just want to farm. Perhaps I'll end up in the colonies — sheep farming in Australia or something . . ." He trailed off. He wanted nothing more than to stay at La Bellule, farming in the serenity of the space he could see from the kitchen window.

"Your turn now, Lex," said his cousin.

Another fraught silence filled the room.

Aurora again helped the young man. "I heard what was said upstairs before you all scrapped over a shirt . . ."

"Yes, well then Aunt Aurora, you must have guessed," Lex smiled his charming and most beseeching smile at his aunt, before saying, "I've written to father and told him I don't want to go to Oxford and study some stuffy classics. I want to fly. Aeroplanes. You know, those new things that are like huge birds. The school knows. The Beak knows, but he doesn't approve. I've APPLIED to join the R.F.C. — The Royal Flying Corps . . ."

"Lex, darling, I DO KNOW what an aeroplane IS. I think if I were young I would want to fly in one. Not as an aviator, but just to FEEL what air is like, how a bird feels . . . yes, I would, Lex."

"Then you shall, Aunt. I shall fly you, high into the clouds, across the meadows and across the sea, right into the eye of the sun; you'll feel the sharpness of the wind, and breathe in air, purer even that the air in the Himalayas. You'll love it, Aunt Aurora, really you will — and you shall — when I am a qualified aviator with my own licence."

They all stared at Lex. Not even Rex realized before how strongly he felt about flying.

"Thank you, Lex, yes thank you very, very much. Indeed you shall fly me — one day. But, now, tell me, HOW do you know what it is like flying. You have never been in a aeroplane."

"But I have. I have. I've even had two flying lessons." Lex had forgotten the family, the kitchen and La Bellule. He was re-experiencing his exploits, re-living the most wonderful experience of his young life. At last his mind returned to earth and he explained, "I saved up my pocket money for the first flight, and a dayboy's elder brother took us both by motor car to the aerodrome where you could get five shilling trips. I used the money father sent for my birthday, sold my meccano, and all these chaps — and Una — helped me; they said it was birthday presents . . . I'm not in the cricket team, nor is Carter, so as a prefect I could visit another boy's home. It was decent of his parents, too; Carter's father lent me civilian clothes — you know, Aunt Aurora, boarders aren't supposed to even taken their jackets off when they visit other chap's homes. I know it wasn't quite the thing for a prefect . . . but . . . well, you know, sometimes there are things that one HAS to do . . . aren't there?"

"Yes," thought Aurora. "Leo had said the same when he decided to leave the army, marry her and settle on the farm, disappointing his mother and his five sisters, irritating his brothers." She supposed he felt the same when he plunged into the sea to fight tumultuous waves in an attempt to save a stranger's life.

"I'm not sure, Lex, if learning to fly is one of those things, but then I am not YOU, am I? No harm came to you and some good came out of it; you KNOW what career you want to follow and it seems the family has been generous enough to help you."

"Oh, but we WANTED to help Lex," Una said. "Lex is always the one to help us. I'd have DIED in that awful school if it wasn't for Lex, well, all the boys, but especially Lex."

"Hm!" added Rex. "That is indeed true. It was Lex who took you back and smuggled you in when you ran away . . . and provided the spare handkerchiefs to mop up the tears . . ."

"Don't, Rex. Don't remind me. It WAS a long time ago . . ." the shamed girl pleaded.

Aurora was drawing new breath with each sentence she heard spoken. She was not sure how much more she could take in one day. "We'll discuss Una and her exploits, later. Much later to-day. Just for now I would like to hear from Ivan. What have you done or not done, Ivan?"

"While he removes that glutinous sized toffee from his mouth, mother, just allow me to state, in public, that Ivan's a stalwart fellow. He took the beating and he took the blame for what all of us did so that we two prefects didn't lose our caps, so that Frank didn't lose his spotless reputation and so that Rolf didn't have to suffer all the questions and jawing and the whacking." Rex's accolade surprised them all. Ivan looked his thanks before rinsing his sticky fingers, then returned to his seat at the table before announcing sonorously, "I am about to surprise you most of us all, Aunt Rora, and Roxana." He rose, bowed to each of the ladies, sat down and his face took on an expression so smug, they all burst into laughter.

"Aunt Aurora, I am going into the Royal Navy — WHEN I pass the exam. Surprised? You see me, here, before you, the rebel, the bad boy, the rogue among rogues, but I have not changed. The career my distant parents planned for me, — with my help, of course — is still to be my chosen career. And when I am Admiral of the Fleet, inviting lesser men to kiss me, you will all kindly remember that I 'stuck to my guns', 'I fought the good fight', 'I held the square', that I 'knew my duty' and I . . ."

"Broke the line," added his twin.

"Of course," he conceded.

Aurora felt a great deal better than she had when the family had been gathered around the table early that morning.

"The sun is shining, the kitchen is hot, there are chores to do later this afternoon, so I suggest we all take a walk along the beach. I would just suggest that SOMEONE lends Ivan a shirt, temporarily, and that you ALL don your football clothes — so much cooler."

A few minutes later the six youngsters, bare-footed and sparsely clad were testing the temperature of the sea. The boys swam in their clothes, watched wistfully by the girl. Aurora watched with pride, Roxana with some amusement.

"I'll give you my miniature shirts and shorts, Una, then you can join us next time," offered her twin as they wandered back to the farm, refreshed in body and mind, full of renewed energy and ready to embark on the variety of jobs allocated to them. Talk, further talk, could wait until later, after the cows had been milked, the animals fed and watered, the stove stoked and fuel carried for the morning, the yard swept, the trunks unpacked, the dirty linen stacked in the wash-house and the elder boys shaved in the new bathroom, and a chalk line drawn across the bedroom floor where Una's partition was to be erected.

Aurora sat at the head of the table, after ringing the gong that evening, thinking, "I shall remember this day always. There will never be a day like it," she could not have known how truly she thought. Awaiting the family, herself, the Roches, their island, the mainland, Europe and the world, was a cataclysm that would bring each individual to the brink of a seemingly bottomless abyss.

Una, most unusually arrived at the table first, her hair freshly washed by Roxana and tied neatly with the black school ribbon. Aurora noticed the sparkle in her eyes and the tinge of colour that even the slightest exposure to sun could produce. "She'll be as dark as a gypsy in a week," thought the compassionate aunt. "She must have been indoors almost permanently to be so pale in July."

The boys swung jauntily into the kitchen, hair sleeked down with water, clothes neatly pressed. "Roxana ironed our things while we were all out doing the chores," explained

31

Rex who stood at his sister's side to hand round the plates of stew that she ladled from the copper pan sizzling on the stove. "Ah, this smells wonderful, Roxana. What a remarkable sister for a chap to have." The young woman was strangely pleased. She had felt utterly defeated a few minutes earlier, while washing her cousin's unruly hair; that had seemed to her the ideal moment to explain to the girl that she must not continue walking in and out of the bathroom while the boys bathed.

"Why?" Una had asked. "We've done it always, and we know what we all look like bare."

Unable to work out a satisfactory reply, Roxana had said weakly, "Well, they're used to being just with other boys — and no girls."

"I KNOW, Roxana; Ivan explained!"

"WHAT did Ivan EXPLAIN?" Roxana held her breath and wished she had not embarked on the topic.

"He said that his little friend — you know, his Thing — didn't like to be seen by people who didn't have one. And I KNOW NOW I won't grow one. The boys said I would — oh a long, long time ago, when we lived in India. It isn't true. I prayed to grow one for SIX years and nothing happened. When it didn't happen, I gave up God. That was last Lent."

Roxana escaped to attend to the supper, while Una added, "Anyway I don't BELIEVE Ivan. He thinks he fobbed me off, so I let him THINK he was too clever for me."

Chapter Three

Roxana's stew had been demolished to the last dumpling and potato. Fruit, bread and cheeses had filled the remaining crevices. The dishes were stacked in the sink covered with a bucket full of rainwater collected by Ivan from the tank outside the door. Bread was rising at the back of the shining range and two huge kettles picked up the rays of the lowering sunlight on their warm copper sides. The large willow-pattern cups and saucers were steaming in front of each member of the family while milk and sugar circulated. This was 'slumping time'; pipes were being lit and three spirals of smoke rose towards the overhead beams; elbows rested on the table, backs were hunched forward or leaning backward on tipped chairs, thoughtfully fitted with rubber feet by Lex, many years before — feet made from old tyres found on a rubbish dump. The table, made from a single piece of oak, was matched by the heavy chairs, in the curved back of which Frank had carved the name of each member of the family, and each chair, as each occupant, had the appointed place at the table, from Rex on Aurora's right in order of seniority to Rolf seated beside Roxana on her mother's left.

"Now," said Rex, "We've had a parley, mother and Roxana, and if you can bear to listen, we've decided to leave nothing, NOTHING, out of a long and complicated story, that ended with Una's expulsion. You understand, we are ALL involved and equally culpable."

Roxana pulled a bag from under her chair and commenced knitting, her four metal needles clicking rhythmically while she watched the faces around her.

"We — all of us — have agreed that I should tell this part of the tale, because everything was new and strange to me when we left the island that first time. Remember, I only left the farm to go to school or church and I was experiencing my first real journey. Ugh. That ship, that day. These world travelled youngsters," he said, waving his pipe around the circle of faces, "they were used to hotels and custom sheds, crowds of people and vast restaurants with flunkeys hovering at every twist and turn. NOW, I am a sophisticated wonder, but THEN, well, then even Rolf here knew which knife and fork to ladle his food with, and I was both bewildered and, I freely admit now, filled with admiration for their undoubted assurance."

"Get ON with it, Rex," interposed Ivan, knowing they could not prolong the moment when they would all suffer distress.

"Yes," Rex took up the tale, "well we stayed in a very grand hotel — all of us — in the middle of London. Every day we went on shopping expeditions with Uncle Augustus, we boys, while Aunt Tera took Una and Anna with her. Most afternoons we went on expeditions without Anna. Nanny stayed behind and looked after her and baby Marc. We went to the theatre — to pantomimes. London was full of post-Christmas entertainments. We saw 'Aladdin' and 'The Boy who wouldn't Grow Up' — Peter Pan. Oh yes, they've just made a statue of him in Kensington Gardens. Well then, after Aladdin, the entire hotel was treated to Ivan's interpretation of that fellow; he had every flunkey and every domestic and most of the guests entertained. WE tried to disown him. Anyway, one cold, wet, snowy afternoon we were all left behind while Uncle and Aunt went to some important function. We were left in the hotel Kitchen with Nanny to guard us. A maid had taken the two little ones out in the pram and we were allowed to put our games and toys all over the huge table. Lex and I started making a model of Tower Bridge from Lex's new meccano set. The other four were re-enacting the Peter Pan story; I expect Ivan was rehearsing for his evening exhibition to the assemblage of grand guests. HE was, of course, the hero and Frank, complete with eye-patch and meat hook fixed up his sleeve, a realistic, and I must say, rather terrifying, Captain Hook.

Rolf was the crocodile which, as I recall, annoyed Una who was obliged to be Wendy, all the Lost Boys, Red Indians and Pirate crew. It did, however give her plenty of scope for getting in the way of the main actors. Which she did! Just when Hook and Pan were duelling with two pokers. Ivan was standing on a chair while Frank parried from ground level. Nanny and Cook and some other slaves were sitting in a little side-room gossiping. I don't really know what happened next except that Una had been pushed, presumably by Frank, fallen on the stove and her hand went down on the hotplate. She screamed. How she screamed! Shook our bridge, it did. Suddenly bedlam was loosed. Cook rushed in, gathered Una in her arms, carried her to the larder and spread something over her hand. What WAS it, Una?"

"Butter."

"Meanwhile, Nanny had grabbed the bewildered Frank, dragged him to the sink, held him down and proceeded to hold his hand under the hot tap. It was boiling hot."

"It steamed." said Rolf.

"Rolf screamed. Ivan screamed," Rex went on dramatically, "Una had never stopped screaming. You can imagine the noise! Suddenly Una had broken loose from Cook, flown across the room and was punching and kicking Nanny, who, rather understandably, let go of Frank, who fled from the room howling. The ONLY time I've ever seen that stoic howl. He apparently fled in his shirt sleeves and shorts, right out of the hotel and vanished into the London vastness. We, Lex and me, rapidly took our bridge to pieces. Nanny sat and cuddled Rolf while Una, oh dear me, poor Una, was stamping her feet and trying to pull Rolf from Nanny's lap, yelling at her, 'Don't you DARE touch my brother, ever again. Satan. Satan. Soor kabatcher' — which this lot tell me is forbidden swearing and means 'son of a swine.' You could only just hear her above Ivan's wheezing, so Nanny HAD to leave us to Cook while she went for his medicine. Nobody knew that Frank had run away altogether, then. Cook sat us all at the table and piled it with cakes and biscuits. After a long time Nanny returned having discovered Frank's absence. Oh, what happened then Lex?"

35

"I don't really remember the order of events, Rex," his cousin replied. "It was all so . . . so fraught. I just remember Una lying on the floor, her skirt wrapped round her head moaning, 'It's his VIOLIN hand, you dirty devil.' I know the maid returned with Marc and Anna, the latter ran straight to Nanny though, oh yes, in retrospect it's actually quite funny. Una leapt to her feet, grabbed Anna and told her not to go near that she-devil as well as all those forbidden words she ever knew."

"I know," said Ivan. "Nanny took the two little ones off, we were cleared away from the table into the sitting room place, while all the staff set to work preparing the evening meal. Only you two older ones stayed up for dinner, so we must've gone to the coffee room place for our high tea."

Una took up the story. "A grand lady, like mother came in with Frank, all wet and his hand bandaged."

"That's right," Frank agreed. "They found me and brought me back and her husband must've been a doctor or something. He put some stuff on my hand. The skin peeled off eventually, but look, it mended." He waved his hand at them all in a gesture they would each remember in the years ahead.

"Well," said Rex, "Here endeth part one. You could say, the start of enmity between nanny and Una."

"Not really," disagreed the girl. "It was ALWAYS there. I ALWAYS hated her TOUCHING me. It was her hands; soft like a tiger's or leopard's pads, but flabby like that chap in David Copperfield . . . what's his name?"

"Uriah Heep," prompted Frank

"That's right, Frank. Like a fish. Nanny had hands like a jelly fish. Ready to . . .to what? I don't know . . ."

"Sting!" offered Ivan.

"We digress," Rex brought the company to order. "What next? Come on Lex, old man."

"The parents arrived home sometime, and then it was next day and we'd all embarked by train to another hotel near the schools. We had lunch there then, as I recall, the infants were left with hotel staff, Nanny, the parents and all of us walked to the Upper School where we all had tea with The Beak and his two unlovely, but gentle sisters. After which we were led, all of us, on an expedition of the school;

from Chapel, to Hall, to Library, Classroom block, the gymnasium, even the fives courts and the shooting alley, ending with the stairs to the dormitory block, where father stayed with us three older ones and the others left. Mother had never noticed Frank's hand?"

"Father did," Frank remarked. "I said I'd fallen on the stove, and he said something about hoping I hadn't blubbed. No explanations required."

"Now, Una," said Rex, "it's your story, I'm afraid."

They resettled themselves in their chairs, had their cups re-filled and Roxana placed a large tin of biscuits and the bowl of toffee beside the vase of flowers and the cruets that occupied the centre of the table.

"May I ask one question first?" asked Roxana.

"Of course. Ask away! and you Mother?" answered Rex, while Una drew a breath of relief at the delay.

Roxana put down her knitting and asked, "Didn't ANY of you ever tell your parents about your feelings for Nanny?"

"No!" said Frank.

"Well you see," explained Lex. "Our life in India wasn't like this. It wasn't cosy like this. We didn't see that much of the parents, really. We went down and kissed mother goodnight whenever she was there, and we had our lessons with her on the downstairs verandah, of course, but our domain was upstairs or on the compound. We rode every day; we played a sort of polo on our mountain ponies; Urjinath's youngest son, Baji, taught us to play cricket; otherwise our life was mainly controlled by Ayahs, Urjinath and Nanny. Urjinath was head of the household; he taught us about people, about animals and about . . . about, . . . well, about the final straw in Una's saga — respect for the individual . . ."

"Where there's mutual respect there will never be war, he said," burst in Frank.

"Pity he didn't come and teach those thugs in Europe then I . . ." put in Ivan though interrupted with some asperity by Rex.

"Stuff his mouth quickly," he said.

They all looked covertly at Aurora who kept her expression as bland as possible. She had not missed the remarks that the volatile Ivan was constantly being reprimanded for making.

"Go ON, Una," ordered Rex briskly.

"All RIGHT then," she snapped, continuing at considerable speed, "Well, Mother went out of the door with Ivan and Rolf, and Nanny took my hand, and I was jolly glad I had on my new school gloves, and led me the other way. I thought she was taking me to the lavatory until we walked on and on and we were right out of town and we passed the pond and turned into a narrow road with school fields each side so I asked when the others were coming and she said they weren't, that I was a very silly little girl and I was going to a Girls' School, of course, and the boys were at their BOYS' School. I just couldn't believe it, then. It sounds silly now, but nobody had told me that Ivan and Rolf would be separate from me. We'd reached the gates leading into the House grounds and I sat down in the drive and wouldn't budge. I don't really know HOW it happened, but somehow I was dragged into the entrance hall and I saw my case, my new case there, and a dragon woman — no dragons are nice, a demon woman in a blue overall came up, then the House Mistress, the Old Hatchet, came, and Nanny was telling them that I was vicious, undisciplined, wilful and so on, then she rolled down her stocking and showed my kick marks. They were BAD. I really had kicked her the night before. I was terrified then that she'd show her stomach where I'd punched her, but she didn't. I remember the Old Hatchet saying, 'You may assure Mrs O'Donaty she need not worry about her daughter,' and Nanny saying, 'Oh, she won't worry. She has another LOVELY little daughter,' then she left. I sat down on the floor and bawled at the whole world about Rolf NEEDING me, and Ivan NEEDING me, and that's when my eyes went half-blind, then the under matron came along and took me to my dormitory and told me to unpack and not sit on the bedspread. I pushed the gladstone bag right under my bed and piled the other things from the case into the drawer; it was a mess; I couldn't see properly, anyway, and then the same woman came back and took me to the kitchen for a meal and I began to feel sick. I don't really remember properly what happened next except that Cook asked me if I ate with a knife and fork or my hands so I said, 'Both,' and the matrons and cook laughed and said, 'Savage,' and I was sick and I went on being sick so I got into bed with all my clothes on until there was some sort of fuss going on round me and I had to undress and wash and get into bed properly and I slept and woke all night with twelve empty beds round me. The girls came back next afternoon, by which time I'd run away twice and finally, left in charge of the gardener I completed my own destruction by pulling my baggy knickers over my skirt and climbing to the top of a tree. By the next evening I understood that everyone had CHEATED me, that I HAD to stay there and they all thought I was some aborigine from the jungle, and because of all my misdeeds I wasn't allowed to go out with Lex for three weeks. I saw him when he called for me and they wouldn't let me go; they wouldn't even let me talk to him . . ."

Lex took up the tale, "So she ran away. Luckily I found her half-way up the dormitory stairs INSIDE our school. I had to break bounds to get her back, but I discovered a back entrance and we bumped into the gardener and he took charge of her, and became our permanent ally and friend. He always met me on Sunday when I took her back, when we ALL took her back, and he had things to show her, pet rabbits, sprouting bulbs, anything to stop her doing her tantrum act."

"Was he the Hermit?" asked Roxana.

"Oh, no," said Rex emphatically, "that's about another two cups of tea away. Rolf, your turn to wet the tea leaves."

"I'll go and close the barn doors," he replied, "the sun's already on the horizon. Ivan can be tea-wallah."

"I'll go with you, Rolf," said Una, who always said a last goodnight to Gamma before dark.

Ivan, restless, and quite ready for some action, leapt to his feet with alacrity, and promptly gave them all a not too exaggerated performance of life in a girls' school dormitory, from the silly tricks to the deliberate spite against one who neither conformed to their code, nor understood why she did not fit in. "They played Truth and dares and you know Una, she'll dare ANYTHING and she is jolly truthful; she hasn't the sense to by-pass questions anyway," he explained,

"The dorm. prefect seems to have been a real bully and always made sure that Una was caught by the matron performing her dares."

"Didn't she make a fool of the prefect that first night?" asked Frank.

"Yes, of course, you're right Frank," Ivan conceded. "She was the only new girl so after lights-out the prefect made them all get out of bed and sit in a circle around her, then proceeded to question her, you know, the sort of things chaps never ask each other, like where she lived, where she went to school before, how many brothers and sisters she had and what her father did — that was the best one because Una naturally said he was a soldier. 'Blacks the Colonel's boots does he?' the bully asked, to which Una replied — and you can imagine HOW she'd say it, 'He IS the Colonel!' It seems some of the girls applauded the prefect's discomfiture, so she made Una take off all her clothes and swing from the cubicle curtain rail, whatever that is, then shouted loudly enough for matron to hear, 'Silence' or something which brought a flood of light and poor old Una well and truly exposed. She told us that girls think it's dirty to be naked — well, dash it, you know Una, absolutely no sense of modesty at all."

They all laughed, more at Ivan's antics than WHAT he said, but Aurora recalled the desperately homesick letters a day-girl had smuggled into the post for her.

"The thing is," Lex was saying as Rolf returned, followed, fortunately at an interval by his sister, "She grew up like a boy, like one of US. We made no concessions for her. The idea of her having a room to herself gave ME quite a shock, I can tell you. I think of her as a boy."

Una heard the last phrase and her whole world filled with light and happiness. The accolade of accolades, and from Lex. Her joy was evident in her face and her sparkling eyes, if anyone had chosen to notice.

Once they had taken their seats and were stirring the sugar into their refilled cups, Rex asked, "What came next?"

Lex took up the story-telling. "It was Ivan, really. When he had a really bad attack of asthma and became delirious, don't you remember, Rex? I had to go over to the Prep. in the middle of Latin, and Miss du Shane, their matron, was in

40

quite a frenzy because he kept shouting, 'Una.' She didn't know what he was saying, so I explained about the twin and she just put on her hat and coat and somehow fetched Una out of lessons, then returned her after tea that evening, when Ivan began to get better. She is a really marvellous person. Somehow she had the ban against Una coming out, lifted, and then invited us all to spend Christmas with her in the Prep. House, even Una, that first year when we were all in quarantine for chicken pox, or actually having it. What a Christmas it turned out . . ."

"Yes," interrupted Rolf, surprisingly. "We had the run of the house, allowed to leave our belongings all over the dayroom, play the piano, even use the gym AND we had TURKEY for our Christmas dinner. Yum."

"And, let it be acknowledged," interpolated Rex, "she just DOTED on you, Rolf."

"And," said Una, "we decorated the whole dayroom with holly cut from the woods, and she gave us a broom to clear up and didn't even MIND the mess."

"She let us wear football shirts and no ties or stiff collars or jackets and the boils on my neck were cured," added Frank with feeling.

"It was through collecting the holly that we found the path through the centre of the woods," Lex continued with the story. "We had to spend two hours out of doors every afternoon, and at first we just did the usual, the traditional three mile walk — a circuit, Aunt Rora, along a country road lined with ancient trees and thick woodlands that have been there since Wat Tyler raised his rebellion; he came from there . . ."

"Some of those oaks were — are — more than five hundred years old," Rolf informed them.

"May I continue?" demanded Lex. "Thanks. The walk is traditional in so far as all, ALL the local schools do it EVERY Sunday of term. Some, like the Girls' High or the Convent, and the Prep Boys go in long crocodiles, two by two and controlled by either one or two slave-drivers. We superior beings go — eh, went — in groups of not less than three. The townspeople go in families, or groups, and all the way round The Avenue, as it's called, there are notices stating that trespassers will be prosecuted. Anyway, we're not supposed to step aside from the road at all. Chaps do. Some take side turnings and visit girls, or pubs, or collect conkers."

"Get ON, man," encouraged Rex, leaning back and re-lighting his pipe.

"Oh yes," Lex responded good-naturedly, "yes, well, we found this path which cut off about one third of the circuit, that holiday, and along the side of the path there were seven ant-hills and three dew-ponds so it became infinitely more interesting than the well-trod track. I should explain now that the woods weren't solid as you might say; they were thick, but they encircled an area of farmland, obviously once a clearing in the old forest, and at the far side from our track we could see a low farm building and out-buildings; there were cows, not like ours, but black and white, busily grazing. I expect it was a dairy farm. We never risked being seen and kept well clear of habitation. There were plenty of narrow rabbit tracks in and out and around the wood. One day while we were making bows and arrows Una found a donkey wandering around and it stuck to her. After that she kept her after-lunch apple and fed the beast every afternoon. I suppose it was only for four days, actually. As Miss du Shane had lent us secateurs, two pairs, to cut holly, we used them to cut saplings and thin branches and began making ourselves a den. The donkey was ALWAYS there. It was an intelligent little beast and it used to nose into that cloak thing Una had to wear at school, and help itself to bits of food she'd stuffed into her skirt pockets. She called it Yaw and even rode it."

"By Christmas Eve the weather had become VERY cold, and when we went along the path there was no donkey. We even risked being caught in the woods by calling it. Una poured tears all over the place, and actually we were ALL a bit concerned; not for the donkey you understand. We knew it had probably been taken into the farm paddocks, but we were still being really nice and kind to Una. She'd had most of her chicken-pox at her own school and she'd been really quite ill, so we weren't our normal beastly selves to her; not like we are here. Actually, we all thought she'd had a poor deal being suddenly deprived of her WONDERFUL brothers, her SPLENDID cousin AND having to live in a place full of GIRLS. So, we searched and searched for old Yaw."

"Then Frank heard him," Una burst out excitedly. "Frank's fine hearing heard him. He was looking for US, we thought. We all followed Frank and he followed his ears."

"Frank also saved his own hearing by shutting Una up by saying the donkey was obviously looking for a stable as it was Christmas Eve," her twin traitorously told them all.

Una, used to it, ignored her twin and laughing with remembered delight said, "And Frank was RIGHT. He had found a stable, Yaw had. Ivan heard the little hoofs stamping on wood and we all went along, in single file, following the sureness of Frank's ears, along a winding path we'd never before seen, and there it was, the Tumbledowns. Two derelict cottages with one of the famous oaks spreading its branches across the roof and right into the eaves. You go on Rex. I want to just remember that moment."

"All right, if you've gone all broody," he responded. "It really was an amazing sight, those two attached cottages, attached but on two different levels, one door hanging from a single hinge and open, and there inside, lit by that strange afternoon December light that's only half-light. Oh, I'm not so good at descriptions. I recall mostly the fabric of the building. One of you others go on."

"It was like a pastoral symphony, that sight," volunteered Frank.

"Yes, Frank," added his elder brother. "That's it. It seemed an integral part of the trees, in spite of being built of brick. Most of the windows were broken, but wherever there was glass there were small splinters of light, and, if you don't think I'm being a bit of a mystic, seeing Una in a navy cloak and long hair with her arms round the donkey seemed just perfect for Christmas Eve. Well anyway we all rushed around collecting bundles of not too damp bracken and beech leaves and made a covering for the floor. Rex and I fixed the door so that it couldn't either fall on the animal or wedge him in."

"It was instinct that made Yaw go to that cottage," announced Rolf.

"Yes," Ivan added, "because it DID snow, and we had a jolly hard time visiting every day with food. Frank and I used to sneak close to the farm and pull handfuls of hay from one of the haystacks."

"That was good sport, wasn't it Ivan," Frank beamed.

Rex took over. "Lex found all the house keys which WE kept. We repaired it bit by bit, dodging up sidepaths and using a quicker route, and that way avoided the embarrassment of being stared at by all those girls, and of being seen by our classmates with two Prep. boys AND a GIRL in tow."

"But, Rex, what was it like, this cottage?" his mother asked.

"How tumbledown was it?" his cautious sister asked. "Was it SAFE?"

"Oh, yes, it was safe enough. It was really two joined together, like the Roches, in a way, except there was an upstairs, but no proper roof. The stairs had collapsed in one cottage. There was a fireplace and a sound chimney at each gable end, and one room at the bottom of each, but two small rooms upstairs. We made a rope ladder from the roof space so we could escape if anyone came in. The place had been derelict for years and years. The bottom was reddish brick, but the top was lathe and plaster with great beams — oak probably."

"The oak, Rex. Tell about the Sacred Oak . . ." Una reminded her cousin.

"I don't know about the sacred part, but there was a magnificent oak tree —- such as you have never seen, mother. Ivan, Frank, Lex and I held hands and we just encircled it. The Hermit said it was more than five hundred years old."

"And WHAT about this hermit? You still haven't explained his presence or anything about him." Aurora queried. "You talked about the hermit as if you were accustomed to meeting hermits every day of your life . . ."

Ivan felt he had been silent too long, so took upon himself the task of describing their first encounter. "Una found him. We were carving boats and things from pieces of wood lying around and we wouldn't let her use our penknives so she went off, sulking, into the other cottage. She burst in on us in a few minutes and said, 'I've seen God! He's next door.' Of course, we just laughed, but in the end

44

Lex went to see what it was, and it was this Hermit. It was after some other Christmas holiday when we'd been here for about four weeks, and he'd moved in. He had the cottage with the stairs, and he'd made the room downstairs like a sort of chapel — well one end of it; there was a sort of altar, and an alcove with a carved picture at the back. What d'you call those things, Frank?"

"Icon," his brother informed them all.

"Yes, that's right, an icon, with flowers — dead ones, he'd dried. He had long white hair and a long white beard, otherwise he didn't look much like God to us. Well, Lex, being polite, invited him into our cottage to share toast and marmalade with us. We bought a loaf of bread most Saturdays to toast on Sundays. So, that was how we met him . . . oh, about four years ago. At first he didn't really trust us, did he Rex?"

"No," Rex took up the tale. "And we didn't trust him — except Una. We thought he may be an escaped convict or something, but as we'd all taken a vow never to visit the cottage without all of us being there, we felt safe. Lex and I were as tall as him and we were fit from all the gym and games we played at school. We helped him dig a patch at the back and Una brought him vegetable seeds to plant; her school gardener gave them to her for her own school garden, so she brought most of them to the Hermit . . ."

Una intervened, "And the potato peel, Rex, don't forget the peel. I picked the peel off the school compost-rubbish heap when the Hermit said you could grow potatoes from old peel. Did YOU know that, Aunt Aurora? Well you can, and he DID. He said he learnt that in Ireland and that was all, ALL his family had to eat sometimes. He was descended from the Kings of Ireland. He said his ancestors had 'sat on the High Seat of Tara' and that the High Seat was a sacred stone, but someone called Cuchulain came from Ulster and stole it. I asked my history mistress about that and she said it was a myth or a legend and I didn't know what those words meant THEN. He thought we were Irish, but Rex explained about our name, or Lex did . . ." she trailed off, having talked at such speed that her breath ran out.

Frank continued, "I think he was very Holy, possibly, in a strange way." He searched for words then went on slowly, weighing each word, "He was a thinker. He believed in a paradise on earth. He was a Roman Catholic on Sunday, he told us, a Mohammedan on Friday and a Jew on Saturday . . . and a Buddhist the rest of the week."

"He knew everything about wild animals," Rolf added.

"He said my donkey chose this place that Christmas Eve because of the Sacred Oak. He said donkeys were Very Special . . ." Una said with pride.

"It's MY turn now," Lex laughed. "Frank and Una will go on forever about the Hermit's thoughts and ideas. He was an old soldier and he had killed men on his conscience. He was JOLLY old; he fought in the Crimean War — at least he was a boy bugler. He said the Irish kept the army supplied with men, but they fought on different sides. He said that most British, German, French and Polish Generals had their roots in Ireland and ALL the Americans. Actually he had the most incredible store of knowledge."

Ivan burst in, "D'you remember his music? He made pipes from wood with the sap taken out. He gave one to Frank when he lent him his violin bow and he showed us how to play a saw — his only tool beside his big jack-knife."

"And, Ivan, the secret writing, he showed us, don't forget that," his sister encouraged.

"Yes, WE used to call it secret writing, but it really IS very ancient Celtic writing. Frank looked it up in the school library . . ."

Aurora decided, fascinating as she found this account of the wonders of the Hermit, to bring them all back to the explanation as to how the Hermit fitted into Una's problems. "Before you explain," she said, "would you see that the field hut and stable barn doors are fixed open. A storm is coming and I like to be sure the animals can find shelter if, and when, they want it."

The exodus gave her and Roxana breathing space.

Distant thunder accompanied the return of the young, to the Truth Table, on which stood a bottle of homemade elder-flower wine and the best wine glasses. While they each sat in their accustomed seat, Rex said, "We had a quick conference outside, Una, while you were washing up, and we decided that we MUST tell EVERYTHING — even the bits you don't want mentioned. Unanimous except for you."

Una shrank lower to the hard seat of her kitchen chair, saying miserably, "Well, don't you laugh at me, then, any of you."

Lex took up the tale. "We've told you about the Hermit, and it would take years to tell you about all our visits to the Tumbledowns. It went on for years. It was our home from home, and we learnt things from the old man that we might have learnt from fathers if we had any — we learnt about how to survive, how to live off the land, and how to look at both sides of a problem and, as he said, 'all the way round the edges'. He spoke like a poet and Una asked him if he was Homer come back to earth. He liked that. Then, four weeks ago we went as usual, to the cottage and he wasn't there. He had ALWAYS been there, waiting for us. We brought him newspapers from our school boiler-rooms; he read them and then made them into bedding with sacks and dried bracken. Rex and Una went into his cottage after we'd waited for about an hour. They went in the back way and up the stairs, and there he was, lying on his sack mattress, sun filtering through the trees and broken roof. They thought he was dead, but Una, imagine Una of all people, knelt down and held his hand . . . you go on Rex. You saw it."

Rex continued. "The old man opened his eyes wider than WE'D ever seen them — pale, pale blue, they were — and said, "Please fetch Father Dominic." So that's what we had to do, but Una had written a poem for him, and she put it in his hand, rolled round and tied with a shoe lace like a scroll. Frank and I went to find Father Dominic and the others stayed with the Hermit. They said he slept most of the time. Well, now mother, WE didn't KNOW who Father Dominic was, so we went to the Catholic Cathedral in the town — two miles away. We had to talk our way through bishops or cardinals or whatever and finally we found, or rather, they found Father Dominic, and Frank said, ". . . he looked at Frank with admiration before continuing," "Father, Sir, may I ask that we have the seal of the Confessional?" It may not be the correct way to address a Priest, but it was impressive. When he said he would treat anything we said as sacrosanct, old Frank said, "One of your flock is in dire need of your services. Will you come?" Well the Priest asked us who and then came with us. He ran part of the way, but when we had to stop for breath — and he wouldn't let either of us carry his case — he said he knew the old man, by sight, at Mass every Sunday until that particular day. By the time we arrived at the cottage, it was time for us to go back to school. We had to get Una back, as well as Ivan and Rolf AND be in Chapel by six o-clock." So we just said goodbye to the Hermit and the Priest and rushed back to school."

"And while they were chasing Father Dominic," said Lex, the Old Hermit occasionally opened his eyes, but he kept telling us to look at the stars, as if it was night. He kept asking us to look at the Northern Cross — Cygnus. We ALL knew he was dying, but it wasn't really sad, somehow. He was so sure of himself, so peaceful . . .Well he did die, and Father Dominic stayed with him. Frank found out afterwards . . . BUT nobody knew who he was, not even the priest. All the authorities had was a poem signed Una O'Donaty, High House School. The police took the poem to the school and Una was kept apart from all the other girls — and US."

Rex added, his voice alone an accolade, "Una told them she was with her twin when she found the old cottage with the sick man in it. She never told about US, she didn't actually LIE . . . so Ivan got the beating and we, Lex and I have unblemished records; less blemished . . . "

"Was it all such a CRIME?" asked Aurora, mystified.

Her son tried to explain the taboos and laws that govern school life. "We were all breaking bounds. The woods were private, but we always walked BEHIND the 'Trespassers will be Prosecuted' sign. In addition, it isn't the 'done' thing to consort with, what the authorities called a vagabond and a tramp."

"At Girls' Schools," Ivan said scornfully, "they do what they call 'owning up'. If someone gets caught doing something unlawful, all the others leap to their feet and say, 'I am also to blame' or something as silly, so everyone gets punished . . . "

"I'm afraid, I still do NOT understand why it was SO terrible," Aurora said. "Do YOU understand, Roxana?"

"No. I expect lots of girls break bounds or whatever you call it," her daughter answered.

Frank tried to explain. "The girls don't have any rule like that. They're not allowed out, unescorted."

Una straightened her slumped body and said, "They said I had 'lowered the standard of the school', but it was my poem . . . they, my housemistress said it was blasphemous, sacreligious, and profane. I borrowed a dictionary from a daygirl in my form and looked up the words and I didn't believe it, so I wrote it down for you, Aunt Aurora, in a letter, but they read my letter — we're not allowed to seal any letters — and they tore it up and told me to write another. I had to sleep in the attic, next to the maids room, and eat at a special table in the dining hall and nobody was allowed to talk to me. The daygirls talked to me in school; I had lots of friends, especially Jill. Her father is a master at the boys' school so she smuggled letters to Lex and in case the boys read them on the way I wrote the important bits in the Hermit's secret writing. Well, I wasn't allowed to see the boys so I didn't have ANYONE to talk to on Saturday and Sunday. I had to go to church walking with matron AND I had to sit on the outside of her in case I infected another girl during the service. I was a leper, you see . . . just because I made up a beautiful poem; well, I think it's beautiful . . . "

"What's it about?" asked Roxana.

"Oh God, and Prefects and People," was the reply.

"Why don't you show it to Aunt Aurora and Roxana," suggested Ivan.

After some persuasion, Una went to the room above. Those below heard something being dragged across the floor.

"That's her precious gladstone bag. She keeps all her secrets locked in there," her twin explained. The boys were laughing when she returned and she looked round at them all, suspiciously, before pleading with her aunt, "YOU won't be cross when you read it, will you, Aunt Aurora? I mean I couldn't LIVE if I was a leper at home."

There was no sound except the dropping of coal in the closed grate, the rumble of thunder, still some distance away, and the salivary sucking of three newly replenished pipes. The sheet of lined paper lay on the table between Aurora and Roxana 'like an offering to the Truth Table' Una thought, many years later, when she recalled that evening. The two women read:

49

"When I was young,
Before I could read
I was taught a Truth
More divine
Than taking the Holy Vessel
And drinking
That Blood in Wine.

When I was young,
Before I could read
I was taught to respect
The Khama,
Moslem's Allah and Jesus Christ
And Buddha's
Dalai Lama.

When I was young,
Before I could read
I was taught to respect
Every Man,
Afghan, English, Mongol and Sikh,
Tibetan
And Hindustan.

Now I am old,
And now I can read
I'll learn no Truths
So Divine,
For I'm lost in a female jungle
Where respect
Is just a sign.

Now I am old
And now I can read,
I'm learning to see
And respect,
In this arid schoolgirl desert,
The customs
Of each Prefect."

Roxana spoke first. "Well, Una, I can understand them feeling annoyed about the last two verses. You have rather suggested that school is a void, or a useless space . . ."

"Not SCHOOL, Roxana," the writer defended, "Only the boarding house. School's different. Even School Prefects are different. I mean THEY don't tell you to do things, KNOWING you'll get caught — like that that that, WORM, Elizabeth Wright did."

"You shouldn't have DONE the things, silly," her twin scoffed.

"Matron SAID, 'Do what Elizabeth tells you and you'll be all right,' so I did and I wasn't — at first." Una thought for a moment, noticing the scorn on the boys' faces, and continued, "I wrote the poem when I'd just done five hundred lines for a Prefect, from Paradise Lost, then I took her my lines — in my BEST handwriting — and she said had I learnt not to run across the lawn on Sundays, so I said I had, and could I borrow her book to read some more, so she said it was cheek and made me do another five hundred lines. I don't see how that could cure me of forgetting about not running on Sundays. So I wrote my poem. It isn't REALLY blasphemous, is it, Aunt Aurora?"

"No," Aurora adjudicated. "It might be considered somewhat profane, perhaps, but I should like you to copy it out for me — in your BEST hand-writing — in my Commonplace Book. Would you, Una darling?"

There was relief on all their faces. A sudden clap of thunder almost overhead and a flash of lightning caused Una to jump and knock over her untouched glass of sweet wine. Everyone laughed.

"Shall I fetch my School Report?" asked Una, after mopping up the sticky white wine. "You'd better read MINE first as it'll be the worst one," she suggested, already moving towards the hall.

The report-reading was lengthy. As each was read, it was passed to its owner who also read it, then handed it to the others or not, as they chose.

It was very late that night when Aurora reached her own room. She had visited each of the family in turn and kissed them before extinguishing their lamps. Too disturbed, and too weary, for sleep she sat at her open window and watched the starlight flickering fleetingly through the occasional break in the heavy clouds that hovered above, threatening storm. She tried to adjust to the new vision of the children that had spread over that great slice of oak which Ivan had named the Truth Table. "Children!" she thought scornfully, "A meaningless and demeaning word. They're people, not some sub-race; they're miniature — or not so miniature — PEOPLE; just growing up people; less articulate than grown up people perhaps; they're PEOPLE with people's rights and a wisdom that is born of visions that they are seldom able to express in words." They had been far from inarticulate during the last few hours.

Tears filled her eyes at the realization that the six young people had created a home from home of their own during all their absent years, a replica La Bellule to which they had arrived with a variety of experiences that had already left ineradicable marks, even scars; she included her own son, for he had been obliged to share his home and his life with five total strangers after losing his own father tragically. She was never to know that he had stood at the window by the tourelle, clutching the stuffed kangaroo that had been his father's and watched the wet body being lifted from the cart, and understood.

The crabs in their subterranean fastness beneath the house scuttled along their ancient, well trod channels, feeling the storm vibrations in their multitudinous strong little legs, anticipating a wealth of treasure being washed on to their beach before daylight.

Chapter Four

A scream split the house and every occupant was alert. Aurora, who had just fallen asleep, sat up and listened. She heard the light bare feet skim across the room and she knew Ivan was waking his twin. She heard the firm young voice commanding the girl to sit up. Above her head she heard the creaking of three beds as the older boys resettled themselves momentarily. While whispering continued at the far end of the other room the windows were lit with a flash of lightning. The storm had arrived.

The human sound had driven the night loving animal world to sanctuary; the bats disturbed in their swooping and diving above the pond; the mice from their peregrinations inside the house walls; and the voracious rats from their empire in the banks and ditches surrounding each paddock; the owl went deeper into the old elm tree and the parent swallows remained on their perch guarding their fledglings in the nest below. The storm followed its ordained course and once the noise ceased and the rain fell in friendly torrents the bare feet sped lightly back to bed.

Ivan understood his sister's nightmares. His were of large snakes, and he had always thought her nightmares had been about tigers until to-night. She had told him that the recurring dream was of a tiger with fat, fishy hands. "She never draws any hands on her people," he thought. He had held his own hand up against the window and she had said, "But you've got good hands, clever hands, and they'll never be anything but good. Most of us should have had wings instead of hands." Somehow her words made him feel very grown up and he slept.

Aurora woke early next morning to find Ivan beside her bed with a cup of tea. She had never had a cup of tea in bed except when she was ill. "I thought it was time WE looked after you, Aunt Rora," he said. "I'm just taking this other one to Roxana." She heard her daughter's exclamation of surprise at this luxury. Ivan too! He was normally the most difficult to rouse and always last at the breakfast table.

There were more surprises in store for the family. By the time mother and daughter reached the kitchen they found Ivan standing over the range, stirring the porage, and wearing a teacloth around his waist and another pinned into a cone on his dark hair. "It's all right, Roxana," he said, "I took the porage out of the haybox, and I found the tray of potatoes and mushrooms in the larder; they're in the oven, cooking nicely. You see before you, the most expert of the six cooks, sorry chefs, who served a long apprenticeship at The Tumbledowns." After such an exhibition it was impossible for the age old custom of a silent meal to be adhered to, they found.

Lex made an attempt to restore the old custom, addressing the self-appointed chef who was busy juggling with wooden spoons. "Clown," he said scathingly, "you belong in a circus."

"I thought I was IN one . . ." came the immediate rejoinder.

His aunt interrupted, "IF this is a circus, then I am the Ringmaster and I want a great deal of action in the ring, under the Big Top to-day. Rolf I see has already been out, helping Old Pierre with the milking. I think we can exclude you Rolf from the list of chores. I know you and Old Pierre will have already planned the days work outside, but please make a list of any repairs that are needed inside the barns and stables; yesterday we only made a rapid survey and then only the outside." Rolf glowed with pleasure as well as with the outdoor air.

"The rest of you boys," she continued, "I would really like you to have a list of everything you need for the partition upstairs and, if it's not asking too much, of any timber you need for fence and gate repairs, then Old Pierre can take the cart and collect it all at once from the timber yard. And you, Una, would you feel it was grossly unfair if I asked you

54

to prepare all the potatoes by yourself . . . and a few carrots and onions? Roast mutton to-night, so we'll have cabbage with it . . . oh yes, and then perhaps you could give Gamma a good gallop along the beach?"

They all laughed. It was no chore to Una to take Gamma out, especially along the beach. She joined in the laughter. They were really going to start on making her a room, a room all to herself, TODAY. Not tomorrow, not next week or in a fortnight's time, but today. This time the previous day she had been lying sick and miserable upstairs after three weeks of shame and isolation at school and suddenly the world was a beautiful place. She had dreaded becoming thirteen, but now it seemed that her birthday was a day to look forward to with pleasure.

"I'll wash your hair for you tonight, if you like," Roxana said, rising from the table before leaving for school.

"We'll start the washing up rota tomorrow," decided the Ringmaster, adding, "I think you boys had better work out a shaving order, unless you can safely shave in concert as it were." She knew there would be arguments if they were allowed to work on a rush and grab system.

"It's all right, Mother," her son assured her. "Rolf doesn't shave yet, Ivan only shaves about once a week and it's only Frank and I who sprout overnight. He uses my razor anyway; they both do."

"Then put razors on the shopping list," she ordered. Ashamed of her own ignorance, she added, "and the things that go with them of course. Ah yes, another thing. Could you make a small bookcase to fit beside each bed? Nail a few planks together or something? You might find it easier to keep your rooms tidy and Frank has all that prize money to spend on books."

They laughed, both with pleasure and with fond amusement. They learnt woodwork at school and knew that a few nails would not be adequate.

Marie arrived and there was a hurried exodus as everyone disappeared to collect the considerable array of dirty clothes she had come to wash in the wash-house behind the kitchen.

Marie quickly at work in the wash-house, stoking the copper with wood from the farmlands, smiled at the good spirits and energy of the youngsters. It was always the same for the first few days; sometimes it lasted as long as a week or ten days, then the squabbling began, the evading of duties and the solitary visitor at her cottage door. They just visited, saying nothing of whatever had caused some unrest, but gathering some sort of equilibrium from the practicality and simplicity of her and Old Pierre. Young Pierre, her son, was different from his father and herself; perhaps he had picked up some of the O'Donaty ideas; when HE felt awkward he sought out Rex and they took the boat, just off-shore, and pretended to fish. "The young THINK more than Pierre and I ever did. We just LIVED. Now they ask questions WE can't answer . . . I don't know what will become of their generation."

Marie need not have worried. The wheels of fate, turned by the hands of politicians, powered by greed, and maintained by lust for superiority, were turning faster and faster as each day followed the one that had passed.

Storm clouds still hung in the sky like grey sheep waiting for a leader to take them to some better pasture, closer to the sun that shone faintly far above them. Smoke from the copper rose in eddies making a herd of lesser sheep in the sky above. Una sat in the yard perched on a small milking stool a bucket between her bare legs and occasionally looked up at the patterns made by the clouds and the wash-house smoke. She was peeling potatoes, neatly and deftly with a knife she had previously ground to a sharp edge on the back door step. Each peeled potato was put into a huge saucepan beside her, and all the eyes from the vegetables were piled separately, to be planted later. While she worked she listened.

All five boys were in the bedroom above discussing the partition they were to construct for her. They had even collected Rolf from his farm work to ensure that whatever was planned would suit ALL of them.

Ivan, standing beside the nearest window was saying, "Yes, Rex, that's fine, but if she has this end of the room, like we thought, she"ll have to walk RIGHT PAST Rolf and me to get to her bed."

"Put her at the other end," said Rolf.

"No," argued Lex, "That won't do. Aunt Rora said she was to have PRIVACY . . ."

"Well?" queried Ivan. "What's wrong with her having privacy THAT end?"

"And HOW would you get to YOUR end?" Rex scorned.

Ivan, irritated by this time, snapped, "We'd just walk through . . . oh yes, of course . . ."he laughed, "We'll make another partition and shut her in," before hastily adding, "Perhaps we can't condemn her to The Black hole of Calcutta, even if she IS a girl."

"And that's the chap who leapt to her aid in the middle of the night," said Frank. A long silence ensued before he added, "There HAS to be a way." Their footsteps tramped up and down, measuring this way and that with their feet and strides. Una, sitting below, worked and listened. Suddenly she heard a loud and distant shout, "Eureka! I have it." Heavy feet moved up and down the upper floor then there was a stampede down the tourelle, voices conferring with her aunt and another stampede up the tourelle. She looked at the pile of eyed pieces of peel and considered where she would plant them and start what the Hermit had called 'new creation', when she heard her aunt's voice saying, "Yes boys, yes, that would be ideal, but do you think YOU can do it?"

"OF COURSE we can do it," they chorused. "It'll be easier, AND need much less timber."

"You'd better fetch Una to see, then," her aunt suggested.

A few minutes later the girl stood at the top of the Tourelle speechless with delight. They were going to make her a very small room on the landing where a large blanket box had always seemed to be a fixture under the window Leo had fitted into the eaves. "Could you make little side windows in the dormer?" asked Aurora, and although they looked dubious not one of the boys was prepared to admit to the impossibility of anything.

"We'll have to take the bed springs from the ends," warned the careful and practical Rex.

"Bolt the base on to timber legs," suggested the resourceful Frank.

"Of course, old man," his cousin acknowledged; "we could all do the same and stop living barracks fashion. Shove the beds under the eaves — a window each, eh? What do you think, Mother?"

Before she was obliged to reply, Frank had another suggestion. "Yes, take the casters off those iron frames and fix them to boxes and we'd have drawers to slide underneath the beds."

"Tremendous," Ivan expostulated. "Frank, you are indeed a BRAIN. An inventor. And I might, JUST MIGHT be able to reach my own bed without falling over Rolf's collection of rubbish that he insists on pretending is valuable pieces of wireless, or Una's beach that also gets spread far and wide . . ."

"Yes," interrupted his aunt, "certainly! Make a corner of your own, each of you. It might result in greater peace on the upper floor." Laughing, she made her way to the kitchen, followed by her niece who threw her arms around her neck, completely overwhelmed with pleasure, while calculations and measuring with the one tape-measure, laughter and good-natured teasing continued above their heads.

When Rolf came down and set off to find Old Pierre, Una joined him while Aurora cut fresh flowers for the hall. She was arranging them when she heard a further discussion taking place on the landing above.

"Here we are then," she heard Rex say. "Let's check that we have EVERYTHING down on this scrap of paper." He began reading the list when Frank burst out, "The door, Rex. We've forgotten the door."

"It'll have to open outwards," his cousin pointed out, "and it might knock someone down the stairs."

"A sliding door?" suggested Lex.

"Difficult," objected Rex.

"Slats then," Lex said.

"Hanging slats. That's it," Frank agreed. "Like we had in India. On the bathroom, remember . . .?"

Ivan's voice, pitched high, and filled with, what sounded to Aurora, like fear, screeched, "Not slats. Not slats. Oh no! Now I remember . . . the snake . . ." A heavy thump was followed by silence and Frank flew down the spiral, into the bathroom, returning with a tooth-mug in his hand, without even noticing his aunt.

Aurora went to her room and listened. She wanted to go and see what had happened, but knew she MUST trust these

58

young people who would so soon be away from her, leading their own lives. They would come for her if Ivan had banged his head and was bleeding. She gathered from their subsequent remarks that he had fainted; he had been up in the night; he had gone to bed with a mild attack of asthma and he had been very excitable all the morning. She sat and she listened.

"You look AWFUL," Lex said.

"Went out clean you did," Rex added. "One minute you were Ivan, the next you were a blooming corpse."

"Why?" asked Ivan.

"You tell us, old chap," encouraged Lex. "Frank was just talking about the bathroom in India having a slatted door, and you were a gonna. . ."

"My dream . . . my dream," mumbled Ivan. "It was real. . ."

"Tell us," ordered Frank. "Dreams are jolly important you know. There's a bloke called Jung who interprets them; works with Freud, you know. . ."

"Don't lecture him," Lex intervened. "Help him. He looks terrible still. He can't face Aunt Aurora looking like this. She'll have him off to the quack and we'll never get these things done."

"I'm not a psychoanalyst," Frank answered irritably. "All I know is that dreams are supposed to be part of some early experience in life, and not as people used to believe, foretellers of future events. He's supposed to cure people by making them tell their dreams."

Rex suggested, "Can you recall it Ivan. You can tell US. WE won't spill it."

"It wasn't a dream, Rex. It was real. I SAW the snake inside the bathroom, through the slats, and Urjinath put his hand over my mouth. I SAW it . . . ugh . . . it was AWFUL. It was hanging over Una and she was asleep on the floor behind the slats . . . it was ready to strike. That's my dream. But it's something that REALLY did happen. Urjinath clamped me against him — to keep me still, of course . . ."

"Go on, Ivan," said Frank gently.

"I know," he struggled to recall, "the water carrier had seen Una and the snake . . . would it be a cobra perhaps? . . . so he dumped the two pails and went for Urjinath, and I followed HIM . . . then he grabbed me and squeezed me close to him . . . and I could see Una and that monstrous THING. I must've been about three, or less even . . ." His voice trailed off until encouraged by Frank, he went on, "I could see through the gaps in the slats, chinks they were, and the window was opposite and THAT had bars across. Was it a skylight? No it wasn't. It was a small window that opened outwards and the bars used to make stripes on the bathwater. Una and I used to pretend we were tigers, making the stripes of shadow fall across our bodies. Then there was a face at the window and a rope came slowly down. It touched the cobra and it sprang at it. I think it tried to climb UP it. I'm not sure . . . I know Urjinath stopped squeezing me, pulled Una through the slats and held her upside down and shook her. I don't think she WAS asleep. I think she was dead, or nearly dead. He shook her and then he blew into her face and she started crying — all softly, weepily . . ." He stopped talking and began to wheeze. After a silence punctuated only by his irregular gasps, Ivan stood up, banging his back on one of the roof beams.

"You are right, Frank," he said sombrely, rubbing his back. "My dream DID really happen." Whenever Una talks me awake, I have a sore back and she ALWAYS says, 'That's where I bit you!' And she DID BITE me. That's why she was in the bathroom. Of course! We were dressing and she and I used to do each other's buttons up, and that day she just bit me. I expect I yelled the place down; I know I saw Nanny rubbing that red soap all round her mouth, in the bathroom, then she smacked her and left her screaming in there . . . that's it."

"The cobra came up the sluice!" Frank told them. "The water carrier's job was to swill the sluices out before we bathed."

"That must be why they fixed all that iron gridwork on all the sluices," Lex remembered.

"It must be almost lunch time," Rex brought them back to the present. "We must have a door on this here room — and no slats, eh?"

"How about TWO thin doors?" suggested Frank.

Ivan, suddenly embarrassed by his exposition and show of weakness, laughed, wheezily and said, "She only NEEDS a THIN door, anyway."

60

While the two elder boys measured and calculated, saying laughingly, "Two thin planks for each door should do." They called out their figures to Frank, adding, "and two extra hinges and the appropriate number of screws," then led the way down the tourelle. Before following, Ivan, said to Frank, "Hey, Frank! how could Una KNOW about the cobra? She was out, stone cold, unconscious?"

"I don't know," admitted the elder boy, "but I believe the subconscious absorbs things. Jung's just published a book about it. I'll tell you when I've read it."

Roxana arrived back from school and was being dragged towards the stairs by her excited young cousin.

After their midday meal the family dispersed; the four older boys to Town with their formidable shopping list, to which had been added, various items of clothing, particularly for Ivan; Rolf and Una to the blacksmith with Alph; Roxana back to school for the last two hours of term, Aurora to her special place along the promontory where she had much to think about and where she hoped she would gather wisdom and strength through the solitude, the now cloudless sky and the inscrutability of the ebbing and flowing wavelets that lapped the great rocks. She could not wander along the beach, knowing that in due course her niece would be riding astride the bay mare, her kilt tucked along the top of its back and she did not wish to see her, officially.

Aurora slept. She had seen the niece for whom she had been weeping, racing wildly up and down the beach on the gentle mare; she had also seen them go deep into the sea where the coast shelved very gently; she hoped this child, so very, very dear to her heart, would be allowed to remain wild and uninhibited for as long as possible. Weary with her almost sleepless night and all the emotions of the Truths she had heard the last day and a half, she slept. When she woke up she felt surprisingly refreshed, but an examination of the heavy hunter around her neck caused her to return to La Bellule at a singularly unseemly pace. Long before she reached the archway she heard the family; shouts of encouragement, yells, peals of laughter filled the air. "What on earth is Ivan up to now?" she thought, smiling to herself.

61

Ivan was doing nothing except laughing uncontrollably.

It was Old Pierre. He was sitting on a dilapidated bicycle, being held upright by his son on one side and Rex on the other, and he was pedalling with both his short little legs. Marie stood watching, wiping tears of mirth from her dark eyes. As Aurora reached the group, the chief acrobat was back on terra firma and his two runners were both pedalling expertly towards her. They stopped with a skidding of tyres and a scraping of shoes on gravel. "Want a ride, Mother?" her son asked. "Look, we can ALL stay on, except Marie and Roxana; they won't try. Even Una can balance; she has to sit on the bar to reach the pedals and we have to stop the machine." One by one they each showed their prowess, while Roxana disappeared indoors to complete the cooking her mother had abandoned.

The family had admired Frank's immense pile of books although nobody was able to genuinely profess any real interest in their content.

"I spent my prize money on second-hand books," explained Frank, "so I felt that a second-hand bicycle couldn't be considered cheating. It cost five shillings."

"And you should just SEE the pile of books, aunt Rora," added Ivan. "Frank NEEDED the wheels to carry them home."

"The Beak'll be impressed by the books. I doubt if he's even read them all himself," Lex said.

"Put that old boneshaker away, Frank and let's all go in and gloat over our purchases," laughed Rex, recalling the delights of their expedition to Town.

The bicycle was duly stabled in the stall next to Gamma and the gloating commenced, supervised by Rex who intended to ensure full credit being heaped on Frank's head. The prize money was the most prestigious prize offered by the school annually and normally went to a boy in the top class; to receive it in the lower sixth was a compliment to the worth of the quiet boy who so rarely found himself the centre of attention. Rex had some understanding of Frank because he himself occasionally felt overpowered by his tall cousins, but Rex had a sparkling personality, and THIS had ALWAYS been HIS home; HIS mother and HIS sister were the rulers of this domain, but for Frank it must often have seemed that everyone except himself radiated their own beams of light.

The books were piled on the kitchen table and Rex had thoughtfully put the other purchases on the sideboard. One by one each dusty tome was passed from hand to hand — a Greek New Testament, an Indian Cookery Book and a Gray's Anatomy besides several dictionaries, a companion to the Bible and a copy of Kipling's 'Kim'. Frank handled each almost lovingly, gazing with complete concentration at the names and dates inscribed in the cover, and saying nothing. Ivan chattered incessantly as each book reached him, lacking interest in the actual content, but considerable curiosity about the previous owners. The one volume that proved to be of interest to all the family was the Anatomy. Roxana alone noticed the exchange of glances across the table as something within produced more than passing interest.

"Jolly impressive stuff, this," exclaimed Lex. "Jolly impressive!"

"Why the Kim, though?" asked Rex.

"Oh," Frank hedged, "an English or Eurasian boy — belonging to two worlds —" He removed his glasses, polishing them as he said slowly and hesitantly ". . . like us . . . eh . . . like me." He replaced the glasses, bent and peered closely at a copy of Milton's 'Paradise Lost'.

"A wonderful library. Congratulations, Frank," his aunt said. "I think the FIRST bookcase MUST be yours."

The moment was charged with electricity — a rare family moment in time when ALL the family felt unadulterated pleasure in the success, acquisition and the honour paid to one of their siblings.

"Want to see MY shopping now?" Ivan broke the brief, charged silence.

"And what was that for?" he shouted as a well-aimed kick from his twin struck his leg beneath the table. "I THOUGHT," he added scathingly, "you'd grown out of kicking, little donkey."

"You spoil things. . ." Una retaliated. "It's Frank's moment, this. . ."

Frank began piling up his books, saying, "Oh, don't interfere, Una. You know it was YOUR fault Rolf had a bloody nose. . ."

"Leave her alone," Rex added, "I mean, she's only a girl. . ."

"Chores!" ordered Aurora.

"Then supper," Roxana added, already busily making gravy in the huge baking tray while the joint cast a calming aroma on the scene.

Una and Ivan, both on their feet looked to Aurora like two trapped animals; each wanted to disappear through the door and into the open air, but neither wanted to risk a collision in the doorway. "If you, Ivan, would help Frank pile his books on the sideboard Una and I could bring the washing in from the line." Peace was thus restored.

No word passed between aunt and niece. Clothes were removed from their orderly arrangement on the lines, folded and placed into a huge wicker laundry basket. Aurora removed the small items from one line while Una dragged the other line down by pulling on pyjama trousers or sleeves, until she could reach the pegs. "She's only a girl . . . only a girl . . . ONLY a girl . . . only a GIRL," rang through her head, beating out a funereal march in keeping with the self-pity in which she wallowed. She dragged Ivan's green and white striped pyjama trousers with such viciousness that the pegs flew off the line leaving Rolf's red stripes hanging dejectedly by one peg. She stood and stared at the line, and from the line to the neatly folded clothing in the basket and planned a painting of washing on the line. If her aunt had not been there she would have rehung the older boys' pyjamas and Roxana's and her aunt's nightgowns; they had all looked so lively and 'Lived in' swaying from their pegs; they looked dead, folded in the basket. Una smiled, forgetting HOW her twin's garment had escaped its appointed order, and thought, "Just like Van to be different . . . and just like Rolf to suffer BECAUSE of his livelier brother."

Whilst the clothes were receiving attention outside the table was laid inside the kitchen, fuel stoked beside the range and Ivan had donned a new shirt and trousers, smoothed his hair with water like his elders and was peering wide-eyed at diagrams in the Gray's Anatomy pointed out to him by his younger brother; pages were turned slowly accompanied by stifled sniggering. Frank hovered at Roxana's side, affecting assistance; Lex and Rex were shaving and life, it seemed, had returned to normality. The instant Aurora and Una appeared, carrying between them the loaded basket, vegetable dishes were placed on the table, the joint of mutton put before the matriarch's place, seats pulled out and occupied and Aurora announced, "After today, you three older boys should take turns at carving whenever we have a joint."

"They may as well practise knifing bodies. . ." Ivan encouraged.

"We bought Rolf a razor, while we were in the shop," said Rex loudly, looking venomously at his thoughtless cousin.

While teacups circumnavigated the table the mail was placed in front of Aurora. There was a long letter from India which she read out to the family around her. It transpired that Anna and Marc would not be educated in England; they were to attend schools in Tasmania where Augustus was to be posted as Commandant of the forces for a few years before retiring from active service. It was too early for him to have received the school reports so there was no comment about changes of plans the boys hoped to make. Most of the letter applied to Rex and ended with, "I suggest you arrange for Rex to spend most of his vacation on horseback, and find someone to instruct him in polo — It is essential out here to play well." They laughed, all of them, quite unrestrainedly. The idea of a local polo team was as unrealistic as to belong to the realms of fairy tales.

"I'll take Alph along the beach, Mother," he suggested. "Una can ride Gamma and Frank can pedal up and down on his bicycle. We can have chukkas, or whatever they're called, up and down the salty strand — when the tide is low, of course. I should think Alph would be pretty nippy; there just might be space enough for him to turn without drowning, around, perhaps a football." As the hilarity died down he added, "I didn't know my revered uncle was such a humourist, I didn't."

"Try pig-sticking, Rex," Rolf suggested, "we have a sow we want killed."

"I THOUGHT," said Rex winsomely, "I was joining an INFANTRY brand of soldiery. I prefer the thought of an automobile to a nag. Nags have a nasty tendency to up-end people. Ah yes, you lot may well laugh. You grew up on the outer edges of civilisation, but me, I'm human. I'm only joining the army because I think I'll look EVEN MORE handsome in uniform AND I fancy being fed, housed, bedded and fêted without too extensive corruption of my brain, and . . ." he added on seeing his mother's expression, "I actually believe that a country is only able to retain a peaceful existence IF it has a strong army — and navy Ivan — and an Empire as vast as ours, needs quite a few splendid fellows like me to keep, it going." He stood up. "Tell you what," he suggested seriously, "Why don't we all go and do some of the outside jobs so that tomorrow we can make a start on that upstairs closet."

The newspapers, already two days old, lay unopened on the dresser.

One by one they returned, made themselves ready for bed and sat for a while with their Aunt. The three youngest lay in bed listening while Frank, accompanied by Roxana played his violin.

It was not until next day that they learnt that two countries in Europe were already at war and that a third was massing troops on the borders of a fourth country.

Two days later, many boy hours later, and a small mountain of sawdust later, Una's room was completed. The entire family sat on the bed, the floor and the chair. "To make it properly lived in," Lex had said.

Una, who had been speechless for the two days, and to the great inconvenience of all of them, rummaged under the bed, dragged her gladstone bag on to the landing and from its higgledy-piggledy mess pulled out a bottle stopper attached to a black shoelace and hung it on the curtain rail. "Look," she said, "My own rainbows inside my OWN room." Rewarded, they began to disperse while Lex, sitting on the chair, turned it to the windows saying, "There you are Una. Just like the cockpit of an aeroplane." He leant forward, moving an imaginary joystick. "Chocks away," he ordered, "Brm . . .brm . . . brm . . ." He spun, he swooped, and finally he landed. They felt they were with him on this airborne adventure. They remembered.

Rex, watching, felt envy for the first time in his life. His deep voice, resonant with emotion, he exclaimed, "God, Lex, I wish I had your dedication." He looked at the faces close to his through the limitations of the space imposed by walls and low ceiling, and continued, "All of you. You're all grasping for something beyond yourselves. Not me." He laughed briefly.

"Oh but Rex," Una consoled, "You know what the Hermit said; he said it was one thing to reach for the stars, but another thing to grasp them, and some people REACH for them, but never catch them while others have them already in their hands. You're one of those who already has them. And we all sort of DEPEND on you . . ." she trailed off, out of breath and embarrassed. The boys would think her awfully soppy.

To his surprise Rex was pleased. "Let's go for a swim," he said.

A few minutes later five figures clad in a variety of clothing plunged into the sea, cavorted and swam, then raced back the way from which they had come and disappeared into what appeared to be a hole in a huge granite wall. Ivan, never the keenest of swimmers stayed behind. Una, pegging wet clothes on the line spied him sitting on the barn roof.

"Don't let Aunt Aurora find you," she said.

He ignored her warning, saying, "There's a Dreadnought out there; it might be one of the Super-Dreadnoughts. Soon I'll be on one of those — after I've climbed the rigging and things on the training ship. Your precious stars'll be all round me. I'll have them in my hands. You'll see. The others might dream, but I'll be doing it."

"Come and watch the ship from my new room," she pleaded. "You gave me the rainbow bottle top. . ."

"I know. I dug it out of a rubbish dump behind the Tumbledowns. All right then. P'raps I'll get a telescope from the parents for our birthday, then I'll be able to see what Lex and Rex and Pierre are doing. They went towards the village like conspirators, all neat and smart, and flattened hair."

While an ultimatum was being delivered to one country from another across Europe, the three young men sat on the sea wall opposite an omnibus stopping place. Two of them smoked pipes nonchalantly and gently tugged at fairly new moustches while the third smoked loosely packed cigarettes, an air of confidence exuding from his whole being.

"What DID you learn at that school of yours, Lex?" asked Pierre, stamping on a growing pile of cigarette ends.

"Oh, book stuff; Latin and Science and Mathematics. . ."

"No, not that sort of stuff," the questioner persisted. "I mean didn't you go about and LOOK at girls even?"

"Not allowed," Lex tried to explain.

"Don't you know ANYTHING about them?" Pierre's voice was full of disbelief.

"Oh well, the chaps TALKED about their exploits. Some of them were jolly lurid, I must say, but we came here in the holidays. . ."

"Sounds like some sort of prison to me," Pierre concluded.

Rex wondered how Pierre could possibly understand the strange and alien, to him, life of a boys' boarding school. He had left school some five years before, but he had frequently taken days off to help his father fishing. "You see, Pierre, EVERYTHING is compulsory most of the time, and on Sundays, a partially free day — well between morning and evening chapel — we had to take the young ones out. . ."

Lex helped his cousin defend the way of life their parents had chosen for them," Some fellows, like the Rajah's sons, the Dungarapurs, they had their own women in London. The elder chap said his father gave him his on his fourteenth birthday. . ."

Pierre, laughing uproariously, fell off the wall, gurgling "You don't need to be GIVEN women. You fish for them. See, there, those three over the road. They've walked up and down twice already. They've seen us. Soon they'll cross the road and walk back THIS side. You watch."

"We'll talk English now and they'll think we're more class," he added, as they had been talking in a mix of patois and English. "It's a GAME," he added.

"A game without rules?" suggested Lex.

"No," pondered Pierre, "there's rules, sort of rules, but some of them are what you'd call a bit elastic."

The girls passed again, as Pierre had predicted, and stopped while he exchanged badinage with them, ascertaining that they regularly walked along the same road,

"Getting some air between work and returning home," they explained.

"We might see you again," Pierre suggested. "If we have time, of course," he added.

The girls went on their way and disappeared. "They'll be here again," Pierre assured his friends. "We'll come back and they'll have discussed us and decided which one likes which of us. But WE'LL do the choosing, you see."

All the way back to the farm they described the attributes of each girl, and Pierre knew there was SOMETHING he could teach THEM, besides fishing and sailing. "It'll last them longer than book-learning," he thought. "It's LIFE."

On reaching the great arched entrance to La Bellule, Lex pulled the others back beside the benitier and said, all frivolity gone from his voice and demeanour, "Look here, you two, especially you Pierre, you do realize that war is only days away, don't you? Well then, we two, Rex and me, we could be called to the mainland earlier than we're expecting. See? We might, we just might be away longer than we expect. It could go on in the far parts of the Empire, looking on the blackest side, you know. We could be away a very long time. What I'm leading up to is this. There are lots of jobs around the place that need our brawn and I think we should really make a stupendous attack on the biggest jobs. You know what's MOST urgent, Pierre, so tell US and we can find diplomatic ways of attacking them."

Pierre looked surprised. "You're serious, Lex!" he said. "Rex, there isn't really going to be a war, is there?"

"Yes," his friend replied, all laughter gone from his face. "I should have thought about the urgency, myself . . . You tell us Pierre and we'll find some way of getting the others to work with us . . . eh?"

Pierre lit another cigarette and looked to sea to stir his memory before saying, "There's the barn on the Roc, Rex. The thatch fell right in with the spring gales. We've got the timber and sheets of iron to replace the old thatch, piled up in the empty cottage next to us. That's very urgent and the next few days will be the perfect tides for landing it . . . Then there's the piped water that Frank has planned; it's a big, heavy job if he plans to bury the pipes, but it would save the carrying of all those pails of water every night to fill the troughs. Frank's already saved a lot of the work with his barrels by the barn collecting all the rainwater."

"So," suggested Rex. "D'we get them all to the Roc tomorrow?"

"Too many," objected Pierre. "There'd be no room on the boat for the timber."

"All right, then. You and me, Ivan and Lex, of course. . ."

"Better to have the small chap. Rolf takes up less space."

"What d'you think, Lex?" Rex asked dubiously.

"I think," Lex replied, "That the smaller gang take the stuff over tomorrow, and we go over the day after and cart it up the cliff and repair the roof."

"Yes," agreed Pierre. "We could get some of the planks up to the top."

Rex agreeing said, "We should be able to get all the timber up in a whole DAY. Right! Lex and Frank start on the water job and we four transport the cargo. I'll be casual about a visit to the Roc. . ."

"You'll have to take Una," Lex added as they moved towards the house, "or we'll have tantrums all over the place." They laughed, and he continued, "Throw the planks in the water and let her swim them to the landing. She's a mermaid or a nereide."

The three young men parted, two to the house, the other to his cottage and an ultimatum was being received and ignored in a distant European capital.

Chapter Five

The party for the Roc sailed from the tiny harbour loaded with sheets of corrugated iron, planks forming seats each side, lobster and crab pots, rucksacks containing provisions for the day and an assortment of tools, nails, screws and ropes. Lex and Frank watched them depart, thankful that the loading had been achieved with few problems. The human load had also balanced out neatly with Ivan and Pierre in the stern, Rex facing Rolf and Una midships. As Pierre steered expertly between rocks, every move watched closely by the boy at his side, Rolf began to wonder why he had agreed to join the expedition and Rex wished with all his heart that it was possible to reach the Roc without the preliminary purgatory of the rolling motion that even the smallest ripple produced. Una hung over the gunwale trailing one hand in the water and encouraging spray to dampen her face and hair; she felt blissfully happy. All of them watched the Roc, some five miles from the harbour, slowly taking shape. Aurora watched the sail becoming smaller and smaller until she saw it lowered and knew the party had arrived safely.

The Roc itself waited, lying in the sea like a huge crouching dragon, its back humped into the air, its hind legs hunched, ready to spring, while one foreleg curved right round, claws stretched towards its tail and its head plunged downwards into the depths as if the eyes were searching for a long forsaken lair; its mouth was open, the lower jaw jutting well beyond the upper, exposing an immense cavern from which four teeth had once been ejected and remained as four sharp pinnacles swept by white eddies.

71

"It spat its teeth out when it was deprived of its liberty," thought Una, "and was forced to stay forever at the mercy of wind and waves, tides and shifting currents."

To Pierre the Roc was nothing more than a malevolent islet that threatened shipping, but provided sanctuary in its numerous rocky outcrops and caves for lobsters and crabs — until he arrived to remove them, when they represented food and a livelihood. To Ivan the Roc was the focal point of his immediate ambition which was to sail the boat unaided from Bellule Bay into the tiny harbourage. To Rolf the Roc represented good arable land and an extension of the farm pasturage, thus an increase in the number of sheep. To Una the Roc was not only a benevolent dragon, but a place for dreams of a land of makebelieve. To Rex the Roc was more home than his own beloved La Bellule; he loved it more than any place or person on earth and felt he belonged to the very fabric of the island. The Roc OWNED Rex. Once ashore his customary lethargy left him and he became both physically and mentally more alive than at any other time or in any other place.

Expertly handled the boat dropped sail and glided into the tiny natural harbour accompanied by the disturbed cry of the seagulls, the swish of water and then the slight grating of the rubber tyres hung overboard as they ground against the granite landing stage. A slight breeze from the far side of the island caused miniature fountains to spurt into the air as the boat displaced water.

While the slow and onerous job of unloading the craft progressed on the Roc, Aurora was amused to see that the two boys who had remained were helping Roxana with the washing up, each vying with the other to attract her attention, and showing evidence of growing irritation between them. Tethered anger suffused Frank's face when Lex side-stepped him and took the last plate from Roxana's hands, while the strong tight-lipped mouth and line of wrinkles on the wide forehead indicated the control the boy was having to exercise. Lex's more mobile face glowed with excitement, his mouth twitching and crinkling at the corners as he made some witty remark that drew a laugh from the object of their admiration. Quickly Aurora organized the work ahead, ensuring Roxana's disappearance from the farm on a shopping expedition into Town and her own supervision of the pipe-laying with Old Pierre also in attendance. When she returned to the kitchen Roxana said, "The wisdom of Solomon, eh, Mother. I DID want to go to Town anyway. I'd like to attend those First Aid Classes they're holding at the hospital and I need to put my name down and find out when they're being held. I hope you don't mind. . ."

"Mind? I'm delighted. You SHOULD have some life beyond the farm and your school. . . oh, yes, and your cousins, especially the young adult MALE cousins. Look at bicycles at the same time. I would feel happier if you had one."

"I thought I might get some material and make Una a new kilt and a couple of blouses, Mother. She did grow just a little, last year . . . and she's growing up now. . . "

"I know. But don't tell her so. . . "

"I thought I might try and make her a little skirt AND short jacket, then perhaps she'd stop wandering around in the boys' cast off jackets and blazers, if you think that would be all right. . . "

"Of course. I know, my dear, she'd LIVE in the boys' clothes if I allowed her to."

Meanwhile the brothers, bereft of their idol, worked with rapidity and skill, gradually moving farther and farther from the house, and entertained by the voluble Old Pierre. Later they would each indulge secretly in their worship at the altar of Venus.

On the Roc the five inhabitants struggled slowly up the winding two hundred feet of rabbit path, each dragging a single plank behind them. Trailing brambles caught at their legs, gorse grabbed at their clothes and their bodies, and each plank gained weight, it seemed, with every few feet. At last five planks lay on the clearing beside the barn and five bodies lay sprawled along them. Rex had manfully carried an extra burden, a rucksack on his back containing bottles of homemade lemon barley water and a bottle of machine oil. While they sat up and passed the drink from hand to hand he said, "Look here, we can get all the things up here if we use the winch. If Rolf and I winch, you, Pierre and Ivan could load couldn't you? Yes, and Una, you could act as

73

messenger and start off by bringing up some of the tools."
Rex looked at the twins, admiringly; neither appeared to be
suffering from either the heat of the sun or from their
exertion, while he and Rolf were visibly oozing sweat, Pierre
was unusually red in the face and his dark hair lay flat on his
head and across his swarthy brow.

By the time the family at La Bellule restarted work after
their midday meal, all the timber and iron lay piled outside
the barn on the Roc and the five workers were sharing out
the bread and cheese in the shade cast by the granite walls.
Nobody spoke. They ate; they took turns drinking from the
rapidly diminishing supply of lemon drink; then they
sprawled.

Rex finally broke the silence. "If one of you chaps could
hand up the planks I think I'll nail them on to the beams.
Hardly less work than piling all this lot INSIDE the barn
really. Oh, Pierre, you can't. You must get your traps out. . . "

Rolf felt obliged to offer, and Una thought she could also
help.

Una would have offered to run to the ends of the earth
when all the boys chorused, "Oh, no, you've done valiant
work lugging all these sacks up the cliff."

By working as a team they carried the unwieldy iron into
the barn, propped the planks against the barn wall so they
could be pulled and pushed to the roof, passed the
remaining liquid round and Pierre with Ivan in tow were on
their way down the cliff to the boat.

"Shall I fill up the bottles from the spring?" suggested
Una, and with a rucksack on her back set off, fighting her
way through yet more brambles along the spine of the great
dragon in the opposite direction from the harbour.

By the time the girl struggled back, four filled bottles
bumping against her thin back and her legs bleeding from
the undergrowth, the roof planks were in position, Rex had
vanished to his secret 'Lookout' and Rolf lay hot, sunburnt
and exhausted in the coolest part of the building. She
handed him a bottle and wandered around the interior.

The barn was, in reality, a cottage and a barn attached
with an internal door allowing passage between the two. The
barn partition was divided into several byres, but the cottage
contained two clearly defined rooms, all around the walls of

74

which were portions of presumably wrecked ships; a brass-ringed porthole had skilfully been made into a convex mirror in which, despite the dust, Una saw herself distorted, at which she giggled aloud; a rope-ladder connected the loft with the lower floor, and Una exploring there discovered beneath a pile of rat droppings the remains of three flags, indistinguishable in design but still showing evidence of bright colours. She climbed down with her booty and found in one corner of the main room a barrel from which a brass tube protruded and, with several joints disappeared through the wall into, as she discovered, another barrel placed under the corner eaves of the roof. "Look, Rolf," she roused the somnolent boy, "they had plumbed water here BEFORE we had it at the farm."

"You'd better USE some of it, then," replied her brother unfeelingly, "and get some of that filth and gore washed off before we have to go on the boat."

"No," she said, "I'll go down to the harbour and wash with sea water. You KNOW what the Hermit said about NOT washing open wounds with dirty water. That's what killed more men than fighting did. YOU and Rex can bring the rucksacks and bottles down," she added aggressively, and proceeded to saunter down the crooked, but wider than it had been in the morning, path. She walked slowly, peopling the cottage with another Hermit, then a family, then a shipwrecked pirate, in her active imagination. Once she reached the rocks at the bottom she longed for a swim, but swimming alone was forbidden and they were all honour-bound never to do so. She washed her legs in the ripples that crept up the great sloping piece of rock that formed a chute or natural slipway. Looking along the edge of the island she noticed a pool, a rock pool. She had never explored this part of the island and she decided it could be her own secret, and she would not tell her unfeeling brothers. It meant climbing and fearing more damage to her feet she replaced her plimsoles and scrambled from rock to rock until she reached the pool. It was large enough for her to lie down in, she judged, and only a few inches deep. She was slightly above it and fascinated by the play of sunlight on the various seaweeds growing in the crevices beneath the water. Suddenly her foot dislodged a round boulder. She slipped. She landed in the pool, one foot striking some sharp protruding rock. She removed her slippers and lay in the cool, refreshing water. "I can't get my clothes any wetter than they are already," she thought. "I can dry them before the boat comes back. Anyway I'm giving them a wash."

Once out of the pool she examined the distance she had travelled from the landing and she began to feel afraid, wondering if she could climb back. She decided it might be better to go UP the cliff where she could just see the barn roof on the skyline. Immediately behind her was a huge outcrop of rock above which a line of thick gorse and blackthorn pointed in an almost straight line upwards, flanked by mosses and carpets of purple heather over which she could walk in the paths and gentle furrows already made by generations of rabbits. Scrambling up the rock was quite an effort and her head began to ache. At the top she felt the back of her head and discovered to her surprise a large bump. The discovery made her feel the pain more intensely and she felt irritated by the cloying of her wet clothes, especially the pleated kilt, so once on the smooth top of the rocks with only the gently sloping heather to surmount she removed all her clothing, spread it around the rocks and lay, lapping up the sun that was already striking that side of the Roc. "Must be after four o-clock," she thought. She shook her thick, long hair free of their ribbon, lay on her front, and Una slept.

Pierre and Ivan having dropped the lobster pots sailed into clear water and netted a variety of small fish, most of which they returned to the sea. Ivan hooked a large pollack, a small brill and between them they caught enough mackerel for the next day's breakfast for both families. They rowed into a cove and swam, then Pierre let Ivan sail the boat around a distant rock while he lolled idly watching this apt and eager pupil. He enjoyed the young boy's company; he enjoyed his vivacity and laughed uproariously when he mimicked people well known to both of them; he seemed to take on the very personality and bearing of the person he portrayed, adopting each inflexion of voice and laugh and switching into each of the three languages used by both of them as well as giving renderings of people from many other parts of the world.

"I don't know HOW I do it," was Ivan's answer to a query. "But you see, Pierre, it will come in jolly useful when I'm in the navy, and anywhere in the world. A few days ashore and I'll be able to get to know people of any old nationality. Think of the girls I'll be able meet, eh Pierre?"

The fisherman smiled to himself thinking. "THIS one won't have to LEARN about THAT side of life. Not him, and not me."

While Rolf slept inside the barn, knowing Rex would shout when he saw the boat round the 'Teeth', giving him time to collect up the scattered clothing and rucksacks, Rex sat on his private 'Lookout', some fifty feet beneath the plateau on which the barn had been built. At some distant time, probably before man walked the earth, volcanic eruption or landslide had caused a cavern to be formed above a slab of rock, high on the rocky islet. The land below had formed natural terraces and there appeared to be little sign of erosion, although the vegetation had grown in strange patches, as if certain species had voluntarily decided to remain within certain limits. Immediately beneath the bare rock a carpet of low growing moss and heather made an apparently even carpet of colour, below which stratas of bushes alternated with more heather, thus giving a striped effect seeming to plunge into the sea. Rex sat in the entrance to the cavern, his burnt bare legs wrapped in cooling dock leaves, his body out of the burning sun. He could see the sea clearly but was shielded from being seen FROM the sea by the gorse and blackthorn that grew in patches immediately in front of the cave.

Rex felt smug. Between them, the gang he had taken to the Roc had achieved far more than they had expected to do; all had worked together well; there had been no quarrelling; not even a disagreement had spoilt the day; all these facts gave him a sense of superiority because he felt certain that his command had probably prevented the usual bickering. He felt he had earned this respite from responsibility and he wanted to think. He wondered just HOW he would cope with army life, even if he was really suited for the career he had chosen.

After a while Rex changed his position, moving further into the cave where a smooth piece of rock offered a more comfortable backrest. Once seated he found that part of a gorse bush obtruded between himself and the sea, so he jumped up, cut down the offending branches, collected fresh dock leaves for his sore legs and returned to his comfortable shelter leaving a neat pile of gorse adding colour to the already colourful heather carpet. The massacred bush looked stark and grotesque, while the golden blooms and bright green spikes looked like a neatly laid bonfire. "One day I'll repair the cottage and barn and come and live here," he thought. He thought of how he could take a few comforts and furnish the cottage; a camp bed and some blankets; an armchair and a kettle and pan to cook meals in; then he pictured himself sitting in front of the grate with red embers glowing while he had the comfort of an armchair, a cushion at his sore back and a pipe alight.

Immediate on the picture came the desire to smoke. Slowly he pulled pipe and tobacco from his pockets, slowly and methodically he filled the pipe, and lazily lit and struck a match; the pipe, in need of a clean, did not light, and the longer it remained unlit the stronger became his desire to smoke. In the end he was obliged to empty the pipe, clean the stem with a spike on his penknife, refill it and light it. The enjoyment was greater because of the delay, and Rex luxuriated in both the tobacco and the vision of himself occupying the cottage on the plateau above his head. When the pipe went out he did not bother to relight it, but placed it beside him, closed his eyes and slept.

Rex slept soundly and dreamt. He dreamed that Lieutenant Rex O'Donaty was leading a platoon of soldiers through the Khyber Pass when they were attacked by a band of marauding tribesmen. Gunfire echoed along the Pass. Then he woke and heard gunfire. On an instant he was on his feet. It was not gunfire, but gorse burning in front of him. He knew HOW it had started and he knew that he must put it out, so removing his shirt he beat at the almost demolished pile of leaves and branches he had created, but in doing so he scattered the ashes of what might have been a small, contained fire into a real fire. The dry weather of the last two days and the strong July sunshine made tinder of the next bushes, and the slight breeze from the plateau fanned the flame. Seeing his mistake and realizing the impossibility of beating out the flames Rex had the choice of either allowing the fire to take its course until it reached the sea or cutting down bushes in its path with his knife. The thought of the fire being seen from his home and the explaining he would have to do decided him, so he went ahead of the immediate bushes and started cutting, but long before he had destroyed one bush he saw it was a hopeless venture. The only thing he could do he decided was to cut the turf, moss and heather on each side of the strange line of gorse. "The cliff will be pleasanter without it," he thought philosophically. On one side of the gorse line the turf and heather lifted easily as he cut deftly and deeply with his knife. When he reached a gap between bushes he went through and began his work on the other side. It was easier to work as he was climbing upwards instead of moving backwards down the slope, but the smoke was being blown into his face and he had difficulty keeping it from his eyes and mouth and nose; the air he desperately needed to inhale was thick with the pungent vapour. He straightened his back and faced the sea where the air was being polluted with spasmodic grey swirls of smoke. He inhaled deeply registering surprise at the quantity of discolouration that such a small number of bushes had created when he saw below him something that filled him with fear. He had never felt fear like that in all his life, for some fifty feet below and in the direct path of the fire should it jump the gap in the bushes lay an inert body. Later, he could not remember how, he reached the rocky ledge; he had assumed that the smoke had suffocated the small child stretched naked on the rock. He had hauled an apparently unconscious child across his shoulders before he realized it was his cousin, when he put her down and dragged her up the slope. He heard a loud sound like a pistol shot and felt his hand contact bare flesh, before he regained any semblance of composure, and heard his voice saying, "Put your clothes on, you little fool."

"I can't," Una replied, standing unconcernedly before him. "They're down there," and she pointed down the cliff where the fire was still spreading.

Throwing his shirt at the girl, Rex angrily slid and jumped until the ground he had previously bounded down he saw to be treacherous shale and almost perpendicular at one point. Sitting and sliding down the last part he gathered up the scattered clothing and finding the long strip of pleated skirt to be quite damp used it to beat out the remaining flames, then stood and studied the spot below him where she had lain. He saw the danger she was in due to his own carelessness. Slowly making the return climb he found himself choking, not with smoke this time, but with relief; tears oozed from the corners of his eyes, drying on his heated face and lingering in the hairs of his fair moustache. He had shed few tears in his life, but at this particular moment he felt there was an unlimited quantity waiting to fall. Once clear of the smoke he became vaguely aware of the small figure swathed in white and lit by the direct rays of the lowering sun against the dark background of the cavern mouth. Drained of energy, he threw the bundle of clothes at her feet, fell on the ground, buried his head on his arm and panted, while trying to will the tears to cease.

He felt the girl drop to the ground beside him saying, "I think you've made a tattoo on my bottom with your hand."

Through veiled eyes he saw, turning his head sideways, the contorted body studying the very red mark on her anatomy, and in a spontaneous gesture quite alien to his normal behaviour, he grabbed the girl, clutched her close to him and hugged her with what strength remained gulping, "I damn nearly burnt you alive. My God, I nearly burnt you to death."

Twisting from his grasp she kissed him on his wet cheek and breathed at him, "You SAVED MY LIFE, Rex. You saved my life," then rolling sideways and pulling his shirt about her body added, "You're a hero. A REAL hero, Rex . . . and you've got hairs all over your chest and they glitter in the sun."

Torn by conflicting emotions and bewildered by his own actions, Rex said irritably, "Well give me my shirt and get dressed."

In one rapid movement she obeyed then started searching for her vest, saying, "Anyway I like your hairs. . . "

"Shut UP!" he snapped combating a strong desire to slap her again, before effectively doing so verbally, by adding, "And you've got bumps on your chest."

"I haven't!" she snapped back. "I haven't and I won't. . ." She studied her body, then moaned, "Well that proves God's no good. I promised all sorts of things . . . and I've tried Allah and ALL the gods. . . " Hurriedly and clumsily Una dressed, forcing the buttons on her liberty bodice to meet the button-holes, sliding her legs into the voluminous navy blue school uniform bloomers, then moving closer to her cousin pleaded, "Don't tell the others, please Rex."

Uncomfortably disturbed, he leapt to his feet growling, "Oh all right, but you can keep this business to yourself. Agreed? AND, don't you EVER come here; this is MY place. Understood? And, WHY were you swimming ALONE?"

He barely listened to her explanation, interrupting to say, "I used your skirt to put the rest of the fire out . . . ah, there's the boat. I'll go and warn Rolf, " then bounded along his private path leaving her to follow.

Dock leaves wrapped around her torn foot, Una limped slowly behind the two boys who had cleared up the barn and were carrying the rucksacks between them. Ivan, having had a comparatively restful afternoon bounded up the path and offered his twin a lift on his back which she declined remembering the hated bumps on her body. Climbing unsteadily into the boat she heard Rex say, "No we didn't swim. Rolf and I finished the roof and Una went off climbing and fell in a pool."

"She carried all the water bottles up from the stream, don't forget, Rex," said Rolf.

"What about the fire?" Pierre asked. "Deliberate or accident, eh?"

"Accident," admitted the culprit.

Pierre advised, "Woodsmen's law, Rex. Never smoke till you've dug out a turf. Ashtray, you see, and no sign left when you put the turf back!"

"The Hermit said that," Una reminded them, which caused extreme ill-temper to flood through the normally easy-going and placid Rex.

Ivan saved anyone having to converse during the trip homewards and Lex met them at the harbour, taking Una back to the farm on Frank's bicycle crossbar while the others unloaded and moored the boat for the night.

After making arrangements for a work-party to visit the Roc next day, they separated, Pierre to his cottage and the O'Donaty family to the old granite farmhouse. Pierre entertained his parents with a voluble account of the day's events. At the farmhouse a silence hovered over the usually noisy kitchen table. Each individual seemed wrapped in a separate and isolated world; plates were passed, vegetables offered, accepted or rejected and the large brown teapot sat forlornly on the hob, burdened with the unconsumed liquid, while the rapidly tidied kitchen and the huge oval Truth Table seemed deserted, bereft of the vibrant life that usually seemed to permeate the whole area even when no human was present. Not only was the small farm and all who belonged there transfixed in time, but the whole world was waiting. All over the world there were young people reaching the abyss that divided them from the world of adults; they waited, fear mingling with confidence, misery with joy, lust with love and curiosity with indifference. It had been the same since before man settled in dwelling places, and it would be the same until man destroyed himself, but during the summer of 1914 there were resonant drums beating in the ether and the young humans, with the instinct of animals, felt the urge to cross the abyss precipitously and without hindrance.

Aurora O'Donaty felt as if she lived on the top of a volcano. She felt the first vibrations of impending eruption during the journey back from Town with her sick niece beside her, but since then the rumblings had occurred with increased rapidity and she needed time, and solitude to THINK. The evening was still and stifling hot and she would have liked to stroll across the beach as the picnic and bathing parties had dispersed, but she felt she should be at hand in case one of the family should want to talk to her. She sat in the drawing room beside the window over-looking the dragonfly pond and thought about the many questions she would like to ask. The mere act of forming some of the queries made them unnecessary as the answer flashed across her mind. One by one she mentally studied each of her charges, beginning with her daughter whose sewing machine she heard whirring away in the bedroom, stitching a new outfit for Una.

Turning from the window at the sound of some movement in the hall, she saw the carpet on which Leo's wet body had been placed, and then the image of the body and the child standing in the doorway holding her white nightgown against her body. It had been Old Pierre, tears pouring down his bearded cheeks, who had picked her up, held her tight and carried her to the kitchen, but it had been the nine year old who had handed out cups of tea and glasses of brandy that night. "I haven't been fair to Roxana," thought Aurora. "I've let her give and give and give; we all have. Even now she is giving her time and her energy, doing the things I should be doing. . . She's twenty-four and is not even courting — and so beautiful . . . somehow I MUST let her become free." Had she but known it, Aurora would have no decision to make for the hands of fate were moving faster each day, but Aurora had been infected by the atmosphere amongst them all and she became fanciful. She wrote on her pad, intending to copy the words into her diary later, "We are like eight clocks, all ticking at different speeds and all at different times." Then she began to list the questions:—

Why didn't you tell me about the Hermit and the Tumbledown Cottages?

Why didn't you tell me about Una's miseries at school?

Why didn't you mention Nanny and the fracas over Frank's hand?

Why did you let me think school was such a jolly place?

"And WHY ask the questions," she decided. "They have been answered — in their own way — I just didn't HEAR the answers." She stood up as the flash of an Emperor dragonfly dived towards the still water of the pond. The translucent electric blue wings picked up the scarlet and orange from the setting sun and kaleidoscopic flashes wove patterns in the air. Looking closer, Aurora saw the swallow-tail butterfly escape the ravenous jaws of the dragonfly and disappear around the corner of the house while the long tailed pair of swallows swooped at the abundant insect life hovering above and around the water. The dragonfly had disappeared, leaving the succulent food to the strongest marauder. In the stillness of the evening Aurora heard the delighted squawks

83

from the nest in the eaves at the return of the two tireless parent swallows, their mouths filled with their plunder. "A pity the dragonflies and butterflies and moths don't make an alliance, an agreement NOT to attack each other, then they'd each have only one enemy to watch out for and evade," she thought. Soft footsteps above her head brought her back to earth. She heard Frank's bedsprings creak and vibrate, clearly responding to a body hurled on to them. A heavy book was thrown on the floor, then a long silence ensued. Aurora wondered who else had gone upstairs; who had caused the anger she could feel below. She heard the springs creak again, footsteps crossing and recrossing the floor, evidently retrieving the books followed by the slow careful steps descending the stairs until Frank was inside the room, his face taut and his glasses awry. "I'd like to take my violin outside to play, Aunt Aurora." Without another word he picked up the battered black case and disappeared through the hall, through the kitchen, into the yard, along the drive, under the archway, across the track and the strip of common and on to the beach where his violin, the seagulls and the sea formed their own pacifying orchestral symphony.

Frank, unused to being thwarted was very, very angry; he seldom asked for anything; he seldom strove for anything until he was certain of success; he had EXPECTED Una to comply with his wishes — she tried to please everyone most of the time. He had only asked her to help him with his medical studies, and she had not only refused, but refused emphatically and furiously. He only wanted to study her anatomy and compare it with the diagrams in the Gray's Anatomy and she had told him to get out of her room AND threatened to scream. It wasn't as if he hadn't seen her body often enough; this time he wanted to study it. . . Frank stopped thinking and tuned his violin, the discordant sounds offending his ears and usurping the other thoughts crowding tumultuously through his head. Slowly he made his way to the water's edge and heard himself playing an old Irish lullaby he had last heard many years before, hummed by his father and picked out on her violin by his mother. The music he was creating had taken him over, the plaintive notes calmed him and he stood, violin dangling from one hand, the bow from the other and listened to the rippling of water and the raucous screeching of gulls. In that instant Frank knew that it was not only scientific knowledge he sought from his sister. Slowly he returned up the beach but did not pass through the archway; instead, he walked close to the wall following it around the perimeter of the farm, crossed the donkey-spattered common and made his way into the small fishermen's chapel where he prayed to a deity he had absolute faith in, to remove all incestuous thoughts from him. He was about to leave the dark little building when another thought struck him. He returned to the altar steps, knelt, and prayed for strength to combat his unholy thoughts.

At the other end of Bellule Bay Rex sat on a rock gazing out to sea at HIS ROC. The object of his thoughts was the same as Frank's, but where Frank felt guilt, Rex felt delight, tinged with enough guilt to make the topic beguiling. "So that's what it's like to feel lust," he thought, "and even a little girl's naked body. . ." He relived the event on the Roc and resampled the parts he had touched. He realized that his own fear for her safety and his unceremonious handling of her had introduced him to the feel of most of the childish frame. "A pity she isn't more voluptuous," he thought, knowing that he would have enjoyed a repeat of the same experience — without the fire — in spite of the meagre attributes. . . "Perhaps next time we go to the Roc. . ." he thought with lust-filled relish, imagining the joys ahead.

The object of the two boys' thoughts barricaded her door with her heavy gladstone bag, removed her clothing and studied her body. "I'm not a bit like that drawing in Frank's old book," she thought. The bumps were still there though. She stretched out and they disappeared — almost. "I'll just have to stretch myself. . ." She was forced to admit that she was NOT the same shape as the boys. The bumps WERE there, very small, but soft, not hard like Rex's chest had felt when he held her close to him. A sudden fear filled her, "Suppose she grew bumps like Elizabeth Wright? Nothing would hide them from the boys." She put her clothes on again, studied her swollen foot, tied a handkerchief tightly around it hoping to push the swelling inwards, but the pain was too intense so removed it, assuming that if she tied something round those bumps they would also become painful. "I'll just have to stretch every night and wear loose clothes all day. . . Rolf'll give me his old shirts. . ." She knew she did not want to grow up; she wanted to be a girl Peter Pan; she recalled the day they all acted the story. "I'll make a stage and a marionette theatre," she decided, sliding from her bed intent on searching the barn for an old box. If she made the theatre first, Roxana would certainly give her cloth for curtains and costumes; the 'people' could be made from pegs. . . . she wished her foot would stop hurting! She made yet another bargain with God. "I'll put up with the pain in my foot if you make the bumps go away." She KNEW in her heart it would not happen, but it was worth trying.

Lex sat in the yard whittling a piece of wood into the fuselage of an aeroplane and dreaming about a future amongst the clouds, high above the farm, the sea and people, free as a bird, the wind singing in the ailerons and joy in his heart.

Ivan lay on his stomach on the barn roof watching the movements of ships far out to sea and wished he had a telescope, that he could be three years older than he was and that somebody would share his interest and excitement at the sight of naval vessels manoeuvring so close to their island. The years stretched ahead unendingly to his impatient outlook; years confined to classrooms, dormitories and playing fields, marking time until he could become part of a ship's company facing the hazards of wild and turbulent oceans, seeing the world and belonging to some close-knit community. He saw himself performing acts of valour. Ambition filled his restless spirit and he longed to talk about his hopes but there was nobody prepared to listen; Rolf thought only of sheep, cows and wirelesses; Lex dreamt of aeroplanes; Rex's mind was tuned to an equally ambitious life in the army and Frank seemed lost in religion and medicine. Perhaps Una would join him in his make-believe world — but Una was only a girl!

Rolf gently scraped the tiny crystal he held in his hand, his penknife removing a few fragments of dust before placing it in the cigar box filled with wires and attached his aerial to the metal plug. He put the earphones on his head, turned the appropriate knob and faintly a voice sounded in his ears. He had contacted London, and he knew that a fresh battery would produce a louder volume. The instructions in the encyclopedia had borne fruit. He, Rolf, had made a wireless. Slowly and carefully he sorted through the heterogeneous collection of coils, wires, clips and strips of metal and knew that he had enough parts to construct a two valve set if he could buy the valves. He unplugged his aerial and decided to tell his sister about his achievement; she would let the rest of the family know and then he might receive the approbation he felt he deserved, but was not articulate enough to demand himself.

Rolf tapped gently on Una's doors. He heard her heavy gladstone bag being dragged from behind it, the door opened and she invited him in, a large darning needle and thread hanging from her shabby kilt. "I'm trying to stitch up the burns," she said. He sat on the bed beside her while she used up the thread, weaving it in and out of the cloth.

"My wireless works."

"You mean, Rolf, you really CAN hear voices miles away talking to you?"

Gratified by the admiration, Rolf nodded. "You can come and listen if you like." Without considering the job she had been doing, Una followed her younger, taller brother to his bedside. They sat, taking turns listening to voices. Neither registered the words being said; it was enough to be hearing voices from, as Rolf explained, hundreds of miles away, speaking to THEM through air waves.

"Like sea waves?" asked Una before examining each piece of the simple mechanism that had resulted in such an apparent miracle.

"When I make a two valve set I might be able to put an extension to your room," said Rolf grandly. He showed her the valves, the coil and the microphone he had already collected before explaining that he had to save up for an accumulator.

"When we get our pocket money I'll let you have mine," offered the admiring girl.

They sat in companionable silence, Rolf straining his ears to catch the words beyond the ether and Una gazing at the confusion of wires that lay around the bed, wondering why the machine was called a wire-less, when the sound of people and crockery moving around drifted from below. Una heard her aunt crossing the hall, then Roxana's door opening followed by her footsteps. It seemed as if each of the isolated entities had decided to conjoin. When Pierre's voice was heard in the yard, followed later by Old Pierre's and Marie's, Rolf and Una made their way down the tourelle and into the crowded kitchen where Ivan was pouring tea into the large willow-patterned cups.

"Troops are moving across Germany," said Pierre. "They heard it on their wireless at the 'Harbour Arms'. Papa and I came back to tell all of you."

"It means war," said Rex.

"They wouldn't dare fight if we join in," Ivan added, "We've got the best and biggest Navy in the world. . ."

". . . and they have people — most of them trained to fight. . ." Lex said.

"We're trained as well," Rex argued. "Look at the hours we've spent learning to be soldiers in the School Corps . . . and Pierre, he's in the Militia. . ."

"Oh yes, we'll soon show them. . ." Ivan agreed, aggressively.

Frank spoke in the moment's lull that followed his brother's remark, "Maybe the politicians will TALK the nations into peace. . ."

"Perhaps," agreed Roxana doubtfully.

"Anyway," said Una, "Rolf's already prepared. HE'S made a wireless that WORKS, and you can hear a man talking in London. . ." They sped up the stairs to listen at the faint distant voice. After each of the young had tried the earphones, the older members of the family listened. Marie hugged Rolf, calling him clever and patient. By the time they were all sitting around the kitchen table, Rolf felt he had grown inches and was agreeing to construct wireless sets for all of them — provided THEY bought the necessary parts.

Meanwhile in the country with the largest and best-trained army in the world, an egoistical Sovereign had already briefed his Commanders while his Politicians prepared Documents purporting to expostulate their own lack of aggressive ideology, or desire for territorial expansion.

For three days the family worked energetically, and together. The visit was made to the Roc without the twins who cleaned and scraped the farmhouse paintwork around windows and doors, a conclave having decided they were the lightest and most agile at climbing ladders. They chose to take each respite at roof level thus watching events at the Roc as well as naval movements in the sea beyond. Una listened to Ivan's talk about ships, the navy and the war, her foot aching so intensely that she had no wish to reply, nor even argue. The assault on each job became almost frenzied, the unity within the family group unnaturally affable and the exhaustion by nightfall consummate. Roxana returned each evening in time for the meal after spending the day at the hospital and attending every First Aid lecture available. Once the dishes were cleared away she demonstrated the skills she had acquired during her classes and they all practised bandaging each other with strips of torn up sheets. By the third evening their combined life had taken on a daily pattern: morning chores completed before breakfast, and a swim, the repairs and repainting performed steadily throughout the morning and afternoon followed by another swim and an abusive game of cricket. The main meal was always jolly and full of talk, then Aurora was ceremoniously escorted around the farm to view and admire the day's work, after which the riot of bandaging and splinting began. Una became the favourite victim stretched out on the kitchen table as Roxana's dummy then turned into an Egyptian mummy by deft as well as clumsy hands; she gritted her teeth when they bound her sore foot visualizing herself as a Jeanne d'Arc, a martyr.

"We should have done this to her," said Ivan, "BEFORE we used her as our Viking chief and sent her out to sea on that raft. . ."

"You did WHAT?" asked Roxana, horrified.

"Oh it was all right," Ivan continued, "we didn't set fire to her. Rex stopped us . . . anyway we wouldn't have let her really burn. . ."

"But I didn't mind," said the victim. "I KNEW they wouldn't let me DIE."

Rex added, "Actually I had a jolly difficult time pulling that raft in, I can tell you. I mean fancy sending her out on a falling tide anyway . . . of course," he added condescendingly, "you'd only just arrived over here — but none of you could swim."

"You've saved my life TWICE, then," said the victim, sitting up and destroying the neat arrangement of bandages.

"Lie down, idiot," Frank ordered, grabbing her foot and pushing her backwads.

A scream filled the kitchen, the farmhouse and even filtered through the archway, disturbing the crabs busily scavenging along the beach.

"What happened?" they asked each other.

"What did I do?" asked Frank.

"Is she dead?" asked Rolf while Roxana feverishly unwrapped bandages from her body.

"She's fainted," Roxana was saying as Aurora hurried in from the garden.

"Whose fainted?" asked Una, sitting up. "Ooh, Van, you look AWFUL."

Accompanied by Ivan's wheezing they laughed nervously and Roxana continued her methodical unwinding until interrupted by Frank saying, "Look, Roxana, it's her foot. I grabbed it and it's a balloon." For a few seconds they stood around admiring the misshappen limb.

"Frank," ordered his aunt, "Go on your bicycle and fetch Dr. McFane. Now."

The crabs were treated to further disruptions of their ordered lives. The cranking two-wheeled contraption vibrated over their passage-ways, and just as they were settling to their maraudings a heavy four-wheeled ear-invading monster rattled along the lane and stopped at the archway with, what seemed to be a massive explosion followed by silence accompanied by choking fumes. The crabs hurried with all their legs towards the safety of the rocks near the water's edge.

A few minutes later the members of the family who had been banished from the kitchen were recalled and the inevitable cups and saucers were being put on a slightly damp, freshly scrubbed table while the kettle complained noisily and its companion teapot was savouring the aroma of its many spoonfuls of tea. The boys were too busy questioning Una to bother with teapots, Aunt Aurora was in the drawingroom with Dr. McFane and Roxana had disappeared to her room.

"Come on, one of you, make the tea," said the latter, returning, wearing a clean dress.

By the time the doctor and Aurora returned the boys were almost sated with descriptions of gore, each recounting some accident witnessed that was slightly more revolting than the previous one. Ivan said nothing; he wheezed and inhaled deep breaths from a jug of hot liquid provided by Roxana.

"I've done TWO disappearances now this hol. Van," and Una proudly, "and you've only done ONE."

Ivan lifted his head from the steam and whistled, "I did SIX last term," before returning to his inhaling.

"I've written mine in my notebook. There were too many to keep count. The last three weeks of term it was EVERY DAY in prayers — but I only missed one line of the prayer. It still counts though, Van. . ."

"What on EARTH are you two talking about?" asked Lex.

Una tried to turn to face him, but her foot propped up on a stool prevented her, so speaking through the back of her head she explained, irritably, "Oh, Lex, you know, like I did tonight and on the Roc when I hurt my foot — disappearances . . . being there and not being and then being there again. Van and I do it all the time. We don't MAKE it happen. It happens. We just compare how many that's all. See?"

Rex changed the conversation by addressing the doctor, "I say, Sir," he said, "that's a jolly good Ford motor car, you have. We looked it over while you were operating in here. Lex here says an aeroplane cockpit is more complicated inside — so if he can drive 'planes, we could easily learn to drive a Ford. . ."

"Not MINE, though," laughed the doctor, rising to leave.

"I'll call the day after tomorrow," he said, leaving the house accompanied by the entire family except the twins.

Once again the crabs were treated to shocks sufficient to cause their shells and claws to shudder uncomfortably while those in the middle of moulting, or newly moulted, received permanent damage to their soft flesh when hard shells banged them so unexpectedly. Had they but known, the human who had caused all their troubles was the only human in the edifice above their world who had NEVER molested them; she neither collected nor killed them; she only watched them, a harmless and natural curiosity since they were thousands of years older than her species.

While an insignificant amount of blood and gore was being shed at La Bullule, followed by a peaceful retiring of the family, a small and almost insignificant state had been invaded by a powerful marching machine equipped with the latest ingenuity of man's creativity, and a politician spoke to a silent throng of representatives of his nation, "The lamps are going out all over Europe; we shall not see them lit in our lifetime," and a war had begun that was to encompass thirty nations and result in eight and a half million dead, twenty-one million disabled, and seven and a half million unaccounted for, besides twenty-two million dead within three years of the cessation of hostilities due to the spread of an epidemic among ill-nourished civilians by the movement of troops. The war was to strike at the heart of every cottage, hovel, castle, tenement and house. The war was to strike at the very foundations of the family that belonged to the newly painted farmhouse built as a refuge against the might of the unleashed sea and guarded by a beautiful, powerful insect, the Anax Imperator, a dragonfly — or une bellule — of the Odonata Order.

Chapter Six

Dr. McFane arrived two days later to find the patient whose wound he had intended to dress, being towed on a couple of planks behind a decrepit old bicycle, cheered by an admiring host of young people. On closer inspection he found the planks were attached to two pairs of wheels that had once known better days on a doll's pram, and the injured limb was supported by a thick cushion. While the 'chauffeur' took the patient to the kitchen, the rest of the family evaporated, taking the opportunity to study the car parked on their own drive. Frank remained behind after parking his own contraption and asked, "May I stay and watch, Sir? I'm hoping my father will allow me to study medicine instead of soldiering."

Aurora arrived in time to hear the request and quietly nodded in answer to the doctor's unspoken query, and once the foot was dressed and rebound the doctor asked, "Why not go with Roxana to the First Aid Classes, young man? Doctors will be needed in plenty before this crazy war is over . . . and don't look so dubious. There are other young men at the classes; two sixth form lads from the College and a medical student from Cambridge — and there'll be others joining. And now how's young Ivan," he asked turning to Aurora while he closed up his brown bag.

"He's out fishing with Old Pierre," she replied.

"As I thought," the doctor laughed. "Only gets his wheezes in sympathy with his twin. Best thing for him the Navy, eh? Nelson was an asthmatic, you know, AND seasick, which is something that hasn't worried these twins has it?" Aurora recalled this holiday in the many years ahead as one in which she had, or so it seemed, constant cause for pondering.

The next few weeks while the rest of the world seemed to be on the move those at La Bellule were waiting, impatiently and restlessly, but waiting for their various fates to be sealed. Lex's chagrin was unbearable as he watched Frank on his buckle-wheeled bicycle leave the house each day beside Roxana, and return every afternoon conversing in some alien medical language. Rex was bereft of his usual holiday companion for Pierre, conscripted a year before into the Militia, was attending an intensive training course. Ivan, though not quite thirteen mixing freely at the town harbour with seamen and fishermen, seemed to have an entrée to every vessel in port and was even earning money from his privately caught fish. Rolf, when he was not with his beloved sheep, was constructing a wireless and they, the two elders of the tribe, had to ask to be allowed to listen to his two-valve set; ask this mere eleven year old! Even Una seemed to be content, spending hours beside the pond drawing and painting the insects and plants, or propelling herself on the trolley to the danger of all pedestrians. The two young men decided to prepare themselves for their future careers and the conflict in which the world had become enmeshed by embarking on a self-inflicted programme of physical fitness and stamina. They swam long distances across the bay and around the rocky headlands; they went on gruelling cross-country runs before breakfast every day and in all weathers; they scaled up some hazardous cliff-faces and they explored the island that was their home and which they scarcely knew; they spent two days and nights sleeping rough and cooking their meagre supply of food on camp fires — and discovered the cold that arrives with night even during summer weather; they waited impatiently for their chosen careers to commence.

During Una's incarceration, Rex exercised Gamma, somewhat listlessly and definitely without enthusiasm, but at least feeling he was contributing something to the household. Lex wandered out to the promontory, followed the coast, and, deep in his own thoughts, became aware that he had arrived at the small fishing harbour where, to his astonishment, a warehouse had become a garage almost overnight it seemed. He studied the two gleaming Ford motor cars that exalted the place, that once, a very short time ago, was a confusion of nets, lobster pots, spars, sails and parts of engines. With a jauntier step he turned and strode towards home. About quarter of a mile on he met a man visibly sweating, pushing and attempting to steer another, though less glittering, Ford. Lex offered to push, allowing the man the chance to both rest his aching body and steer more competently. The cavalcade came to a standstill in the garage beside the new machines and the man explained, "Only sold THIS one three months ago, and look at it. Paint knocked about, bent mudguard, dry water tank, no petrol and the gears ground to nothing." Whilst speaking he was indicating all the injuries that were visible. "I'll have to strip it right down," groaned the man, "and no assistant; he's been called to the Militia."

"Can I help?" asked Lex, adding, "I don't know much about engines, but I've time to spare — until they put ME in uniform."

Every day Lex appeared at the garage, old clothes on his body and an ancient cap of Uncle Leo's on his head. At first he tightened or loosened bolts, cranked the starting handle and passed tools, but his master, Jim Solange rewarded his industry by taking him for a drive, then driving lessons besides giving him responsible jobs to do on the variety of engines that came for minor or major repairs. The evening Lex made his first driving excursion without Jim beside him, friends were waiting for the garage man to go 'on the town'. They shouted their approbation when the driver returned after a faultless performance and heard Lex say, "Whew! I hope my first solo flight will be like that." It was the first indication he had given of his future hopes, and he had won the admiration of all the company; not because he intended flying, but because he had not mentioned his awe-inspiring and glamorous future. He became 'one of them' that day for he had successfully bridged the gap between two distinctly different cultures. He had also learnt something that no education, nor lack of it, could offer.

By the time Una was walking again Frank had also crossed one of life's bridges. He no longer arrived home with Roxana, but, according to his cousin, pushed his bicycle and walked home with one of the young ladies attending the classes. When teased and questioned he merely answered, "She has copper coloured hair and bright blue eyes," but nothing would induce him to tell them the girl's name and Roxana loyally kept silence.

Rex was delighted to hand back responsibility for Gamma to his cousin. "Nothing," he thought, "can be more boring than sitting bare-back on some ancient nag and walk it or canter it up and down a stretch of sand. Even in the desert there'd be dunes and even the occasional mirage to break the monotony." He had never seen a desert, nor a mirage, and he had no idea what Una did when out with Gamma, but to Rex, it was all right for a girl to do dull jobs, while far from all right for a man.

Una was happy. The tide was well out so she marked a rough circle on a part of the beach invisible even from her window; she removed her old, patched kilt and rode the patient mare round and round the circle; she used hands and legs to control Gamma and having achieved a steady canter stood up on the horse's back. Certain that she was very unlikely to be seen she tucked her long hair into the nape of her shirt, performed her gymnastics then, still on the creature's back took her into the sea, sliding off and swimming while still holding the reins. Slowly she returned up the beach, picked up the kilt from a nearby rock and was just wrapping it around her when a voice startled her.

"A nice performance, young man."

A small, white-haired old man appeared from the direction of the promontory and if Una had been dumbfounded by the voice, the stranger was shocked to discover a girl holding the reins, waiting while he limped uneasily across the spongy sand.

"I was going to ask you if you'd like to exercise my two horses. I, er, didn't know you were a girl," painfully embarrassed he asked, "I suppose you haven't any brothers, have you? I'm keeping my nags for my two sons, serving overseas and I can't make the back of even a donkey nowadays — one no good leg and the other side — well, no leg." Since Una had not uttered a word, he asked again, "Have you got any brothers?"

"Lots!"

"Would any of them like to ride my chargers, d'you think?"

"Come and see them," said Una, her ready friendliness and lack of shyness exerting itself. "You mightn't like them, of course . . . we live over there," and she pointed to the arched entrance.

While they walked slowly through the archway Una said, "I'd ride your chargers. I THINK I can ride ANYTHING and I wish I wasn't a girl. The only thing I can do as a girl is join a circus. THEY can do ANYTHING. If I was a boy and still me I'd join a cavalry regiment and there's Rex, he's going in the army and all he wants is to ride motor-cycles or drive an armoured car."

"I've found someone on the beach, Aunt Aurora," Una called through the kitchen where her aunt could be seen busily preparing the evening meal. It was thus the family adopted, or was adopted by another equally isolated household. By the time Una had finished with Gamma all the family except Frank were sitting around the table drinking cups of tea with the flotsam 'found on the beach'.

"Bought the cottage and the two paddocks round the back of your farm," said the stranger. "Both my sons abroad you see, and the quacks thought my legs might behave better over here. It's terrible damp where I came from, the middle of Tipperary. We have to have quiet, me and my missus; she's deaf you see, stone deaf, but noisy vibrations, now they hurt her ears, they do. Deaf when I married her, poor old thing. She used to hear, oh yes, and sing they say, but an explosion made her deaf. Good pair, aren't we?" he laughed, an infectious, musical laugh without any trace of bitterness, adding, "No ears on the one side and almost no legs on the other . . . and there's me filled with the Irishman's love of talking, a stranger here, and nobody to talk at." Una came in at that point, and the man turned to Aurora and apologised, saying, 'I THOUGHT this young lady was a boy. I'm sorry I spoke to her. Wouldn't dream of accosting her if I'd known." He had pulled himself to his feet while he spoke, and with a graceful old-world action, bowed to the lady of the house, then the young girl, and finally Roxana.

"I expect she was riding without a skirt," suggested Ivan, receiving a look that should have shrivelled him, from his twin, but actually just glanced off him, before she turned her attention to her aunt, who, seeing BOTH looks said, "My dear Una, I do know. I've seen you often enough from the promontory."

The gracious stranger cooled the atmosphere by saying, "I'm sorry. I haven't even introduced myself. Here I am, sitting drinking tea in your kitchen and I might be a vagrant or tinker . . . or . . . but I'm not. My name is Fyne, spelt with a Y, and it depends where I live what I give as my given name. In Ireland it's Séan; in England it's John, in Scotland it's Ian and when I served in South Africa it was Jan or John depending whether I was a Boer prisoner or a cavalry sergeant. I suppose I should be Jean, here, d'you think?"

Aurora and Rex walked back with Sergeant Fyne, met his beautiful little wife and a friendship began that was to last closely and almost lovingly to the end of their lives. In addition it was the beginning of a gruelling time for Rex, Una and Rolf who all volunteered to ride the chargers, and be TAUGHT 'cavalry fashion'. Serge as they called the old man, was very dubious about accepting a girl, but at first she rode Gamma, however when the instructor saw how fearless she was, and how quick to learn he almost forgot she was not one of his old troopers. Rolf had surprised all of them, but he explained in his usual laconic fashion. "I'll have a sheep station one day."

Rex found himself enjoying the training, enjoying the feel of power under him and the technicalities of real horsemanship. Unknowingly he learnt something far more important, even more important than the self discipline and instant obedience of horse and rider, horse through rider, to commands; he learnt about life as a trooper, as a human lacking the luxuries enjoyed by officers, adding to the Hermit's memories; these things were to stay with Rex all his life; not a word, a tale or an experience was to be wasted.

Augustus' long awaited letter arrived eventually. Permission was granted for Lex to join the R.F.C. although by the time it arrived the choice was no longer his. Rather less generous permission was granted for Frank to enter himself for medical school, after which was the addition, "he can always become an army surgeon." Ivan was to receive coaching in mathematics and it was to be expected that he would pass the examination to the Naval College in the spring. Una had disappointed both himself and her mother, but IF their long-suffering sister was prepared to put up with her, then she could attend a local school and make herself useful around the house. Aurora did NOT read the letter aloud. She paraphrased the verbosity into bare facts which excluded any criticism. Una's overjoyed letter of gratitude must have surprised her parents who, if their daughter chose to consider them the best and dearest parents in the world, did not reciprocate the sentiments regarding this particular offspring. The home-made wine circulated at La Bellule that evening.

Besides the thick package from India was a parcel from England addressed to Una. Parcels being a considerable rarity, this was passed from hand to hand and each tried to guess the contents. Clearly it MUST be some article left at school. The last guesser and addressee was furthest from the truth when she suggested resignedly, "They probably found the liberty bodice I stuffed behind the boiler last year."

All eyes on her, Una opened the package and pulled out a letter, reading aloud,

> "Dear Una,
>
> The old man you befriended asked me to give you the enclosed carving before he died. Please thank your brothers for fetching me in time.
>
> Dominic Fr.

There was complete silence as, with shaking hands and tears veiling her eyes, Una unwrapped the carved icon that had hung behind the 'altar' beside the Hermit's sacking bed. She turned it over then ran from the room, returning swiftly with drier eyes and a small piece of card in her hand. "The secret, ancient writing," she croaked.

On the back of the carving was a line of scratches.

///// I IIII III III / IIII II IIII IIIII III

99

"RHETT MCLEIF," she translated.

Holding the carved piece of wood so they could each see the marking on the reverse side, Una said, "His name. The Hermit's name."

Later that evening, when the three younger members of the family had gone to their room, the others went out together for a walk. They ambled along the edge of the strand then followed the bay round until they reached the promontory where they stopped and lapped up the stillness of the evening and the magnificence of the sky reflecting a dramatic sunset taking place on the other side of the island. The two ladies perched on convenient rocks and the three young men lolled against others, less smoothly polished, and lit their pipes.

After a long, companionable silence Aurora posed one of her very rare questions. "Tell me," she said, "about this Hermit. What was he REALLY?"

"Ah," said Rex. "WE don't actually KNOW. Certainly an old soldier; certainly a man of some education and certainly Irish; an ex-soldier, with no money to pay his journey to his home, a tramp, vagrant, expelled gypsy thrown out of his tribe long ago, perhaps. We didn't think he was some sort of religious recluse; that was Una. She thought the donkey had LED us to meet God. Well, you know Una — all dreams and imagination . . ."

"We had to do something for her," added Lex. "She was so unhappy at school, or, let's say, she was unhappy at being deprived of US."

"But WHY did you go on and on, all those years, visiting him?" Roxana asked.

Rex tried to explain. "WE found the cottage and then he moved IN, remember. We wanted to keep the place for ourselves. Look, the alternative to spending Sunday there was to do the three mile route march being leered at by lines of girls, the entire Prep., AND the townspeople. We were CONSPICUOUS, you can see that; five handsome boys and only one little girl, all in school uniform . . . well it was jolly embarrassing. The cottages were a Godsend . . . ha! ha! ha!" he laughed mirthlessly, "What a wit, me! Una thought she'd found God there. We thought we'd found a hiding place where we could relax, make toast, and generally treat the place as another home . . ."

Lex, realizing that neither of the ladies had any conception of school life elucidated, "You see the other chaps went to their own homes — if they weren't too far away; others went out to day-boys' homes; some had parents visiting and the rest went on the three miles walk. Of course chaps slipped aside and went off elsewhere; most of the overseas fellows went off to one or other of the country inns, but they were frightfully rich."

Rex added further explanations by saying, "IF old Lex here hadn't taken Una or the small-fry out, they'd never be able to go out anywhere except in those dreadful crocodiles. It was all right for most people, but THIS tribe coming from all that adventurous life in India, well, I mean to say, it'd be like caging a . . . swallow say."

"Rex just came to support US," Frank offered.

"Quite a few other chaps had to take sisters out, but they all seemed to have aunts or friends to visit where they dumped the girls — so they say," said Lex.

"Did you LIKE your Hermit?" Roxana asked.

"Yes," said Rex, dropping his bantering tone of voice. "We liked him. ALL of us did. He was like . . . like a sort of grandfather . . . you know . . . what we never had . . . eh?"

"You mean a sort of substitute father, don't you?" his mother asked.

"Probably," her son replied. "These chaps hardly ever saw their father, you know. Their servant fellow was more like a father to THEM . . . like Old Pierre, to me, perhaps."

"EVERYONE needs two parents!" stipulated Frank. "The hermit liked US. We FELT it. He made us THINK, too."

"We were USEFUL to him, as well." said Lex, as always trying to see two sides to everything, "We brought him newspapers, notepaper — well old exercise books, and food and seeds for his garden; we kept his place secret . . ."

"Suppose he'd been an escaped convict though?" Aurora asked.

"IF he was," her son said with conviction, "then he was wrongly convicted. He was the most gentle, and gentlemanly old man. You'd have liked him, Mother."

101

"Look closely at that carving he gave Una," Frank seriously suggested, "it's four separate pieces of different kinds of wood overlaid one above the other; at the bottom in almost black timber is a Buddhist prayer wheel, above it is Star of David, with a Crescent Moon just across it and on top in almost white wood is a Celtic Cross; set into the Cross are five tiny metal stars, the Northern Cross, or Cygnus the Swan the other way up. The same five stars Aunt Aurora, that are inside our Bellule in the archway."

"That's why we call it an icon," Rex added the final explanation.

While they slowly walked towards the house Roxana remarked that the old man had a tremendous effect on them all. "Even Frank becomes loquacious," she said.

"More than that," her brother laughed, "he told Una she was the Queen of the Fairies and had immortality, and she believes it probably. Through HIM she's able to leave her school, a school she just didn't fit. Other girls fitted, but not her."

"Too like a boy, and they didn't like it," her eldest brother added.

By the time they reached the archway, the boys and Roxana were laughing and joking, imagining what Roxana would have done had she been sent to the school.

Aurora listening to the badinage and verbal sparring in which her daughter was taking a very active part, realized that the age gap had almost completely vanished. The four young people were no longer children and an adult; they were equal adults, young adults, enjoying each others' company and speaking the same language. Aurora felt strangely alone — almost lonely. It was time to stand aside, like the swallows driving their young from the nest, stand aside with the door wide open, and always open — and with a smile. "These four are the future," she said to herself, "and I'm the past." She started planning how she would release her daughter from her self-appointed jobs that segregated her from the young.

Aurora wandered round the house to the pond instead of going in immediately after leaving the group in the archway. Whilst they were studying the huge sculptured dragonfly above their heads she watched the rapacious activities of the magnificent Emperors. Whirling and circling gracefully while their death-dealing masks entrapped any insect small enough to make a tasty mouthful. The flickering light from the red ball of the sun shone through their almost transparent bodies, illuminating them and enhancing their already considerable splendour with streaks of purple, gold and emerald green. While the dragonflies searched for their quarry, they were also being attacked, ineffectively, by the entire family of swallows whose refuge was under the eaves of the farm-house itself. Aurora stood still and watched. The ways of the insect and animal and bird world were, after all, natural to them; they killed another equally magnificent species in order to live; they killed to eat to live. Men were killing for no good reason, their own kind. Already in the depths of the pond were the larvae that would become the dragonflies of the future — next year and the year after. While she watched, an Emperor successfully drove off one of the few Agrion Virgo demoiselle-flies from a somnolent fly, only to be frustrated by the swift dive of a long streamered adult swallow. "There's plenty for all of them," she thought, turning towards the house where she noticed a spider sitting in its web which was spun across a corner of the drawing room window.

Back in the kitchen Aurora found the four young people preparing an evening milk drink. All four were at work; one mixing powder in a jug, one hovering over a saucepan, one putting cups and saucers on the table and the fourth raiding the larder for biscuits.

"Roxana said we should allow you three more minutes of your well-deserved peace," said her son, "then we were all coming to carry you bodily inside. We can't sit down without you."

Aurora's face wrinkled with pleasure.

While they sipped and nibbled she said, "Augustus enclosed three cheques in his letter — one for each of you young men to open a bank account, and I wondered if you could all arrange to meet Roxana in town and she can introduce you to the Bank Manager, would you mind, darling?" she appealed to her daughter. "I have to compose a letter to him and should get it into the mail as soon as possible."

She watched the pleasure spread round the faces of the four, then continued. "There are very precise instructions on the use of this money. It's a substantial amount for you to handle after your two shillings pocket money. He says one third is to be kept in the bank as emergency money," she fetched the letter from the drawing room and unfolded the numerous pages of closely written spidery scrawl. "Yes, here we are," she continued after a silence only broken by the rustling of wafer-thin sheets of paper, "one third is to be used for equipping yourselves with whatever is specified by the establishments and one third is your term's allowance and," she began reading, "I trust them to be circumspect in their spending and that Frank will not abuse my trust by using his money before commencing his training."

"Uncle Augustus has included ME, Mother?" asked Rex.

"Yes," she replied, "Oh, he says later in the letter, that you had all become one family living under one roof . . . and so on." She handed out the cheques, watched them study them with disbelief and changed the conversation, leaving them to make their own arrangements with Roxana. "While you are in town, I wonder if you could enquire into the fitting of telephones. I see there are telegraph poles coming closer and closer to us, and I think we should have it. I know. I know. I'm old fashioned over most things, but I would like to have the telephone, for me, and for the Pierre's . . . and perhaps that Sergeant Fyne would like it. If it COULD be done before you all leave you could show me how to use the contraption . . ."

While they all silently digested this revolutionary suggestion Aurora was thinking, "I'll be almost alone soon. How would I call Dr. McFane if Una had another accident and Roxana at school?"

Once again Aurora broke the silence, having glanced through the first page of the letter, whilst folding it. "To-morrow, I shall have to go out and visit various schoolmasters and find a tutor for Ivan. I cannot write to Augustus until I have completed all his orders." She laughed. "Perhaps I shall take Una and search out a school for her. The Headmaster at the College will advise me. It's time she learnt to drive the buggy . . . before I'm too old to teach her, don't you think?"

"Aunt Rora," suggested Lex, "Why shouldn't WE coach Ivan? Rex had to coach some of the smallfry at school during the influenza epidemic last spring. I had to take Latin lessons and even Frank here was coaching football. You had Ivan in your cricket juniors didn't you Frank?" he ended, turning to his younger brother.

"I could get him up to standard in maths," Rex acknowledged.

"Would he do as you told him?" Aurora asked dubiously.

"Of course, Mother," her son answered confidently. "Don't forget WE were AUTHORITY at school. The young feared us more than the Beaks. Ivan was very law-abiding. He clowns around, but he actually LIKES discipline. It's only here he goes wild; his time isn't ORGANIZED FOR him here."

"And you," Roxana admonished, "have just broken the rule of the house. You've been talking about one of the family in his ABSENCE."

"He's probably awake listening," said Frank. "He never sleeps . . ."

Lex skipped lightly into the hall and called up the tourelle, "Ivan," with no response. He returned and said, "No, sleeping . . . well Aunt Rora, what you'd think?"

"Wait a minute," Frank interposed, "Why not send to that postal tuition place that Mother used to teach US. They run courses for entry to all schools and colleges . . ."

"Of course," Lex added, "and they provide books, practise exam papers, and they EVEN arrange for pupils to sit the exams. All over the Empire people use them — India, of course, but Outback Australia, the African continent, Aden . . . well, everywhere. We, Frank and I were well ahead when we started school. I got lazy the first year because I'd done most of the work."

"It sounds to me like an excellent idea," said Roxana. "After all, Mother, you had ALL your education at home and you don't seem to be lacking anything . . . except perhaps, practical science."

While she was talking, Lex had run upstairs, rummaged in an old cabin trunk kept beside his bed and returned with one of his old exercise books from the age of about ten. "Here it is," he said, placing the book in front of his aunt, "There is the address."

Rex and Frank lit the oil lamps and the decisions were made.

By the time the bracken had turned copper around the edges, and the heather begun to fade, a cable had arrived from India, requesting Aurora to keep all three younger members of the family with her, and arrange local schooling for them to leave 'shipping for troops and essentials', the three young men had departed, one by one, and been seen off by the remainder of the diminishing family. Ivan was well advanced mathematically, and had even, to his surprise liked the subject. Both boys were equipped with College uniform and it was decided to let Una learn at home — from the postal course. An expelled girl, it appeared, was not considered a suitable adjunct to the local girls' school. Young Pierre resplendent in uniform, awaited shipment to Ireland to complete his army training. The telephone was installed in the farmhouse, the Roches' cottage and the Fyne's home and a shiny new wireless occupied the rose-bowl table in the drawing room, Aurora's pride and delight. On the back of the wireless was an engraved copper plate with the words, "With all our love from Roxana, Rex, Lex, Frank, Una, Ivan, Rolf, O'Donaty." YOU KEPT US ALL IN HAIL AND BEQUEATHED US NO TUMBLED HOUSE.

The presentation was made on the twins' thirteenth birthday, the day before Lex departed for the Royal Flying Corps training barracks, and two days before Aurora's birthday when Rex was to sail followed by Frank on the next boat, a few days later, as the mailboat had ceased to make daily crossings. Aurora also treasured the birthday cards each of the family had made for her; she kept them standing by vases of roses all round the room, but on her bureau was Una's card — a painting of the front of the farmhouse showing the stables and the pond and underneath the words:—

TIR TAIRNGIRÉ
(Promised Land)

Years ahead, a whole age, an aeon ahead, Aurora was to look back on that summer when the world began to fall apart with conflicts that rolled on with the never-ending ripples of the future, as the most peaceful at La Bellule. The four-roomed farmhouse had, with the family it owned, become firm, solid and secure and ready to withstand the oceanic forces of war.

The crabs, unchanged in shape and mechanism for ten million years, were aware of the changes taking place amongst the earth's newcomers living above them. The crabs, busily engaged in the daily business of foraging for fresh flesh, mating, reproducing their kind, moulting and growing and moulting, smelled, heard, saw and felt the earth vibrations of the world of humans, but none of it was especially new. They had experienced it all before and before that and even before that; sudden explosions under the water sending tremors to their stronghold and temporary alterations in the tidal flows were not new; the smell of cordite was not new; the departures, silences and sudden arrivals at the construction above them were not new; what was new was the exaggeration of all the experiences. Explosions were louder, vibrated for longer and sent more pungent fumes in their wake. More departures occurred above them; the silence was longer and there were more solitary walkers disturbing their evening beach forays and some of the solitary walkers were unsteady with uneven thumps shaking the sensitive sand.

Above the crabs the dragonflies also continued their own well-ordered lives. By the time the swallows departed they had guaranteed the survival of their own species, leaving the future under water to add to the apparent debris of the pond, whilst aerating it and keeping it pure — and, with growing maturity reducing the number of other inmates, attacking the abundant supply of worms, snails and small fish without leaving its stalk or weed to which it seemed permanently attached; the viciousness of this maggot-like creature only equalled by its excessively ugly appearance. It remained like a solitary sniper in a fortified terrain and reduced the enemy while the seasons passed until it finally changed shape, crawled its benevolent stem and became the magnificent death-dealing creature that fought for aerial supremacy over flying insects with the swallows that had returned from their winter habitation. Year after year the combat continued until 'peace' arrived with the seasonal change in weather after the non-survivors had guaranteed the survival of their own species.

The master race of humans had, during their own evolution, lost the art of guaranteeing survival of their species, thus, while season succeeded season the world of men successfully decimated their own supply of active reproducers.

Chapter Seven

Four years of war had decimated the youth of the 'civilized world'. The bones of lord and labourer, clerk and coalman, banker and barrow-boy lay side by side in cold mud, hot desert sand, dense forest and the ocean depths — and MOST had offered THEMSELVES on the sacrificial slaughter stone of war. By asking for volunteers the finest of one nation went first — the smooth-faced boy from the classroom with the working boy far removed from council school and education. The disintegrated youth of the nation had NOT endorsed the right of their government to embroil them in war, for, although they had been deemed of age to die for their rulers, they had not been considered old enough to have any say in WHO should govern them. The future fathers of a generation had vanished, leaving tenement rooms, cottages, terrace houses, mansions and castles to a breed of stoical women who may not have condoned, but understood, why they had gone. It was not the waving of a spectacular three-coloured flag, nor a be-whiskered face behind a pointing finger that had sent them to their deaths. It was the RIGHT TO DEFEND their inalienable right to dance around maypoles, gamble at races on green-swathed downs, gather together on heaths and in market squares, get drunk in mean city streets, belong to semi-secret fraternities, and burn effigies, annually, of a man who had dared to try and extinguish rulers whose claim to rule had not been affirmed by their ancestors, but, above all, it was for their freedom to speak against their government, even if their voices were not heard. It was for THEIR RIGHT to exist in their muddled way, led by confused politicians with perplexing principles, and to OWN THEMSELVES, mind and body, for which they fought — and died.

The wholesale slaughter was over! The war had ended and had even been given a name, a title, like the others that had preceded it through the aeons — The Trojan War, the Punic Wars, The Hundred Years War, The Thirty Years War, The War of Devolution, The War of Jenkin's Ear, and now, the latest had the title of The Great War, the war to end all wars . . . and so there was 'a new heaven and a new earth for the first heaven and the first earth were passed away.' The GREATNESS of the war made itself manifest only within the remnants of the 'old heaven' where the celestial skirl of bagpipes, throb of drums, blast of bugles and shouted orders were accompanied by the screams and groans echoing and re-echoing between the 'old earth' and the celestial spheres from the unwilling citizens, the flower of mankind, on their journey from the living sufferers to whom they entrusted 'the earth'.

In the cultural centre of the 'new earth' a pantomime was being performed on a stage surrounded by mirrors and haunted by decapitated ghosts, for here, at Versailles, was the Never-Land where all the Lost Boys of the 'old earth' were represented by four Nations. Alien actors, nationalistic, inexperienced, self-motivated, power-greedy and intransigent avengers rubbing shoulders while enthroned on crimson, gilt-edged chairs. Here in the Hall of Mirrors they smashed to smithereens the tablet of fourteen world-embracing laws suggested by their messianic, self-appointed leader — the representative of the newest of the New World. The curtain fell on the first act with the mortified exodus of the chiding, haranguing, cajoling 'messiah' — not to a high Place to commune with his Deity, but to a gold-decked plinth and superficial congregation in the new land across the sea. In his place there remained the shadow of the boy who would not grow up and a Star illumined by Belief in a society, a club, a League of Chosen Nations; a Union.

When the curtain rose on the Second Act a new Never-Land was revealed; a lagoon surrounded by forbidding mountains, glaciers, reflections, a land of unrealities, of mermaids, sprites, and untouched by the recent conflagrations; a land where resolutions were never adhered to or concluded, where territorial adjustments were never agreed, from where a deep-rooted fear never vanished, but where belief in the single Star never wavered. The Star sparkled, glittered and expanded, Nation by Nation, deaf to the ticking of a clock inside a crocodile warning the Chosen Nations of an embryo Captain Hook, but the warning went unheeded.

The final scene was the same as the first and the pantomime ended as pantomimes should end; satisfactory justice was meted out, villains were suitably punished, heroes rewarded and signatures inscribed for posterity. The cast crowded the stage for the final curtain call and to accept as their prerogative the tumultuous applause of the audience.

Inside the crocodile the clock tick-tocked relentlessly, invisibly, the pendulum swinging left, right, left, right, left, right, measuring Time in seconds, minutes, hours, days, weeks, months, years and with a hair-spring that would last for two decades when a new, vibrant youth had replenished the recently decimated, and, once ripe for harvesting had also filled the silos of the Celestial Spheres, and another generation of Lost Boys would throng the Never-Land. The crocodile warned of tick-tocking boots, of the gradual emergence of the Pirates and their Pirate Ship captained by a fanatic with an iron-hooked hand, but listening to omens had ceased; belief in fairies had faded; the Star, like the Phoenix was in ashes and buried beneath a carpet of blood-red poppies.

With the ending of the pantomime the imposing facade of the cobbled 'foyer' teemed with the 'old earth's' pleasure seekers, mingling with the survivors, exotics from the five continents of the 'new earth'. Flimsy sarees and crisp kimonos rustled against sombre suits and smooth flannels; kaftans whispered brushing the flowing burnouses; khaki breeches and corded blazers glittered against the flimsy cloth that was world-produced, but transformed locally into feminine spectaculars. Above the kaleidoscopic movement pink, black, brown, tan, yellow and red faces sported their extravaganza of blue or white turbans, red fezes, flowing cotton veils, scarlet mitres, embroidered skull caps, golden straw hats, dingy felt hats, black bowlers and the lustre of gold-edged military caps. The cobbles, that little more than a century earlier had run with blood from the citizens and throbbed with the roll of tumbril wheels, sang with the gentle tap-tap of heeled leather, the ring of metal-braced boots and the benign shuffle of soft sandals.

While the post-war pleasure seekers mingled with the procreators of a new appreciation of earth through art, they were, unknowingly, setting the scene for a future rolling of tumbrils down the wide boulevards and cobbled, once blood-stained streets. Most of the numerically few survivors waited for the pantomime promises to be fulfilled and for the benefits to be made manifest. Having been deprived of the opportunity to acquire skills, they searched for Causes to embrace and combats to Champion — thus using the only accomplishments they had learnt. Invisibly and irrevocably, earth was being fertilized in preparation for the spring sowing of seed that was to mature into an abundant harvest to fill the silos of the Celestial Spheres of the newer 'new heaven', and the compost heap of the newer 'New Earth' with deadly, malignant weeds.

Few listened to the clock ticking away Time inside the crocodile. A new 'messiah' was being searched for, and inevitably, several self-acclaimed 'messiahs' appeared. As two thousand years previously, fear controlled human reactions, so the satanic coming messiah was locked behind bars where he wrote a new 'bible', 'koran' Confucian script to be used when release arrived for him. The Holy, Godly messiah languished in an Asian jail BECAUSE he decreed a creed of unity, non-violence, universal love and equality — incomprehensible to the young, bred on unquestioning obedience, violence and hate.

Spring had arrived in the half of the world most battered by conflict. Daffodils sprang from the muddy fields where the poppies would bloom in their appointed time, before pouring unnumbered seeds back into the earth from which they had been conceived. In this not-so-new earth there was a constant struggle for survival, competing with the desire for gain in an increasingly fast-moving race. Literature, music and art flourished, entertainment supplied the masses through the wonders of the ether or by means of celluloid projected through the ether on to large white squares; books were mass-produced, galleries and pavements exhibited the visions of the dwellers in the 'new earth', and halls shook with the uninhibited movements of abandoned dancers. The 'new earth' moved at a speed it had never known. Greater speed became greater daily and the earth dwellers conquered domains above the earth, and beneath the earth's surface. The tarnished earth, the newish earth, was found to be good — by a small minority.

When Cygnus, the Northern Cross, had returned from its southern sojourn to the northern hemisphere, names were being engraved on huge stones throughout the 'new earth'. The blocks of stone were large because there were so many names to record. Perhaps for each name a blood-red poppy sprouted. Certainly for each name there lived the mourning women — four to each name, hiding their sorrow, their desolation behind veiled eyes, holding together deprived young as best they could within their brick tenements, country cottages, terraces of identical houses, tenement slums, mansions, castles, mud huts, igloos, skin tents or a few feet of busy street paving. Before the soldierly hard-capped poppies were in bloom and while the elegant daffodils nodded gracefully, the new young adults had taken their oaths of allegiance to whichever killer offered the best reward or they waited with infinite patience for the rewards that eluded them.

Chapter Eight

"Keep — the young — generations — in hail, — and bequeath — them no — tumbled — house. Keep — the young. . ." The bay mare's hooves beat out the rhythm of the words while she splashed along the rain sodden tarmac road out of Town. The wheels of the buggy she pulled rolled smoothly. The thin spring drizzle spattered on the hood of the buggy, then dripped through leaks on to the hooded figure huddled inside. From the hood of the ulster the rain made rivulets down to the shiny black goloshes, filled them and overflowed on to the floor of the shabby vehicle from whence they were ejected to the road beneath. The workworn hand tightened on the reins once the tarmac ended and the cobbled road commenced, but the body remained statuesque, misery exuding from every inch while the stream of tears poured down the wrinkled face, the brain beat out the words and the rhythm, altered by the terrain to a jerky, "I bequeathed THEM no tumbled house . . . it is THEY who have bequeathed ME a tumbled house. . ."

By the time the buggy rolled across the common the horizon was marked by a wavering puff of smoke mixing with the watery pink of the setting sun and the veil of light rain. Aurora raised her head and tearfully acknowledged the puff of smoke that escaped from the cargo boat on which her beloved niece was a passenger, on her way to join her almost unknown parents at the other side of the world.

Gamma quickened her pace when the coast road curved and the roof of the old farmhouse was visible on its fortified mound. A warm stable and a dry coat awaited her. Aurora noticed the leaking gutters, the salt-smitten paintwork and the abundance of moss sprouting from the stone slabs.

Inside the farmhouse would be her daughter and her foreign son-in-law and her much loved youngest nephew. Soon they would be gone — one to follow his sister and rejoin the unknown parents in an unknown land, the other, her daughter to a farm life half across Europe from where her husband had come. The four and a half years of war was being celebrated by the return of the participants to their roots.

Four and a half years earlier, Aurora had sat at the head of the huge kitchen table celebrating her son and her nephew leaving school, the young admitting changes in their future careers; they had celebrated the new indoor bathroom, the bedroom the boys had made for Una, the telephone and finally the wireless set they had all given her. They had worked as a team, painting the farmhouse, and repairing fences, barns and gates. THIS had been their HOME, their security and their refuge. It was from this place they would be kept 'in hail', from THIS house that would never tumble. They had either been born in it or had been brought to it by parents whose lives were too dangerous and distant to allow for the upbringing of children. Now the father of the young people was to retire and return to HIS roots — and he required the return of his own offspring. One would never return anywhere, his existence marked by a white cross and a blood red poppy; another was already on his way aboard a naval vessel; another son awaited his call away from the farm and the animals he loved; another son lay on his bed in the loft, his violin beside him and pain in the right arm he no longer possessed and Aurora's own son was serving in the army, following the profession of his uncle. Una, the much loved and difficult niece was beneath that puff of smoke.

The drizzle ceased. Puddles sparkled with rainbows from the drips of water and the watery sunset. After making Gamma comfortable Aurora splashed into the kitchen, kicked off her goloshes, threw off her wet ulster and sat in her usual seat at the head of the oval table. Roxana had made tea and left it ready then allowed her mother the solitude of the kitchen, the hub of the house and family, to adjust to the depleted family.

Each chair had its owner's name engraved on the back; each was in its appointed place, but few had a place laid on the table. After allowing her eye to circumnavigate the table Aurora announced to the empty room, "I shall keep the young generations IN HAIL, despite a tumbled house."

Una O'Donaty hung over the rail of the ocean liner, her light green eyes fixed on the horizon, searching for a glimpse of the island she had left the previous evening. Long, thin icicles hung down her throat as she recalled her last sight of her frail little aunt huddled inside the buggy, enveloped in the well-known ulster and her face wet from the mixture of tears and drizzle. The last sight of 'home' had been Rolf's bright hair above the long, dangling legs that festooned the harbour wall like flags waving the noisy little boat away. Somewhere to the west, Una knew, lay the islands; somewhere within the confines of the recently hard-defended Channel. Una also knew that the remnants of the family would be performing their evening chores before sitting in that familiar kitchen around the oval table with its many empty chairs, and its intense sense of 'belonging'.

She SHOULD be feeling wildly excited. More than ten years had passed since she had last seen her parents and her baby sister and brother. She was embarking on a great adventure. She was, after all, returning to her roots. With characteristic suddenness she switched her thoughts back ten years and tried to relive that other journey through this same Channel, but travelling in the other direction. Life on board that other ship had been tremendous fun for the five children. She and Van had made friends with each member of the crew, the Captain and most of the male passengers. They had raced around the deck to the danger of carelessly outstretched legs, on scooters and on tricycles, encouraged by the many young subalterns on 'home' leave, who had betted on the winner. In their cabins all five of them had acted out the latest stories that Mother read them, and Nanny, dreadful, hateful Nanny was permanently seasick. Father was distant — an austere and highly respected soldier who did NOT stoop to playing with children. Then there had been a change of transport, a night on board the rolling Mail Boat and the meeting at the small harbour with the kind little aunt who had led the entourage in their hired chaise to what had then seemed little more than a doll's house built on a mound, surrounded by a large secure wall and moat, facing the sunrise and an ever-changing sea. That was the one place that Una felt safe — and truly herself.

The smooth passage of the liner and the small ripples of sea decorated with the foam from the bows almost hypnotized the girl high above the water whose eyes were unfocused, veiled behind middle-distance vision and an escaped tear.

Everything about that moated and fortified house seemed to be lovingly secure. The menacing dragonfly insignia embedded in the arched entrance was somehow protective towards the family; all of them left little offerings in the benitier at the entrance; the huge oval table around which the family gathered at least twice a day was benevolent; it was solid; it was alive; and it was the one physical point of contact between the individuals who argued, debated, laughed and sulked around it; Van had baptized it 'the Truth Table' when she had upset her homemade wine once. All the inanimate objects in that friendly kitchen seemed to have life within them; the copper pans and kettles sparkled in any light, and glowed in sunlight; the dresser covered with willow-pattern crockery, told a continuous story. The black range had to be fed twice a day with logs, brushwood, driftwood or coal and in return it provided the household with cooking heat and hot water. The uneven stone floor seemed alive and each chair had its legs sandpapered to different lengths to comply with the idiosyncrasy of its allotted portion of flooring.

While she peered through the spray and mist, Una thought she was back in the security of La Bellule, sitting on her chair between her brothers Frank and Van, looking down the length of the scrubbed table at her greatly loved aunt, flanked by her own son and daughter. "But we were really ALL her children," Una said inside her head. "How will she live without us?" She then made the decision to write to her aunt every day, to keep her aunt in touch, even though the letters might not be posted for weeks at a time.

Still hanging over the rail Una began to think about the family. She recalled Roxana's wedding to her Jewish Polish husband. She thought about her cousin, Rex, whom she might see whilst in India. She pictured her twin, Van, handsome in his naval uniform with his dreams of becoming an Admiral and his gift of mimicry. Rolf, big, blond Rolf with no great ambition beyond farming and rearing more and more sheep at La Bellule, but soon to be sent for to join their parents in Tasmania. Last of all Una thought about Frank who wanted to become a missionary, but now lay suffering pain in an arm he did not have and blaming her for the pain. "It is a good thing I had to leave," she thought. "Perhaps he will now forget that awful scalding of his hand and recall the way a sniper shot him while he tried to give first aid to a soldier."

A ship's steward slid silently to her side requesting her to join Mrs. Sutton in the Forward Lounge. She followed him resignedly, already finding the prescribing of her every moment onerous — but she was in the care of Mrs. Sutton and shared a cabin with her daughter. Both girls were to be groomed to grace the social scene of British India.

"Oh, my dear," said Mrs. Sutton, when Una was led to her side by the stiff-faced steward, "you should tidy your hair before coming in here. Sit down, my dear. I'm afraid you have missed tea. It is VERY punctual on board ship, and dinner will not be served until eight o'clock."

Una sat down on the seat indicated and wondered! "Tea? Dinner? AND lunch? Was life on board ship all eating?"

She felt disapproval in the atmosphere, so she asked, "Where's Georgina, Mrs. Sutton?"

"Georgina is in the cabin, my dear, getting ready for dinner."

Una looked at the large, brass-framed clock at the end of the lounge, and remarked, "Golly! already? There are two HOURS to wait!"

"You will find, my dear, that all the well-bred young ladies, rest and compose themselves before the evening meal. It is a SOCIAL occasion on board ship."

"Oh! Well I'm not well-bred, and I'd be a MESS in two hours."

"If I may say so, my dear, you can learn a lot from Georgina. You ARE after all, the retiring General's daughter, my dear."

117

The constant 'my dears' were beginning to grate on Una. "He'll ONLY be a Colonel, anyway, when he retires. He wasn't a FULL General, only a Brigadier General and they don't have them anymore."

Mrs. Sutton's husband was a colonel and the 'only a colonel' demeaned her as well as her husband. She had only undertaken this annoying chaperonage as a means of assisting her husband, she erroneously hoped, to promotion. She felt certain there would be some kudos attached to her arrival in India with the daughter of the man who was being given banquets, honours and speeches at his long-overdue retirement. He had, after all, been at Delhi when the siege was broken and the mutiny ended. She forgot that the inclusion of this strange girl in her party had allowed her to enjoy a cabin to herself, the two girls occupying the next cabin. Georgina's education had been thorough and expensive and the finished product was to be 'brought out' where women were in the minority and acceptable men of good family to be found in abundance.

The ship began to lurch in an unseemly fashion, and Mrs. Sutton decided to retire to her cabin, admonishing Una to, "Be ready dressed by ten minutes to eight — sharp, my dear."

Una escaped to the lighted promenade deck and watched the rising waves with exhilaration and delight, until cold drove her to the warmth of her cabin, and the sight of a prostrate Georgina.

By the time Una presented herself for inspection at precisely ten minutes to eight, Georgina had moved on to the couch in her mother's cabin and both ladies lay suffering, stoically, the turbulence beneath and around them. Una, escaped, leaving them to the ministrations of a steward, and, marvelling at the magnificence of this ordinary liner, slowly made her way to the grandeur of the dining saloon where a splendidly attired steward showed her to a table set for six. She sat studying the elaborate menu that decorated the table and waited, anticipating the arrival of the three unknown people who would be joining her. She waited. She watched anxiously as groups appeared, seated themselves and studied the menu as she had done. She began to feel conspicuous and alone, wishing one of her

118

brothers were beside her, when the steward leant over her and said, "The Captain's compliments, miss. Will you join him for dinner?"

Would she not? She and Ivan were great friends with the Captains of each of the mail boats that had carried them between home and school and back again, and all of them were informative, responsive to questions and kindly. This was no exception. She was shown to the one vacant seat at his table, was introduced to the assorted passengers and junior ship's officers already re-seated after standing to acknowledge her presence, and was introduced as, "Miss O'Donaty, on her way to join her parents in India."

It transpired that her three missing companions were three other young women, rejoining parents after their schooling was completed. The purser, in his infinite wisdom, had put the three unattached and unchaperoned young ladies under the supervision of the Colonel's Lady; they had cabins adjacent to theirs and thus, thought the purser, or perhaps he merely hoped, they would be less of a problem to the young ship's officers. Years of transporting the heterogeneous British across the world and back again had turned him into a cynic who aimed at keeping his side of the ship's company as efficient as possible, despite the often wayward aspirations of his passengers.

Surreptitiously Una studied her companions whilst they, having already assessed each other, studied her during the soup course. At last the Captain asked courteously, "Just finished with school, Miss O'Donaty?"

She had not realized he was addressing her at first, unused as she was to being called anything but Una. Confused by the stares around her, she said, "Oh, no. I was expelled from School, YEARS ago!"

If she had set out to create interest she could not have succeeded so effectively. The two young officers' eyes sparkled with interest. A wizened elderly lady seated on the Captain's right smiled, her eyes alight with intrigue and curiosity. A military-moustached gentleman snorted and his wife sniffed. The taller of the two young men, reminding Una of Ivan, asked, "You must have done something awfully exciting to be expelled?"

119

"Oh, no," she responded to his evident interest, "I just consorted with vagrants, they said, AND wrote blasphemous poetry about the school prefects."

Suddenly questions were poured at Una as she struggled with fish and some sauce that was quite foreign to her.

"What a curious crowd you must be thinking," the wizened lady said in the most melodious voice Una had ever heard, unsung.

"I don't mind," said the naive girl. "I mean I didn't steal or lie or anything really awful; my twin had the beating and my other brothers and cousin had unblemished school records and I didn't have to go back to being a young lady, which I'm not."

The Captain blessed the compulsion that had caused him to invite the small, mousy-looking lonely girl to join him for dinner. Una did not know, then, that she had found in the wizened lady, Mrs. Hope, a friend for life. The sniffing lady offered to translate the main course for Una who replied, "Oh, thank you, but we speak a sort of French at home, most of the time. We call it patois; but I learnt proper French at home."

"Try the lamb. It's the Chef's speciality," suggested the Sniffer.

"I'll just have vegetables," Una told the attentive steward. Before he had passed from earshot her clear young voice announced, "I COULDN'T ever eat lamb. I saw one being born one night and it had such a fight to survive it would be cruel not to let it grow into mutton, wouldn't it?"

By that evening there was not a steward nor a member of the deck crew who did not know her. At the first dance, some nights later, she was sought after by every young officer and many older ones on board. She had become the childless Captain's special protegé, she had found her first woman friend, albeit old enough to be her grandmother and with her the most discreet of chaperones, one who seemed to walk the promenade deck when Una was showing young men that she KNEW the names of the constellations. Una never discovered the significance of an invitation to see the stars until many, many years later.

From Gibraltar, Una sent off an extremely frank description of her fellow passengers to her aunt, ending with, ". . . I'm not allowed to go ashore because Mrs. My-dear Sutton doesn't feel well and she won't allow prissy-Georgina off the boat — nor me. But, Aunt Aurora, thank you a thousand times for making me go to those dancing classes with the boys. Rolf and Ivan would be proud of me dancing like all the other girls. I DO miss you all. I unlock my gladstone bag when Prissy has settled for the night and I take my old kilt to bed with me — silly isn't it? It smells of sea and the farm and all of you. . ."

From Marseilles a brief letter was posted stating, ". . . I'm not allowed off the ship, but a few more passengers have come on board. Gibraltar isn't nearly as impressive as The Roc, even though it is larger; it lacks SHAPE. Mrs. Hope and THE CAPTAIN are going to take ME ashore at Port Said. Mrs. My-dear couldn't refuse the Captain who is VERY proud of Mrs. Hope. Have you heard of her? She is a FAMOUS authoress, the Captain says."

The letter posted at Port Said was filled with lyrical and ecstatic descriptions of sunsets followed by the admission '. . . but I expected to see pyramids rising above the delta and the Sphinx peering down on the ship as it passed. One minute we seemed to be in open sea and then ordinary bungalows seemed to grow from the water's edge with a few bedraggled palm trees standing sentinel before them. In one minute I am to meet Mrs. Hope and go ashore, leaving the dreary Suttons to wallow in the misery of closed cabin portholes and fear of being robbed by Arabs. It's hard to believe I have been on board this floating palace for only twelve days. It's sixteen days since I last saw all of you, oh dear, I do wish you could be with me seeing these wonders. . ."

From Suez a letter was sent on its way. Una wrote, "I think just WATCHING the people from the ship is probably better than being in the streets with them. They are all nationalities and in all stages of poverty or wealth, but they keep TOUCHING you as you pass, and plead for alms or to sell you something. But, Aunt Aurora, they are REAL people, people-people, not like the stuffed clothes of many of my fellow-passengers. I think I would have been easier if I had travelled second class or steerage. While we slowly steamed through the wonderful emerald green canal I went down to the second class deck and they are more ordinary

121

passengers. I told a group of children a story I made up as I told it — about a family of dragons, and then they crawled all over the deck BEING dragons and nobody told them not to, or to keep clean.

Desert and wilderness stretch as far as the eye can see, and camel caravans with a few sad-looking donkeys are ridden at the side of the canal by imposing Arabs. I expect to see Lawrence waving his scimitar or whatever Lawrence waved when he crossed the desert. Mrs. Hope says he is supposed to be writing about his adventures. I think, while I write this, sitting demurely in a deck chair in the sun, that what I see stretching to the horizon must be like the world was before man.,"

Mrs. Sutton has given up trying to make me look tidy. I dance EVERY dance and I'm the only ugly girl here. Georgina is not as fortunate and she does NOT approve of me. The indelible pencil is invaluable for writing my journal and, of course, this letter. My next letter will be posted in Bombay and you will know I have arrived SAFELY. I shall send news of Rex IMMEDIATELY I have seen him, but it might be quite a long time before he has leave in Kashmir. . ."

Before she disembarked at Bombay, Una had posted a letter outside the purser's office in the box provided so her news of the arrival waited some days before it began its lengthy journey by ship and rail, van, rail and another ship, to La Bellule.

She wrote, "We have now been seventeen days at sea and absolutely EVERYTHING has changed. Desert stretches on each side, and I mean real desert with massive dunes and a formidable, but wonderful spaciousness. Everything has changed on the ship. Great screens drape the promenade decks as protection from the sun, and I am not allowed on deck, not anywhere on deck after six o'clock in the morning; you'll never guess why so I'll tell you. All the gentlemen go wandering around in their pyjamas. EVERY-ONE — well almost everyone sleeps on deck which makes the rule rather funny. Georgina makes a steward carry her mattress up to the foreward deck which is for women, and then she and the three Simperers — not my name for the three girls who share our table — but bequeathed to them by a subaltern called Ted Morris — well the Simperers and

Prissy TALK ALL NIGHT. I don't have a mattress — much too hot for these still nights. I just take one of the deckchairs with a footrest and sleep cool and aloof. One lady objected to me taking a deckchair because she said it was part of their barricade of privacy as the men slept the other side, so I just blocked the gap with myself and the chair. That's how I heard what Ted said about the you-know-who.

I find this Red Sea wonderful. It IS hot, but I have lots of cold baths and the sleeping outside all night is worth the heat. Do you know the sky looks so close you think you really can grasp the stars.

The deckchair bed is the first advantage I have found in being small. The second is that I haven't suffered from prickly heat and I don't have to wear corsets like Georgina; well I suppose they're corsets; they're stiff and tight. I found out by having to be in the cabin when she was dressing. I fear I have not impressed the Suttons.

I saw two children yesterday, just like Van and me, scooting up and down the deck between the line of deck chairs and the rails. I felt like asking them to let me have a scoot, but, you will be pleased to note, I refrained, most unwillingly. When Van and I did it, the men used to lay bets on who would win — until Nanny dragged us away. Now I play deck quoits with anyone not too exhausted by the heat.

We reached Aden today, just twenty-one days at sea. Once more dear Mrs. Hope took me ashore. She hired a driver with a thing not much bigger than your buggy who drove us around a narrow road so that we could look right down on the flat roofs of the houses of the port. If there had been time she would have taken me to a place called Crater which is an Arab village built inside one of the volcano craters. Imagine living INSIDE a crater. Oh, yes, Aunt Aurora, and Mrs. Hope told me to give two messages to you. One: that you don't need to worry about women alone being in danger because Arabs have very deep ideas about women. Two: she thinks you educated me and brought me up VERY WELL and she would like to meet you. I suppose that makes message number three. I found Aden absolutely fascinating but Mrs. Sutton said it was the place originally referred to as 'The White Man's Grave'. I thought that was Africa, but I expect I'm wrong. Aden is a huge orange lump of rock split part of the way down the middle, and it is very hot. I should very much like to see what is the other side of the volcano. I must now go and think up a fancy dress for the night after tomorrow. I wish Roxana was here. I really wish all of you where here to share all these sights and wonders. We must have been too young to notice when we left India all those years ago. Georgina brought a fancy dress ready made; she is going as a Spanish dancer. I must ask the Simperers what they are going as. Perhaps I'll go as a ghost in a sheet from my bunk.

I went to the fancy dress as the Mahatma Gandhi AND I won a prize, but Mrs. Sutton said it was in bad taste. I think it was now, but for a different reason. She said he was a trouble maker and upset the army. I think now, that I should not have mocked a Holy man. But I did look like him with my hair squashed down with water and hidden in the sheet and pencil wrinkles on my face. I borrowed some steel glasses from Mrs. Hope — well hers were gold.

Two days have passed since the Fancy Dress Dance and the edge of India is visible — lots of bungalows with white walls, tin roofs and verandahs. I am, at last excited about meeting the family. I have packed most of my things and Georgina is busy turning the cabin upside down packing her VOLUMINOUS quantity of dresses and things, oh yes and corsets; I saw them spread all over her bunk and she's only eighteen, the same as me.

We are now at Bombay. I DO remember the smell of rancid water, the shouting of hundreds of people, on the quay, on the ship and on the little boats — launches — that are taking luggage off and other launches taking people ashore. Our luggage has gone, but I wouldn't let them take my gladstone bag, so I'm sitting in the cabin, as I was told to do while Mrs. Sutton and Prissy Georgina are fluttering around in her cabin waiting for Colonel Sutton to come on board and take us to the hotel. I've said goodbye to Mrs. Hope and her wraith like companion or friend or relation called Miss Law. They will be at the same hotel so we agreed to meet again this evening; I hope I'm allowed to. I shall now seal this letter and wait patiently for the order to move. . ."

Una sealed the carefully addressed envelope, sat on the bunk and looked at her locked, much labelled gladstone bag, longing to unlock it, burrow into its secret depths and find her kilt, to hug, sniff at and, through its shabby folds, feel the warmth and affection that she had left behind in the sturdy old farmhouse, so very far away. She shook herself, rather like a terrier, kicked off her shoes and climbed on to the bunk so that she could see through the porthole. "I bet I'll recognise old Colonel Sutton," she said to herself. She tried to pick out one army officer amongst the throng that moved up and down the quay, but they were hidden constantly by groups of sailors, naval officers, police, and the kaleidoscopic unending collection of coolies, vendors, traders and beggars. "What a WEALTH of living life," she said under her breath. "Where have you all come from? Where are you all going? Why are you here and what do you think of this monster that has sailed in from the ocean, emitting smoke from its nostrils, and great whistles and gongs from its throat? Do you know that it has another world of humans inside it, humans just like you, that it is vomiting in small vomits, and I am one of them." A sharp knock on her door almost unbalanced her, but, still almost hanging from the porthole she turned her head and called out, "Come in."

Into the cabin walked a well-known figure, smartly attired in shorts, long socks and stiffly laundered, much pocketed shirt.

"Rex," she shouted, leaping from her perch, sliding across the polished floor in her stockinged feet and landing in his supporting arms.

The two cousins were still embracing each other, still balancing themselves after the unexpected contact, when a voice in the open doorway spat sharply like a rifle shot, "Una! Una O'Donaty, WHAT are you doing?"

Mrs. Sutton stood there, flurried and visibly shocked.

Una had no idea why Mrs. Sutton should be so angry, but introduced her cousin, who was left to explain their relationship to the very benign colonel, and Georgina.

"My uncle sent me to join the escort party attached to Una. I believe you leave the train at Rawalpindi and I have to take her to her father at Peshawar."

Noticing the surprise on Mrs. Sutton's face, who perhaps thought she was not considered a suitable chaperone, Rex

125

added, "I had to execute some commissions for him in Bombay, and, of course, he did not know you would be here, Sir," he added turning to the Colonel. Still looking in the same direction and straight into the eyes of the older man, he continued, "It's not every subaltern that has the chance to escort a train of young women up country, is it Sir?" both men knew that civil disturbances were becoming frequent and many trains had been ambushed since the end of the Great War.

"I see you've still hung on to your precious gladstone bag, Una," he remarked. "Am I allowed to carry it from the ship?" He turned again to the amused colonel and the gaping women and explained, "She's humped that bag with her, backwards and forwards to and from school. NEVER let her brothers or me so much as touch it." While Una slipped into her shoes and crammed her hat on her already untidy hair, Rex picked up the letter, saying, "Shall I write on the back of the envelope, Una?" She nodded, still speechless with joy at seeing a part of 'home' so unexpectedly.

By the time the party boarded the northbound train next evening, compartments had been organized and meals telegraphed for along the route of the three day journey; baskets of fresh fruit and quantities of permanganate of potash in which to wash the fruit, packages of month old English newspapers and tins of ice had been delivered and their luggage stowed carefully under the direction of the two men servants whom the Colonel had brought with him. Una had been taken shopping and provided with the compulsory topee and bedroll, and, looking round the sumptuous compartment and recalling the many times she had travelled in the same fashion across the length and breadth of the vast continent, she felt a strange sense of belonging. Here, after all, were her roots. It was from this colourful, noisy, multi-racial throng that she had first emerged into the world.

Rex and the Colonel slept in a two berth compartment between the two larger ones occupied on one side by the Sutton party and on the other by Mrs. Hope and Miss Law. At each station the men and Mrs. Hope left whichever space they had previously occupied and strolled up and down the packed platform. When there appeared less of a crowd than usual they took Georgina and Una with them, the latter revelling in the lively tapestry that was part of the life of the great railway.

"I'm like Kipling's Kim," she said to Mrs. Hope. "NOW I understand why he loved The Great Trunk Road. Everyone here is ALIVE, and very living."

"Some are barely living, if you look well, Una," the writer countered.

"I know. I know. but, I um mean, they're filling their lives with being just with BEING themselves, I think."

"Aren't you?"

"No, I'm not allowed to, am I? I have to BE and DO things that are just for the look of it."

"Do you HAVE to?"

"I do now. I didn't have to at La Bellule."

"Well, now, what sort of things do you HAVE to do that disagree with being YOU?"

"I HAVE to eat more than my stomach WANTS, I mustn't hug young men when they say goodbye, and now I mustn't even kiss Rex goodnight like I've done all my life."

Mrs. Hope smiled. "I'm an old lady and I'll take the liberty of giving you a piece of advice. Don't eat more than your stomach requires, and you'll keep healthier in this strange climate. Nobody can FORCE it down your throat." She searched for words and phrases before continuing. "Perhaps it is better NOT to hug every young man when he says his farewells, in this country where young women, young white women are not too plentiful. What do your brothers and cousins do when they say goodnight at your La Bellule?"

"Oh, the boys go round and kiss all the girls and ladies, but you see I had to go to bed BEFORE the older boys; I went with Ivan and Rolf, so I just followed them round the table or all round the drawing room if we were in there."

"Of course, Una you are now one of the ladies. The men leave your compartment as if they were leaving the drawing room, so why not leave it to them."

Una sighed, then said, "do you know Mrs. Hope, I was just getting used to being a grown up — on the boat — but seeing Rex made me sort of thirteen or fourteen all over

127

again. That's how old I was when all the boys, except Rolf and Ivan, went to the war."

Having, she hoped, successfully offered advice, the elderly woman asked, "Did they all come back safely?"

"Only Rex. The others either didn't come or only half came. . ."

"And your twin?"

"Ivan? Oh, Ivan is indestructible. Two years unscathed with the Channel fleet and he's now training to be an officer. Ivan is FUN, like Rex. EVERYONE loves Ivan. He's the other half of me; I'm the solemn, thinking half and he's the joking entertaining clown. He's as graceful and neat as I'm awkward and untidy. He was the STAR of our dancing classes and I was, I was the piece of meteor. I grasp for the stars but he has his feet safely on earth. I was born just before midnight and he brought in a new day with his birth. That's what Aunt Aurora says. I'm talking too much. I am sorry, Mrs. Hope." The slightly husky young voice ceased and a deep red fought the brown of the sun-tanned face and made Una's ears burn with heat.

Miss Law threw down the book she had been reading and said, "We must be coming in to Kishangari. I shall join the Suttons after tiffin for a hand of bridge, if you don't mind Margaret."

Trays of food were brought to each carriage by white coated boys when the train stopped at what was little better than a large clay brick hut surrounded by dilapidated wooden shacks with drooping thatch roofs. On their left the great plains edging the Indian Desert stretched out, dotted with bundles of sticks forming villages and minute patches of struggling pasture, while on their right the dun coloured foothills seemed to smoke in the dust and haze. The Suttons, Una and Rex lolled back in the spacious compartment, their bodies sticky slipping on the leather upholstery of the bunks. Mrs. Sutton lay back on the low bamboo chair, and before giving herself to the drowsiness that soon encompassed them all said, "Una, my dear, you really must try to eat more. It is no wonder you look childishly thin."

Rex, seated opposite slowly winked, and Una began to giggle silently, thinking how he would enjoy her exploits as Mahatma Gandhi, when she told him.

They were awakened with a jerk at Kishangari, and the two men entered their own compartment, Rex to collect the revolver he had thoughtlessly left there, and the Colonel to assure himself that nobody had entered, in spite of the locked doors and windows. It was not uncommon for untried travellers to lose all their possessions apart from the trunks that held them, for thieves would crawl the length of the train across the tops of the carriages, and, by almost impossible means, slide through the smallest of cracks left by unclosed windows. Rex would have preferred to remain alone in his small cabin-like compartment, but Mrs. Hope walked to the door and invited him to join herself and Una while the card players were indulging their skills.

"Bring your book and a towel. You can take a bath in my bathroom if the heat becomes too unbearable," she invited and he felt it might be churlish to refuse such consideration. By the time he had collected his things and taken a seat in the other compartment, Una was sitting, bare-footed and bare-legged on one of the bunk-seats and was busy making drawings in an old sketch book. In the centre of the floor was the gladstone bag. The three sat in comfortable and well-tuned silence enduring the extreme heat as the train rattled its smoking way across a great empty, low-lying plain. Rex took advantage of the invitation to soak in the bath and wished he could wear the looser clothes of the Indian instead of the well-fitting army uniform. "What a way to spend my leave," he groaned inwardly, wondering how to spend the time since reading was almost impossible due to the jerks and jolts of the train.

"I see your ancient baggage has accompanied you, Una," he said, "And it is unlocked. . ."

She rose to the bait as he knew she would, saying, "And don't you DARE touch it, Rex. It's only open because I trust you both."

"As if I would! I'd be torn apart if I so much as peeped," he said affecting fear.

Mrs. Hope's face wrinkled even more, smiling at each of the young people in turn.

"Tell you what, Una," the young man bantered, "I've invented a new game; it's guess the contents of the gladstone bag."

Una snorted. "You wouldn't guess them in a thousand years — neither of you."

The game proved entertaining, mainly because of the girls's derisive negatives at many of the suggestings. She had forgotten that Mrs. Hope was a new acquaintance, a famous authoress, and an unrelated hostess; she thought of her as Aunt Aurora. The suggestion that there may be dolls in the spacious interior brought forth most derision, and evoked much greater interest in the already fascinated older woman.

At last the two competitors had delved to the bottom of their inventiveness and Una, who had been making ticks on the edge of a sketch counted them.

"All right," she said, "Mrs. Hope had five right — paints, pencils, sketch pads, bible and purse; Rex had six right — Gamma's shoe, the prism, an ormer shell, photographs, journal and the Hermit's button. I'll show you," and she laid the treasures in a row on the seat beside her, and then added the contents they had not guessed. Rex, holding one side of the bag rigid while she eased out a newspaper wrapped treasure noticed a familiar object at the bottom.

"You HAVEN'T brought that old kilt, Una?"

"Of COURSE, I have," she replied, lifting it out and rubbing it against her face, sniffing the sea from its folds.

A surge of tenderness engulfed Rex, momentarily, as the kilt was held out to him to sniff at, but it passed while the wrapped article was slowly held up.

"See, the priest posted me the Hermit's carving and my poem."

"They never traced his family in Ireland?"

Mrs. Hope, who had been looking at the dog collar, well worn and still with a faint smell of dog about it, and the faded badge from a much worn blazer, looked up at the beautifully carved object before her, then at the sheet of paper that had slipped to the floor. Una handed it to her, following Rex's eyes peering still at the depths of the bag. "What's that?" he asked, "That box, hiding under your old guernsey. She extracted the darned garment that had reached her after each of the boys had worn it and outgrown it, and tenderly lifted the box tied with quantities of string. On the lid Rex read in Una's large, careful handwriting. 'For mother — from Lex.'

"I thought I ought to give them to her," she explained, her voice catching.

"Tell me," interposed Mrs. Hope, "about this wonderful carving."

By the time the sun had set and the train was leaving Delhi, Margaret Hope had determined that she would not lose touch with the two young people who had helped her to enjoy the most wearisome part of the long journey. Until far into the night she made copious notes in her new exercise book, and confided to her niece. "Just when I thought there were no more vital and unspoilt young about any more, here are two who seem to have come from a different planet or a different time. Would you mind very much if we went on to Peshawar and stayed a few days there before going home? I would like to meet the rest of this interesting family."

Rex and Colonel Sutton sat facing each other in the masculine privacy of their compartment, a folding table containing whisky glasses and bottles of the beverage and the soda that usually assisted its consumption. The older man poured generous quantities, saying, "Forget the seniority, boy. We're on the same task, you and I, escorting women half across India, and we're both more used to the company of men. At least I am. In pyjamas there's no rank, eh?"

Rex scratched at his leg, relieved of the irritation of woollen socks, and looked surreptitiously at the brown paper parcel Una had thrust into his hands as the whistle was blowing for departure from Delhi. Her face had been contorted with misery while she said over and over again, "I'm sorry, I'm sorry, I was so excited at seeing you I didn't remember the parcel I brought for you, from all of us — especially Aunt Aurora." He thought he had better open it in the privacy of the bathroom once the Colonel was safely inside his bedroll — or judging by the heat — on top of his bedroll.

"Prickly heat, eh?" queried the veteran, pouring himself another liberal drink.

"No, Sir. Just a scar that doesn't approve of woollen socks."

"Polo accident?"

"No. A Hun bullet."

"I didn't know you were in Flanders, O'Donaty. You look too young."

"I wasn't, Sir. I'm twenty-three, almost twenty-four. I was in West Africa."

"How on earth did you end up here, then?"

Both glasses were refilled and Rex resigned himself to what looked like being a long and liquid night.

"I was already enrolled at military academy when the war sprung on us. I was hurried through then shipped out to Quetta. They retrained me there and shipped me to Africa with the Baluchistanis. Hardly had time to learn enough Urdu to talk to them; I'd picked up more Hindustani from my cousins."

"Much the same lingo. Refill?"

Rex was not at all sure that he wanted to actually get drunk with a Colonel; not just the two of them; the old boy might reveal some best left unknown facts. He had already suffered from the consequences of being a too-willing listener to a 'misunderstood' memsahib, and he could well imagine Mrs. Sutton to be of the same ilk.

"I think I'll take a cold bath, if you don't want the bathroom, sir."

Rex returned from the bathroom not having opened the package; the room was even more airless than the compartment. To his relief, the Colonel followed his example having almost drained the whisky bottle, so he stretched out on the bunk and undid the lovingly tied cover. A letter from his mother lay on the top and he laid it aside to read later, then examined each of the contents filled with nostalgia and a very real homesickness. Each gift spoke volumes about the giver's desire to send him something that would be in constant use; there was one of the new fountain pens from his mother, a tobacco pouch from Frank, a safety razor from Roxana and her stranger husband, Dan, a small pocket-sized album of recently taken photographs of the family and the farm from Ivan, and a neat little penknife from Rolf while from Una, the least practical and most imaginative member of the family was a minute tablet bottle containing, as the minuscule writing on the label specified sand, sea and seaweed from Bellule Bay; there was also a reed pipe that he assumed came from the same quarter. The latter made him laugh. The idea of him sitting on some rocky escarpment overlooking the Khyber Pass playing a Peter Pan pipe was wonderful to visualise. He had just put the gifts into his small bag and read his mother's letter when the Colonel returned.

"That's better," he said, brushing his hair down.

Rex's eyes filled with admiration. The man had consumed almost a whole bottle of whisky, seemed almost inebriated, soaked in a bath and reappeared looking completely sober, sounding sober and was apparently intent on restarting the session.

Rex helped himself to an orange, cut it in half and sucked the juice.

"That's a good idea," exclaimed his companion. "Haven't done that since childhood," and proceeded to follow Rex's lead. They sucked in companionable silence for the time it takes to reduce two halves of an orange to a withering shell of pips and membranes and to wash the resulting juice from face, hands and moustaches.

The older man broke the hot, steaming silence asking rhetorically, "Want some advice, young man? Course you don't. Here it is, just the same! Get yourself a wife while you're still young; don't wait until you can keep her in the luxury her elderly Colonel father has done . . . and don't marry one of the girls whose been hanging about learning how to be pukkha burra-memsahib, marry a girl straight out from home — one of the 'fishing fleet' if you like. This damned country ruins most of the women, makes them think they're God's gift to the native, the army and the politicians — and they teach their daughters to think the same. They put up with hell here in their amazing fortitude, the heat, the dust, the rains, the germs, the infant deaths, the separations from their children, BUT, my boy, they demand a PRICE for their fortitude — and the price is success and RECOGNITION. I wish I'd known at your age, O'Donaty, what I've just spilled out to you."

Rex grunted, then noticing his companion lighting a cheroot said, "May I join you, Sir? I didn't know you smoked at all."

A cheroot was thrown accurately into the young man's hands before the thrower remarked, by way of answering the slight query in his companions voice. "I don't. Not allowed to. Keep it for the Club and the Mess. Never in my own home."

Rex looked at his fellow traveller with some compassion mixed with surprise, which the other man noticed, then asked, "Your father ruled YOUR home perhaps?"

"No. My mother. My father died when I was three."

"Did she permit smoking?"

"Yes, Sir. But we'd all been smoking at school for years before we actually produced pipes IN PUBLIC."

"Big family, eh?"

"Seven of us, with my cousins."

"Remember my advice, then. Think about it. And get that little sister of yours married off before she's ruined by this place. How old is she? Sixteen?"

Rex was beginning to dislike the conversation in some strange fashion so he did not bother to correct the Colonel about his 'little sister', he answered briefly, "Nearly eighteen!"

"Look around, boy, fast, then. Find her a nice young subaltern with some money behind him — before they turn her into a germinating memsahib." He stumped out his half-smoked cheroot, smiled, almost grinned across the compartment and said, "You smoke all you want in here, my boy. I'll blame you when my women smell it on me, eh?"

While the two men slept through the night, Una in the next compartment lay restlessly awake, as did her two companions, until finally mother and daughter swallowed some sleeping tablets and Una felt alone with her thoughts. At each station she peeped through the blinds leaning precariously from her top bunk, watching the somnolent bundles rise from the wooden platform, gather crates of hens, bundles, and often children, to climb into the nether reaches of the great iron monster, accompanied always by shouts, screams, orders and loud vocal demands mixed with abuse. Above and around the human medley there was the hissing and whistling of escaping steam. Between stations she kept peering out to the plains, hoping to see the Great Trunk Road and the distant foothills beyond. Her school atlas and a battered copy of 'Kim' lay beside her pillow, while her imagination peopled the road she could not see, but knew to be nearby with the figures of the veteran of the Mutiny who wore the Order of British India about his neck, his three gambling Ressaldar-major sons, the palanquin with the talkative old lady with bazaar invectives pouring from her dowager throat, the old Babu and the red-coated men of the cavalry, and around and behind each other the mixture of walking, riding, carrying nationalities, so vividly portrayed by the great master of the art of using words to evoke images of the sounds, colours and even smells of India in one volume.

The air became cooler at Umballa and Una knew the iron dragon was making its way into the foothills, the lower foothills perhaps, but still the foothills above which the massive Himalayas stretched forever, sideways, backwards, and upwards into the stars. She fell into an uneasy sleep wondering if that vast ridge had anything at its roots, imagining a tangle of potatoes and their side roots reaching into depths to the very centre of the earth. "If there's an UP there must be a DOWN," she thought sleepily.

The train crossed the River Sutlej while the two families and their friends slept, but in the strange pre-dawn light it shuffled noisily into Amritsar, disturbing all the passengers. Una slipped from her bunk and dressed, to the annoyance of Georgina beneath, whom she attempted to placate by saying, "Don't you want to TRY and see if the Sikh's golden Temple is visible?"

"No I don't."

"We'll be at Lahore soon," whispered the undefeated Una.

"Go away."

Silently Una said to herself, "All right. Stay in your bedroll and miss what's supposed to be one of the most beautiful cities, inside massive walls. School doesn't seem to have taught you much. Anyway, I want to think about the Shah

135

Jehan and his Shalimar. His Shalimar what? Garden? Or river? Or lake? I must ask someone." She pulled the blind up slightly and watched the scattered houses gradually closing up, nestling together, and pictured a dirty, turban headed boy sitting on a green verdigris covered bronze gun outside a 'Wonder House' inside a crumbling walled city. She could see, as if she had been there a tall, yellow-skinned lama walking away with the boy trailing beside him, carrying his begging bowl. Her eyes must have closed. She was jerked awake by the grinding to a stop, of the train, the whistles and shrieks and clamour of the normal arrival at a large railway station, and from within the train the voice of Mrs. Sutton.

"Close that blind, AT ONCE."

With a second start she obeyed. Later it registered that, for the first time in their relationship, Mrs. Sutton had not called her 'my dear'.

"I'm sorry, Mrs. Sutton," she said.

Mrs. Sutton was bustling around the space, in and out of the bathroom, in and out of her trunk, in and out of each of the numerous cupboards that lined the walls.

"I'm glad someone wants to see Lahore," thought Una.

The bustler was back again saying, "Wake Georgina, my dear — quickly."

Una did as she was told.

The voice called from the bathroom, "Your father is meeting some men here. Dress quickly."

Suddenly the Suttons, all three of them, had vanished into the interior of the station building and Una was put in Rex's care, which amused both of them to the point of rather childish laughter.

Rex joined Una and they sat companionably drinking quantities of tea with slices of lemon while the sky became resplendent with the rising of the sun somewhere above the distant mountains.

"That's something I haven't remembered," Una said slowly, "The sun sets so quickly that you have to be sure not to miss it, but it takes AGES to rise."

"There'll be lots of things, Una, you'll find you've forgotten. The whole way of life here. It'll be NOTHING like life at La Bellule. . ."

136

"What DO you mean, Rex?" she almost snapped at him.

There was something Rex wanted to warn her about; here was the opportunity and he was finding it difficult, very difficult. She didn't help by snapping. At last he said, "Well, for example, you can't just take your horse out and ride into the hills, alone. You must have an escort, or at least the syce, and that means you need your parents permission."

"Oh," she exclaimed, "why?"

"It just isn't done, that's all. . ." he explained, unwisely, then quickly added, "It really isn't safe."

"I see," she said, and Rex knew she did not see.

"You'll be expected to ride with a saddle and stirrups, properly dressed, not bareback with your kilt wrapped round your waist." They both laughed.

"I won't have to ride SIDE-SADDLE will I? Because I can't?"

"Anna rides astride, but she wears these new jodhpur things that women have taken up."

"But, Rex, I haven't any whatever they are. Where can I get some?"

"The dhersi, the tailor'll make you some I expect . . . ask Anna. Oh yes," he rushed on, "Don't forget Anna isn't the little toddler she was when you last saw her . . . um . . . she's quite a young lady, now."

"She CAN'T BE. She's only fourteen, Rex; she's still a schoolgirl except she doesn't go to school."

Rex remembered the fearful misunderstanding Una had suffered when she thought she would be at the same school as all the boys, so he persisted, "She's a very grown up sort of schoolgirl. The centre of the family — and very, very . . . well, very treasured. In some ways she's more grown up than you, Una."

"Hm. Oh well, she'll be MORE of a FRIEND for me, then, won't she. I never had a girlfriend after Jill — when I left school. I didn't NEED one, anyway, but now, NOW I haven't any of you, I WOULD like one, Rex. Yes, I would."

"Well, I hope you and Anna like each other. Don't forget Marc, though; he's a really nice little boy. As a matter of fact he's very like you — small, wild hair, wild ways too. He's always in trouble with your father, or so he told me."

"He was only a bundle in long dresses and shawls and nappies and all red face and screams, when I saw him. I hope he doesn't still scream."

Rex laughed heartily at the idea of the tough, lively little boy he had met, screaming. He still had more warnings to make, whilst the chance offered, "Your father's a very old man, Una. He must be coming near to eighty. He was a coronet at the siege of Delhi, so he couldn't have been more than sixteen years old then he was promoted to Ensign; d'you know he wasn't much older than you when he led a platoon into Afghanistan." Rex did some quick mental arithmetic and corrected himself. "I suppose he was about twenty-one or two. They gave him a medal for that tribal war . . . what a man! He's quite deaf, now, Una. Really quite deaf . . . and shouts his orders, bit like a rifle shot sometimes I. . ."

Mrs. Hope stood at the door saying, "I wondered if you two would like to join me for the morning — to leave the Suttons free to pack; I expect their servant will be using up quite a lot of the space."

They both accepted, Una taking her precious gladstone bag and Rex his own small case — with the revolver.

The four sat writing letters 'home' for sending away the moment they reached their destination. After a long silence when the only sound apart from the rhythmical music of iron wheels rolling along iron rails, was that of rustling paper and the scratch of pen or pencil, Rex asked, "Una? What can I write to Frank?"

Mrs. Hope looked up and Una explained Frank's predicament ending with, "you see he NEVER wanted to kill. He wanted to cure people — and convert heathens. I don't believe in changing people from one belief to another, myself, but he's VERY sincere . . . well he was."

The wrinkled face looked sad and she said, "Perhaps, if he could come to terms with his own disablement he could help others do the same. THIS country is riddled with deformed and limbless people. They either beg in the cities or they go on scratching a living, fighting back at their 'sickness' and accepting it as their fate. He could TEACH in one of the mission schools out here, perhaps?"

Una's face lit up and her voice became tense, "Tell him that, Rex," she said. "He was born here. He hasn"t forgotten all his Hindustani. He COULD teach out here."

Leaning forward towards Mrs. Hope she added, "He needs something to come alive FOR. Then he'd learn to stand without overbalancing. He could still ride, one armed; he could exercise Gamma for me to start with . . . he needs a CAUSE."

The train puffed and spluttered into Gujerat and a company of sepoys was marched into the bowels of the machine. Colonel Sutton stepped down and stood in animated conference with the Major and young Captain who had accompanied the sepoys.

"More trouble on the frontier," said Miss Law. She turned to Rex and explained, simply, "It was from Gujerat that MY fiancé, about the age of that Major, there, took the train, and didn't return. A long time ago." She had so seldom spoken that both young people stared at her with interest. "My aunt, here, gave me a home and a job that I perform most inadequately." They all laughed for no apparent reason, except that the mousey Miss Law had the ability to laugh at herself, which she proceeded to do. "Yes," she added, "I typewrite my aunt's beautifully written manuscripts, but I am quite UNABLE to spell. There are the long words, neatly written, accurately spelled, and I think I am copying them, but no, every word of more than five letters has each letter copied into the wrong position — just like a children's puzzle. I think I should just make puzzles for young people to work out." Both ladies laughed; their laughter was not the polite teaparty laughter of most ladies, but of two friends genuinely enjoying a huge joke.

"We call it 'scrambled spelling', laughed Miss Hope. "We keep talking about employing a secretary, but shrink at the thought of sharing our home with some thoroughly efficient young woman who would deplore our irregular hours. Emily, Miss Law, is quite wonderful with figures; she keeps our accounts, our engagements and she ALWAYS wins at bridge — almost always. The Suttons did not invite us to play with them, you notice; not after our first session."

"Will you be writing more books?" asked Una.

"Certainly. I am half way through one novel and have the germ of another waiting to be started."

"I used to think I'd be a writer — or a poet," confessed the young woman.

"And you've changed your mind? Why?"

"I just couldn't make up stories about people, not real people. I make stories about dragons and unicorns, witches and leprechauns."

"You should WRITE them down. You can draw. Illustrate them. Make books for children to read — less sad than Uncle Tom's Cabin, or Jackanapes."

"Do you know, Miss Hope, what I wish? I wish I had written Kim. that's about people-people. Not about his spying and things; just about the Great Trunk Road people." She broke off suddenly, stood at the window and said, "Look. Oh Look, Rex. The Jhelum. The Jhelum river. That's where Van and I were born. And there are the real mountains. Somewhere up there, at Srinagar I started life. Van and me. We're coming to MY roots, Rex, like I came to your roots."

The stop at Jhelum was short and desultory. The Suttons did not invite the young people to return, so they remained with their friendly hostesses.

When the train restarted Mrs. Hope said, "We often spend a week or so on a houseboat by Srinagar. Our little home is at Gulmarg, a day's ride from Srinagar — a beautiful ride through the Pir Panjal hills. You must both be our guests sometime and we shall take you to Srinagar. Don't you agree Emily?"

The nod of acquiescence given, she announced, "I shall call on your father in a day or two. How long is your leave?" she asked Rex.

"Six more days."

"Very well. I shall call the day after tomorrow. I have a second reason, or excuse. I shall offer to write your father's biography."

The train chugged its slow way up the steady incline rising up to some three thousand feet and settled its weary wheels at Rawalpindi, where the Suttons disgorged themselves, leaving a considerable quantity of luggage for their smartly attired servants to carry to their house. They parted from the travellers with whom they had spent so many weeks with the usual casual, almost conventional farewells, the likelihood being that they would meet again at some polo match, gymkhana or regimental ball. Una thanked them for escorting her and had no great desire to meet them again.

"You'll soon become accustomed to our ways out here, my dear," were Mrs. Suttons parting words, before she was bustling through the space cleared by her husband's impressive frame.

When they had gone Una said, "I don't think I'll EVER be like Georgina — and, awful though it is, I don't terribly want to be."

"I hope you won't," consoled Rex.

"Oh, it would be so NICE to always say the right thing instead of the wrong thing."

Mrs. Hope, overhearing said, "Stay as you are Una. Don't let them make a burra-memsahib of YOU."

The soothing words provoked great excitement in Una. She would soon be seeing her mother for the first time after eleven years. Her mother would be reassuring like Mrs. Hope and Aunt Aurora.

The train collected itself, took the bit between its teeth and sped down to Peshawar Plain, beyond which rose the lofty hills and mountains of Afghanistan. Una consulted her atlas. If the train failed to stop at Peshawar it would rattle right through the famous Khyber Pass. She was far too excited to speak and just gazed silently from the window until an exhausted shriek, a belching of smoke and a jolt indicated that they had arrived.

"I won't recognise them, Rex. You must show them to me," she gasped.

Rex's servant slid up to him and was instructed to remove the luggage while Rex scanned the narrow platform. At last a chuprassi arrived wearing the red bandolier and sash of the General's household and indicated a tonga to which Rex gently edged his cousin. Mrs. Hope and her niece, having said their goodbyes, stood and watched the disbelief spread across the girl's face. While they watched they became aware of a small figure running along the platform, pushing people aside like a fragile yacht ploughing its way through mighty breakers, and, as they looked on fascinated, a small boy hurled himself at Una, stood back and solemnly shook hands with Rex, then once more hugged Una. Marc had arrived to claim ownership of the sister he had never consciously seen.

Chapter Nine

The tonga strolled through the crowded street of Peshawar, pushing aside people and livestock as it rolled from side to side, and causing the three occupants to jostle each other with a companionable, almost embracing series of physical contacts. Marc kept up a steady flow of chatter and queries which only Rex responded to, aware of his cousin's hurt. Una watched the great flow of life around them, but pictured arrivals at home. Memories of departures and arrivals at the small harbour flooded her mind, for she had almost always been one of those meeting the boat. She and Aunt Aurora, old Gamma and the ancient buggy – and, as the war-victims returned, an ever increasing collection of people arriving on bicycles, in trucks drawn by Alph, or walking. The entire household waited, hours sometimes, to greet the returning member of the family. They had gathered to welcome the remnants of the once splendid Militia, with the frozen-faced Pierre; Pierre had joined them when they welcomed Roxana and the stretcher-borne Frank; frequently they all turned up to welcome the resplendent Ivan; Rolf even played truant from school to join the welcoming party, and, a greater sacrifice, abandoned his sheep to join their ranks. After an absence of eleven YEARS her parents had not foregone their siesta to meet their daughter – just because the train had arrived some two hours late. Only an unknown chuprassi had been sent, and Marc, the brother she did not know, had crept out of the house to welcome her home. For Una supposed this was now to be her home.

Once beyond the town the road became a sand lane lined with rambling bungalows on one side, and flanked by tiers of rocky escarpment rising to some considerable height on the other side. At the end of the lane the tonga entered a wooden gate being rapidly demolished by white ants, and Marc leapt out, saying, "I'm resting, remember," and disappeared from sight behind and then beneath the wooden building. The two servants who had been running behind the tonga smiled; the tonga driver smiled; Rex and Una smiled. "Lucky he's so small," said Rex. Una's luggage, a small leather covered trunk, or yakdan, and a crocodile skin suitcase were being unloaded and placed on the wide verandah, Una stood, clutching the gladstone bag and nervously twisting and untwisting her handkerchief. She watched the syce, or groom, emerge from the nether regions and heard Rex speak to him, as in a dream. "I've ordered ponies for us – you'll need a ride and a chance to ask ME the things that you will find bothering you. I remember Una! Turning your handkerchief into a Turk's Knot whenever you're confused . . . ha! I see you have Lex's yakdan and case . . . Come, let's have a cool drink before the family descends on you . . . yes?"

Una gazed around. The house was different; the place was different; but this was assuredly the same home she had left eleven years before. There on the wall were the huge buffalo horns attached to the grisly skull of the grotesque head, the elegant ibex antlers, the disintegrating tiger skins and, draped across the bamboo sofa the soft pelt of the snow leopard. All the glass eyes inserted into the various eye sockets caught and reflected the sunlight, throwing green, brown and shades of red stripes in rainbows across the bare wooden boards of the verandah. Suddenly, while her eye went from object to object a tall, impressive figure filled the doorway into the house interior. "Missi-baba, Missi-Una-baba," said the figure. Una saw the great height of the man, the impeccable, white turban, the vivid blue eyes in a coffee coloured face and the unforgettable grizzled beard, though no longer jet black as she had remembered from the past.

"Oh Urji," she gasped, "Oh Urjinath, dear, dear Urji." She was clasping both his hands while she gulped, lifting them and holding them against her face. "Truly," she thought, "this man is God."

143

Evidently Urjinath was a God who knew his place in the hierarchy of service. He stood back and studied the young woman who had left as a very small child. "Memsahib," he said. "No more Missi-baba! And the Ivan-sahib? He is well?"

"Tall as you, Urji; tall and very well, and a midshipman in the navy. And VERY handsome, Urji . . . oh, yes, and very clever. We never stopped remembering you, Urji . . ."

"Ah," said the old man, filled with pride. He was the major domo of the household, but before he retired into this situation he had served at the side of the General for fifty years; they had been little more than boys when they first attached themselves to each other. Each of the two old men felt the sorrows and joys of the other, and the twins were Urjinath's greatest pride. It was probably thanks to his devoted care that they had survived their premature appearance in the world. While the ayah, his wife, fed one twin, he bottle fed the other. Also, twins being a rarity among his people, they seemed as gods almost, reincarnations of Yama and Yami, the sun and the moon – not unlike the Norse twins Sol and Mani. Urji alone could cope with the twins and they were still crawling when nanny had passed them almost completely into his hands.

The luggage had been carried on to the verandah and Urji explained, after sending the bearers away, that they could not be carried into Una's room until the family appeared from the afternoon rest, however he called a young boy and ordered him to bring barley water for the Sahib and Memsahib, and, once it had arrived, he disappeared into the back where he distributed orders and instructions like confetti among his array of underlings – most orders revolving around the little missi-sahib. The seal was thus set. She had found favour with their lord and master, therefore THEY would take greater than usual care of this newcomer.

When Rex and Una had sat and cooled themselves with several glasses of the sweet, cool drink, Urji himself returned to remove the tray.

"You have forgotten your Hindi, Missi-memsahib?" he asked.

"Not all, Urji. Listen. You taught Van and me – listen:
Humpty Dumpty baithnakehr chapt,

144

Humpty Dumpty ghilghear fut;
Rajah khiyalaska,
Ranee kigora,
Humpty Dumpty khubinai jaura. Hai!"

Una just had time to register the pleasure that crossed the old man's face when a startling apparition swept on to the verandah from another doorway, and Urjinath withdrew.

Tera O'Donaty swept into view. A prima donna's polished stage recall could not have been so dramatic, so perfectly timed and so graceful. The clock struck four, a gong rang out sonerously and a silver tray containing silver objects appeared.

"Una, my dear," said the magnificent goddess who was Una's mother. "I hope you had a pleasant journey," she continued, holding out her hands and clasping her daughter's, whilst breathing a butterfly wing of a kiss on the girl's hot cheeks.

"Yes, here she is," said Rex with obvious false heartiness, but trying to give the girl time to recover from her stupefication. "Pity the train was so late; a lot of time spent loading troops on for the frontier, Aunt Tera."

While Rex was speaking Tera had seated herself and indicated a chair for each of the others. Una sat uneasily on the edge of the bamboo chair watching her mother infusing the tea – as she had long remembered – in the fluted silver teapot with the serpentine spout and pixie-hat lid, pouring the water from the same slender silver kettle kept boiling above a methylated spirit lamp. The moment Tera had closed the teapot lid another gong rang through the bungalow and there arrived, like puppets manipulated on strings, or Una's own marionettes, three others through three different entrances. The General, her father arrived from the corner of the verandah, kissed his wife on the forehead and then embraced the already standing figure of his daughter, then held her at arms length and studied her saying, "Well, well, well, a bit of a foil for young Anna, eh? Well, well, well, Una!" There was warmth in the old man's greeting, even if his moustache scratched and the voice boomed in her ears, Una thought. Anna had arrived from a door behind Una's back, and this little sister was the greatest shock of all to the already bewildered young woman.

145

Anna was the same age that Una had been when her school expelled her, and despite Rex's warnings, she HAD expected a scraggy little schoolgirl. Instead she saw a beautiful young woman, tall as herself, taller perhaps, with hair the colour of golden syrup and eyes like cornflowers, enhanced by a complexion that could only be described as delicate peaches and cream. Not a freckle marred the smooth cheeks or short straight nose, and she moved with the lightness and grace of a butterfly, her neatly curvaceous form enhanced by the blue and white dress she fitted like a glove. "She's like a Chalk Hill Blue," thought Una. She seemed to skim to her chair after planting a kiss on her sister's cheek, and sat with the relaxed grace of an experienced dancer, or a well-schooled debutante. While Una gaped and Rex sought for some means of diverting all the pairs of eyes that held her in focus, young Marc bounced across the verandah, threw his arms around her neck, saying, "I'm Marc, your long lost baby brother, ha, ha, ha!" Una hugged him, wanting to cry, and whisper, "AT least YOU are real!" However she was brought to reality with what seemed like a cannonade.

"Where's Nanny?" barked the General, stirring his tea and causing the cup to rattle in the saucer.

Una jumped, spilling her own tea down her travel-stained dress. "Nanny?" she queried. "I though she was dead!"

"Dead? Not yet, Una my dear, not yet."

Una turned to face the voice, dropping her saucer which clattered to the floor scattering in fragments, which seemed to reverberate their bell-like tinkling throughout the house. A miracle of juggling saved the cup from meeting the same fate, and then Una found herself engulfed in a flabby, but masterly embrace, held at a distance and examined from head to toe, from her untidy hair to her dust-stained and inelegant footwear, almost denuding her as it travelled slowly down the body, and certainly and effectively depriving her of the last remnants of dignity. "Well, well, well, so THIS is what our little Una has grown into, oh dear, oh dear. Never mind my dear, we can do SOMETHING with you. Do you not think so Mrs. O'Donaty."

"Of COURSE, Nanny," Tera answered kindly, "Now come and have your tea."

146

Una sat miserably watching the boy sweep up the scattered china and tried not to allow her hands to shake when she lifted the replenished cup to her lips. A picture, a moving picture, a film ran through Una's mind even while she answered the occasional question directed at her; she saw a young man, an armless young man, lying on the grass with violin beside him and superimposed on him was a little boy with his hand beneath a tap of steaming water. At last Rex's voice penetrated and erased the 'film', "I've arranged with the syce, Aunt Tera, to have a couple of ponies saddled. I thought Una could do with some exercise after sitting so long in the train. I thought I'd take her out and show her where to ride in the mornings."

"Of course, Rex," his aunt replied, then, attracting the General's attention, mouthed the information to him.

Anna and Marc showed their sister around the bungalow which had a verandah encircling it. "You see," said Marc, we use it as a passage, mostly, although father has his afternoon nap on HIS bit of the verandah. See, Father's room, Mother's room, Visitor's room – Rex's at the moment, my room, Nanny's room, and now yours and Anna's room. We don't go any further – OFFICIALLY – that's kitchen and servants' quarters."

Once the tour was completed, Anna and Marc disappeared across the compound beyond their verandah saying, "We're off to the Padre for lessons." Rex came to the room and collected Una for their ride, and explained the niceties of the bathing system.

"The Bhishti, water carrier," he explained, "brings buckets of water and puts them either IN the bathroom – that place behind the slatted swing door – OR if the room is occupied he leaves them on the verandah. There will be additional hot water supplied early in the morning, in time to have a bath before breakfast, and again around six o-clock to allow time for a bath before eight o-clock dinner. You will find, Una, that EVERYTHING in this household is controlled by the CLOCK – and EVERYONE obeys that inexorable controller of their lives. Oh yes, and you tip the tub slightly when you want the water to completely run away. You'll notice the floor slopes towards the corner where the sluice is; a sluice with a strong grid to keep the snakes and things out . . . Come on then. We ride, eh?"

They rode up a gently sloping, spiral pathway up the rocky escarpment, dismounted and sat on a rock high above the neat little bungalow roofs, glittering in all their corrugated iron glory, that was the British residential out-of-town area, as Rex explained.

"This reminds me of The Roc," said Rex.

"Yes," Una replied, "and nobody except Pierre and Rolf go there, now."

And then they talked. Rex asked endless questions, trying to fill in the gap of five years, but neither of them referred to either Lex, or to Frank's injury. Long silences were all they managed, each knowing that the other was thinking their thoughts. Only while they tightened their girths for the return ride did Una broach the subject of Frank obliquely though.

"Rex," she said, "I don't think I'll stay here. I don't think I CAN stay . . . not with Nanny there . . . I don't BELONG . . . and I don't know HOW I can NOT stay. I HATE NANNY. I'm sort of AFRAID of her and I keep thinking about Frank feeling pain in the hand that isn't there and crying out in his sleep 'No, Nanny, no . . .'" she finished in one breathless rush.

"Just a minute Una, old thing. You've only just arrived. You're tired and it's all VERY strange and different for you. They are YOUR PARENTS and they'll decide FOR you whether you like it or not . . ."

"Aren't YOU on my side, Rex?"

"I'm always on your side. I'm just trying to be IMPARTIAL . . ."

"If YOU abandon me, Rex, . . . well . . . it'll be like . . . like . . . being left at school by myself . . . it'll be like Lex being killed all over again . . ."

"I'll never abandon you, as you call it. Just give it TIME, Una. See how you feel when you've been to the gymkhanas and balls and experienced all the fun of the cold weather season," said Rex doubtfully.

"Hm. All right, I'll see. I'll TRY to be a silly little burra-memsahib, . . . PERHAPS." Una laughed her old infectious laugh before adding, "And I'll be about as successful as I was at being a nice little English school-girl. D'you think I might find another old Hermit and get myself expelled from HOME. D'you think I could write a blasphemous poem to Urji? or better, Mahatma Gandhi?"

"Back to normal, I see," Rex laughed.

They had arrived back later than they should have done so both had to take hurried baths as they were expected to appear for 'drinks' with the head of the house. Anna was already bathed and changed when Una wandered into the room, and Anna burst out into peals of laughter at the sight of her sister.

"You DIDN'T ride out in THAT?" she shrieked. "Oh, Una, you're just as funny as Nanny said you'd be . . ."

"What's wrong?" asked her sister.

"What's WRONG, Una? What's RIGHT? I mean look at you. Where did you get that shirt, and those breeches things?"

"They're Rolf's cast-offs. I ride at home in my old school baggy bloomers. Nobody SEES me, except Sergeant Fyne and he doesn't mind."

By the time Una was dressed she felt like Jane Eyre being inspected by Mr. Rochester. Anna had laughed at her very limited wardrobe. Anna had laughed at EVERYTHING Una possessed.

"Well what's in that dreadful old bag, then?" Anna asked pointing to the gladstone bag.

"Oh just private things. Drawing pads. I keep it locked, ALWAYS . . . Oh, I've just remembered, I have a package for mother . . ." She unlocked the double lock, pulled out all the contents and dragged to the surface a shoe-box carefully tied with ribbon. While searching for the package she had not noticed Anna. Suddenly her young sister stood up waving the burnt and tattered kilt and the much darned guernsey.

"What on earth is THIS, Una?" she taunted Una, already tired and bemused by the days events, holding it just out of the older girl's reach, who, goaded beyond her very limited endurance, grabbed the treasured articles, thrust them in the bag, locked it and burst out, "Don't you EVER do that again, Anna."

149

Authority rang in the voice and Nanny, standing in the doorway, heard it, and saw her treasure's ruffled hair and heated face. "And Una, dear, don't bring your wild ways here. We don't want Anna to grow up like you, my dear." With which she led the young girl from the room. By the time Una joined the family on the verandah, Anna had obviously told her mother that poor Una had no suitable clothes and the arrangements were already being made by Urjinath, for the dharzi, or tailor, to appear next morning with samples of materials.

Her first day with her parents, thought Una, was not exactly propitious.

"Oh dear," thought Una, lying sleepless under her mosquito net. "It's exactly like that awful first day at school, and I just do EVERYTHING wrong and say everything wrong and even THINK everything wrong. I wish I was back home with Aunt Aurora. At least I just remembered in time to give Mother the box of Lex's things. I hope she won't be too sad when she sees them . . ."

After an early morning ride with her brother and sister and Rex, Una found herself embroiled in a plethora of materials, patterns and tape-measures, with the little dharzi, Nanny, and from time to time, her Mother. She was draped and swathed and forced to examine her rather puny body in Anna's long mirror; she was asked to differentiate between one material and another – and make choices; she found it all exciting but very unrewarding as well. When she made some vigorous decision about material, either liking or disliking it, Nanny invariably reversed the decision. On two things alone did Una feel determined to retain her own wishes; one was colour and the other a refusal to wear anything with frills. She even won some admiration from her own mother when she defied Nanny over colours, saying "No, sorry, Nanny, I will NOT wear red, purple or blue. Never. Ever. No!"

"And what colour DO you THINK suits you?" Nanny asked irritably.

"I don't care if it suits me. I care about what I am happy WEARING."

"Oh yes, Una, and which of these colours would you condescend to wear?"

"The gold for best, and yellow and green for ordinary wear . . ." Her mother re-entered the room at that point and overheard the reply Nanny gave, "Una, dear, the gold is a little dramatic for YOU isn't it?"

Tera made the decision, saying, "Yes Una. With your brown face and arms, the gold will perhaps tone down the Eurasian look of you. Have the gold, by all means."

Una, like any girls, would have revelled in this apparent wealth of clothes being provided for her, but during all the measuring and draping there were always Nanny's leopard-like pads, touching, prodding, pinching with the fleshy, slug-like fingers.

Once the fashion designing and discussions were over Una was left to her own devices, Rex having gone into the town to meet some friends, so she sat on her bed and made some sketches to send back to her aunt and her brothers. Lost in her own world she was rudely shaken from it by the voices of her mother and Nanny talking on the verandah – about HER.

"I just do not know what we can do with her, Nanny," her mother said.

"Some girls find husbands within three months . . . but not Una, I'm afraid," Nanny replied.

"She IS my daughter. I have to make some attempt to settle her."

"She will not find a YOUNG man. Perhaps a middle-aged . . . do you think?"

"Too childish. Too unsophisticated . . . and regrettably, no talents."

"It is a problem. Here you are, Mrs. O'Donaty, with two daughters; the youngest like the most perfect rose, and the other, the one we must arrange some future for, a wild rambler."

"Anna could marry to-morrow, she is so sophisticated. She must be watched at the gymkhana – and especially at the ball. I hope you will keep a constant eye on her, Nanny. I shall be occupied with the General and all the farewells."

Nanny laughed. "I shan't have to watch poor little Una!" she concluded as they moved into one of the rooms, adding in a voice that seemed to vibrate through the listener's head, "Fine feathers do NOT make fine birds in this case . . ."

151

Una put down her sketch pad and pencil and laughed. She pictured herself recounting the conversation – with a few additions – to the family at La Bellule, sitting around the great Truth Table in the friendly old kitchen. At least she had the evening rides with Rex when home seemed very close to both young people.

By the time the family had to leave for the polo ground to attend the gymkhana, Una's new riding outfits had arrived and she passed her Mother's scrutiny without a single unfavourable comment. "Though very immature," thought Tera, "my daughter looks extremely neat!" Una was delighted with the close fitting jodhpurs, although she had no idea that riding astride and in men's garments would be generally regarded with great disfavour by both sexes. However, by the end of the afternoon Una was in demand by all the young men as partners in any riding, running or ball throwing games, and her antics during the musical chairs created a furore as she leapt both off and on to the back of the pony, disregarding the array of syces standing by each chair to assist the remounting of the young ladies. The family watched with very different feelings. The General felt an unwilling pride in this hoydenish daughter of his; Tera felt that the girl could do SOMETHING, however trivial; Anna was openly jealous; Marc equally openly admiring; Rex was amused, though not surprised, but felt himself slightly irritated by the attention HIS cousin was receiving from fellow – and more junior – officers; Nanny felt a strange venomous fear of the girl who was taking the limelight from her beloved rose; and Una was scarcely aware of anything either unusual or untoward.

"Where DID you learn to ride?" asked one young subaltern.

"A cavalry sergeant taught me like a trooper," she had replied. A reply that was to reverberate around Peshawar for a few days.

Once more she answered truthfully when asked by the mothers of the other young women, "Where did you go to school?"

She told them, adding that she had been expelled so gave up school at thirteen.

152

Miss Hope and Miss Law were at the gymkhana and Una was able to introduce them to her parents, resulting in an invitation to dine two nights later and Rex's last evening.

Una returned to the house quite certain in her own mind about one thing; she did not WANT to become like the other young people she met. "It's as if they all have corsetted actions and laughter and talk," she explained to Rex.

While the O'Donaty family was beginning to absorb their newest, and greatly censured member into the fold, the highest British Power in India had refused the most honoured of the Indian symbols of unity, power and peace, a withdrawal of a new and harsh piece of legislation. Resulting from the refusal, the man of peace, the Mahatma Gandhi, instituted satyagraha, disobedience of the laws by passive resistance, and non-violence. The result in a country of mainly very poor people who could not afford even the basic necessities of life, salt, grain, oil and cotton cloth, was an ever increasing country-wide series of demonstrations. Demonstrations by vast concourses of humans inevitably led to the inclusion of many with less desire for peace, the leaders of mass-hysteria, the fluent talkers, the Robespierres of a more destitute country than France had been over a century before. As inevitably as the ebbing of a high tide, the agitators, over-excited, encouraged the damaging of their power-filled masters' property; equally inevitably lives were lost, including five Englishmen killed and one woman beaten by one small, unruly mob. Arrests had followed. Other mobs caught the epidemic and, gaining confidence, burnt banks, railways and government offices and the perpetrators, arrested with the innocent by-standers. While the gymkhana was running its pleasantly delightful course, huge concourses of peace-loving demonstrators were gathering with their wives and children, enjoying an unexpected and self-decided holiday in parks, gardens, polo grounds and anywhere that offered space on the outskirt of many towns and cities. They were obeying their new leader, a man of themselves, a man like themselves, but a man comparatively few had ever seen. In the same way their 'masters', their 'rulers' from whom they wanted freedom to govern themselves, would congregate in great parks and on heaths to listen to speakers urging them to political, religious or social changes in their own country, far across the sea.

The morning after the gymkhana the family had an unusually silent breakfast. Anna had not joined the morning ride. Marc had been ecstatic about his elder sister's performance the previous day, until told to stop talking, after which he also sank into an uncomfortable silence. The General, never loquacious, merely listed the day's duties – the time Marc was to leave to spend the night at the Padre's house, the time the ponies were to be returned after the last ride, and, most emphatically, the time ALL were to be ready and on the front verandah, for departure to the Ball that evening. Rex and Una had planned to ride high into the hills soon after breakfast, partly to exercise the two other ponies that had not been out earlier, and partly so that Rex could show Una the path where she could ride in his absence – with a syce in attendance.

"I'll wash my hair first," Una told her cousin as they all spread out around the bungalow. "It can dry on the ride!"

"Half an hour, then," Rex stipulated. "Half an hour ONLY. If you're not here I'll come and fetch you."

"Half an hour!" thought Una. "I can write my journal as WELL."

The two girls went to their room together, Una excited and looking forward to the new experience of a REAL BALL. It was to be Anna's first ball as well, but Anna was sullen; SHE had always been the centre of attention at gymkhanas – and now this, this waifish sister had supplanted her.

"I hope you won't show-off, to-night, Una," the younger girl snapped.

"Of course not, Anna. Why should I?"

"Well you DID yesterday, didn't you, Una?"

Una flushed. "Did I?" she said.

"You behaved like a little boy. Like Marc; worse than Marc . . ." with which unkind thrust, she called to her brother and walked across the compound, books under their arms.

Una sat, blushing furiously and trying to find out for herself if she had really been showing off. "I'll ask Rex," she thought, closing the outer door and hurling her clothes across the room, anger and hurt fighting for supremacy in

154

her mind. She flung open the lattice door into the bathroom, and even whilst pouring jugs of water over her head she could hear the creaking of the hinges as the door swung backwards and forwards. She continued angrily smearing soft soap across and over her scalp, her long, thick hair piling up in a turban, then being roughly pulled down and rubbed with her long hands.

Suddenly she jumped.

"I'll do your hair, Una dear," said a voice immediately behind her.

"No, thanks, Nanny," she replied, still shaking from the unexpectedness of the silent entry, and standing upright to face the intruder, soap dripping into her eyes and streaking her naked body. She turned back towards the bath tub to reach for her towel hanging over the rim, when the deceptively strong hands grasped the nape of her neck and commenced pouring the jugs of warm water over and down her head. Una felt like a kitten being shaken by its mother. She wriggled and water poured down her body disappearing under the slats and gurgling into the drain in the far corner of the room. She remembered the strength of those soft pads that might have been hands. Still held in a grip of iron, rubber clad iron, Una felt herself pushed on to the cork covered stool, her head and face smothered in the large towel and being rubbed. She was gasping for breath when the rubbing ceased, her ears filled with water which she shook and tipped once she had caught her breath, by which time the soft voice was saying, "And now some oil, dear." The pads poured oil down her body and proceeded to rub it gently, but very, very firmly into every inch of her body. No part was left unexplored, untouched. She was squeezed, pinched, prodded and even pulled and tugged. Even the scar on her foot was explored. To Una, her body was no longer her own possession. After the door had stopped swinging backwards and forwards, the invader long departed, Una sat. She knew it was a nightmare from which she must surely wake – and then she was sick; unable to reach the commode, she threw her breakfast down her body and all across the slatted floor.

Rex stamped up and down the front verandah. Up, down, up, down, and at each down, he banged on the railing around the verandah with his short cane. "Twenty more turns and I'll drag her out," he said to himself. She was late and becoming later and even more late. He had ordered a packed lunch so that they could remain out, and travel high into the hillside. He had put up with Urjinath's saying, "ALL day, Rex-sahib, all day and no syce?"

Rex had answered irritably, almost, "All right, Urjinath. I shall look after your little baba-log; as if she was the most precious of precious jewels, the Koh-i-noor diamond even."

"Yes, sahib, but may I, sahib, intrude enough to ask you sahib, is it proper? She is no longer a missy-baba."

"She is as my sister, Urji . . . and I know, Ivan told me, how you breathed life into her when she was dead . . . I know . . ."

"Forgive me, Rex-sahib. Yes she is as dear to me as my own grandsons . . ."

Rex recalled the conversation, appreciated the concern of the old man, and gently laughed to himself. "Dear, funny little Una . . . an object of lust . . . " However he was delighted that this opportunity had fallen into his lap to be alone with her, talk about home, feel as if he WAS at home – before he went out on frontier duty. The General and his aunt were dining with friends at the club, and Nanny would be at home to supervise the two youngsters' lunch and rest time.

He had walked twenty times up and down, so on the last up-walk he continued around the verandah, passed all the bedrooms, and, seeing the door open into the girls' room, knocked and walked in, when he met an overpowering smell of carbolic; he caught his breath; he had not met that smell in such force since he left the hospital in Cape Town.

"Pouff," he said, then felt fear. He saw the bathroom door swinging back and forth, propelled by the foot of the object of his search, who sat swathed in a large white towel, tears pouring down her face, and huge sobs racking her body while she kicked.

"What is it Una?" he gulped. "Not a scorpion . . .?"

A harsh laugh burst through the sobs, that were now close to his ear as he knelt, clutching her. "I'm kicking Nanny to perdition. Oh Rex, Rex, thank you for coming. Please, please get me my tissane from my gladstone bag; it's in a jar; please mix a spoonful with some water . . . I can't see, Rex, not properly . . . the key's under my pillow . . . a teaspoonful or I'll sleep all day. Then get me out of this place . . . "

"You've not been bitten . . . stung . . . hurt . . .?" he asked while moving rapidly to do as she had asked, then, while she drank the concoction, he continued, "But what has happened? It smells like six hospitals in here."

"I'll tell you when we're out of this evil place . . ."

"Is Nanny all right? The servants?"

"Oh SHE'S all right, that she-devil, Beelzebub, Moloch, Satan . . . Devil. That one is all right, IF what she IS is all right . . ."

"Where are your clothes, Una? Now you seem to be back to nearly normal hadn't you better put some clothes over your nakedness?"

"Rex!"

"I'll go and wait on the verandah again . . ."

"NO, NO, NO, please, stay. Please, Rex." The urgency and fear in her voice stopped him in his tracks. He returned and sat on Anna's bed, watching while Una walked around the room picking up jodhpurs and shirt, opening drawers and extracting articles of clothing he should not be seeing, correctly; while she stooped and collected, the towel slipped from her shoulders slightly. She laughed, almost giggling,

"Sorry, Rex," she said.

Rex, delighted that the fraught atmosphere had relaxed said, "Oh, that's all right, Una. You've got bumps."

Una was behind the door slats by then, and he heard her giggling, "Have I? Well you've got hairs on your chest," and both of them laughed and laughed recalling that terrifying episode on the Roc, and one which Rex would like to forget, even now. "Nice bumps – bump! I only saw one."

"Rex!" she expostulated. "The army has NOT improved you. You're ruder than Van, even . . . Funny though, he wouldn't DARE say that to me . . . and I wouldn't LET him. You're different . . . I suppose . . ."

"I should jolly well HOPE I AM different from Van. Now COME on. We're taking our tiffin with us . . . I fixed it. Threw your parents out for theirs, shut Nanny in a cupboard, and here we are . . . see?"

157

Rex received another hug, a kiss that landed on one ear, and was almost knocked off his very solid feet by the impetus of the onslaught.

By the time they had mounted the ponies and loaded the unnecessarily large basket of provisions, Una's eyes were focussing correctly once more and she had stopped giggling. They rode in silence, one behind the other, high into the great rock hill, interspersed with small crevice-rooted plants and shrubs. At last Rex called a halt where there were three flowering trees and a tiny trickle of water bubbling from rock to rock. They tethered their steeds in the sparse shade, which Rex accentuated by throwing his numnah, or saddle cloth, high into the centre tree; they hung their saddles over two rather frail, but adequate branches, placed Una's numna on the ground and sat, the basket between them. After a long interval, Rex lit his pipe, removing a small square of turf as he puffed and sucked "my ashtray," he said.

"I KNOW, I REMEMBER Pierre telling you to do that . . ."

"Well, now. While I'm lazily smoking, you UNA can be my dancing girl, my entertainer . . . no, no, no . . . you need not dance. Just tell me about Pierre, then all the others – properly – not just polite for the parents telling – Tell me REALLY, about them all."

Rex knew his cousin, perhaps too well. He knew she would not be able to talk about whatever had happened between herself and Nanny, immediately, if at all to-day, or even tomorrow. First, she needed to talk about family, the things both of them could understand.

"Now," said Una, "Let's eat!" She had told Rex almost all the news, ending with the message from Aunt Aurora that she would cable the family immediately Roxana's boy was born.

"Boy?" asked Rex.

"Oh, it HAS to be a boy. Roxana's going to call him Leo, and Dan agrees. He's going to choose their daughter's name – later, you see Rex."

"I see that you think yourself the Oracle of Delphi . . ."

"I am, Rex. There are things I just KNOW. Like Urjinath. Perhaps he breathed it into me when he made me live, and I don't remember, but Van does. I just KNOW things. Like I know it will be a boy. I think it's the third eye. Like I KNOW

158

that Nanny is EVIL for me, but GOOD for Anna. It was Nanny who made me almost dead that time when I bit Van and she soaped me strapped me and shut me in the bathroom with the snake. And I only bit Van's back because it was so nice; I licked it; it looked nice and it tasted nice and I LOVED Van, so I ate him. That's not so strange for a very little girl, Rex. I was only three – or less, two perhaps; Rolf was a baby in a basket so I might have been only ONE." Una then tried to explain about the morning's trauma with Nanny by saying, "She was strong, like when she held Frank's hand under the boiling tap, but she wasn't BOILING ME; she was, eh INTRUDING, touching, oh I can't explain, Rex . . . feeling me . . . all over. It was DISGUSTING and humiliating . . . and wrong. You know how I HATE being touched, Rex. Only SPECIAL people . . . like family."

"Hmph," said Rex, feeling strangely ill at ease. "What about dancing? What about the ball to-night? People will touch you while you dance . . ."

"Of course, silly! I learnt to dance. It was my bargain with Aunt Rora. I could have lessons at home if I went to dancing lessons and later to tennis lessons. So I did. And I LOVE dancing. That is completely different."

"Yes, I see! Well, what about marrying someone, eh?"

"Oh, Rex, I know all about THAT. I asked Rolf when Roxana got married, and Rolf told me – it's just the same as the ram and the ewes except they cuddle each other one way round and we cuddle the other way round, we humans. Rex, don't you know all this?"

Rex sat up and laughed and laughed and laughed, and Una, without knowing why, joined in his mirth. "I'll go and see to the horses," he said, still laughing, "It's time we started back. Mustn't miss the tea gongs! AH yes," he turned to face her again, "Next time you wash your hair, get Marc to sit outside your room, eh?"

While he was away, Una packed up the remains of the food containers, then wandered towards the edge of the apparently sheer cliff, looking down on the desultory traffic that meandered along the dust road beneath. She did not hear Rex's light-footed return, but felt her untucked shirt pulled from behind, twisted into a rope, and heard her cousin breathe close to her ear, "NEVER, never do that again, Una!" Her foot caught in one of the low-growing tufts of herbage, she stumbled and fell backwards into Rex's arms, both of them overbalancing and sliding on the hard rock beneath their feet. Rex still held the girl in an iron grip, panting, "Never do that! You know better than to stand on the edge of a cliff – that rock is ready to fall any moment; just your weight could do it."

"YOU knocked me down instead," she laughed. "And we might be right on top of a krait."

Still holding the twisted shirt tail, Rex looked around them and under them, for the lethal stick-like snake. Nothing moved on the ground. Flies and the entire airborne world buzzed and flurried above and around them. He was still breathing hard. Unimaginative by nature a vivid picture had flashed across his mind – the picture of a naked child on a rock in the vanguard of a marauding fire, lit by himself.

"Can I? MAY I have my shirt back now, please?" she asked twisting her lithe body so it faced him.

He lifted the excessively long piece of shirt that had almost become a rope in his hand, looked at it, and recovering from the momentary fear he had suffered, bantered, teasing, "YOUR shirt, did you say? Indeed? THIS I may say is MY shirt. MY shirt with MY initials on it, in MY mother's red embroidery thread, stitched by MY mother's fair hand . . ."

"But she gave it to me when you went to the war," laughed Una, knowing that it might appear large on her, but Rex could not even squeeze into it.

"Because MY mother sees fit to bequeath MY possessions to all and sundry does not mean, in law, that those possessions become theirs. I think I'd like MY property returned FORTHWITH – I'll take the contents as interest."

As the young man was speaking, Una contorted her body, and the buttons burst from their button-holes. Rex loosed his hold on the roped material, clutched her tightly close to himself, and, unaware of his own actions, kissed her firmly on her laughing mouth. He let her go almost immediately in a strange haze, heard her say, "I liked that; I'll give it back." And she did.

"And the interest?" asked Rex, still bemused at his own actions

A butterfly flew over them, hovered, and shimmering with a rainbow of colouring disappeared into the sun.

The interest was fairly divided, when Rex pulled the girl to her feet, croaking, "That was very, very nice . . . The nicest kiss I ever had . . ."

"I've never had one, so it's MY nicest too."

They rode in silence back to the bungalow. Rex was thinking that Urjinath did perhaps have a third eye. He was standing watching for them when they rode the ponies into the stables.

"I'll have at least six of your dances to-night, Una; the first, the last two and three in the middle," stipulated Rex as they hurried to the teatable, having heard the first gong ring as they dismounted.

While Rex and Una had been spending one of the most memorable days of their young lives, Nanny sat in her room, exhausted, hurt and bewildered. She sat rubbing the shins a little girl had kicked almost twelve years earlier and her small mouth squeezed into an even smaller split, creasing her cheeks and the fleshy skin below the mouth, pulling her cheeks down-wards into valleys and hills that met on the hard little protuberance that was her chin. She would give her life for this family; she had served them for most of her life and they had always been good and kind to her, never treating her as a servant, or one subservient. This was all the real family she had ever known. Somewhere in the almost buried past there had been a frightened little mother – a thin, scraggy, mousey haired little under-sized person, and there had been a big, rough sea-going father, who, unhappily returned periodically. There had been a neat little house in a long row of neat little houses on the edge of a harbour wall. The neat little, shining house suddenly became an inferno of noise and destruction as periodically as the big sea-going man returned to it. Then china and furniture lay in fragments all over the four rooms, and the frail little mother was marred by bruises. Her screams were stifled with a big red hand while her body was pulverised and worse, treated to the most unbelievable humiliations, and the child even dragged from her bed to sit shivering

161

and watching. When the man turned his attentions on her, the child, bruised, bewildered and terrified had sought refuge with the local vicar, where she acted as an unpaid nursemaid to the children of the vicarage until a place was found for her – with the O'Donaty family. She had travelled with a mission school-teacher and his wife and two children, to this haven, this heavenly existence and this easy-going household. For almost ten years she had looked after the mistress, then, on her marriage, and the rapid arrival of children, she had become their Nanny. She had loved each of the children, but the twins defied and defeated her, and something inside her, deep inside her, seemed to enact the cruelties she had witnessed herself as a child – but only against the one child – Una. Had she had the mental capacity to do so she would have arrived at the conclusion that this girl reminded her of herself: her fragile body, her screams during the night, even her ungovernable temper tantrums were like herself – and like the mother she lived with when the man was away at sea. She passed the twins to Urjinath whom she feared, but respected, and poured her frustrated maternal instincts over Rolf; he became her doll; he neither walked, nor talked, nor even crawled, thanks to her ministrations. She loved him with the tenacity of the possessiveness of the jackal. When the beloved doll was six years old he was taken away and another doll had replaced him, and had not been taken away. Anna was her pearl, her possession, and above all, a pearl of considerable worth; she was the perfection of all the deprived woman had yearned for; this pearl could be exhibited, framed, mounted and constantly moulded, and nothing must ever be allowed to take away this petty power; certainly not a scraggy, mousey haired little nobody. Nanny confused her passionate worship of her charge with love. She did not understand that love gives freedom; she had never watched the swallows – love or instinct – the result was the same.

Nanny rubbed her shins once again, hating herself as much as she hated the girl who had been the centre of attention at the gymkhana – and had no idea how to use it. Her darling would know how to make use of the glory.

It was with relief that Nanny discovered that she would lunch alone with the two younger children, and have them to herself most of the afternoon.

As the family separated after tea, Anna nudged Una saying, "I'll have the bathroom first, IF you can get rid of that disgusting smell of carbolic. What did you do, Una, cut yourself?"

Una flushed and said, "No, I just can't abide the stink of jasmine, that filled the room. Sorry! I scrubbed it from ME with that pink carbolic."

"Now Una, dear," her mother gently admonished, "We don't use that sort of language out here."

"Sorry, mother!" she replied, unaware of what she had said.

"What did I say?" she asked Marc and Rex as they walked along their verandah in the wake of Anna.

"Stink!" said Marc. "You know, I smell, you stink, he, she and its stinks and smells! Ha, ha, ha. No lessons to-night and I'm off to the Padre. We're having a midnight feast, Mark, Paul and me!"

Una avoided being anywhere near Nanny from then on. She walked out of her room when the other walked in. She sat as far as possible from her whenever she had any choice. She even avoided walking on her shadow. Above all she barricaded the bathroom door with both stools, effectively obstructing any silent or swift entry.

While the family readied themselves for the ball, and Una exchanged the priceless pearls she had received on her third birthday from an unknown Rajah, with her sister for a cut glass sphere on a gold chain, police in all the cities where the satyagraha was being followed, arrested and imprisoned vast numbers of the peaceful demonstrators. While Una plaited her hair and wound the two long plaits across her head, 'putting her hair up' for the first time, peaceful demonstrators were being bound or manacled in dingy cells. While the two girls admired each other and were in turn admired by the adults, peaceful demonstrators were, in a few instances, being stripped naked whilst being interrogated without regard to their religious scruples regarding the exposure of their bodies – especially to those of an inferior caste, or to an alien and foreign power. The family party drove off in a hired gharrie, resplendent in uniform or gorgeous in attire, and watched by the immaculate retired Ressaldar Major, bursting with pride in them and for them.

Chapter Ten

The morning after the ball, only Rex, Marc and Una rode
out before breakfast. It was a silent ride. Marc's midnight
feast had been ruined by the Padre's wife, Mrs. Grayson,
discovering the hoarded food, removing it, and leaving an
admonitory note in the tin in which the store had been
concealed. Una was filled with the glow that follows any
girl's first social engagement; she had danced every dance;
young men had queued up to sign her dance card and she
had been invited — several times — to visit the kala jugga,
the black place, where she saw couples sitting close together,
almost concealed behind screens and potted shrubs; Rex
had said she must on no account do so, and she had obeyed
Rex. He had walked her outside when she needed air after
eating too many savouries that were handed around. To
Una it was like living in some fairy tale world, unreal and
theatrical. She had told Rex that she felt like Cinderella, but
he had only laughed and told her she would soon lose her
freshness and become like the other young ladies, languid
and brittle and always searching for some new diversion. She
had been most surprised at how well Rex danced, and they
moved together with ease, able to listen to the music and the
rhythm because they had no need to talk. Rex also thought
about the previous evening's ball as he rode ahead of the
brother and sister. He had been taken aback at his cousin's
appearance when she emerged from her room. He thought
her beautiful that evening; the rich gold dress enhanced her
dark colouring and seemed to shimmer in the glittering
green eyes. Even Nanny, he recalled, had gasped when the
goldsheathed girl stepped lightly into view with that multicoloured hair swathed around her head like a turban in a

165

very out-dated style. Perhaps nobody had appreciated the beautiful lines of the girl's face when her untidy hair seemed to spring across it from all directions. Rex's silence was mostly due to the fact that he left for the Frontier next day and she, HIS little cousin, would be at the mercy of all the other young subaltern locusts, not only in Peshawar, but in Simla where they were about to go, and then in Srinagar, and finally Bombay, before they sailed for Tasmania. On the other hand she might be plucked from the nest before the family sailed. A lot could happen in India in three months. The party returned as silently as it had left.

After breakfast Una found herself left to her own devices. Rex had gone to the bazaar and had not offered to take her, so she sat swinging her legs, perched on the verandah rail watching the preparations for the evening's dinner party through the double doors that had been propped open. The great circular table had been dissected by means of a huge handle, like the starting handle of a car, being turned and turned and turned, then reconstructed by the insertion of matching boards that had, it seemed, been cradled beneath the spherical disc. It became a table, though highly polished, exactly like their own kitchen table at La Bellule, the Truth Table. Instead of copperware, silver, sharply glittered in the light of the vivid sun. Disconsolately and solitary she awaited the evening with apprehension.

Augustus O'Donaty stood on his verandah feeling irritable. He was immaculately dressed for dinner, much earlier than was necessary and without enthusiasm for the evening during which he was obliged to entertain some writer woman he did not know, nor wished to know, her niece about whom he knew absolutely nothing, and, to complete his misery, the Padre and the excellent Mrs. Grayson whom he knew only too well. He would have preferred a quiet evening with his wife, two daughters, his nephew and his son, but he was expected to entertain these confounded women with his memories, regurgitate experiences he would prefer to forget and many that he had tried to forget besides the more recent events that he had almost forgotten. Other more flamboyant and loquacious men had told the stories — Roberts of the Bengal Artillery made Earl of Kandahar, Nicholson of the Kashmir Gate,

166

Wyllie and the others who had been, like himself, outside Delhi; they may not have recounted their own tales, certainly not Nicholson who died in the breach of the Kashmir Gate, but by their very exploits of extreme bravery their lives had been recorded, rewarded and recounted many times. They were different. He, Augustus, was a plodder, unimaginative and obedient to the letter of the law, be it army or civilian. These women would find nothing in HIS life of the deeds of daring and verve; only the story of one who had climbed steadily up the promotion ladder, often stepping into dead-men's shoes. He had nothing to offer journalists except a formidable list of campaigns from the march on Delhi from Madras, through to Lucknow, from Afghanistan to Bengal and from Burma to the Punjab, always successfully increasing British rule, widening her dominions and being rewarded with a line of medals, steady promotion and inevitably, loneliness. What could he tell these people that they could not find out from the London Gazette, army records and the records of the one time East India Company with which he had originally served. He had become an old man and was about to leave forever the country he loved, the only land he had ever really known, the birthplace of six of his seven children and the place where he had met and married the woman who had come out to marry his own younger brother. He was about to return to the land of his own birth, to enrich the soil of the earth that had bred him, but ejected him after ten years into an alien and terrifying world, bereft of his mother and adoring sisters forever. Bereft of any woman until, late in life, he had married, bred his children and discarded them to the care of another, far across the sea — the two who had remained would shortly, at his wife's insistence also be transported to the opposite side of the world from where he would be disintegrating.

Disintegrating he may be, but the old veteran still stood at his full height, short though it was, as erect as the day he had been enrolled at military school — aged eleven. His white hair was just beginning to thin, but his snowy moustache still burst across his firm, long upper lip and his eyebrows curled up to meet the white thatch above, beneath

167

which the once hazel eyes, glittered pale green and horizon-focussed.

He saw two figures emerge from the shadows cast by the deodars and felt the vibrations beneath his feet as the ponies clattered into the compound. He heard no sound of either voices or hooves. His deafness had become more than a slight annoyance; it was the mark of his impending disintegration, it imprisoned him as surely as a barred cage and it made social evenings such as he anticipated with some vexation, both a torment and a humiliation. His beloved Tera would answer questions that he was unable to hear, but she could not, and should not, know anything about the life of a man in action. He supposed this interfering writer woman would want gore and gallantry, not the foot-slogging in clothing unsuitable for the heat of this land, of men dying on the march, sleeping on the march, of dust and filth and the bungles of non-existent re-inforcements, of food, water and tents. He slipped quietly down the rotting steps and into the garden, out of sight of the two young people, his moustache twitching at his angry thoughts. He felt that he would be polluting himself if he recounted his life history; it was HIS; HE had lived it. However, he knew that he could deny his wife nothing, so if she invited some busy-body to dinner to plague him with her questions he would have to try and answer them, and one day, not too far distant, his wife would be alone and still a comparatively young woman. For that, as well as for marrying him at all, he owed her more than he could ever repay. His thoughts wandered to the two young people he had seen ride into the back of the house. Tera planned to marry the girl off to some successful officer as she had planned that the beautiful little Anna should go to England to be polished after presenting her to Tasmania, that their youngest son should be educated like his brothers before following in his father's footsteps, and returned to this land to become, all in the fullness of time, a General of some prestigious regiment — not some native field force as he had been. There was one thing she had not considered, the wishes and the will of their offspring. There was another thing she could not consider — that India in its present form, under British rule, may not exist much longer.

There was no sign of the two riders so he assumed they had crossed the verandah and were preparing for the evening. He would miss his nephew, he knew, fondly imagining that each of his stranger-sons were like him; silent when silence was all that was required; ambitious probably; a strong sense of duty — and a good polo player. Perhaps he should do something before he was forgotten, to further the young man; nepotism, but never mind. An allowance would help him pay mess bills — and marry rather earlier than he had himself.

General O'Donaty felt less harassed at the thought of doing something useful and when Tera glided on to the verandah from the dining room beyond, his eyes were alight with anticipation, becoming almost adoration as they re-focussed on the magnificent vision that was his wife. Together they awaited the arrival of their guests.

While they walked to their rooms from the stables Rex said to Una, "Look here, there's a tremendous ritual about your father's dinner parties. Come to my room when you're dressed, we'll have a drink together and I'll explain it all to you. I've had MY orders, and you and I are to emerge for the fray together . . . ah, and it's all right YOU coming to MY room. My chairs have been placed in the doorway AND whisky and a decanter of barley water for you . . . and, before I forget . . . hm, would you like to see the sunrise over the mountains because we can ride out very early tomorrow and you'll see it — before you go south . . . and eh, I go elsewhere."

"You think of the most wonderful things, Rex," said Una, grabbing at his arm. "Oh you really do have good ideas. You understand how much I want to see EVERYTHING."

"Of course," he acknowledged, "just you remember young Una, I am the greatest, the thinker of thoughtful ideas and planner of great events, me."

Una was so quick bathing and changing that she arrived whilst Rex was still wrapped in a towel and shaving. "Oh good, Rex, now I've caught YOU in a towel. Now we're equal."

"Are we? well you just sit in the doorway like a well brought up young lady, while I pour myself into this paraphernalia that duty demands I don this evening."

169

"Can't I watch you shave, even? You look like the Hermit or Urji with all that soap all over your face. You've even given yourself a white beard. MOST unbecoming. . ."

"NO! Go and sit in your purdah place. You're upsetting me and I don't need blood streaking my handsome visage, on this, my last evening of leave."

She WAS upsetting him. Her hair was once more in a turban-coil, and she was not his little cousin any longer. She was a young lady, and a very desirable young lady. Rex was bewildered as he had been for several days.

By the time Rex sat down with her, Una had lost her excitement and was ready to listen seriously to the instructions while Rex smoked and drank his chota peg.

"Here we are, then," he said. "EXACTLY one half hour after the tonga rolls into the driveway, we will hear Nanny plod along the verandah, well, we'll see her, as she must pass us, and that should precede the arrival of the Graysons by about five minutes, after which we wait fifteen minutes then make our appearance, and another ten minutes later Anna and Marc will arrive. The meal should commence some ten minutes after THAT."

"I should think we'll all be starving by then."

"Oh, no. It all begins quite soon. You see your father still has the old idea about not drinking anything but tea after the meal, so his generation did all the drinking FIRST."

"But Rex, does EVERY household have this sort of army discipline in the home?"

"No, of course not. Your mother devised it when he began to go deaf. This way he can do all the niceties of the host and concentrate on newcomers one by one. He can hear your mother's voice, and Anna's and Nanny's and Marc's, but he can't hear the deeper pitched voices like yours and Mrs. Graysons and I doubt if he'll hear that Miss Law. It must be terrible at Regimental Farewell Dinners where they are men. I think he will be really glad to get to Tasmania and throw off his Generalship. He's the last survivor of a very tough breed, you know. All the fellows who were young officers at Delhi during the Mutiny are dead, I think. Robert's death when just putting morale into the troops in the trenches upset the old man, terribly. Anyway there's always a reason behind everything that goes on under this roof, Una . . . Funny, me telling you about YOUR home and YOUR parents, really."

"My home is really La Bellule, Rex . . . and my mother seems to be more Aunt Aurora, really . . . I don't fit this sort of life. . ."

"You've only been here four days, silly. Now then, about dinner. It'll go on and on. ALL the servants will be running around, just like a Mess dinner, and I expect there'll be about five courses, then, before the dessert, Marc will depart; Anna is allowed to eat one thing, then she has to leave, and usually Nanny follows her. Then we sit over dessert until your mother gives you a LOOK and a NOD, and she'll rise and invite the ladies to follow. You HAVE to go to the drawing room, Una, and drink tea; sometimes Nanny returns for the tea. NOW two VERY IMPORTANT things. Until the dessert the conversation is general; after that, with no servants around and the doors closed, anything may be said. The other thing is the wine, Una. Anna and Marc are given barley water or some other drink, but you'll be served wine. It's not like our homemade stuff at La Bellule; take small sips and not your usual great swigs, because your glass HAS to be filled up every time it's empty and if you drink it all as you do at home, you'll be DRUNK and shame ALL of us."

"Well, you've made me so nervous I'll drop EVERYTHING, and I'll NEVER be a burra-memsahib . . . and I don't want to be one either."

"You look really quite stunning when you're angry, little non-burra mem-non-sahib," Rex concluded as Nanny 'plodded' past.

While Rex was educating his cousin in the ways of her father's household the General, to his surprise was entertaining two delightful women. He could even hear what they were saying with considerable effort and by watching their lips as the sound penetrated. They had congratulated him on his wonderful daughters, Mrs. Hope adding, "They're like the sun and the moon, day and night, so different, yet both so attractive."

"You won't have any problem FINDING them husbands, General," Miss Law said, "Your problem will be to keep the potential spouses away from them."

"And at least one of them so talented," Mrs. Hope assured him.

"Which one?" the General enquired, having not considered 'talent' as a particular adjunct to womanhood.

"Oh Una, General. She draws, she writes, it seems she rides and dances superbly well. Quite a diversity of talents, in my opinion."

Nanny had entered at that point, and heard the final remark. After the introductions had been completed and a few polite interchanges taken place the Graysons arrived, and very shortly the General, sitting beside his wife was able to relax and listen to Mrs. Hope and his wife discussing books. It no longer mattered whether he heard accurately or not, because his wife, the wonderful Tera, would assuredly manage to keep any pressure from his aged shoulders, or more correctly, his aged ears. He gathered Mrs. Hope was asking about the life of women married to service men — not only Generals and Officers, but the other ranks, the ill-used ranker and N.C.O. Then, after answering the questions as fairly as she was able, the old man heard Tera ask her question.

"Why do you come back again and again to this country, Mrs. Hope?"

"For several reasons," the writer replied. "There is SO much to write about and each book takes so long to write and even longer to correct. . ."

Miss Law intervened, "You see Mrs. O'Donaty, I CANNOT SPELL. I type all the books, and my aunt has beautiful clear, large handwriting, but I CANNOT copy the words, the letters of the words, in the correct order. I think I have a piece of my brain missing; all the letters get typed, but it becomes a veritable jigsaw for my aunt to decipher — or her editor. . ."

"As a matter of fact," Mrs. Hope continued, "we wondered if you would lend Una to US while you complete your grand tour? IF she was willing, of course. We travelled from England with her, sat at the Captain's table with her and we came to know each other quite well. She has probably told you, we went ashore together at Aden. IF she would learn to type, I'm sure she could type my latest book as I write it. . .?"

Nanny heard and beamed inwardly.

172

"Ask Una herself first, Mrs. Hope," said the General. "Ah here she comes."

Una was at first bewildered and embarrassed by the attention and the silence while everyone waited for her reply, which was an emphatic, "But, Mrs. Hope, I would just love to do it — if you think I really could do it."

"Of course, you can do it, Una," said the beaming lady.

As Rex later described the occasion to Una. "Everybody beamed. Nanny was like a cat with a saucer of cream and half a shark. Mrs. hope was obviously delighted. Miss Law was relieved. Your mother looked as if she had shed a load, and your father seemed to beam with pride in his hopeless little daughter — and even Mrs. Grayson beamed. I can't think why."

Tera, the practical asked, "But Mrs. Hope, Una isn't QUALIFIED for ANYTHING. She has had little schooling — as she has doubtless told you. She is excessively proud of her expulsion from school. . ."

Mrs. Hope snorted. "Expelled for that poem! Expelled for writing a poem! A mere thirteen year old. . .!"

"She was twelve, actually," Rex spoke up for the first time. "She's more qualified than most young ladies out here. She has matric haven't you Una? Mother wrote and told me so."

With the entry of Anna and Marc, a whole life had been altered.

After the silent-footed servants had been dismissed with a nod from Urji and he had withdrawn from the room with his habitual dignity, the family and their guests remained seated around the table, idly picking or peeling fruit, cracking nuts and sipping the light wine. Augustus had managed to evade questions by acting out the part of the perfect host; introducing topics of general interest by posing the queries himself. The past week's social round had been discussed, comments made and performances credited — all knew that whatever was said could be imparted from one back-quarter to another, from house to house and all around the bazaar, so nothing more than glowing or mediocre remarks issued. By the time they were alone and the dessert remained as their only uniting subject they had re-lived the gymkhana, the polo match, the ball and the newly arrived Highland Regiment and the old General knew

173

that he would shortly come under siege. He cracked a walnut into two neat sections, extracted the kernel and began to munch where teeth still remained in his mouth, watching his wife closely. He saw her brief nodding remark to Anna and to young Marc, both of whom promptly rose from their seats, one with the same grace as his wife, the other like the awkward colt he was, made their excuses, adieus and departed followed by the pompous nanny.

He continued watching his wife after the impact of their departure had subsided and he heard distantly some sound made by the lady sitting at his right hand. He watched the lips he knew so well, mouth the words, "Mrs. Hope says 'How did you come to serve in the army out here in the first place?'" He chuckled. There was a story he could remember in each and every minute detail and with greater clarity than he was able to recall last week's polo, or the Coronation Durbar at Delhi eight years earlier, or even Kings Edward's Durbar eight years before that. "I didn't exactly COME here; I was SENT here; I am probably still here for the same reason that I WAS sent — because I was the runt of the litter," he laughed without bitterness, but the faintest touch of cynicism. He continued, "Too small to be of much use to anyone, BUT also too small to be singled out for demolition by snipers or assassins, unlike my father and two of my brothers. Huh, my father didn't even notice I was born — too concerned with my strong, healthy brother, my twin, born AFTER ME, but registered as the elder of his sons, WHEN I had refused to die." Augustus noticed the interested eyes watching him, all round his huge oval table, felt some stirring inside himself, some alien desire to recount that part of his history. He had noticed that his taciturnity had been hard to hold on to as his deafness and age increased, and frequently wondered if it was a sign of the proximity of death or merely the wandering of an aged and well-stored mind, but whatever the cause or effect he felt inclined to recount events he had barely thought about for nearly seventy years and a man he firmly believed he hated; the man who was his own father.

"He was a rogue, my father; not only a rogue, but a huge fellow, tall as Urji, thin as a pole and as strong as an ox, besides being handsome, extrovert, gregarious and a gifted story-teller. The tales he told, chanted or sang to us children all sounded like true adventure stories, and all were about his own ancestors — or so he claimed. He chanted the probably mythical account of a rowing race to find a new land — Ulster — and how the captain in the other boat cut off his own hand and threw it on the shore to claim possession; according to my father his ancestors' boat would have been first to beach. He sang us another song about one of the old sea warriors; he sang it over and over again until we learnt it and sang with him." The old land warrior leaned forward slightly, and, his voice creaking with age, but still tuneful, he half sang, half chanted:

"Tall and straight as a sapling spruce with eyes horizon turning,
Golden hair of his Nordic race, skin with sunray burning.
Born a prince of the northern lands, lands of splintered coastline,
Golden lights of the summer nights, lands of midnight sunshine.
Prince in line of the rich Sea Kings, rich, and gold-band givers;
Pride in place and his lordly race, lord of seas and rivers.
Break of light in the winter night men came fiercely crying,
Berserk fights in the flaming lights of homes and Norsemen dying.
Heir at dawn of his father's throne, hills of slender spruce trees,
Timber halls and longboat thralls, now the lord of the seas.
King of dust in the noonday sun, eyes bewildered, burning;
Child of three on a burial mound, eyes awash with yearning.
Sold a slave where the Volga flows, sold by berserk raiders;
Princely air and horizon stare slave of Volga traders.
Youth of grace in a noble place, youth of rapid learning;
Healing sore of his blazing door, eyes ambition burning.
Pride of place in the longboat race, prince of oar-blade dancing,
Learnt the Code of the Viking road — eyes horizon glancing.
Held as bride his ruler's pride, hearts aflame with wonder;
Wedded bliss from the first shy kiss too swiftly torn asunder.

Three years wed and the bride lay dead, love forever
    sleeping;
Frozen tears for the unlived years, grief too deep for
    weeping.
Shrouded pall and the ocean squall, slender longboat
    beaching;
Icy eyes under leaden skies wildly longblade reaching.
Prince of grief for a love so brief, eyes of berserk blazing;
Flaming path to usurper's hearth, return to land of raising.
King by right in the sunlit night, Lord of fiord and river,
Viking Law and the ocean's roar, Chief, and gold-band
    giver.
Eyes turned west in the golden quest, gold and new lands
    founding;
Rewarding search in the Saxon church, gold and faith
    abounding.
War withheld for the Saxon geld, Christ and the Crucifixion;
Took the Host and the Holy Ghost, and a Bishop's
    benediction.
Forced the Creed on his Nordic breed, sons of land diurnal,
Ousting Thor, razing Odin's lore — faith in God Eternal.
King of lands and sunsplit strands reft by warring nations;
Final sight of the Northern Light in ocean immolation.
Stiff and tall in a funeral pall, regal longboat blazing;
Life at rest on a briny crest — eyes horizon glazing."

There was a brief silence and then the old warrior
continued with the saga that might or might not be the
history of his own ancestors. "That Olaf left a son behind at
some place, along the Volga; the child who had been the
cause of his wife's death. Before he sailed away with his
oarsman though, he had a gold chain forged around the
baby's neck and from it he hung five gold rings — the rings
he had worn around *his* neck when *his* home was left in
ruins, and had managed to keep in his possession even as a
slave of the king of the Volga, predecessor of the Cossacks
probably. When the chain became too tight and the child
pleaded to be released from its embrace, no person would
help him until, in pain and desperation the boy toddled into
the hovel of some old crone who took pity on him and bit
through the links of the chain until it was free from his
strangling neck. In gratitude he gave her the broken chain

to repair the teeth she had broken as she gnawed. The giving of gold has ever been a sign, a symbol of some agreement so the grateful woman is supposed to have told the boy that the significance of the five rings was that somewhere his kingdom would lie among either five rivers or five fingers of land jutting into the sea. So, in the fullness of time the boy became a man, built a boat, encouraged other adventurous young men to join him and set out upon the search, but, through the giving of gold to the ancient woman he had continued visiting her and she, on her part had filled his head with ancient tales, even older than herself, her mother her grandmother and her great grandmother — as old as man she told him. Because of the long stories that he had memorized through constant repetition the boy believed himself to be descended from kings, and more, descended from kings with the gift of song and story — a royal scald in fact being his most distant ancestor; one who had been rewarded originally with gold, like a warrior and leader of men, but instead of arm rings, the reward was finger rings. Each ring had a flattened upper side on which was engraved a four-winged dragon — a dragonfly — with five stars marking wing tips, head, thorax and tail and on the underside of the flattened disc was another dragonfly flying in the opposite direction and with only four stars, the thorax one being omitted. Now had there been only one ring we would assume the difference was some accident, but there were FIVE, each identical with the others — and here IS one." He held his right hand across the table, fingers turned slightly to the palm, indicating the heavy gold signet ring on his small finger.

"Can't take it off, I'm afraid. Enough trouble pushing it on. Knuckles get larger and fingers get thinner with age, it seems. Carried it on a watch chain under my uniform until I was finally put out to grass."

Each person seated at the table leant forward and looked at the very clearcut engraving decorating the General's hand, while he spoke in his normal laconic way. The story had gripped them like any fairy-tale, but the exposure of the ring had given it some memorably dramatic effect, stencilling the whole occasion on to their minds. His hand back on his knee and out of sight, the guests beginning to

177

wonder if the performance was at an end the punkah having ceased its monotonous whirring, he threw another pebble into the pool of interest that surrounded him. "Tera, my dear," he said turning to her, "would you show our friends your locket?"

Slowly and gracefully Tera removed the golden locket on its fragile chain from her neck, ensuring that not a hair was disarranged as she did so, then clicked it open and passed the flat, light disc to Mrs. Hope, from whom it circulated accompanied by the occasional intake of breath by those to whom it was quite new. The General stood up, walked across the room, stamped once at each end and, as by magic, the punkahs began to whirr with considerable energy. When he re-seated himself he asked his wife to tell the story of her home, of La Bellule, the extraordinary carving in the arch and her meeting with his young brothers. "You see," he said to them all, "I did not give that locket to my wife, neither did either of my brothers. She and her sister have one each, given to them by their father when they married, as their mother had requested. They must pass them on to their daughters. Well, of course, Rex, young fellow, Roxana must already have your mother's, eh?" Una replied for her cousin, for she had been at the wedding and remembered vividly Roxana's joy at receiving a much coveted treasure.

"Yes, I remember the moment when Aunt Aurora gave Roxana the locket, but I've only just this moment seen the significance of the two dragonflies." Una had flushed a brilliant red while she spoke, but she had to go on, in spite of the circle of eyes glued to her burning cheeks and glowing eyes. "The dragonfly with the five stars is the Odonata with the Northern Cross embedded in its wings and body. The other way up it would be the constellation Cygnus, the Swan, apart from the missing star, but it IS the Southern Cross . . . eh . . . um . . . well it must have been designed, if not made, by some traveller who had crossed from one hemisphere into the other, wouldn't it? I'm not sure about it, but I THINK you can't see one of the crosses from the other half of the world . . . I . . . er don't really know much about stars; only what I've seen really, and the Children's Encyclopedia."

Tera passed the locket around the table again, then rehung it around her neck, stared hard at the daughter to whom she would have to give it, hand it over forever, and unwillingly, but she had promised to do so. She rose from the table saying, "We will leave you gentlemen to smoke," and, followed by the other ladies led the way into the drawing room where the lamps had been positioned in such a way that the creatures — moths, mosquitoes and flying beetles hypnotised by the bright glow remained some distance from the area containing the usual cushioned bamboo chairs. The three visiting ladies asked numerous questions which Tera, in her element, answered factually and with no attempt at exaggeration or additions. It was such an unlikely romance, the basis for some highly flavoured novel, but nevertheless strictly true. The two handsome young men HAD stood inside the strange entrance to La Bellule, looking at the great sculptured dragonfly above their heads; they HAD assisted her father in the cowshed and remained for supper; they HAD both proposed to the two sisters shut away by their shyness, their distance from other families and their father's necessity to fill with work more hours than there were in a day. "Of course," the hostess added, when the questioning had finally been exhausted, "it is possible that the two young men had been TOLD of the existence of the bellule in our farm entrance, and that they had also heard that there were two unattached young ladies of their own age, almost sequestered within the walls of that dreary old house. The island is very SMALL, by most standards, and most people know most of what is going on elsewhere. We were isolated by rarely going into town, but noticed at church every Sunday." Thus did Tera, in her habitual practical manner and orderly thoughts destroy for her listeners any suspicion of strangeness or of the supernatural.

Una was sitting with the ladies, but not hearing the words her mother was speaking. She was planning a series of pictures she would draw, illustrating the extraordinary saga her father had just recounted. She had visualized a picture in which a dragonfly rested on a smooth stretch of water with a demoiselle fly superimposed over it, thus she would have the two insects with their wings in different positions, the one with the wings open and the superimposed with its wings folded above its back; if she curved the body, the outline would become that of a swan, a cygnet, and the open wings, a line of long oars while the folded wings would represent the sails of a Viking Longboat. In the sky she could draw the Northern Cross, and, by positioning it carefully, make it reflect only four stars, thus creating the Southern Cross in the water. She wished she could escape and make the sketches at once . . . she was trying to work into the whole the five gold rings. Perhaps they could be large globules of dew on the folded wings of the demoiselle-fly, perhaps they could be hoops around the body of the great dragonfly!

There was something else she had not mentioned — afraid she might be showing off . . . each of the Odonatas in the locket had five ovals, or elongated rings holding the thin glass to the golden case . . . She would surround her picture with five thin ovals as a frame, perhaps coloured like the rainbow. Her mother's voice impinged on her thoughts.

". . . of course they were distantly related as were my two grandparents. You see ladies, where I used to live and where my sister still lives, is on a low-lying part of the island, that was regularly, and still is at very high tides, cut off from the main island, and at one time there were several La Bellule's with adjoining properties. Now, with the incorporation of at least two other farms, there remains just one family bearing the name."

Mrs. Hope asked, "Has nobody ever thought of researching into the family and the lockets?"

"It IS possible that my father did — but nobody has ever looked through his writings. There was nobody to do it after Leo's death; the farm took a lot of time and energy. . ."

Una heard her own voice asking, "Couldn't Frank do it?" Her ears felt hot at the sound of her words that seemed to ricochet across the room, and she sank deeper into her chair as the three men came through the double, open doors.

Tea, silver kettle and tray appeared, carried by the inconspicuous house-boys, and once the cups and sugar were dispensed the old General had been persuaded to continue his saga. "Which," Tera suggested, "might well be researched into by Frank — as well as the La Bellule Treasure!" She laughed. Tera was convinced that the idea was her own, and that it was born of a genuine desire to help her armless son.

"Frank you say?" boomed the young man's father. "Just what the boy needs; get him out of himself; give him something to do. Give him something to think about besides himself."

Una O'Donaty winced. A steaming tap, a hand, a sleeve flapping!

"According to 'the most charming rogue in Tasmania'" began Augustus, "my father, OUR ancestor set off with the five gold rings and searched the world for the five fingers of land or five rivers. They called the land Tir Tairngiré — the Land of Promise. They saw Greece as a land with fingers in the sea, but found kinsmen already living there; they followed the Mediterranean coast to coast, went northward along the Scandinavian coasts, but there they found hundreds of fingers in the sea, and unfriendly kinsmen. They settled for years in Ireland where, at Kerry, they found the five fingers pointing south into the sea. They bred generations in the hills and coves and each son set off on his own adventures; sons with names like Red Bodb, Aed and twin boys called Fiachra and Conn, each following his own course in the search for the Tir Tairngiré. My father said we were descended from Red who left other sons in other parts of the world, but still kept in his own possession the five rings until several of them took ship with Dampier landing in Australia. They quarrelled and went their various ways, or were destroyed by the climate, until eventually the five rings arrived in India, and my father was born to inherit them — in the Punjab, the Land of the Five Rivers. How he came to Tasmania I have no idea. Wouldn't be surprised if he sailed or rowed from Malaya in a coracle, or corwg as he called them. I watched him make one — a coracle — when I was a very small child. There was nothing that man could not do, and there was one thing he would not do — part with those gold rings except to his sons; even then he may not have given them to us. He was dead long before I came of age and before young Rex, my brother, was born. All we know of that man, our father, is what he told us — his sagas and the fact that he was born in the Punjab the year of Pitt's India

Act, and that he was one of the first people to take up the Land Grants in Tasmania when they were depositing convicts there AND how to know if we found the precious Tir Tairngiré — by the rings! Uncanny, heathenish, I call it, eh Padre?"

While the story-teller sipped his tea the clergyman nodded benignly. He was well accustomed to stories of pagan beliefs and superstitions. He had served in many parts of the world and was long past being surprised — even by the fanaticism and credulity he met among his own flock. "Did he find his five rivers or five fingers of land in Tasmania, then?" he said in his well-trained pulpit and parade ground voice.

"No. Only a mountain of some five thousand feet and a river and its estuary — and bush; plenty of bush and scrub. No gold. It was his search for gold that killed him in the end, but first he gained land and begat, as the bible says, sons — and daughters. In those early days, and but briefly, a man could claim a piece of land that he could walk round in a day; I suppose to ensure he could maintain his fences and defend it himself. That rogue, my father, set up his tent with food and drink, installed his two witnesses and set off with his ball of yarn — RUNNING. For twenty-four hours he ran! He took the sultry river as his boundary and he ran, unwinding his cord like Theseus in the labyrinth, through scrub, bush, prickly pear, long hard grass and amongst trees. He ran and while he ran he stretched his arm out at intervals and nicked trees with his long knife, an arm's length from his cord; a tall man's long arm's length. He ran with his long loping strides up hillocks, down small valleys and high into the mountain. That man ran for a whole day — a day of twenty-four hours — then claimed the land he had circumnavigated, and received the lease. After a sleep he walked with an axe around his new property and cut down each nicked tree or shrub, building a rough fence as he went. Work it out! The scoundrel had gained some few acres. After fencing his kingdom he 'found' or acquired or probably stole or rustled a few sheep, cattle, pigs, goats, hens — whatever immigrant ships or immigrants brought in, then told his livestock to go away and multiply. And, believe me, my friends, they did. By the time he had built a dwelling place his land was stocked and all he had to do was tame the creatures.

"And what a dwelling place that man built. Not one of your wooden colonial bungalows, like this, like all other settlers build for themselves. Oh, not my father! HE built a great stone fortress. Dug stone and rock from the ground he owned, dug sand from the estuary and carried it about twenty miles on his back perhaps. No idea HOW he built that monstrous place. If fitted into the lower slopes of the mountain, Legge's Tor, so it was two storeyed at the front; three storeyed almost, if you count the byre underneath where the house trained cows were kept. Massive steps led up to a heavy door inside which there was just one vast room with a curving staircase leading to some sort of balcony from which three small rooms were recessed — into the actual wall I rather think — and under the high-pitched roof. I remember there was a huge curved fireplace at one end of the downstairs room into which a black range had been fitted, while at the other end was an identical arch that led into a tower with ladders up to a tesselated top; exactly like some mediaeval castle turret. Inside that strange place were floors, three, I think, used as storerooms, but the ground floor looked like some tiny chapel with small arched niches all the way around the thick walls, between the slit-thin windows, glazed with old bottles, would you believe it? What strange fiendish idea took hold of the man who can tell, but he installed little idols in each of the niches —, including, Padre, a crucifix; there were Hindu gods and goddesses, a Buddha, a seven-branched candlestick with a star of David, oh, all manner of bazaar oddities AND in one there was a really beautiful dragonfly on a sphere; perched on a sphere as if it were resting on some bullrush, all carved from a single piece of pure white stone — onyx, quartz, alabaster, something of that sort. As a child I loved that sanctuary, as my father called it, but now I am an old man I begin to wonder if perhaps, he was hedging his bets — ensuring his future life in eternity. He was some pagan, of that I am convinced."

His audience was still attentive, even eager. He had seen as yet, no hand covering a stifled yawn, no feet fidgeting, no movement except to brush off the attentions of an over-curious fly or mosquito. After some considerable silent time Augustus added, "The church didn't like the sanctuary. Objected vocally and often, but since there was no altar, no sign of sacrilege, or witchcraft, they went away and more or less washed their hands of the sinner while de-polluting the area with the building of an Anglican church around which a flourishing little community had been growing, mostly Cornishmen. Called the place St. Mary's. My heathen father called HIS place Odin Hall. He used to tell US that our name should be Odinaty, loved of Odin, but the signet ring HE always swore had ODINATA engraved on the edge of the seal — too small to see without a powerful magnifying glass. And, that my patient and long-suffering friends that is the scientific name for the dragonfly family, is it not?"

"Is the house still there?" enquired the gentle Mrs. Grayson, fascinated and bewildered by the loquacity of this man she and her husband had known for some twenty years or so and yet had not known at all.

Augustus had not heard the words except the one word — house. Tera nodded encouragement while she poured more tea for their guests. "A house," he began hopefully, "is, according to my father, a shell; and that is all our house was, an empty shell — then. I doubt if it's much different now, with only my brother Alexander to occupy it, and he an old man like me." He laughed, "but one hour younger than me, do not let us forget; one hour younger, whatever his birth registration decrees. I have our baptism certificates, ha! Yes, a house is a shell for a family to use as a retreat, as protection like a crab or a snail, but a REAL HOUSE, he used to say is a FAMILY. A BLOOD LINE. 'We,' he used to say, 'are The House of Odin or Odonity or even O'Donaty. WE ARE THE HOUSE.' that's what he used to say and so, having constructed his shell he had to do something about the HOUSE. And that man, my handsome, charming father, did just that. He set off walking from Launceston to Hobart where he arrived with a horse and governess cart, and sat on the harbour watching the boats come in."

"Probably that man worked and earned money while he waited — he never had the ability to be still for an instance. However it was in reality, he watched the boats and those who disembarked — immigrants from immigrant ships,

184

cargo boats, tea clippers. At last his patience was rewarded. He used to tell us he knew when the boat was sighted; he made out the name 'Cygnet' and THAT was a special sign. Told you Padre, the man was a heathen. When the Cygnet had moored and before her cargo, and sailors disembarked, off the ship came the Master, his wife and his beautiful young daughter — on their way from troublesome Ireland to settle in a new country. Of course, my father married the beautiful girl; a girl with eyes as green as his own were blue and hair as dark as his was fair. his new father-in-law, once the love time and marriage was completed — and I, even I, believe it was a genuine love-match, no doubt of that — sailed his Cygnet round the coast to Launceston and unloaded a house full of furniture, including a harpsichord, while my father drove his new wife right through the country in his acquired buggy. My father waited then for the sons who would inherit his five rings. He had five daughters: Regina, Augusta, Alexandra, Leonora and Victoria, then no infants for more than three years. Imagine his joy when he had TWIN sons — me first and Alexander an hour later. I was taken over by my sisters, puny little me, wrapped in wool from a lamb newly killed for the purpose, and put in the rising oven instead of a loaf of bread. By the time I had risen my father had almost deified my huge, strong brother with his bright blue eyes and fighting fists. My sisters and my mother poured love over me, coddled me, spoiled me and yet all I wanted was for my father to notice me. It was nine years before another live baby arrived, another boy, Leo, young Rex's father, eh Rex? Leo was another strong blue-eyed Viking and it was my father's plan that those two should be sent to Europe to become military men. So it would have been if my father had not had that inner urge that made him believe in his own fate, his own khama, to find gold somewhere in the world. He BELIEVED in some special role for him in the world, so off he went, to join in the Victoria Gold Mining venture. He said the Odonata, the dragonfly would lead him to gold, but he left his rings with my mother, — and an unborn son. He didn't come back alive. My mother hung the rings around her neck when the news came and took ship to Adelaide, returning with a long narrow rough wooden box and some story of a fight over a claim; a fight that lost my father his life, but was more than likely caused by HIM. We buried the old rogue — he must have been about sixty-seven — along with the other tiny mounds at the side of his precious sanctuary, and then Rex was born; another Viking had come into the House of Odin. It was Vikings they all needed to make something out of the land, so my mother, with the rings on a ribbon about her neck organized her children — each to their own special section of farming, and arranged for me, the useless boy, to take Alexander's place at the military college in England and then in Prussia. She taught my sisters and brothers all they ever had a chance to learn, but I was shipped with my grandfather to the other side of the world — an over-coddled, petticoat clinging little fellow of ten years of age." He laughed relishing the looks on the faces of the ladies, of sympathy, sorrow, even misery. "No, ladies," he went on, "it was the best thing my mother could have done. I NEEDED discipline. I NEEDED to be taught that I was not a doll. And MORE, I might have caused another Cain and Abel tragedy if I had stayed at home with the fear of my father no longer hanging over me. I was eaten up with envy of my twin, and all his kindnesses to me were of no avail. For possibly all of my ten years I had hated him. And now my friends, my twin sits in an empty castle — alone — never having the time or energy perhaps, to build his own family HOUSE. It is I, the runt, who has kept the House of O'Donaty standing — although those Prussians who trained me, did their best to destroy it. They took Lex. They took half of Frank, but three boys remain. One day one of them will take ship to Tasmania and rebuild Odin Hall."

After a pause as his eloquence failed, Augustus hesitantly said, "I have nothing to leave my sons. Nothing. I don't even KNOW them. All strangers who bear my name and carry my blood-line. Strangers. Even Marc! Much too old when he was born. Too old when they were all born. Too old when I married. Passed on the blood, that's all — and the sign of the House of O'Donaty — Twins; one big and blue-eyed, the other small and green-eyed, like Una here.

Una squirmed uncomfortably, but to her relief, a flying fox found its way into the room and Tera suggested they walk on the verandah until it had either settled on a rafter high above their heads or taken itself off on some other visitation.

While the ladies walked slowly back and forth, shaking out the creases that sitting had made in the back of their dresses, Rex slid beside his cousin leaning on the railing and looking up at the sky. Both together they said, "I've discovered something about the rings." Both looked out, wrapped in thought and felt the mixture of exhilaration, excitement, contentment and security, that the proximity of the other seemed to evoke. As if from some great distance they heard the Padre's voice proclaiming the marvel that is woman, especially their own grandmother who had done, more or less, the same as had Rex's own mother — kept a family going alone, without a man to take the burdens.

"Oh yes, Padre, you're quite right. Quite right," boomed the General. "My mother not only had that farm running as it had never been run before, but having no money, no money whatsoever, she applied for the grant to carry the mail from Launceston to Hobart. Drove the carriage herself and took paying passengers as well. When highwaymen became a problem she carried two pistols in an apron pocket — loaded pistols AND employed two ex-convicts to guard the coach. Then she thought about marrying off my sisters — dressed them up and showed them off in Hobart, one by one. All except Regina married and she lived on in the house looking after Alexander, until she died."

The flying fox had settled down hanging from a beam in a dark corner so they returned to the drawing room and Augustus hoped the guests would soon stir themselves to depart. He dearly wanted to take his usual evening stroll around the garden, enjoying the velvet feel of the night around him and storing up memories of an India that had nothing to do with soldiers; nothing to do with any act of his. This country had been 'home' to him and he was on the verge of leaving it forever without having truly experienced the peace that underlay the machinations of ambitious men. That was what he would like to take away with him, this kaleidoscope of scented nights, brilliant stars, low heavens, majestic mountains and above all, the living, pulsating stillness that was the anachronism of the land itself. He felt his wife's hand on his and saw the words she was using. Mrs. Hope wondered if he had any regrets.

Regrets! He had plenty of those. Oh yes, when the heat of battle was over there were regrets — for opportunities missed, but more potent, for the dead of all sides that lay around. Oh yes, he had regrets. However he said, "My greatest regret, Mrs. Hope, is that I didn't marry my wife ten years earlier. I knew her for that number of years, but never believed she'd have me. Now, here am I, an old, old man with a comparatively young wife. When I go out for good I am adding yet another woman to the millions of others left to fend for themselves. Do you realise, Mrs. Hope, that for each man killed for instance, be it in the Khyber Pass, the Punjab or the trenches in Europe, there are women left behind — mothers, daughters, sisters, grandmothers and wives; five women for each dead man. They bury the man, honour him, inscribe his name on a tablet, remember him. But the women, eh? They are forgotten, left to exist on their own, exploited, condemned to an imprisonment as binding as any cage. Is it any wonder that here in India they commit suttee. Nobody ever wants to be reminded of them — embarrassed as perhaps you are. Forgive me, my friends. Blame the score of years I have notched up and the silent, saree-villages I have marched through in my terribly long life."

The Padre was talking and the old soldier was able to lean back in his chair and listen to the pulpit man — at last. He admired Grayson immensely. The man went to the forefront of battles, unarmed of course, acted as a medical orderly when there were no men to bury, or send to their death with the comfort of his presence and the sacraments. He tried to 'convert' Hindus, Moslems, Sikhs, Athiests, and Buddhists with equal impartiality and certainty in the superiority of both his creed and his faith — but his skirling voice was monotonous and often excruciatingly dreary.

"Have you never thought of writing a novel about the women left behind, Mrs. Hope?" the Padre asked.

"Yes. But never a story about a whole village of women, Mr. Grayson. It has possibilities. At the moment I'm rather intrigued with the image of the General's mother. Don't you think, Mrs. O'Donaty, it has possibilities?"

If Tera were strictly honest, rather than a polished hostess she would have disagreed. She had met her mother-in-law during their one visit to Tasmania, and had not found her specially prepossessing, while the life at that monstrous house was very like that of her own childhood — lacking any comfort and having little graciousness about it. She would like to figure in her husband's biography, but etiquette demanded that she agree, and agree she did, with every appearance of sincerity.

At last, and to the General's relief yet again, but more permanently this time, the Graysons made the hesitant signs suggesting an imminent departure. Miss Law rose from her seat followed by Mrs. Hope. While they all waited for the tonga to carry the town visitors to their quarters, one last question was hurled at the tired old man by the writer. "What advice, General," she asked, "would you give young people today — especially, of course, the young people out here?" Of course she meant young Europeans, the General assumed.

"Don't be too practical or too ambitious. Marry young, get to know your own children — and give up a promising career if that's the only choice."

"Really?" queried Miss Law.

"Yes, really. At the end of a very long day, be you General or Corporal, you become nothing more nor less than an old man. Yesterday I was somebody, by the time I arrive at my birthplace I shall be Augustus O'Donaty; all the C.Bs. and the rest won't make me the man who was my father — the man who RAN for twenty-four non-stop hours to stake his claim on land to leave his children. I have nothing to leave; my wife owns a rock in the middle of an unpleasantly tumultuous sea, too small to even build a hut on. My daughter's dowry." There was bitterness in the words and sadness in the voice. The progeny of a house of bards or scalds had made his first and last oration, during the last dinner party he was to give in the country he thought of as his own — or as owning — and the words he used, the stories he told, if he could only have known, were to seed, flourish, bloom and propagate.

Footsteps faded into the space beyond the compound; clopping hooves and rolling wheels bumped and rattled, receding clank by clank until they too, became lost in the distant sounds of a thriving, somnolent town lazily collecting itself for sleep; lizards scratched and scraped travelling up walls and across beams; hard-winged beetles flicked their tiny scales, collided with the glass lamp-funnels, rebounded and thudded on the wooden floor; the floors and walls groaned gently, contracting after the heat of the day had at last, seeped from their once living sap-channels; a stiffened silk gown crackled across creaking boards, and with the briefest, "Goodnight," Tera had retired. Una followed after kissing her father and then, unaccountably shyly, her cousin. Two bamboo chairs complained while two men settled down on them, and into them, arms fidgeting with pipes, tobacco, matches and match boxes, until finally the sucking and blowing indicated a companionable stillness; the stillness of two people each wrapped in their own thoughts, but with the common denominator of the source of those thoughts. The source was the saga and the orator of the evening.

For Rex a whole new horizon seemed to have emerged around that dining table, an almost unlimited horizon, such as those mythical — or not — ancestors had searched. His horizon was emotional though, but with all the excitement and unpredictability of an ocean.

Augustus' thoughts were blurred by his discovery of a self he had never known, never suspected existed — except that he had, since he was sent away from his home, visualized himself in his brother's form and with his brother's confidence; that was how he had survived; he had BEEN Alexander in his heart. He had gone to war, fought in battles, defended almost hopelessly indefensible positions with his twin's shoes on his feet — metaphorically — and his eyes had seen the unheroic dead through his brother's lenses, and through those lenses he had marched through the saree-villages without a glance, not even knowing he had noticed; above all he had seen a rightness in all that he was called upon to perform in the way of slaughter through those other lenses, but his own eyes saw other things. His own eyes saw the starvation that followed some border squabble; his own eyes saw the two lines of puppets:— his under the thumb of politicians; his opponents' being manipulated by some feudal chief or some distant foreign

190

power. Either way and either side was little more than a piece of chess in some master game. Politicians — faceless names eaten up with a thirst for power, slaked by greed, dribbling fear and forming pools of hate that grew into streams of hate making rivers of hate and oceans of hate, and the biggest haters were the unknowing, ignorant nobodies who, in the end, were the sufferers, the starved, the dead, the neglected sarees, and their spindly-legged offspring. Perhaps that strange little spindle-legged man in a dhoti had the right idea after all; perhaps behind his glittering spectacles HIS eyes saw more clearly than anyone else; perhaps the time was right to return this wonderful land and its disunited people over to a single cause, a uniting force, especially this man's cause, this man's creed of selflessness and non-violence; but, could ONE man hold millions forever, in the palm of his hand? Other men had tried. Jesus had tried and that resulted in centuries of the bloodiest wars of all time. Well, if Gandhi could do it, now, surely was the time with the world at peace, more or less. There was one enormous world problem though:— a generation had been TAUGHT to hate, TAUGHT to kill, and TAUGHT to think; those same young people — those who had survived — were now free of restricting orders, thinking their thoughts, pursuing their ideals even, uninhibited by the enclosed horizons of their parents. Could one man without using force, channel those new young minds? The old General hoped so, but feared for the land if left to its own devices.

He looked around the dim verandah and smiled. Possessions and prestige! Causes of friction and of world wars, but he, like old Urji, had neither. He and Urji would soon part company until they meet somewhere in eternity, he to live in a strange community among people he would be unable to identify with, and Urji to go to the small Sikh community from which he had come, in the middle of a Hindu village, surrounded by mainly Moslem peoples. Nobody would bother either himself or Urji for they owned no land, no house, except the House of their blood-lines.

"The world is a bridge, pass over it, but build no house upon it." He said aloud.

191

"I beg your pardon, Sir?" Rex asked, aroused from his daydreams.

"The world is a bridge, pass over it, but build no house upon it," repeated Augustus. "Words inscribed by Akbar nearly two hundred feet above the main gate to a desolate city not far from Agra. A city with citizens of wild bees, bats, monkeys and ever and always, ants. The Emperor Akbar was quoting another man — a carpenter from Palestine who claimed to be another sort of king. Take a look at the city of Fatehpur Sikri sometime, Rex, my boy. It reduces one to size, ant-size, and makes it more certain that those old ring-givers were handing on one truth, eh? Five rings, five sons to pass them on to so keep the 'House' of the family flowing while searching for a Tir Tairngiré, a Promised Land, that doesn't exist outside the heart. Good night, my boy." General Augustus O'Donaty stumped out the dead tobacco left in his pipe and, stiff back walked into the darkness beyond the verandah as the last of the oil burnt out in the smoking lamp.

Chapter Eleven

The morning after the dinner party Una was awake long
before Rex had stirred. She had slept fitfully. An uncanny
silence seemed to be holding the household and the distant
town. There had not been the usual chatter and chanting,
clatter of bowls and knocking together of metal pails and
wash basins. The sounds of coolies shouting as they
struggled along the dirt road bearing heavy baulks of timber
or bundles of planks for the building of more bungalows
had not lulled her to sleep. The silence was more complete
than that of La Bellule, where the washing of tide on
pebbles could be heard at all times. Finding herself wide
awake and the faintest tinge of light in the heights above the
town she rose, dressed and silently crept into the stables,
hoping to saddle two ponies without disturbing the syce; she
did not realize that he slept beside his charges. He was only
a teenage boy, perhaps not even into his teens and he
looked terrified. Obviously he thought he had mistaken the
time, and Una was at a loss as to how to explain, but the
fortuitous arrival of Rex cleared the miserable expression
from the boy's face. It stretched into a wide grin when Rex
added that the mem-sahib always looked after her own pony
in England because she could not find anyone as reliable as
him.

Once the cousins had reached the place Rex expected
them to have the clearest view he said, "You should never
take over one of the servant's jobs, Una. THEY lose face; not
only might they lose face in the eyes of the other servants,
but, and more important, they lose face in THEIR OWN
EYES."

"How is it then, Rex, that you have learnt so much about these people? You've been here such a short time."

"I learn the language. I listen. And I wander in and out of bazaars and railway stations — always listening."

"Well, if you listen so much, tell me, what was wrong last night. There was a silence and stillness EVERYWHERE; it was like the strange stillness we get at La Bellule before a storm. Uncanny quiet."

"It seemed jolly noisy to me. It's just that third eye of yours, working overtime after your father's marathon talk. To ME, that was uncanny! That silent old boy suddenly bursting out like that, rhetoric, song, legend and fact, myth and history all locked together, yet pouring out like some waterfall. THAT WAS uncanny, that was indeed uncanny."

"No, Rex. There WAS a silence. The servants didn't gather around and eat and chat, like they do night after night. There was nothing — no water carting, no washing up. Nothing."

"I went to bed to SLEEP, me! You seem to have been exercising your Delphic oracular practices. I think you are not a human, but a Triclops. . ."

"What on earth is a Triclops?"

"I've invented it. A Cyclops has ONE eye; so a two-eyed being must be a Biclops — like most of the animal world I imagine, but you, you're a bit of the unreal with your third eye — a Triclops, see. And now my little monster, turn your attention to the mountains over there, and see the chink of light growing."

They stood leaning against a rock and watched the great kaleidoscope of light and colour turning the imperious mountains from icy white to pale yellow and through to orange streaked with blood red splits until the whole panorama seemed to hover, blush and the blush spread, fading as it spread to a shade of pink that even the flowers had been unable to imitate. The great football that had been the sun, vanished in the blink of an eye it seemed and slowly the pink outlined the great forests of trees, the clearings and ultimately, the lower hills.

The young people remained speechless. There was nothing to say. They had surely been at the gates of heaven in that brief passage of time. They stood still as time itself seemed to switch off after the performance.

Rex stirred the transfixed girl in the end by saying, "There. A daily performance. Just to remind such mortals who witness it that WE are but mere mortals . . . even if we are Triclopeian mortals. Wake up! I have a present for you to commemorate this day, this moment perhaps. . . ah and ME."

He pulled a small package from his breeches pocket and handed it to his cousin, which, on opening, she found to contain a fine golden chain.

"It's to hang your gladstone bag key on, see? Actually, I'm quite sure your parents WILL let you go to Mrs. Hope, and that old Gorgon, Nanny, won't be THERE, but I don't know how long Anna will respect your secrecy; she's a normal little girl, really, beneath the lustre and spoiling. Like it?"

"Rex, I LOVE it." She fell on him, hugging him and kissing his cheek, turned to him, and kissed the other cheek.

"You can do better than that, eh, Triclops?"

Several minutes later when she had proved the truth of his query that was more a rhetorical question, he said, "Well, now then, I wish I'd brought a pocketful of trinkets. I haven't. I have just one more, Una. . . here it is. It's NOT a gift. It's something I want YOU to keep for ME, till I return . . ." Rex slowly pulled the Odonata ring from his small finger and held it out for her to see. "Keep it safe for me, will you, Una? Hang it on the chain and wear it all the time, UNDER your clothes so nobody sees it, eh? Look, I'll show you the secret of the ring. It's a seal for letters, obviously, but see this," and he turned the ring on its side as he spoke, "this tiny obtruberance here; it's a catch; you push it down like this and there you are, inside the oval is the world, perhaps — onyx or quartz with the two constellations, like you said last night at dinner; see the Northern and the Southern Crosses embedded into the stone with diamonds; nine diamonds. Wear it for me." He hung it on the chain, fastened the double clip and slipped it over her head, sealing the gift with a long, gentle seal.

Una had still said nothing. There were no words in her mind to speak. She looked at his well-known face and something she had never seen before glowed from his hazel eyes that compelled her to hurl herself at him.

Grunting he held her close for a moment then, pulling her to her feet said, "Keep that sort of abandonment for me. . . will you, Una?" he almost pleaded. "I'm CHAINING you to me . . ."

"But I AM you, Rex. I'm your khama or you're my khama. We belong, don't we? You've been spending your life SAVING me, now I'm saving your Odonata for you, Rex."

"Yes, we belong . . . ah, and we belong on the lower ridge where the other two should be arriving shortly with Habibi — the head syce. Learn their names Una, as quickly as possible . . . Now, come, my tethered Triclops . . . and . . . take care of yourself while I'm away — for ME. I'll leave you a little pistol. It's powerful. I bought it in the bazaar, but I didn't want to bring it up here and spoil all this. If you ride out with a syce he should have a game rifle, but slip the pistol into your pocket as well — wild animals and with the present unrest . . . well, who knows . . . and don't forget to load it and keep the safety catch ON unless you need it. It isn't an air pistol with useless slugs. You KNOW you mustn't ride out alone, don't you?"

"You really DO care about me, don't you. Oh Rex. I PROMISE. I won't look after ME — that's too . . . too . . . trivial. I'll look after the ME part of YOU."

They reached the escarpment to find only Marc and Habibi so each wrapped in their own united thoughts they followed them back to the bungalow.

Arrived on the front verandah Marc, Una and Rex stood still and stared. An empty space of dusty boards should have greeted them, but instead they found the General and the Padre walking up and down, up and down, turning at the small carved table that held a teapot and two cups and saucers. These two elderly men should be in bed still, sipping tea and cogitating about making the effort to rise and soak, in their warm baths. They shouldn't be visible for at least another hour, and here they were, not only visible, but exercising and causing the whole structure to vibrate as they turned on their heels before returning.

"Ah, my boy," said the General when he noticed Rex. "Glad you went out early. We've just had terrible . . . oh terrible . . ." the tough old man's voice creaked, "Oh dear, oh dear . . ." he continued, "It's appalling the news. Something awful has happened at Amritsar. Awful. Awful. Unbelievable . . . The Gurkhas . . . the Gurkhas of all regiments . . . have fired on an unarmed mob of men, women and even some children. I know. I know. I can't believe it . . . They telegraphed to Peshwar . . . that's all I know. Urji has gone . . . the train was taking medical supplies . . . Urji thinks his two grandsons are in Amritsar. Oh dear, Padre, surely WE would never give the order to fire on a mob. Imprison, yes, that's been bad enough — and foolish of the police; but bullets, oh no, oh dear me, no."

"It will all be exaggerated, General," said the gentle padre. "A mistake at the Telegraph Office . . . Perhaps someone deputizing . . ."

The short upright little man had not heard the voice that issued from the willowy, stooping figure of the padre, but he had caught sight of his youngest offspring, to whom he barked, "And WHAT are you doing, young man? Five minutes to breakfast and see your sister is SILENT during the meal. Move."

Marc moved. He was as much surprised by the tone of voice as he was by the fact that he was being addressed at all. Una followed, but as Rex was about to do the same, the General held him back saying, "Stay one moment please. You should hear this." He then addressed the padre, "I suggest, you discreetly pack a small case for each of you. If this news is true, we may, oh God forbid, have another Cawnpore. If it is true, perhaps we deserve it, my friend. If there is any trouble, we'd be best together, d'you think?"

The Padre, having assented hurried towards his own bungalow, saying, as he went, "Lessons as usual, I think, General!" A query answered in the affirmative by Tera, who had been out of sight, but within earshot of all that was said. As Rex moved off, he saw his aunt lead the old man to his chair, and once seated, her arm remained locked in his.

"What a man!" thought Rex. "The prepared campaigner. And what a woman for a wife!"

Not until breakfast was over did anyone speak beyond answering the offers for more tea, or toast. As it was always an unattended meal neither Nanny nor ANNA was aware of the fact that Urjinath had departed, but as the last morsel was being swallowed the General spoke. "There is some trouble at Amritsar," he said, "and Urjinath has gone to find out what has happened. Meanwhile, nobody, and I include EVERYONE around this table, except, of course, Rex, NOBODY is to go beyond the Graysons' house, the compound and this house. No riding out. You will exercise the ponies round the perimeter of the compound in full view of the two houses." He then glanced at this wife who nodded. "In addition," he said, "you will NOT cause the servants any embarrassment by asking them any questions. I understand that yesterday was a special day, requested by the Mahatma Gandhi, of fasting and prayer, and I, in my ignorance, chose to give an extravagant dinner party when they were all going all day without food or drink." Again he exchanged a look with his wife, and HE nodded.

Tera turned her attention on Una, saying, "Una, your father and I have discussed the offer made by Mrs. Hope. We have decided that you may go and stay with her, but we think you should stay until the book is finished, if she needs you longer than the three months we shall be in India; we shall ask her to arrange for a suitable chaperone for the journey to Tasmania. We have also decided," she continued, turning her attention to Anna, "to take you to Tasmania until you are seventeen and then we may send you to a Swiss Finishing School." One by one Tera spoke individually to each person around the table. She told Marc that he was to both travel and remain with the Graysons, attending school as planned, but spending his holidays with his friends in their home in England. She told Nanny that she would be most welcome to continue her life with them, but if she wanted to return to England that would be arranged and finally and most apologetically she said to Rex, "I am so sorry to ask you to do something for us, but we would be most grateful if you would occasionally visit Una, when you have leave and can spare the time. She will be living at Gulmarg and perhaps you could combine a restful time on a houseboat at Srinagar?"

The house, the state, the whole country was, that morning in the deepest sorrow — or anger, but sitting around General O'Donaty's breakfast table there were only satisfied smiles on that dreary day. At the Grayson house there was open jubilation for Mrs Grayson had not anticipated with any real pleasure taking Anna to live with them; she outshone the much cleverer Mary Grayson by her beauty and vivacity and she had a way of always getting her own way in everything. The boys were delighted, though, at the thought of having their amusing friend with them in the holidays. Nanny could not imagine a life without this family so the decision found favour with her as she was to have Anna and the comfort and company of the only people who had ever seemed to care for her, and Rex did not think that visiting his cousin would be a trial. He smiled again at the thought as he strolled down the verandah beside her. "I shall shadow you," he said.

"Hm. Well, Peter Pan you won't find ME shut away in a drawer . . ."

"Ha! So you are prepared to be MY shadow, even if I must shadow YOU? In that case come and collect your little pop-gun from me and say goodbye, temporarily."

Rex rode out on his horse, looking smart and very efficient. Everyone smiled as he departed, and once the sound of the hooves faded the old couple walked, arm in arm, up and down, up and down. The only words spoken were by Tera who said to her husband, "He looks exactly as you looked when I first met you, my dearest, and you were TWICE Rex's age." They continued their walk and after Una had retired to her room she heard the walk extended to include the side verandah — as far as Nanny's room.

"They use the verandah like the deck of a ship," thought Una, beginning to compose a letter to her aunt. She had barely made a start when she heard her parents talking again. She sat still and listened.

"I wonder if our boy was like Rex!" the General said.

"We will never know," his wife replied. "His birthday yesterday and we kept it to ourselves . . ."

"I know, my dear, I know. I DO know how great was your sacrifice — for me."

"It was MY choice, Augustus. I shall give Una the box of our son's things. We'll keep only the medal and the wings, I think . . . we knew only a little boy, younger than Marc is now . . ."

199

The steady, rhythmical heel and toe of four feet touching and lifting from the rough board beneath continued on and on, finally being punctuated by the sound of two bodies sinking into two bamboo chairs.

Riding with his squadron through increasingly familiar country between Peshawar and Landikotal, Rex's thoughts drifted from the events of the previous evening to events of years long passed. The family saga, as told by his uncle had re-awakened memories of his mother reading stories to himself and his newly arrived cousins, stories about the mythical gods and goddesses who peopled either Mount Olympus or Asgard, stories that he and his cousins had relived and re-enacted in their own versions for weeks. The farmhouse had become Troy with Una, the only girl, as the beautiful Helen whom he and his men were rescuing from the wicked Paris in the shape of Ivan. When those games palled they had become Vikings, and, after hearing the tales of Olaf Tryggvasson they had taken planks to the beach and even sent Una off on her last trip — to Valhalla — stretched on one of the planks. As the only strong swimmer he had been obliged to bring her back to the shore, after which his mother had banned further games in the sea, so they had, like Beau Geste and his family, held a Viking funeral on the dewpond. He remembered the screams of the little girl when it was evident that the dragonflies and their larvae were being destroyed by the smoke. It seemed to Rex, all these years later that his most vivid childhood memories involved him in the act of rescuing that same little girl, clutching her naked or sparsely clad body from some dangerous environment. She was right when she said that she belonged with him and had always done so, and now she guarded his insignia, his ring that had come to him from his father, and to his father from that extraordinary man, their grandfather, teller of tales and believer, perhaps, in some special blood-line that involved the five rings and the periodic arrival of twins — one with blue eyes, the other with green eyes. Not that Una's eyes were really green, more grey-green as a rule but when she stood on the grass they seemed to reflect the colour, and when they looked into his he supposed they picked up his own dark hazel colouring.

While Rex was riding through the Khyber Pass dreaming about his young cousin, the General methodically packed papers and sorted out his few personal possessions, and Tera segregated her unwanted clothing from those to be packed, Nanny sewed name tapes on Marc's clothing, Una added to her daily letter to her aunt and the elderly Rissaldar Major Urji na Singh stood outside the Golden Temple in Amritsar, as if in a nightmare, unwilling and unable to comprehend the horror of sight and sound that enveloped his senses.

Only in the Holy city of the Sikhs did the tall, straight man remember his own correct name; Urjinath had been easier for children to say, and such he had come to name himself; but here, he was a Sikh and proud of his unity with his brethren, his fellow believers. He felt himself on this day, to be in an alien city and he feared to enter the Temple in case that too would be changed. The city was a city of tears and wailing. At last he removed his shoes and entered the magnificent Temple, stepping with great care around or over the signs of dripped blood. In spite of his great height, Urji felt dwarfed by the splendid doorway with its huge frescoes of intricate carving above his head. The interior struck almost night-dark until the old man's eyes adjusted between the brilliance of the sunlight beating off the white paving without and the sparsely lit inside. He waited. He had accepted this blight of the passing of years, this slow adjusting of eye focus, with some irritation; he was a man born and bred in the mountains where eyesight needs to be clear, wide and long. While he stood just inside the doorway he was jostled by others silently entering and departing. Their feet were silent; their footfalls were soundless, but Urji heard the faintest sob, sniff and gasp from each who passed.

Urji was bewildered. He did not know how he could find his two grandsons in this city where he must hesitate to accost anyone, since all seemed to be suffering from an overwhelming sorrow. He decided to walk slowly around the great empty space, just looking at faces, although most were hidden while their owners crouched in prayer. He returned to the blazing sunlight, re-adjusted his eyes and walked from pillar to pillar and around the two great concourses each side of the central paved way, where covered heads bent forward bowed and still; still like statues, Urji thought. While

201

he walked, searched and wondered he failed to notice the young man until he touched the old one's shoulder. Urji had not found his youngest grandson, the grandson had found HIM. In the young man's eyes, Urji saw the same look that seemed to have transfixed the entire city; bewildered eyes, a twisted mouth causing beard and moustache to become distorted, and nostrils of his long, fine nose, closing and opening and closing again. Urjinath, the grandson, was wearing only a singlet on the top half of his body, his shirt having been used as a sling and bandage for his arm, the blood gushing through, thanks to the sudden movement made by the young man.

Urji looked at the wound and said, "It needs stitching together . . ."

"I know," his grandson replied, "but the doctors and everyone else are working all the time, all night, all to-day, trying to save just one more life, one more limb . . ."

"Ah. It is as I heard . . . Stay here in the shade of this tree," he pointed to a single, thinly leafed sapling. "I will return." The Rissaldar Major almost marched off. The young man slept. When his grandfather returned he had with him two bazaar rough baskets; one filled with rice and broken nuts, the other with a pottery, roughly made bowl, filled with water. They ate and they slaked their thirst, after which Urji said, "Now we will go to the well and dress that wound."

Once the wound was expertly dressed by the seasoned campaigner, using the washed out singlet, the shirt washed by a kindly old crone and drying on its owner's back, they walked slowly back in the direction of the Temple.

"And your brother?" the old man asked.

"In the place there — with the others," bitterly whimpered the young man who had become almost a small boy again.

The two men rested and waited while the sun slowly went down, once they had found what was left of the other young man. Then they waited until the flames had died from the line of funeral pyres. They waited on and on while the ashes were scattered on the waters of one of the five rivers of the Punjab, to be carried on and on, purified by the melted snow that sped the remains of so many humans out to the unfathomable and unlimited oceans of the world. Walking

202

away from the smouldering ghats Urji became aware of a metamorphosis taking place in his companion. The silence and acceptance changed into anger and from anger into hate, so the old man, instead of leading him to the railway station, led him along the edge of the River Ravi, following cart tracks, then west toward the railway. They did not board the train; they followed the line of the glittering tracks and they walked with long, easy, strides. The young man talked as they left the ghats. He spoke furiously about the gathering of happy peaceful crowds who were observing the Mahatma Gandhi's day of fasting and prayer; a small crowd became a large crowd and as more and more people filled with delight at this holiday, anxious to enjoy it as well as obey the Mahatma's request, joined the crowd, there was one particular centre — the enclosed gardens near the Temple — the Jalianwala Bagh. The crowds pushed their way through the one entrance long after the space could hold no more. Small people were being crushed; some tried to change direction and get out; panic resulted; already people had been trodden underfoot. He and his brother tried to move backwards, but, tall as they were, it was useless; they were pushed further and further forwards until their faces scraped the boundary wall, then they forced their bodies the other way around and faced the oncoming wave of humanity. He heard, but did not see the marching men. He heard the click of their safety catches, and he heard the order to fire. An Englishman gave the order. He saw his brother fall, but pulled him to his feet. "The soldiers had been firing across the space, until someone near us made a remark — shouted an insult at the officer, and then at the Gurkhas. It was then they fired downwards. The officer, oh my grandfather, was not a subaltern, was not a corporal; he was a fully uniformed Brigadier General — so, it was no accident, no incident, no misunderstanding on the part of the English. They sent a fully-fledged Brigadier General to subdue a few hundred holidaymakers. It wouldn't have been necessary for such a high rank to be sent, or to go, to subdue a contained crowd of rioters. He MUST have seen from his high wall, what I saw from the ground, that the crowd was intent only on surviving by then . . . I shall never follow in your footsteps. I shall never join the army of those foreigners who see fit to subdue US, govern US, make laws for US and only give us the right to fight FOR THEM. There is a burning hate consuming me. To-morrow I join the Party and avenge my brother's death."

"To-morrow," said the grandfather, "and several to-morrows, you heal your wound . . . and we walk. You cannot travel in a jolting train or my mending will be to no avail. We walk, you and I."

For four days the two men walked. For four days and four nights, they walked, and they slept in short snatches, but often; they ate little and drank whenever water was available. They scarcely spoke more than a few words. In four days the bitter young man and the elderly grandfather covered a distance of over one hundred and fifty miles, and by the time they reached Wazirabad an arm was almost healed; an angry heart was a controlled angry mind and a man who thought he had finished his life as a man, felt he had lost years with each mile covered. He would return shortly to his own village, but not as one of the 'useless ones', not to spend his remaining days sitting in the shade of a Bodhi tree, but to walk firmly as a man among — perhaps not too many men, but men.

Urji was convinced, while he walked, that there would be just retribution extracted by the British Raj for this terrible deed; a deed that was already being referred to as a massacre — as it was in deed as well as in title. Relatives of the mob who had been fired on had died far across the sea in the service of the Raj, fighting FOR a cause they did not understand and on behalf of a nation that was not their own. The best of their own land had died in cold muddy trenches, in hot waterless deserts, in jungles and in the middle of oceans, and they had died under a flag that was not their own, but which they served with a patriotism as fervent as if it HAD been their own. Those who returned had energy, ambition and a desire to offer to their own land all they had offered their rulers. They found, under the leadership of one man that they had a new power — their voices, and it was their voices and the power to withdraw their work that had sent them hurrying to the Jallianwala Bagh. Over three hundred died, trapped like wild animals in a cage; over a thousand were injured. Urji was certain that the officer who gave the order would be summarily court martialled and either shot or dismissed. Throughout the huge continent that was India, and amongst the numberless nationalities living in it, few believed otherwise. British Justice, though all too frequently lacking understanding of the ways of the people of the land, was, according to it own creed, just. There were few still living who could remember the bloodbath that had been his own, and his General's baptism of fire; they had been boys then. Urji believed without one moment's doubt that justice would be done.

Events were to prove Urji, and the multi-racial population who had his faith, wrong. To the disgust and horror of every shade of colour from the dark skins of the Madrasi to the white of the Europeans, justice was not done; the officer was dismissed the service, and that was just; he was then rewarded with a very handsome pension. The wound that the massacre inflicted, was never to heal; it became gangrenous in time, and one man alone kept the poison from spreading into the entire body of the land. That man, Mohandas Karamchand had completed his education in the capital city of the great Raj, in the bustling city far across the sea. On his return to his native country he became extremely wealthy through his legal practice, but gave it up to live like a peasant in another strange land where his own countrymen were being discriminated against, and returned to his own birthplace in order to support the rulers of his people in their conflict. The conflict over, he demanded the right of his people to govern themselves, and to show the solidarity of a nation with this aim he had asked for the peaceful show of unity throughout the land. Heartbroken by the result — 'a Himalayan miscalculation', he was to hold tenaciously, from within and without prison, to his belief in the justice of Swaraj — Home Rule.

Urji-na-Singh and his grandson returned footsore and weary to be greeted by the symbol of their tragedy, but when the young man saw the agony of his grandfather mirrored in the eyes of that symbol, the last remnants of violence evaporated from his thoughts, and he used what little energy remained, consoling his bereaved mother.

The General's house had been wrapped in a mixture of apprehension, controlled confusion and excited anticipation during the four days of Urji's absence. Cleaning of silver, brassware and carved wood ornaments and tables had been vigorously performed; curtains and chair cushion covers had been removed, casting a bleak air on the rooms; pictures and photographs had been busily cleaned and left in neat piles approximately in the position they habitually occupied. The chamra-wallah, the leather worker had spent a day at the house repairing snags in luggage, oiling and replacing locks and making a pattern of Una's gladstone bag which he was to copy in crocodile skin for Anna's birthday, and it was the chamra-wallah whose report on events and attitudes in the town that convinced the General that it would be safe to withdraw his siege orders and permit the family to visit the bazaar to buy necessities for travel as well as gifts for the young girl. "And NO chit signing," he instructed, counting out rupees into the hands of the three young people. The old man had seen, all too often, families embarked on the train when a running mob of tradesmen had begged and beseeched them to honour their chits before leaving. It was usually through carelessness and the ease with which money could be signed away on scraps of paper, but it was certain that the debtors generally paid far more than they owed to rid themselves of the excited and romantically verbose craftsmen and traders. They would appear with a limitless list of starving offspring and elderly relations until the last anna was paid in cash and they would then claim the payee to be their mother and their father and an indescribable array of further relatives which, for those who bothered to think about the words, or even heard them, gave one cause for horrific speculations.

In the bazaar the family had parted, the Graysons taking Anna to choose a length of material to take to Tasmania and have made up there, when she discovered what the latest fashions were in that country. Nanny was haggling over an intricate evening purse, while a few stalls from her Marc had chosen a leather purse, and, using Una's design, was having Anna's name marked on it. Una was a very long time having her gifts made so Marc, with more money than he had ever seen, and with guilt in his heart, bought himself a small dagger with an intricately carved handle and a worked, leather sheath — the nearest he could find to a genuine

Khukri, for he secretly hoped to join a Gurkha regiment one day. Una had chosen a small Kashmiri sycamore box from the silversmith which he covered with a thin sheet of silver after embossing ANNA on the lid. Una then chose another box, showed a small copy of the Old Hermit's design to the craftsman and asked to have the box with the design, in silver. She had copied the original in reverse so that the Celtic Cross was at the back and the Wheel of Life on top with a dragonfly each side of the design — one insect flying upwards and the other downwards, the latter with four stars and the other with five. The little Kashmiri looked at the design with interest, obviously pleased to be asked to do something other than the normal curves and roses, and the endless number of silver bowls with parts of the Kama Sutra embossed, and then sold to the foreigners who had no idea what they were buying since only the very rare mem-sahib bothered to find out about the religious significance of the bazaar objects they bought and hoarded.

Una weighed her rupees against the sheet of silver the man produced, when the scales balanced he asked for one more; she knew it was too much and she was supposed to haggle, but she could not bring herself to do so. She watched while he scratched the design on to the silver, swiftly and accurately, then, with barely visible rapid movements pressed around the lines with a thin felt underneath, turned the sheet on to a marble slab and pressed on the reverse side, returned it to the felt, to which he had added a second felt and pressed again, repeating the process over and over again until the silver sheet had been stretched and moulded to perfection. She noted every action with care; the paste he spread into the reverse side of the work, the drying by gentle waving it backwards and forwards, the gluing it to the wooden box with some evil smelling substance, and finally the rubbing and polishing with a red powder. Before he wrapped the box in thin paper she asked him to engrave a tiny plaque and fix it inside the lid, with the inscription RISSALDAR MAJOR URJI-NA-SINGH FROM VAN AND VNA.

"Ah! The Rissaldar!" said the Kashmari, and refused any more money for the plaque.

207

By the time Marc returned with his illicit purchase, the craftsman was busy working yet another sheet of silver with the Khama Sutra extracts ready to mould yet another rose bowl.

Back at the bungalow the young people behaved like young people the western world over; each had something to show one or more of the others, but each had some article they kept hidden. Even Anna had bought something; a foolish article. She had bought herself a string of artificial pearls, not knowing that her sister intended giving her the magnificent string she had lent the girl for the ball; the silver covered box was to contain them, once the older girl had lined it with a black velvet hair ribbon she had not yet used. Anna's last birthday in the country she had lived for all but one of her fifteen years was to be made memorable for her by the giving of gifts that should remain with her to the end of her life.

While the family was in the town, the General and his old friend, his one time Rissaldar Major, talked and walked, each unwilling to waste one minute of these last few they would spend alone together, or in each other's company — ever.

Chapter Twelve

Forty-eight hours after the return of the Rissaldar-Major and his grandson after that fateful April massacre, no human sound disturbed the General's bungalow outside Peshawar. The neatly piled, cushionless bamboo furniture creaked as the heat went out of the day. The heavy teak furniture had a decoration of fine white dust covering the mirrored surface. Faded marks on the walls indicating the shapes and sizes of the pelts and monstrous skulls that were packed in naptha balls, coffined inside wooden packing cases and being jolted in a goods train, bound for a great noisy port. A reddish dust spread across the floors, slowly covering the memorials of tigers, bears and mountain deer, sprinkled by the energetic white ants busy tearing the bungalow rails to fragments. Lizards, spiders, mongooses, the occasional flying fox and the monkeys were the occupants and would remain in possession until another set of humans arrived with almost identical trophies to hang on the walls and spread across the floors, and the ever busy dusters and brooms caused death amongst the existing owners. An empty kerosene tin remained, blinking at the sun and collecting fragments of dew to deliver to the roots of the little rose bush that would, despite drought, heat and dust, squeeze a few blooms into life, to be plucked and placed in a silver bowl embossed with the illustrations of the Khama Sutra. The stables were empty, cleaned to the standard of a hospital ward, while the occupants were slowly wending their way to a small mountain village – a small caravan of hardy, sure-footed ponies, one drawing a tonga inside which sat two mourning ladies. A tall, upright young man led the party, rifle slung behind his shoulder, watchful and alert for the sound of a

209

crouching panther, a wild dog, or a snake; he feared only the crawling, wriggling snake. But the young man, though barely seventeen, felt himself indeed a MAN, to be entrusted by his grandfather, to escort the family and their possessions – few as they were – through the great mountain passes to their home village where their arrival would be as splendid as that of Rajah. The old man would arrive with the two horses after he had made his last farewells to his General and seen his friend's train disappear down the metal road, the first time he would not be with him, and the last time the other old man would travel along that magnificent metal snake that curled around the entire country.

The O'Donaty family sat in the Club with Mrs Hope, Miss Law, two Highland Regiment gentlemen who were both attempting to interest Anna, and two strange civilians who stood, hovering on the perimeter of the group. The General alone was missing from the family party. There was laughter amongst the young people, and deep quiet conversation amongst the elderly; Nanny and Una, far removed from each other seemed, each of them, isolated mentally. Into this conventional gathering a draught of gale arrived. The General, Augustus O'Donaty, moustache and eyebrows rising and falling with his jerky footsteps and his lips forming the words, "incompetent dunderheads!" He acknowledged his wife and the assembled company, thinner already by four – the two Highlanders having melted towards the bar and the two civilians, although still within earshot, occupied in ordering drinks for themselves. "What do they know, these boxwallah, lying scribblers? Nothing, I tell you. Nothing!" He waved two newspapers in the air and continued, "Look at these misinformation sheets, these travesties of the truth, these rags. Two opposing versions of one ten minute tragedy – one claims 'a massacre of unarmed innocents', while the other claims, 'quelling of a rioting, howling mob'. And WHAT may I ask, is the general public to believe? Beside these travesties of the truth I have demeaned myself by agreeing to be interviewed by one of these wet behind-the-ears sensationalisers. Huh!" The old man stopped for breath before adding to his already blistering diatribe.

"I've met them before you see, Mrs. Hope, Miss Law, my dear wife, oh yes I have met them and I have read their jargon. These journalists! Huh! They write about campaigns so you wouldn't recognise them as those you had fought in. Soldiers, you see, just obey orders that begin with politicians and end in bloodshed; soldiers then find they are GIVING orders because they must fulfil some promise or treaty made by some fellows half across the world who've never seen the country nor met the inhabitants of the country THEY have ordered shall be smitten, reduced, tethered or punished. That fellow who gave the order to fire at the Jallianwala Bagh won't get a fair trial, because people will BELIEVE the words of whichever paper they happen to read. If it's in PRINT, they think, it MUST BE TRUE! I've read the scribblings of the verbose reporters; I've seen reports of my campaigns that bear no resemblance to my own official reports. Why? You may well ask. Well, I'll tell you: Because they get paid for each and every line printed – so many annas, pence, pice, rupees even for each elasticated line. You'll see, when I'm stretched out stiff under a small mound of earth – in the not so distant future – they'll look up their records, not army records remember, and they'll write some magnificent obituary – probably it's already written, just waiting for today's interview to complete it – then they'll print it in a suitable position in the news rags. They will, in fact, BORE the general public, or the reading public, about my place of birth and date, the steps by which I became educated, and then list the campaigns in which I was a participant. They will certainly mention who begot me and who I begot – and the latter will fill up a few lines, ha, ha, ha, yes I've done them proud in that line. They get paid for every line remember! Then, to earn themselves a few more annas, pice, pence, rupees, shillings, oh yes, and even halfpence and farthings, they will inflict on the long suffering public an account of my farewell salutation and the ritual depositing of my shell and THEN to add to the superfluity of garbage they will list all the mourners – the officials, family and minor notables. But will they mention, Urji-na-Singh, the dhobies, punkah wallahs – all the people who have kept me alive, and comfortably alive for sixty-three of my seventy-eight years. Of course not. They'll see me safely put out of sight and before the ground is shovelled over me they'll be off looking for something REALLY exciting – a good murder or a hanging. But when I am only a name on a block of stone, and a piece of spoilt turf, it is THEIR WORDS that MY grandchildren will believe. What about my great-grandchildren and their grandchildren? What will they think, eh? I rather think they will think of me as an ancestor who has brought shame on the family; an example of the tyrannical use of power. If that little brown man in a dhoti is to be believed, and I believe in him, his words, and all he stands for, then the day will come when England will be, as I am now, a benevolent parent watching the children of her Empire ruling their own destinies – all of them, black, brown, yellow, pink and white and multicoloured.

"I am an old man and I have seen too much in my life, but perhaps I will, once away from this country, that has been my home for so long, think more about the words than the deeds. The printed word is all-powerful so these reporter fellows – who, I see, are not even punctual, – they will write what they will write. What was it Pilate said, 'What I have written I have written?' and like Pilate they will wash their hands of the responsibility." Augustus laughed, looked searchingly around his companions, and his tone became gentle, all the hectoring vanished and said, "Anno Domini, my friends. The ears lose their competence, but dear me, the tongue gains, daily."

"Augustus, my dear," said his wife. "The journalists are waiting behind you."

The General turned, rose, walked across to them and shook hands and with the slightest bow, said, "Gentlemen, my apologies. I see now why my wife was signalling to me – it is not my habit to insult people to their faces. I was, of course, gentlemen, generalising."

Both men smiled. Both had taken aboard rather too much alcohol to boost their failing courage, and they found themselves with an old war-horse who was truly out at grass, gentle and even benign.

"I have already talked more than I have done during most of my years out here," the old man said, "but I would ask you during your reporting days, to remember that every coin has

212

two flat sides, different in design, but similar in structure; it also has an edge that connects together those two similar sides – that's how events such as the tragedy of the other day, really are, you know. If and when you wash your hands of any responsibility for your words, try to remember that it is YOUR account of events that will become the cartoons, paintings, sculptures and novels of the future. I suggest YOU ask ME the questions to which you would like answers, but speak up." The three men excused themselves and moved into a distant corner, leaving the others, joined by the whole Grayson family, to talk idly amongst themselves and await the summons to their lunch tables.

The first, an anticipated question the General was asked was what he thought about Home Rule for India, Swaraj.

"Overdue," was the unexpected reply. "Overdue, but it must come slowly whilst remembering that India is not one country; it is one great slab of land swarming with innumerable nationalities, each with a different creed, a different language and even different appearances."

"Do you think, sir," asked the taller of the two young men, "that we should just walk out, abandon the land when we have built railways, roads, a telegraph system all over it?"

"WE built them?" asked the old man. "WE built them? Oh no we did not build them. WE designed and planned and organised and controlled the building and the laying. It was the men of the country, the coollies who did the work."

"We financed it then," persisted the reporter, a terrier with a rat, determined to hold it alive until it suited it to kill.

"Theoretically, yes! We provided the money that paid for the goods and the miniscule pittance we paid the workers, but where, gentlemen, did that money originate, eh? We have not been a benevolent society in this country. We have grown rich FROM it."

The other journalist entered the fray with, "What would you do about it then if you had the power, sir?"

The General laughed. "I would never either want or earn such power. I am neither more nor less than a very old soldier. All I know about the politics of this land is what I read about in your papers, written by you. There has only been one unifying power in this land since Akbar – and he seems to have been a bloodthirsty villain – and that is the

213

British presence, – until now, gentlemen, and now we have a man born of the land, educated partly in England, educated in English Law, remember, and he and his uniform of a spotless white dhoti seems to have the power to hold the people together – but for how long? How long before the tribal strife becomes universal. Perhaps the Mahatma could govern, backed by OUR army and our undoubted expertise until we have trained enough people to slowly, very slowly step into our shoes."

These were not the answers the two men had expected. The smaller was leaning forward, intensely interested whilst the other became almost bored and lolled in his chair, crossing his long legs and fidgeting with a slim silver cigarette case.

"Perhaps I can ask YOU a question?" the General posed. "While you absorb my answers and think out your next questions, let me ask you why YOU came out here?"

"I was BORN here," said the keen young man. "My father was a Sergeant in an infantry regiment; he was killed soon after I was born. Name of Allen, sir. I was born at Lucknow and always wanted to return to the country."

"And you?" asked the old man, turning his attention on the languid figure draped across the chair. "And please smoke if you wish," he added since the cigarette case was being clicked open and clicked shut at regular intervals.

"I missed the war so I came out here for adventure," came the reply.

The General only just heard the young man's words and he felt anger rising inside him.

"Too young for the war, were you?" he asked.

"No, not too young, but I had to complete my university course – then it was too late, unfortunately."

"Did you think you were missing some rugby match conflict then?" the old man asked.

Before he could reply Allen asked hurriedly, "Have you any regrets, sir, now you are leaving the country and the service?"

"Regrets? Oh yes, I have regrets, millions of regrets, young man. I regret the bodies left all over this country, throughout Afghanistan, across the mountains, into Assam, Bengal, Burma and right down to Madras. The bodies are buried or not, but they are dead. Kaput. Finished. My regrets are not for the dead, Mr. Allen. My regrets are for those left behind. Who could appreciate this better than you? For every dead body, left to the jackals and tigers, ashes floated down the Ganges, or under white crosses there are the women mourners – four women at least, to mourn each dead man; a mother, a wife, a sister, a daughter and in this country where boys grow up young and die young, a grandmother. Bad enough in England, but here, in this country, there is nothing but semi-slavery and disgrace or being traded with some elderly man as little better than a concubine – or suttee . . . After that hartal the other day, that day of fasting and prayer, just think, there are now at least one thousand six hundred mourning women – more than the number wounded in that garden; someone will have to support them – or there is the honourable, though distasteful to us, suttee."

"What advice then, sir, would you give ME, a new reporter out here?"

"Learn about the PEOPLE of the land. Go on shikari and – you only need to PRETEND to be shooting – as your guides take you through villages, use your eyes. You will pass through the Saree villages; they litter India."

There was silence and Marc slowly approached the group, but just as he reached his father's chair, the General entered the fray once again, "D'you know how the half dead soldiers who had walked and marched for mile after mile to reach the besieged Delhi, d'you know how they were roused to even greater efforts? I'll tell you. An NCO, a soldier, an officer, anyone in that bloodbath roused his comrades with the words, 'Remember Cawnpore! Remember the memsahibs,' and miraculously anger rejuvenated the men and they fought – and died – like tigers."

The lethargic young journalist sat upright with a jerk. He had smoked a cigarette, and that combined with the dry weather, his throat felt inclined for a drink; he thought he would end this interview, cleverly, "What advice, sir," he asked "would you offer your young grandson?" He smiled broadly at Marc.

The General rose to his feet. "My grandson?" he asked. "I have no idea, young man because I shall not live to see any grandsons. That gentlemen is the other great regret I have. This is my son, the youngest of five sons. I shall be unlikely to see this one reach adulthood, but my feelings are nothing compared to that of my wife. You see gentlemen, I told you, it is the women who suffer – my wife parted with her children, left them the other side of the world for others to bring up. Our eldest son was the age of this one, Marc, when we left him at school in England and his mother will NEVER see him; he is buried in his Sopwith Camel somewhere in Flanders, aged twenty-one." The General was upset. He had talked too much and it worried him. He was irritated by the manner of the young man with his manicured hands and slim silver cigarette case. He had posted Lex a similar case, but he was killed too soon! He was going to MAKE this arrogant young fellow THINK, even if it meant tearing himself into pieces. He turned to his son saying, "Escort your mother into lunch for me, if you please, Marc. I shall join you all in two minutes." He then looked directly at the object of his attack and continued, "That boy has never knowingly seen his eldest brother! You see, whilst you were just too late for the fun, boys were partaking in what was NOT, young man, fun. Another of my sons DID NOT take up his university place where he intended reading medicine – to mend people – instead he went as a messenger to Flanders, messenger and Red Cross worker, but too young to wear the badge on his arm – the arm, Mr . . . eh . . . the arm that is no longer there. Yes I have regrets for myself, but overwhelmingly for the mother of those boys. Thank you, gentlemen, and now please excuse me, my wife will wait until I join the family." The General shook hands with the young man called Allen who had risen to his feet when the old man rose, nodded to the other who was still rising from his chair, and, his back like a ramrod, his step quick, and light, the retired soldier joined his family at the table.

Both the men watched. They saw the beautiful and stately woman who was his wife, and clearly almost a generation younger than her husband, and then they saw the two daughters, one as startlingly beautiful as her mother must have been, and last of all they looked at the small boy in neat khaki shorts and shirt. "What a man. What a GREAT man he must be," said Allen.

While the General was being interviewed and interviewing his questioners, the Rissaldar sat in a quiet, shady spot outside the Club precincts fingering and often scrutinizing a small silver box with a strange, but intricately beautiful design on the lid. The little Baba the Missi-baba had given it to him from herself and the little Ivan-baba; the twins he almost worshipped. "We will BOTH come and see you one day, TOGETHER, and then you'll see what grew out of your care," Una had said.

Three weeks after Anna's birthday the Ressaldar Major stood, a solitary figure, watching the serpent of smoke hang in the evening sky, growing longer and fainter at one end fusing with the pink edged clouds at the other. When all movement ceased he strode with his loose-limbed mountain gait, collected his two tethered ponies, turned their heads to the north and began the long lonely journey towards his mountain home – his roots. He felt inside his loose shirt and his fingers encountered the oval silver box with the strangely beautiful design on the lid. While his large, long-fingered hand turned it over and over he thought, "I shall keep my medals in here, and inside the lid I shall glue the photograph of me holding the hands of the twin babas." Urji na Singh recalled the day it was taken. In those days his beard was thick and jet black; at the end of each of his long arms was a child, head level with his knees, and underneath were the words 'Urji with Van and Vna – one year old'. He had seen Vna, or Una as she became, settled with the two eccentric memsahibs at Gulmarg. He had accompanied the family across the mountain pass to Srinagar and returned with them after the stay on a houseboat and endless dinners and banquets. He had made his last farewells and with the disappearance of the last puff of smoke from the train he had parted forever from the one person he understood, and who understood him. A sense of deep desolation filled his heart as he thought about his hopes for his own grandson – the hope that he would ride through a career in the army at the side of the young Lieutenant, nephew of the General he had served, and an identical model. The Jawallah Bagh had ended that hope. Urji na Singh would have commenced his life as a pensioned off Ressaldar Major more happily if he could have seen into the future and the fulfilment of his khama generations later.

While Urji embarked on the loneliest journey of his life, the young man about whom he had been thinking lay on his canvas camp bed in his tent, a day's march from Kabul. His men were settled, the horses picketted, sentries organized and the cooks busily preparing the hard-earned meal. Rex had showered under a kerosene tin of mountain water and lay wrapped in a towel dreaming of a girl clad in a towel, a very young version clad in no towel, a girl who was the other half of himself. He looked at the tiny bottle of sea water, sand and seaweed wrapped in a piece of green tartan and thought himself back in the homely kitchen and safety of Bellule Bay.

Augustus O'Donaty had fallen asleep with the suddenness of the aged while the train rolled its way southward towards the last public appearance, his last regimental dinner at the place where his army life began. This time there would be no Urji na Singh at his side. A sudden jerk in the even rhythm and Augustus was wide awake and with consciousness came the loneliness, the utter desolation and an overwhelming desire to hide. Briefly he visualised the place of his birth, the monstrous, but secure, structure high in a mountain with only sheep to witness his disintegration. He had stoically watched the boat leave Bombay with his friends, the Graysons on board with their children and his youngest son. He knew he would never see Marc again. He had seen his eldest daughter ride into the mountains with the writer woman and he wondered if he would ever see Una again. He had seen Urji na Singh standing like a statue watching the train leave, and knew they would never meet again; imprisoned by his deafness he had come to value the silent comradeship that had existed for so long. In the next compartment were his youngest daughter and Nanny, talkative and accompanying him. Beside him his wife stirred on her bunk; he glanced at her with his usual adoration and said, "Do you know, my dear, I can ride hour after hour and feel little fatigue, but after a mere TEN MINUTES talking I was exhausted. It is not at all surprising that politicians who TALK ALL THE TIME make mistakes. They're OVERWORKED WITH TALK."

"Yes, my dearest!" agreed his wife before returning to her interrupted slumber.

At that moment in time politicians, tacticians and senior military men were TALKING – and planning the future of Afghanistan as a result of the sortie in which Rex O'Donaty had been involved. The result of their TALK was to ricochet for half a century and onward as a bullet ricochets within the Khyber Pass. While they decided the future of a country they had never visited, mathematically, strategically and politically, the watchers in the wings girded their loins in anticipation of the rich pickings that would inevitably result from the TALK. Before that barren inhospitable land felt the final onslaught of an exchange of masters, other politicians were carving up another continent in such a way that the unborn would be involved in yet another blood-bath that was to end in global changes to which there would be no final cessation.

By the time Augustus was settling into a wooden bungalow in Hobart, a small mound existed beside the pond at La Bellule. Another Leo lay buried, but this one had not even breathed.

Chapter Thirteen

The swallows, owners of the eaves of La Bellule, had effectively driven their young from the nest and were hatching their second brood of the season. The flycatchers had taken up their disputed residence on the other side of the farm and the birds of both species were united in their attacks upon the few dragonflies that had emerged from their lengthy period of pupation. The lambs had grown, skipped less and ate more than when they had been delightfully playful infants. The crabs beneath the earth, without any parental instincts, had provided their millions of eggs and abandoned them to their own devices, knowing that, by the law of averages, sufficient grubs would become crabs to ensure the survival of THEIR species; but the crabs had millions of years of experience to assist them in their insurance against extermination. The two-legged parent from the farmhouse that harboured the creatures working so busily under the ground, on the ground and in the air above the ground, sat on the rocky promontory that overlooked the wide bay and jutted into an ocean that covered the globe; the only parent with nothing to do; the only parent who was no longer necessary for the survival of a species.

The light from a marbled sky shone on the distant Roc, glittering from the golden gorse and enhancing the splendour of the huge white daisies and dainty campions that spread up the jagged cliffs. The gentle wavelets trembled up, and around the sandy bay leaving patterns of wavy lines interspersed with small pools. Aurora O'Donaty had nothing to do. She had performed her few daily jobs; a huge chicken pie was baking in the oven; peas lay ready for

cooking; potatoes boiled gently on the hob filling the air with the smell of mint. Marie 'owned' the kitchen, ironing with her rapid strokes all the washing she had removed from the lines — which were promptly taken over by the two swallows busily preening. Roxana was taking her first walk since leaving her bed after weeks of sickness, ably supported on the arms of her husband and Frank. Rolf and Pierre were dividing and sub-dividing the sheep and lambs into different pens; the horses and cows were out in the meadows as were the pigs and the hens. Aurora felt unnecessary. She pushed her hand into the pocket of her skirt and took out two letters; both had arrived the day before, both had been read by each member of the family and both came from India. She unfolded the single page letter with tiny, neat writing, held it close to her eyes and re-read her son's brief news:—
Dear Mother,

The war with Afghanistan is over. I don't think there were any winners or losers beyond the fact that they held the rocks, the hills, and every blade of grass or scrub by the thousand. We were easy targets as we rode through the low-lying plain. The finale came one night when we had abandoned our horses and were thus on more equal terms; the nags were held in rings in a convenient nullah, about ten to a single man, but these mountain men attacked the camp one night, slid right through our pickets, fired a few shots down the nullah and the horses stampeded, chasing the enemy for miles, followed by US on foot. Wasn't it some Persian King who used this means of terrifying some other nation, long ago? Our horses returned to us having enjoyed their private sortie, we returned, not having enjoyed it, and finally the big mountain guns arrived and that was the end of that. The PEACE has been splendidly celebrated with bonfires, firing of Verey lights and a certain degree of refreshment (liquid). I have to have some repairs done to my face and will thus miss the regiment's return to Bangalore and polo. I hope the box-wallahs in London will make a sensible peace treaty, but doubt it. If we decide to punish these courageous mountain men by reducing the subsidies we will drive them to the Bolsheviks' care and protection.

221

Once I have been patched up I shall take sick leave and spend it with Mrs. Hope — and Una — at Gulmarg. I shall make the most of having THREE females to pander to my every whim. Am hoping for home leave THIS year — after taking a couple of exams. Love to all, devotedly, as usual, Rex.

Aurora sat staring at the page of flimsy paper, trying to visualise having her son home again. The rest of the letter, even the injured face, waxed into insignificance besides that one phrase, 'home leave THIS year . . .' Slowly she folded the letter and returned it to its envelope then gazed out to sea, to The Roc. She shook her shoulders. "That," she thought, "is something I CAN do. I'll make patchwork curtains for the Barn. Rex said he would like to make a little home there . . . all those years ago, when he had just left school and was sucked up by the war . . . patchwork curtains and a cover for his camp bedroll, and the chair he said he'd take there . . . all the little bits and pieces of all the children's outgrown clothes . . . almost a history of his childhood in patches . . . and my old clothes and even Leo's." Aurora felt she still had some use left in her. She pulled out the thick package that was Una's letter knowing that of all the children, THIS one would understand the value of the patchwork. She spread the pages across her knees for the girl's large clear handwriting did not require squinting eyes to decipher.

Aurora smiled while she read:–

O My Best Beloved Aunt Aurora,

You will understand that I am reading Kipling's 'Just So' Stories and each begins with O My Best Beloved. He must have loved his children very much like you love us. You really ARE my Best Beloved. I am so glad you took us to your home and your heart. Mother didn't approve of me. I am not like Anna. Now they have gone and left me with Mrs. Hope and Miss Law I am able to write properly. My little sister was no respecter of private things and Nanny IS a SPY. I think father liked Rex better than me. Did you know that he is a **VERY BURRA GENERAL** out here? When he brought us all home he went to the Palace, did you know? He was made something called a Commander of the Order of the Bath. A very rare distinction according to Mrs. Hope who knows EVERYTHING. I think it a very humorous distinction because what father did not have was a bath. He had a shower made from an old kerosene tin with holes in it. His 'boy' had to pull the tin up on a pulley and father stood underneath the dripping water to wash and then the 'boy' had to let the tin down and refill it — several times. The 'boy', father's personal servant, was about a hundred years of age! He has gone back to his village now; the same village as Urjina-Singh. Did I tell you that Urji's sons were all killed during the war and his eldest grandson was shot in the Jalianwala Bagh horror? The Colonel who gave the order to shoot on the weaponless crowd was born in India, but it must be said — the only thing that can be said in his defence — he was rapidly becoming paralysed from a leg injury so his judgement may, no must, have been impaired. Mrs. Hope said the authorities extract a terrible duty from the officers, keeping them active, or on the active list far too long because they give them such miserably small pensions to retire on that few can afford to retire.

I have mastered this typewriting. I am now keeping up with Mrs. Hope's daily writing, riding every day with Miss Law and avoiding the social things I am invited to attend. Rex is going to spend his local leave here with Mrs. Hope so I might HAVE to go to functions if he wants to go, but I am really happy here with such kind people, and I am doing a lot of painting and drawing. Mrs. Hope said she might ask her editor if one of my pictures can be used in the book!! I am running out of pencils, but Rex said he will bring me a 'gladstone bag full' of indelible and drawing pencils — and an india-rubber because I am using lick and an old tyre.

Now I must go back in time. Kashmir is indeed 'the Garden of India'. So many things we didn't notice particularly when we were young and living here. Of course, children just accept whatever is; like the people of this country, who also 'accept'. This fertile state is watered by the beautiful Jhelum River where every variety of fruit and flower abounds and the pastures and rice fields are truly verdant. I expect this is why so many British families have settled here, preferring to spend the years of retirement in this climate than face the fogs of their native shore; here too, are many British children too young to be sent home to school. To possess a house is a rare and coveted honour which only state officials can be sure of obtaining. Thus the majority of residents, unable by Kashmir Law to own land, solve the problem by living in houseboats. All along the river on either bank are these homes, some most pretentious and beautifully furnished, others rough and rather primitive — known as doongahs and being little more than a large open boat with roof and sides of woven matting.

Our houseboats were of the pretentious standard and exceedingly comfortable. I think they would compare very favourably with an English home. Our living room was about sixteen feet by twelve feet — about the size of the drawing room at La Bellule I would think, and very pleasantly furnished. Of course father, Mrs. Hope and the Graysons were renting, but many English people possess their own floating home. Ours had five bedrooms, each with its own bathroom, and the bedroom area separated from the living room by the pantry. The cooking takes placed on a doongah attached to the main living by a plank, over which all the food is carried on trays. The staff also live there and their families — except on ours because mother refused to have wives and children living so close. I thought it very hard-hearted until I heard several wives on a nearby doongah squabbling; they have VERY high voices and an unlimited supply of colourful invectives. I learnt some very useful Hindustani by just listening. Mrs. Hope says she learns about the problems of the women of the country by listening to their quarrels and gossip and chatter; she is fluent in the language. I must tell you about the meals here. We have quite simple meals really, but it takes about five servants to prepare and cook them and one other to prepare the bath water and keep the place clean.

English people who live here all the time have great fires blazing INSIDE the houseboat, but even that isn't as dangerous as the Kashmiri habit of carrying his own personal fire around WITH him, under his top garment; it is a little fire made inside an earthenware pot, a charcoal fire, and then carried in a wicker basket; it is called a kangri and they even sleep with the kangri on their chests. Tiny children carry these fires around with them, but only wear a single garment.

I could live permanently on a houseboat. It is so soothing to sleep to the gentle rocking, to move up or down river if the neighbours are annoying or the scenery has lost its appeal. No packing, no inconvenience, all you do is call the 'manjis' to move you. They call their satellites and chanting 'Illah, Allah,' they sort of punt you to the new desired residential area. The ONLY disadvantage seems to be the lack of garden, but it would be possible to grow a garden in pots on the flat roof where we sit in deckchairs and watch the kingfishers diving and wheeling. I'm not QUITE sure, but I THINK that living on a houseboat might be EVEN preferable to living on The Roc. A houseboat on the pond at La Bellule, perhaps?

My love to all of you. Don't ever think that, in all the excitement here and new scenes and experiences, I forget any of you.

I had a note from Rex saying that now the Afghan War is over he will be spending some time at Ambala and will then come here to Gulmarg at Mrs. Hope's invitation.

My very special love to you, O Best Beloved Aunt, with a very special hug for you and for Roxana, Marie, Dan, Frank, Rolf, Pierre, Sergeant Fyne, Gamma and Alph from Una.

Aurora hurried back from the farm, a new lightness in her step and a determination to commence work on the patchwork curtains immediately after the meal was over — patchwork for Rex's Roc, but with Una's approbation in her heart. To Rex curtains were curtains and to all the other men of the household; Roxana was more capable that she was at making things; Una would study the design and recognise each fragment of clothing the finished article had been contrived from; inspiration would come from thoughts of her niece. She, Aurora O'Donaty still had some uses, she thought, smiling.

By the time family parties were spending whole days on the beach at Bellule Bay laughter rang out night after night in the kitchen of the old farmhouse. Once the dishes were cleared away, the Truth Table took on the appearance of a jumble sale, as each member of the community discovered unusuable or unwanted articles of clothing and offered them for Aurora's patchwork. They even offered each other's clothing in bursts of generosity. Roxana even offered her mother's ancient ulster on one occasion.

"No! Absolutely NOT and NEVER!" the owner stipulated, "Especially now it has that beautiful sheepskin lining that Rolf gave me."

"Well, then," said her daughter, completely recovered from her long illness, "I think I'll take Una's old kilt."

"You're too late," she was told by all the family. "Una took it with her."

While the two women were bandying words they did not notice Rolf quietly removing some of his most treasured pieces of clothing. Like his sister, he had the greatest difficulty in accepting that even clothes have an ultimate life span. Once the evening's badinage was over they sat with cardboard templates and cut shapes from the material, handing them to Frank to sort by colour, material, size and shape. While they worked they talked, and it was decided after a great deal of discussion that Frank should be dispatched to England to visit his unknown little brother in September, soon after the boy began his first term at school. They discussed and wondered, about the decision to take Anna to Tasmania instead of sending her to school near her brother.

"I expect the parents are still ashamed of Una being expelled!" decided Rolf.

By the time the second brood of swallows had become demanding fledglings they all had some other news to cogitate over, surmise about and generally reach the wrong answers. It was contained in a letter from Rex. As usual, the letter consisted of bare facts. They read:–

Dear Mother and all the family,

The army has done a very creditable job on my handsome countenance. Perhaps they will regret it as I have applied to my C.O. for permission to marry. Meanwhile I am performing some excessively dull duties here as Adjutant at this repair factory for the battered, which will last until September when I can expect an additional affliction in the person of my cousin, Ivan whose ship has the lack of judgement to waste time in the waters between India and Burma. I fear he will visit me. I wish he could sit my language exams for me.

Love as ever, your devoted son, brother, cousin etc . . .
Rex.

PS. The Brass Hats have discovered that I have not graced the family hearth since the beginning of the war so they have assured me that I shall have leave, home leave about November. R.

PPS. I assume you have NOT given my bed away and can accommodate me plus wife; She's quite small.

Aurora had taken herself to the promontory, noticed nothing of the view, but cried; it was one of the few times in her life that she had just sat and let the tears fall and fall and fall. A schoolboy had gone away and she wanted the schoolboy back again, before he became a husband and belonged with some other woman. She knew she was having selfish thoughts, but she thought the thoughts and felt the feelings that suffused her whole being. Self-pity totally overwhelmed her and she indulged in it to the full. She had asked so very little of life. She had offered so much. She had given up her son to that great school. She had given her son to the army, to the country, the nation. She had waited with infinite patience for his return when he would fill in the years of his absence, as he had done during his last holiday when she had learnt so much about his secret life away at that school. She did NOT want to share him with some other woman — not yet. She opened the great watch that hung from her neck and saw that it was time for her to return to the farm and put the supper on and she rebelled. Climbing down from the promontory she walked along the empty beach, kicked the small fragments of rubbish left by the picnickers, and felt the swooping of the swallows above her head. Seven of them swooped, wheeled and swooped again, just circling the ripples of sea. She bent down and splashed her face with salt water, wiped it on her skirt and, watching the swallows, began to smile, crookedly. Of course, she had been like the parent swallows; she had not exactly CHASED away her own brood, but she HAD made it easy for them to leave her — and to return, unlike the swallows. Yes, she had loved her son, and her nephews and niece and her daughter, enough to GIVE them the only, but the greatest gift she had to give, their freedom. Roxana could have gone to Poland to her husband's home. She could have pleaded

227

with Rex NOT to stay in the army. Una had gone and might never return; Rolf would leave one day, and even Frank might go; Ivan's life was at sea. Rex's wife would add to the family, either here at home, or overseas. He was young to take on the responsibility of a wife, but he had been responsible for all those cousins for the years of their schooldays. Rex and Lex between them had looked after the younger children. Lex had died BEFORE knowing the joys of married life. It was quite wonderful that Rex was going to bring his new bride to La Bellule.

Roxana had cooked the meal and Sergeant Fyne talked throughout, except when he was obliged to cease his verbosity in order to eat, when Frank or Dan kept up the steady flow. Nobody mentioned Rex's news. They avoided the subject with such scrupulous care that Aurora began to feel genuinely amused. When Frank rose to make the tea she said, "Shall we celebrate Rex's future marriage by opening some bottles of elderflower wine?" Backs that had been rigid during the meal, slumped, or leaned backwards, shoulders dropped, eyes began to sparkle and they all began to talk, surmise, laugh and interrupt each other — as usual.

"I really will have to finish the patchwork for the Roc," said Aurora. "He's sure to want to take his wife there!"

While they cut and sorted they decided on the young woman's colouring, her nationality, antecedents and qualities. Unfortunately they were unable to agree about anything. Rolf went over to the Roches and brought Marie and Pierre to help celebrate and join the discussion.

"He always fancied blondes," Pierre told them.

"How do YOU know?" asked Aurora, and Marie together.

"Oh," said Pierre, "We used to go out and talk to girls, me and Rex and Lex . . ."

"Oh, did you?" Aurora said, smiling thinly.

"I expect he met plenty of those in South Africa, and dark girls," Pierre continued, "and all those beautiful Indian girls out there, and the English officers' daughters. He'll probably find it difficult to decide between them, nurses and rich idle girls. What a wonderful life!"

"Perhaps it's the Colonel's daughter," Frank suggested.

"Suppose she's like that awful Georgina, Una travelled with?" Rolf offered as his contribution.

Roxana reminded them, "We KNOW it isn't that awful Georgina, anyway, because Rex says she is small, and Georgina, according to Una's letter, was and presumably is, far from small. Rex wouldn't WANT to marry anyone who didn't fit in with US. Let's get on with the patchwork. If we need extra help, Rolf, we'll put YOU on to machining the patches together."

"I think I'll try MY hand at sewing," said Séan Fyne, to the general amazement of all. And he did.

Frank arranged the pieces and held them together with drawing pins on a piece of board. Séan Fyne tacked pieces together and Aurora and Roxana stitched night after night, and often joined by Marie, left on her own by Pierre who was 'walking out'. Dan and Rolf confined their assistance to praise or, more often, derogatory remarks about the prowess of one or all of the workers.

"La Bellule is back to pre-war NORMALITY, almost," said Aurora one evening feeling the warmth of family around her. Una's latest letter had been read out loud by Aurora and passed around for each to read — and to enjoy the tiny illustrations with which it was sprinkled. Frank had it open on the table and commented, "At least she DATES her letters. I wish Rex would."

"SHE dates hers all the way through!" complained Rolf.

"Now we're all settled with our work," Aurora suggested, "read it aloud to us, again, Frank, will you?" Frank would have had to sit idly for the next hour or more and this was exactly what he needed; to BE useful, not just FEEL useful. He read:–

O Best Beloved Aunt and Roxana, Marie, Dan, Frank, Pierre, Rolf and Sergeant Fyne, You will understand that I am still reading The Just So Stories. They were written for children, but absolutely DELIGHTFUL for adults — like me. You MUST read them. Mrs. Hope has GIVEN me a copy, printed in Bombay on gold-edged, very fine paper and bound in deepest red leather. It fits into my jungle coat pocket and I have made a little tartan bag for it; guess where the tartan came from! My old kilt, of course.

3rd July 1919 since starting my letter I have been to Ambala with Mrs. Hope and Miss Law. Dearest Aunt, you have NO need to worry about Rex. He looks wonderfully fit, though somewhat UNbeautiful, at the moment. He seems to have everyone doing precisely what HE wants and the army surgeons are re-mending his leg injury which has given him a lot of trouble; and irritation; he has to wear SILK STOCKINGS under his socks. The enclosed photograph was taken by Miss Law. Your WORTHLESS son is being worthless even though is is SUPPOSED to be Adjutant; he is the chap sitting on a table playing a banjo. He bought the banjo from a cousin we discovered here, Guy Waley; he is the handsome blond beside Rex with his arm in a sling. We've worked out that his mother is one of my father's sisters who lives in Hobart. Rex has besmirched MY reputation by telling everyone highly exaggerated stories about my escapades — as a child. The result is that ALL the convalescent crowd plan to visit Mrs. Hope in Gulmarg AND to visit YOU ALL when they have home leave.

Van will be with us we think/hope/fear for our eighteenth birthday. Love to you all, as always Una.

Packages arrived weekly from India. Pages and pages describing places, people and experiences were read out while the family sat around the Truth Table at La Bellule and constructed patchwork curtains, bed covers and cushion covers. Una was being taken on wonderfully adventurous journeys, and shared them with the family 'at home'.

The days were shortening and the bracken turning copper when her shortest letter arrived:–
Dearest Aunt Aurora, And all the family at La Bellule,

I have written to my father and asked permission to marry. Expecting him to agree the arrangements have been made and the padre will perform the ceremony on YOUR birthday, dearest Aunt. Van has been granted leave and will 'Give me away' — with alacrity, no doubt. Mrs Hope is arranging EVERYTHING; she says it is payment for my typing. Her book is finished and she says she needs something to DO. My love to all, . . . oh, PS. I really should be asking YOUR permission, Aunt Aurora, but the law demands otherwise . . . I WANT to write millions of words, but I'm afraid I can only add to the above — THANK you for EVERYTHING. My everlasting love, Una.

Chapter Fourteen

Swallows were collecting in large family units on the telegraph wires that spread over the countryside. A few more sunrises and they would be gone to join summer elsewhere in the world — and their flying larder that was disappearing daily. Lights shone from the windows of the old farmhouse and the birds were thrown into a frenzy of bewilderment, but the pair of longer-tailed creatures had experienced the phenomenon in the distant past and twittered their reassurances to the inexperienced.

The pair of blackbirds sang their dawn song without the certainty that a later time would have inspired.

The crabs, already scattered along the beach, returned to their shelter beneath the house to sense, hear, smell and see what the newly arrived mammals living above them were doing in their strange leg-impoverished world.

Aurora O'Donaty arrived in her kitchen to find a pot of tea made and put at her habitual place at the table. She saw a light outside the stable and heard the familiar sounds of a horse being harnessed to the old buggy. She drank slowly from her large cup until, as she had already anticipated, the door to the yard was flung open and the tall figure of her nephew filled the aperture before slamming the door shut. Rolf could do nothing quietly.

"It's a cold day," he said. "I hope you've got plenty of warm clothes on, Auntaury."

Frank walked into the kitchen, a smile bending one end of his straight thin mouth and upending the thick reddish moustache. Aurora felt the usual wave of tenderness swamp her as she greeted this young man. It was to meet him, on his stretcher, that she had made her last dawn journey;

Frank brought back by Dan and Roxana. It had seemed then that he would never come to terms with his disability, but now he could smile; he could walk without falling over and he did not, at first sight, appear to have anything wrong with his physique. He had laboriously, and one handed, stuffed an old stocking of hers, with scraps of material he had cut with scissors, left handed, then stitched the object inside his guernsey. Once he had his jacket over it and the end pushed into one pocket he appeared to have two arms. He taught himself to balance by walking beside Gamma, leaning against her soft body, and one day he managed to mount her. Nobody saw the stages before he achieved that result, he just rode INTO the kitchen, the first smile they had seen for years, lighting his face. He had risen especially on this special day to see his aunt depart.

"It's time you left, Aunt Rory," said Frank. "You don't want to feel rushed — and it IS dark."

Roxana and Dan strolled in, Roxana adding, "Yes, Frank's right, mother."

Aurora put on her old ulster, climbed into the buggy with the patient Gamma seemingly also filled with the importance of this day, stepping out briskly without needing so much as a flick of the reins on her back. Aurora, to her intense surprise, felt tears streaming down her face. She found a cushion had been placed for her back and a foot warmer for her feet. She slid the goloshes off her feet and felt the heat penetrate the old pair of football socks she had purloined from her son's drawer. Twelve years earlier she had made this same dawn expedition to take into her home, and into her heart, her sister's children. If she had been their mother they could not have repaid her with more affection. The absent members of that family shared their lives with her by writing long and vivid letters; the farmhouse blazed with lights thanks to the generosity of the eldest nephew who did not return from the war; and today, on this very special day, they had all decided to see her on her way — and not one of them had suggested accompanying her. They knew she would not have refused them; they knew she would prefer to go alone. As she swept around the corner of the massive wall she saw all the lights flick off and then on again several times. When she reached

Séan Fyne's cottage, his lights did the same. Aurora had added the Fynes to her 'family' for Kitty Fyne had followed the baby Leo, and then Old Pierre. Sergeant Fyne had said, "It was a Sunday when Leo went, so two more would be bound to follow; now he has two parents," and he worked even harder with Frank, pushing him to more and greater spectacular riding achievements — and to the regaining of his lost confidence, and a will to live.

By the time the buggy reached the fishing village with its potent aromas Aurora was thinking about Rolf. She could not love that boy more if he was in reality, her son. He had kept the farm going during Roxana's long illness after the baby had been born. He had abandoned school and somehow never returned. He seemed to be always at hand during each of the many emergencies that followed that harrowing event. His noisy presence, heavy footed, door slamming, but silent tongue was the only live substance inside the farm; a welcome reminder, day and night, that life continued.

Still deep in thought when the Town clock was visible, Aurora realized that she had not once looked behind her to see if the mail boat smoke was visible. She looked out to sea, and there was the mail boat; another twenty minutes and it would be squeezing itself through the harbour heads — and Gamma still trotted briskly, forgetting her age, but somehow recalling the process of turning herself and her burden at precisely the correct point so that they would be visible from the gangplank, once it was lowered. Then Gamma snorted disapprovingly. Instead of Alph being driven, turned and parked in front of her, a noisy contraption arrived, moving smoothly BACKWARDS and almost under her nose. She snorted again at the gust of smelly smoke it discharged somewhere near her polished hooves. Her final snort accompanied a great slamming of metal against metal and the appearance of her one-time friend, Young Pierre.

Aurora's eyes searched the rails as the boat went through the usual mooring gyrations. Nowhere could she see the smart little whiskered man in military dress with a fashionably smart little woman by his side. She slipped her feet into her goloshes and climbed from the buggy. "They can't have missed the boat," she whispered into Gamma's

233

ear. She backed Gamma a little further from the lorry — the apology for a lorry, made as it was from bits and pieces attached to a broken down motor car. She turned her eyes again to the stream of passengers pouring from the gangplank on to the quayside, but her view was blocked by a very faded blue guernsey that engulfed her. Rex was home. After five years her son was home. The same Rex who had gone to that awful war, a lot older looking, browner skinned and fairer haired but the same deep hazel eyes, laughing mouth mostly covered by a very fair moustache, unchanged voice and above all, essentially it was Rex.

After what seemed to be an eternity, Aurora asked, "where's Una?"

"Her eyes went funny. She's gone to her old bag to find her tissane. She said she couldn't risk being sick all the way home, AGAIN."

Aurora laughed. She wasn't sure if she wanted to laugh or to cry, but laughter came more easily to her, so she laughed. She laughed with real relish when the girl appeared, clutching the same gladstone bag, wearing the much too short school cape over her untidy skirt and hair wisping from its braids. "How could she have expected this girl to turn into the smart model of her mother?" she wondered. "Surely this girl SHOULD have been her own daughter, surely, surely," she thought as Una hung on to her.

"I've only been gone six months and it seems forever," the girl said in her strangely husky voice.

"You haven't changed, darling," said the aunt who felt that this girl was really her daughter.

"Both women turned to watch the two men. It was as if neither had been away; they were walking around the mechanical contraption, Pierre pointing out its few qualities, Rex admiring the ingenuity that had resulted in such a conglomeration of working parts.

"Been waiting for Una to paint a bellule on the side," said Pierre.

"She'll do better," Rex answered. "She'll do one in pressed metal." There was pride in his voice, which was not lost on his friend who responded with, "You're a lucky fellow, Rex — ah, and so's she, eh?" They laughed and then side by side and together loaded the luggage on to the planks behind the old car engine.

"I'll take Una with me. She's a lighter load for Gamma to pull," Aurora called out.

"AND the gladstone bag, mother?" laughed her son.

Pierre pulled up in the fishing village and tinkered with the engine while the fishermen greeted Rex, then once the buggy came into view, passed them and made its leisurely way by the sandy coast track, Pierre and Rex followed the road, thus they arrived together at the archway leading into La Bellule.

The crabs, the swallows, the blackbirds and thrushes and even the dormant chrysalides of moths, butterflies, damsel flies and dragonflies were awakened, startled and bemused by the sounds that exploded from the interior of the old stone farmhouse. When the machine driven by Pierre ceased its noisy vibrations and Gamma was being led by him to her stable a new version of the Trumpet Voluntary echoed from every granite block of the building. A bugle replaced the original trumpet and the orchestra was composed of a piano, a banjo, a mouth organ and a saucepan lid being beaten with a wooden spoon.

The travellers stood like megaliths in the centre of the yard until the 'music' ended with a solo bugle call, followed by a stampede by the 'orchestra' towards the megaliths who were engulfed in hugs, handshakes, back-thumping, and the incoherent welcome sounds of a family being reunited.

Somehow they all squeezed into the narrow kitchen door, spread themselves around the capacious room until the gong was sounded in the hall and Roxana said, "Your wedding breakfast!" and they seated themselves around the Truth Table. Ten of them sat down, for Pierre, Marie Roche and Séan Fyne had joined the O'Donaty family.

While Roxana ladled out porage, Frank remarked, "And the groom was appropriately attired in his usual uniform of faded, darned and outgrown guernsey over tweed. . ."

". . . and the bride glittered in a most becoming school cloak, her hair in the latest half-braided wispy style . . ." Roxana added before being interrupted by Rolf.

"A cloak, unadorned by sick. . ." he offered.

"Carrying a most original bouquet of battered gladstone bag. . ." said Frank before he was again interrupted.

"It IS WONDERFUL to be home!" exclaimed the happy young bride.

Dishes piled up in the sink as the last egg, fragment of bread and mushroom vanished, and bread, honey, butter and the inevitable tea circulated. In direct proportion to the quantity of internal fuel being consumed, the external talk flowed until a high tide of talk crossed and criss-crossed the great oval of oak. Two broad gold wedding rings were held out for all to see the engraved Odonata on each. "You see," explained Una, "Rex can't wear his Odonata ring in uniform so I wear it on a chain . . . for him."

Aurora left the room, returning swiftly a moment later. She placed a locket around the bride's neck, saying, "Your mother sent it to me to give you, Una darling." In little more than a whisper Una said, "Oh, thank you, thank you, I didn't think she'd give it to me in the end. I thought Anna would have it. She approved of Anna, but I was, I am, well, all wrong. I didn't fit."

"Good job, too," Rex conceded, "or you mightn't have had permission to marry me . . . well, not so easily, eh?"

Not knowing whether she was laughing or crying, Una added, "Well we were almost at the church when their cable arrived, anyway."

"Oh well, good old Van was going to take the blame if they objected," said Rex. "He gave his twin away with absolute delight and took about a hundred photographs to prove we were married — and to bring to you all, our nearest and dearest who could not be there with us."

"Why didn't you wait to marry here, Rex?" asked Frank, voicing the question each of the family wanted answered.

"We couldn't have travelled together otherwise," Rex explained, his face stiff and serious. "I'd have been sent in charge of troops probably, and, you see, Frank, the army paid for Una — as my wife. I quite wanted to look after her, too, you know. The war in Afghanistan showed me that there is no such thing as peace throughout the world, and, as we know, life can be short. Uncle Augustus has been fortunate, even lucky, and I intend to follow his example, but HE advised me not to wait too long to marry; of course he didn't know I was going to marry HIS DAUGHTER, then. I'm not sure that I knew. . ."

"I am overcome with delight that you two married," Aurora announced, bubbling with excitement and pleasure. "Just look how my family has grown and all collecting around this table at least once a day."

"They will ALL be here for supper," Roxana warned. "Marie and Pierre will bring the two ex-servicemen who live in one of the cottages and supply the fishermen and their wives with lobster pots and fish baskets; Taffy is blind and Jock is paralysed. You can meet them this afternoon when Séan Fyne and Frank take them riding."

The early morning sunshine was trying to break through clouds and light up the kitchen when they all went on a tour of the farmhouse.

"It's just like the day we left school," said Rex, picking his way around and over the luggage piled in the hall.

Aurora led the way up the tourelle saying, "I've put you both in the 'Boys' Room' and left it for you to rearrange."

Una stood in the hall reliving the day she had first arrived at this 'Tir Tairngire', this Promised Land; she had been a very small child and the spiral staircase had seemed magical. Once shown her little bed beside the window overlooking the stables, and noticed that there was no mosquito net to billow in a wind, fearfully, she felt secure. Twelve years later she followed the family around the tourelle. They stood recalling the making of the little room and seeing again the effervescent Lex pretending it was the cockpit of an aeroplane. It was now a study for Frank, lined with books with Lex's model 'planes hanging from the ceiling, moving in the draught.

"Let's hope each of us finds our dreams coming true," said Dan.

From the other loft window they could see the pond, the willow and the tiny grave that marked the place of Dan and Roxana's son and the ending of his dream, of returning to his homeland with a son — in spite of his Gentile wife.

Rex, looking down the tourelle recalled the day he had seen a wet, still body carried in, knew it was his father and clutched his stuffed kangaroo more tightly. Nine years later he had viewed the arrival of his cousins, his aunt and his uncle; it was then that he began to consider the army as a possible career, a way of acquiring the respect that surrounded his uncle and a means to becoming a leader instead of the follower that was his role in life, so far.

By the time the evening meal was nothing but a huge pile of willow-pattern plates soaking in the sink and well-satisfied stomachs the young couple had walked the boundaries, watched the Sergeant and Frank at work with their pupils, admired the basketry piled up at the Roche's cottages, and Rex had sat with his mother on the promontory watching Una riding the elderly Gamma along the beach. The oak board had been wiped down, the stove fed for the night, and dough sat rising and whispering accompanied by the hissing of the copper kettle. Outside the rain poured steadily in straight sheets promising a storm in the next few days. Photographs of the wedding passed from hand to hand. Una sat beside Taffy and described each picture while the rest of the family passed judgments and asked questions.

"You look almost human," Rolf remarked to his sister.

"How did Ivan behave?" Roxana enquired.

"He made a wonderful speech," Rex admitted, "then had a sword fight with his sister, MY BRIDE."

"When he saw me in all my finery he said, 'You needn't have gone to all this trouble. I expected to give you away in a brown paper parcel'," Una added.

Rex produced another packet of small snapshots explaining, "We, Una and I camped and walked through the mountains and visited Urji na Singh at his village. And look at this snapshot! Yes, it is Van. He appeared in uniform, left in mufti, and somehow joined his ship at Colombo — and is now safely in, or near, Australia."

The door to the yard burst open and a bedraggled apparition appeared shouting, "The Banshees are here! Happy Hallowe'en." It WAS Ivan.

Aurora recovered first. "Upstairs and change NOW," she said. Then explained to those around the table. "That was Ivan."

"But Van is in Australia. He wrote from Colombo and said he caught his ship," Una almost shouted across the table.

Rolf thumped up and around the tourelle to keep an eye on his possessions in the room above.

Having mopped up puddles, Roxana busied herself, re-heating remnants of joint and potatoes and adding more and more succulent titbits to an already substantial-looking meal. From all around the table instructions were hurled at her. "Don't FEED the beast!"

"Starve him until he EXPLAINS!"

"Bread and water's enough for convicts!"

"Be careful, Roxana, it's the devil in disguise!"

"You mean it's that devil, Van PRETENDING to be angelic!"

"NOT ONE CRUMB, Roxana, until we've found out how he got here!"

"How ANYONE can get to La Bellule at nine o-clock at night. . .!"

"How ANYONE can be going to Australia at the end of September, well, on the 20th, and be here, at home, on 31st October. . ."

"He could have FLOWN. . ."

"P'raps he had to walk the plank and this IS his ghost. . ."

"He's been EXPELLED — just like I was five years ago . . . This is just like five years ago happening today . . . He MUST HAVE BEEN EXPELLED!"

"No I haven't," said the subject of their discussion. "I have been PROMOTED!" He twirled round and round, swinging Una's school cloak which he wore around his shoulders. "By the time we reached Aussie waters the scrambled egg battalion, the chaps with heavy gold mines dangling from their caps and shoulders, said, 'this virtuous young gent should be sent on a flying course,' so they sent me. I did myself a bit of good off Darwin by saving a poor old shark from digestive troubles by removing a Snotty, or Midshipman from his jaws. One of them, the boy, or the shark belonged to some Admiral. I thought the creature was a WHALE or I'd never have gone within a mile of it. The Navy acts in a mysterious way; in many mysterious ways. Someone thought that as I could SWIM fairly fast it must follow as the night the day that I must be equally as adequate in the air. They sent me home by battle ship, but I met a Froggy in Pompey Harbour with his own, HIS VERY OWN seaplane, so I said I'd navigate him to here. I left him down in the Bay, but I'd shown him the Town Harbour so he's going there for the night. Nice chap — for a Froggy. I'll be carrying out naval creed; I abandoned ship LAST because I carried the Captain's case ashore — behind him. Funny world the navy is; a world of its own. Bells instead of clocks and time existing in its own special measurement. 'Naval time is five minutes before time' they teach you when you're new and raw and trusting; it isn't; it's a one way rule; it's five minutes BEFORE time going ON duty and five minutes or even five hours AFTER time when you're going ashore. The Admirals and Sea Lords get water on the brain with spending so much time surrounded by oceans and seas. Tragic really. They have MESS decks and MESSES and the one thing those places are NOT allowed to be is MESSY . . . and I could think of a more appropriate name for the Heads . . . oh . . . sorry! Forgot the ladies were here. I think I'd better eat before I really DO say something I shouldn't."

The family sat in silence and watched, wonderingly, at the dexterity with which the plate of food found its way to, and into, Ivan's mouth at an almost immeasurable speed, until, extremes of hunger evidently satisfied, he looked around, waved his fork in the air and said, "Please, please feel free to talk — and smoke; I'm too busy to join you in the former and too fragile in health for the latter; I shall take up either opium or snuff — depends whether I'm a pirate chief or an admiral. I gave up tobacco when I was fourteen." Nobody spoke. The fascination of the disappearing food held them all enthralled until the last crumb had vanished and the tall, lean recipient had deposited the clean plate in the sink, saying, "Thank you, Roxana! That was a wonderful, wonderful meal! Whose turn is it to wash up? I'm very good at it now. Experienced, you might say. That's one of the Navy's humourous methods of getting free labour — it's a punishment for being 'adrift' on some ships. It's a comedy you know. You find yourself adrift — or late as humans term it, — because the LIBERTY boat which is not concerned with liberty at all, but incarceration, arrives late to take you aboard. Your name is taken and next morning there's another comedy. We used to call it Assembly at school — which it IS; an assembly of people; the Navy calls the gathering together of unseen troglodyte souls once a day, not an assembly, but DIVISIONS. If you've been adrift your name is called out and you have to FALL OUT in front of the entire Ship's Company, but you may FEEL like falling out only that is PRECISELY what you DO NOT DO. You smartly, VERY SMARTLY I might say, MARCH out — and collect your INAPPROPRIATE punishment. So, I'm a good galley slave! I would gladly do ALL the washing up in gratitude for that meal. . ."

"You are sure you've had enough to eat, Ivan?" his aunt asked.

"Oh, yes thank you, Aunt Aurora — for now, anyway," he replied.

"As for washing up," Roxana answered, "we each manage to find part of the process to do: usually, I wash, Taffy and Jock dry and Frank puts away, while Dan and Rolf go round the barns: Mother and Sergeant Fyne, as befits their seniority sit and talk."

The work commenced while Ivan picked up a wet kitbag they had not noticed before. "I've got a few presents for you," he said, "That's why I didn't have a change of clothes. Another chap's taken my gear on to the flying school . . . oh yes, and sorry to disappoint you all, but I leave by the mailboat tomorrow. The course starts on All Saints' day; that IS the day after isn't it? Is there a Saint Ivan yet?"

He fumbled inside his kitbag and produced a leather-bound photograph album for each of the family; each volume had the owner's name printed in gold lettering on the cover, and inside each was a packet of wedding photographs. While they were admiring the unexpected gift, Ivan hurriedly produced two more packages, each carefully wrapped, and handed one to Séan Fyne and the other to Frank saying, "Found these gadgets in America. A pad for your leg, Serge, and a sort of jointed doll's arm, Frank, which I see you don't need." There was a silence that hung in the atmosphere of tobacco smoke and mint and rising dough. Ivan flushed, watching his brother's face, the tightened lips slowly relaxing, the glasses removed from the eyes and then a spontaneous burst of laughter, real laughter, such as none of them had heard since he left to join the army.

Frank remarked through his laugh, "Remember us operating on Una's hated doll, Van?" to the relaxing faces around the table he explained, "She hated it, so WE, Van and I obliged by chopping it up with my new penknife."

"Yes," Ivan continued. "We disjointed it, poured water through it, then took its appendix out. We didn't know what an appendix was so once Frank made the hole and all the stuffing fell out, I fetched — eh, STOLE — Rolf's toy rabbit and we stuffed that in. We were playing at conjurors when Nanny caught us. She beat Frank, but I ran away."

"Her horror, Van!" Frank laughed. "As if we could have known about things like that!"

Aurora watched and listened and thought, "Yet another bridge has been crossed tonight, thanks to the Truth Table."

In the silence that followed the laughter she asked Ivan, "How did you find your parents? Have they settled into their new life? How was Anna enjoying it?"

"Ah," procrastinated the usually glib young man. "Hm, well, this being the Truth Table, I'd better tell the truth. The house looks like any colonial-ex-India bungalow; verandah all round and walls festooned with dead animals and skins and skulls amongst the arsenal of weapons that destroyed them — boomerangs, rifles, swords and blow-pipes. Macabre! But Nanny was the most macabre thing there. She vanished to her room with a headache when I arrived and looked terrified of me. I thought it was Una who treated her so badly!" He exchanged a quick flicker of a glance with his twin, then answered the rest of the question.

"I think they have settled amazingly well, Aunt Aurora. Mother is VERY social, giving prizes and opening fêtes and having tea-parties in aid of immigrant Irish girls, and so on. She has only ONE household slave — a VERY pretty Irish immigrant. Anna said I mustn't be too familiar with her because she 'isn't nice'. Intriguing! If I'd had longer leave I'd have taken her out, away from the skeletons." He paused and waited for any questions, but none was forthcoming so he continued, "Mother is absolutely BEAUTIFUL. Very young looking and regally aloof. I don't think Anna likes having such a YOUNG-looking mother. She's tall and grown up, sophisticated, and vain, and always rushing off to tennis parties, boating parties, picnics, gymkhanas and balls. As for Father, well, he spends his time travelling to and from Odin Hall; he must be getting on with his twin because it's a

242

ghastly journey — all night on the train from Hobart, a bumpy car ride from Launceston to St. Mary and THEN the climb up the mountain. I didn't have time to go there, but I did try to interest Father in the idea that Rolf might farm sheep up there, but he said, 'I've made Odin Hall over to my brother, legally — in perpetuity for himself and his heirs.' He then said Rolf will have to find his own land like his grandfather did . . . I tried Rolf," Ivan added, turning to his younger brother. "Anyway I didn't think Uncle Alexander HAD any heirs, has he?"

Nobody answered so Ivan added yet another shock to the evening's total by suggesting HE should make another pot of tea.

"He's got water on the brain as well as his Admiral," Rex said. "Has he EVER volunteered for ANY job?"

"Never," they choroused.

"Ah, now," Ivan explained. "I can use all my job-avoiding talents in the Navy, so I can now be virtuously helpful at home."

"Roxana. Mother. Quick," Rex shouted. "Find the man JOBS. Twelve years of missed jobs plus interest."

"Make the tea, slave," said Frank.

Whilst making the tea Ivan turned to Taffy and Jock and said, "Sorry I haven't brought you two a present. Didn't think you'd still be here, really. . ."

"Nowhere else to go even if we wanted to," said Jock.

Taffy added, "We both grew up in orphanages — me in Wales, Jock in London. THIS IS OUR FIRST HOME, you know. Orphanage to boy-soldier to the trenches and now in HEAVEN."

"You've made me feel young again, tonight," Jock claimed. "We had fun at my orphanage — all of us Scottish lads — but we couldn't have made the noise you've made today, all of you, but we had fun. Taffy didn't. His place was all silence and prayers, wasn't it Taf?"

"And SINGING, man. There was always the singing," Taffy said in his melodious voice.

"We were lucky," Ivan conceded. "OUR ORPHANAGE was HERE, and OUR AUNT MADE us into HER CHILDREN . . . without any money. Father was supposed to have retired when the war began, and with the usual army efficiency they didn't go on with his payments to Aunt Aurora, here. He only discovered when he really retired a few weeks ago and his back money turned up in Tasmania where they've made him Commandant of British troops — nothing much to do and probably quite well paid for it. BUT HOW DID OUR AUNT feed, clothe, educate and make good the damage we did here. FIVE of us when war came. . ."

"No, Ivan," remonstrated Aurora, "that's not strictly true. Lex, Frank and Rex were arranged for . . . there were only you and Rolf and Una. . ."

"Well, how did you feed and clothe us, Aunt Aurora?" persisted Ivan.

Aurora glanced around the table before explaining, "We all worked together — Roxana's salary, Old Pierre's fishing, Young Pierre's lobsters, Marie selling the fish in the market . . . We managed. . ." Her look of appeal was answered by Roxana.

"When you were all away at school, mother did the milking, fed the animals, delivered milk and eggs, and we all collected driftwood for the range, dandelion leaves and nettles for vegetables, and fruit for pickling and jam making. We cured hams and harvested the potatoes. . . We all ENJOYED HAVING YOU. . ."

"Why didn't you TELL us?" Rolf asked. "WE could have collected driftwood and gorse after school. You let us all go ormering. . ."

Séan Fyne interrupted. "I'll tell you why," he said. "I know because I know what Kitty did for OUR sons. Your aunt didn't want you to FEEL POOR — not with you going to that grand school. That's it, isn't it?" he asked, turning to Aurora.

"Partly," she parried until interrupted by Una whose voice scratched with emotion as she grated, "But we STOLE Rex's birthright. I mean he must have felt like Esau. Or at least he must NOW. And we were SO AWFUL — especially ME. We sort of TOOK OVER the house and Aunt Aurora's time and Roxana's energy. He must have felt SWAMPED by us."

"Oh, no, Una," Roxana disagreed. "Not at all. It was difficult for Rex when you first arrived, but mother and I had spoilt him, coddled him and we actually thought we were somehow making up to him for not having a father. Rex had been the centre of our lives from the age of three, and, by the time he was eleven and you arrived, he had become quite a little toad . . . well, a near-toad; a tadpole . . . wasn't he mother?"

"Well, thanks," said Rex, "Thanks so very much all of you! This near little toad, this toad tadpole, as my sister so delightfully terms it, was FURIOUS at the cousin-invasion; not to mention the humiliation at finding they were so knowledgeable about almost everything; they weren't even seasick when we went to The Roc; they talked to each other in a strange language and when Pierre and I talked patois in front of them — to pay them out — ONE of them picked up patois and the others weren't too slow at getting a smattering. This little near-toad would probably have done away with them if they hadn't had just one redeeming quality. They couldn't SWIM. They couldn't even float and I had to teach them. I THINK I began to secretly admire them then. They put up with my scathing comments AND they stayed in the sea, BLUE with cold and persevered. They even swam in the winter until mother stopped it — they were all so SKINNY, but the twins were almost skeletons. THEN we went to school — my first time away from home, and small for my age, like now, and without Lex I would never have survived the attempts at bullying me. I can't imagine what MY life would have been WITHOUT them — anyway I've stolen one of them for keeps . . . I freely confess to this august company that I WOULD have become an adult toad WITHOUT them . . . and I enjoyed Una's awfulness, usually; it was quite a strange and exciting experience to see her throwing missiles at her brothers, then rolling around the floor screaming . . . It's mother and Roxana we should all pity, perhaps. . ."

Aurora thumped the table. She had never had recourse to such an act before and they all stared at her until she said,

"Let's put everything into perspective shall we? I ALWAYS wanted a large family. This farm and house is right for children and I HAD my big family. I wouldn't have been able to send Rex away to school unless Augustus had paid the fees and I wouldn't have willingly let him go away, all alone. It seems I benefit all the time. The young return of their own free will. They even bring GIFTS," she concluded, waving the photograph album in the air whilst rising and removing her ulster from the hook behind the door. "Look at this," she said, holding it open in front of them. "A sheepskin lining made by Rolf!"

While eyes were peering closely at this well-known article that was an integral part of Aurora, Rolf burst into a great peal of laughter — a sufficiently unique occurrence to attract the peering eyes to his, as he informed them and reminded his aunt. "They were YOUR sheep, Auntaury, and I used YOUR sewing machine and broke twelve of YOUR machine needles. . ."

"Well," said Rex, "You're all making me feel jolly inadequate, I can tell you. . ."

He was interrupted by Frank growling, "Oh no Rex! Who kept peace between all of us?"

"Who shared his HOME with us?" Rolf asked.

"Who shared his sister and his MOTHER with us?" Una contributed.

"And who," asked Ivan, striking a pose, "Who's taken our sister off our hands?"

"And brought me another daughter, a legal daughter, ensuring the continuity of house and family — of La Bellule," said the proud mother.

"Spoken like a true Matriarch," Dan added.

"A true Matriarch," Roxana continued, "who might have read in a poem called 'The Empty Purse':—

'Keep the young generations in hail.
And bequeath them no tumbled house.'